Shoshana Ishboneh had lost her first
husband and two children in the gas
ovens of Europe in 1944. After the war
she remarried, moved to Israel and
started to build a new life. The two sons
born of this second marriage, Uri and
Gadi, were growing into fine young
men with promising futures – and then
came another war . . .

With both her sons fighting at the front,
Shoshana faced tragedy for the
second time.

Harry Brodie
and Laszlo Deutsch

A Place to Live
and A Place to Die

CORGI BOOKS
A DIVISION OF TRANSWORLD PUBLISHERS LTD

A PLACE TO LIVE AND A PLACE TO DIE

A CORGI BOOK 0 552 10283 0

First publication in Great Britain

PRINTING HISTORY
Corgi edition published 1976
Corgi edition reprinted 1977

This book is set in 10pt Times.

Corgi Books are published by Transworld PublishersLtd.,
Century House, 61–63 Uxbridge Road,
Ealing, London, W.5.
Made and printed in Great Britain by
Hunt Barnard Printing Ltd., Aylesbury, Bucks.

Acknowledgments:

To the journalists, overseas and Israeli, whose detailed stories helped us to check the many confusing and conflicting accounts of the war, and also suggested valuable background information – to the Army Spokesman's office, the Ministry of Foreign Affairs and their Publication 'Features of Israel', for similar assistance – to Ralph and Michael Brodie and their fellow-soldiers for checking the authenticity of many of the battle-incidents – to Alice Gurarie, Yael Stein, Vivian Brodie, Rena Weinreich, Rachel Lough, Ros Brodie and Rose Brodie, for research and help in typing, checking and editing the manuscript.

This book is dedicated to the fallen,
the wounded, and their loved ones,
who paid the price of the 1973
Yom Kippur War.

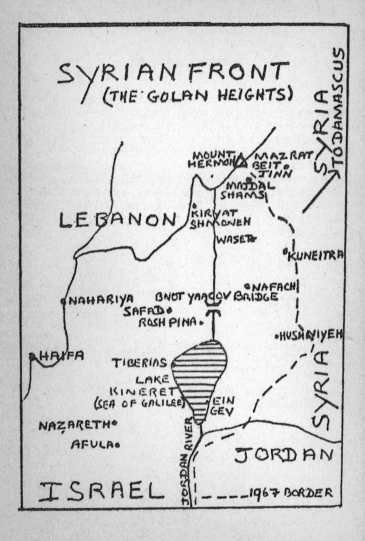

EGYPTIAN FRONT

MEDITERRANEAN SEA

GAZA

RAFIACH

EL ARISH

PORT
SAID

PIZZA

BEERSHEVA

BALUZA

SUEZ CANAL

KANTARA

ISMAILIA

SERAPEUM

CHINESE
FARM

TASA

RIFFIDIM

DEVERSOIR

CROSSING POINT

FAYID

GREAT
BITTER
LAKE

SMALL
BITTER
LAKE

GIDI PASS

TO
CAIRO

KM. 101

SHALLUFA

MITLA PASS

SUEZ

JEBEL
ATAKA

ADABIYE

STRAITS OF SUEZ

ABU RODEIS

JEBEL
MUSA
(MT. SINAI)

Authors' Note:

This is a novel, a work of fiction. In essence the story it tells is true, but any resemblance of the main dramatic characters to actual persons living or dead, is purely co-incidental.

Where well-known persons have been given their real names, the stories and incidents are based on authentic reports, allowing for literary licence to preserve the even flow of the narrative.

Where characters have not been given their real names, especially in relation to Generals who actively conducted the war, the reader is specifically cautioned not to associate or identify any one character completely with any one living person. These characters are fictitious composite characters. Some of the conversations and incidents ascribed to them were reported in widely differing and contentious versions, and free use of literary licence has been made to blend them into the story.

Similarly with military operations and strategy. Some incidents and items originally set out in the manuscript were deleted or altered by the Censor, to avoid giving potentially valuable information to persons hostile to Israel. Others have been freely adapted by ourselves in accordance with the literary demands of the story.

Friday, 5th October

Uri Ishboneh was sitting quietly in the library of the Tel Aviv University his left elbow resting firmly on the dark mahogany table. A lock of straight fair hair fell down across his forehead, and sub-consciously he stroked it back with his right hand, repeating the action again and again as he concentrated fiercely on the book propped open in front of him.

Since nine o'clock in the morning he had been working on a project for Middle East Contemporary History to devise a policy for the Israeli Government to deal with the 'Palestinian Refugee Problem'. This entailed considerable background reading on the 1948 War of Independence (which took place two years before he was born), the 1956 Sinai campaign, the 1967 Six Day War, and the War of Attrition which had ended only three years ago, in August 1970, a month before his first tour of duty at the Suez Canal.

The book he was consulting was written by a well-known Israeli leftist politician and began by describing the jubilant atmosphere in Israel after the 1967 war – when it was felt that peace was at hand, and the Arabs would now have no choice but to sit down at a conference table with the Israelis and find a way to settle the problems which confronted both sides.

In 1967 Uri had just turned seventeen, and he still vividly remembered his father, Meir, talking to him in the quiet unassuming way that Uri found so endearing.

'This victory is a wonderful thing,' he told Uri, 'now we will be able to bring up our children without them being forced to kill. They will no longer learn to hate. It will be good for everybody, the Arabs as well as ourselves.'

His father, and two million other Israelis turned out to be bad prophets, and the book described the frustration of Israelis as they gradually came to live with the idea of no war and no peace. Like the previous wars, the 1967 war had

9

been forced on Israel and from the point of view of achieving peace it had proved as sterile and futile as all of them.

On the problem which directly concerned Uri, the writer expressed strong views about the position of Arabs who had lived in Palestine previous to 1948 and then fled. He advanced the thesis that the State of Israel had come into being largely because of the guilty conscience of the world for the suffering the Jews had endured in Europe. The Arabs of Palestine had not caused this suffering, but in the end result they were punished for it, and rendered homeless.

In the course of the book the Israeli 'establishment' was criticised on almost every score. Uri felt that many of the arguments put forward were exaggerated, but he nevertheless took copious notes to weave into his project.

He glanced at his watch. Tomorrow would be the 'Day of Atonement', the holiest day in the Jewish Calendar, and the library was closing at eleven to enable everybody to get home while there was still public transport available.

Most of the students had already left when Uri returned the book to the librarian's desk, put his notes into a file, and went out. It was a beautiful day, and he felt a physical excitement beginning to take hold of him as he walked over to Zeev's apartment, where Aliza had promised to meet him.

Uri had many good friends, but Zeev was the one closest to him. They had first met when they started basic training in the armoured corps. An initial spark had sprung up between them, when Uri, who was good at anything to do with guns, used to help Zeev get ready for the dreaded inspections. One speck of dirt could bring about a thunder of criticism from the sergeant-major, and often an unpleasant punishment such as a six-kilometre stretcher hike carrying a 'wounded' soldier. In the three years of compulsory service that followed, hundreds of small happenings had cemented a bond which was stronger in many ways than the one he had with his younger brother Gadi.

At one time or another they had happily shared everything with each other, except their girlfriends. Only a few months earlier, Uri had been best man at Zeev's marriage to Vered, and when they moved into their apartment at Ramat Aviv next to the University, there had been an added bonus for Uri and Aliza, because it gave them a place where they could make love comfortably, without fear of being disturbed.

Uri pressed the buzzer at the entrance to the apartment, and when Vered opened the door he saw Aliza standing behind her. They made a nice contrast, Vered with her blonde curly hair, and Aliza with her huge dark eyes, white teeth, and straight black hair that fell below her shoulders.

'Come inside, quickly,' Vered teased him, 'Aliza's all worked up waiting for you.'

Uri blushed deeply and the two girls burst out laughing. Aliza had an advantage because her olive skin didn't reveal any traces of embarrassment. They had coffee and biscuits in the kitchen, and then Vered good-naturedly shooed them out, maintaining that she had work to do and that they were in her way.

They went into the bedroom, closing the door, and with the complete naturalness of two young people who love deeply and trust each other implicitly, they undressed, lay down on the bed and made love.

In the warm after-glow they relaxed with their arms wound around each other, eyes closed but neither of them wanting to sleep. Uri's thoughts drifted. He was essentially a serious person, conscious of his happiness, and aware that this was something which one did not always have, and that when it was there one should recognise and cherish it. In his daily life he was cautious, inclined to analyse and often to hold back on what he thought and felt. With Aliza he felt no barriers, no secrets that he could not divulge, no dream he could not share. And he had complete confidence that she believed in, and felt the same way towards him.

It was no accident that Aliza was a nurse. There was a warmth and gentleness about her which wrapped itself around her patients, and played not a small part in the healing process of those who were under her care. Uri thought she would make a wonderful mother. For a brief moment he envied Zeev, married with a place of his own, but he knew it was only a matter of time before he and Aliza would also enjoy these blessings.

A noise outside disturbed them and they realised Zeev had come home from work. It was already one o'clock. They dressed quickly and came out of the bedroom.

'Thank goodness,' laughed Zeev, 'we thought you'd

retired for the weekend!' They sat down and talked for a while but refused Vered's offer to have lunch as they would be eating early that evening, sharing with their respective families the big dinner which customarily preceded the twenty-four-hour Yom Kippur fast.

* * *

Sergeant Gadi Ishboneh, Uri's younger brother by just over a year, was on the last lap of his journey. He had left his base, Tasa, twenty kilometres from the Suez Canal, at six o'clock that morning. Unable to get a flight from the airport at Baluza, he had been forced to hitch-hike the four hundred or so kilometres to his home in Herzliya. It was now eight hours and five lifts later, and he was in the back of a Volkswagen travelling along the highway which by-passed the crowded business section of Tel Aviv. He would be home in less than an hour, revelling in a hot soapy bath, and with luck he might still have time to slip over to see Rina before the Yom Kippur dinner.

Gadi fancied himself, with some justice, as being the good looking one in the family, black curly hair cut short for the army, six foot tall, blue eyes and a dark tan nurtured by the sun in the Sinai desert, where he had been stationed for the last twelve months. He was tired from the long trip, and was thinking of Rina, recalling the afternoon he had spent with her on his last short leave, the memory of which had been running through his mind like a recurring daydream ever since.

They had gone down to the Herzliya beach for a late afternoon swim. He had dated her steadily on his last few leaves, but somehow they were always in a crowd, and this was the first time they had gone out just the two of them. They had swum far out, and he'd returned to the shore before her. He watched her as she waded slowly through the shallow water towards him, smiling. The sun had mellowed to its pre-dusk orange and her tanned skin shone bronze in its reflection. Tiny waves lapped against her legs, and a light breeze blew strands of gold-tinged hair around her face. For Gadi the moment was magic. Each had understood what the other was feeling. He'd held out his hand to her. She came towards him, and they stood locked in an embrace, oblivious to the stares of scattered beach-goers getting ready to go home.

'I love you Rina,' he whispered.

'I love you Gadi,' she whispered back . . .

Gadi had always played the field. He had had many girl friends, lots of affairs, and regarded himself as an experienced man of the world. He often affectionately chaffed Uri and Aliza, declaring that he wasn't going to get himself 'tied down' to a woman, even if he could find one as lovely as Aliza. Gadi had everything all worked out. He had been counting the days to the end of his army service, now only fifty-eight to go. He intended to get a job and earn some money quickly, enough to get him to Europe and from there to hitch-hike wherever his fancy took him, seeing everything, tasting everything, experiencing everything. He wanted to be free from army discipline, free from home restrictions, free from obligations to everything and everybody – just free.

It had all seemed so exciting, and now suddenly it was flat and uninteresting, and all his plans were new and serious, and all revolved around the little seventeen-year-old blonde who had only just finished school and was still too young to go into the army.

The Volkswagen pulled up with a jerk as a traffic light changed to red quicker than the driver anticipated, and Gadi realised that he had almost missed the turn-off to Herzliya. When the light changed to green the driver moved forward and pulled over to the side. Gadi climbed out and walked away from the throughway, up a short steep hill.

At the top he stood for a moment taking in the green beauty of the Sharon Valley. He could see the apartments where they lived, only two kilometres down the road. Directly behind him and just as close, the beautiful blue Mediterranean sea shore sparkled in the bright sun. Gadi had no difficulty getting his last lift of the day, and five minutes later he was bounding up the stairs of his block and letting himself in with his key, while Shoshana was still running from the kitchen to throw her arms around her 'baby'. She had on her usual floral apron and her bright eyes shone as she let Gadi crush her in his embrace.

Shoshana was in the middle of cooking two big meals, the dinner preceding the fast, and the dinner for Saturday

13

night, with which they would break the fast, and which she was not allowed to prepare during the day of Yom Kippur. She had a round pleasant face, a surprisingly smooth complexion for a woman in her mid-fifties, and brown hair turning grey and tied simply in a bun behind her neck.

'Hi Mom! Did Rina call?'

'Rina! Rina!' she replied with mock jealousy. 'Can't you think of anything else these days? . . . Yes, she called. She's waiting for you to come over, but don't forget we're starting dinner at four forty-five sharp.'

'Okay Mom. I'm going to have a bath first. You can come in and talk to me if you like.'

'As if I've got nothing else to do,' snorted Shoshana with a happy smile all over her face. All her three men were now accounted for, and she went back to the kitchen cheerfully preparing to feed them until they could eat no more.

By the time Gadi had dressed in his one civilian suit and left to see Rina, Uri was already home and Meir had awoken from his afternoon sleep and was waiting patiently for him to finish using the bathroom.

Meir sat on a faded wicker chair on the patio with the weekend edition of *Uj Kelet*, the local Hungarian daily paper, open on his lap. The traffic was still heavy on the road outside as people made their way homewards, and Meir found it more pleasant to close his eyes and relax than concentrate on the newspaper which was full of election speeches and propaganda.

He could hear Shoshana busy in the kitchen and a feeling of affectionate pride went through him. They had been through so much together, and on a day like this, with the Yom Kippur festival approaching and their two grown boys home to spend it with them, who could say that it hadn't all been worth while?

Outwardly there was little to distinguish Meir and Shoshana Ishboneh from half a million other East European Jews who had made their way to Israel after the Holocaust. Each Jew had his own story of the horror he had been through. Few of them were able to talk freely about it, and what was unspeakable remained bottled up inside them, surfacing at unexpected and uncontrolled moments, sometimes in extreme joy, sometimes under stress or fear, and sometimes in nightmares, when they would awake scream-

14

ing incoherently and sweating out the terror of a long past crisis. With Meir and Shoshana there was a difference, a quirk of fate which had somehow made the unbearable bearable.

Meir had been born Michael Bauman in the small Transsylvanian town of Zilahborsa. His father was a prosperous wine merchant and Mickey, as he was affectionately called, was the third generation of Baumans to be born there. In 1814 the founder of their small dynasty had wandered into Zilahborsa as a pedlar, fallen in love with a young Jewish girl whose father owned a small plot of ground on the outskirts of the town, and was more than amenable to accept the plot as a marriage dowry. Part of the ground was already cultivated with vines, and the young pedlar using a homemade recipe that he had learned from his mother, soon found that there was a good market for his wine. The family prospered, bought the grape harvests of neighbouring Gentile farmers, and over the years built large cellars for the wine to ferment and mature.

More of the Gentile farmers switched to vine cultivation and the Baumans contributed substantially to the economic progress of the town. Over the years problems developed as the Bauman family grew noticeably rich and the farmers demanded higher and higher prices for their grapes. There was envy and anti-semitism and veiled threats, but the family, like other Jewish families in the town, learned to grease the right palms, and somehow no real crisis developed. Pogroms in other parts of the country simply meant a temporary increase in the amount of 'protection money' needed.

Mickey grew up almost without a care in the world. He loved the fields around them, the smell of the grapes when they were picked and crushed, and the coolness of the cellars with their huge vats. He married young, a beautiful blonde girl from Budapest, and somewhat against his will, had moved to the city and gone to work in her father's wholesale food business. Hilda had given birth to twin girls, and life was good until the Germans came.

In 1944 Mickey's world came to an end as he watched Hilda walking up the ramp at Auschwitz with the girls clinging to her. In his heart he felt that he had died, that nothing could ever have meaning for him any more, that he could never again know happiness – never love.

15

And then when the war was over, by sheer chance he had met Shoshana, who also came from Žilahborsa, when they both stopped to look at the same shop window in a side street in Budapest. They recognised each other immediately. She was a few years younger than he was, and had been married to Janos, an enterprising and highly-respected notary. He and their two little boys had died in the ovens at Maidanek.

Drawn together by the bottomless horrors of their common suffering, they had clung to each other, and a miracle happened. They were born again! Within two weeks of their meeting they were married, and on their way to Israel to start a new life together ... and Uri was born, and then Gadi.

Meir felt at peace with the world, happy with Shoshana, happy with his two boys, a lovely family, a complete family, what more could a man ask for ... ?

At three o'clock the radio and TV transmitted the last news bulletins before closing down. Outside the road was already bare of traffic, and an air of quietness and peace took hold of the country as everything came to a virtual standstill.

At a quarter to five they all sat down for dinner. From experience none of them had eaten lunch and it did Shoshana's heart good to see the chicken soup, the roast chicken and crisp roast potatoes disappear. Both Gadi and Uri asked for second helpings. Stewed fruit and black coffee followed, and when they finished, Shoshana lit the Sabbath candles and the light in remembrance of the dead, and Meir recited the short blessing to God ending 'who has kept us in life and has preserved us and enabled us to reach this season'.

Groups of people were already walking past on their way to prayers at the modest neighbourhood Shul. Shoshana tidied up quickly and the four of them left the house together. Meir felt a warm glow inside as he walked with the two boys towering above him. He was not an observant Jew, but for him and hundreds of thousands like him, this evening was a special one, embodying a mixture of intense seriousness and joyous pride of identification with God and His people.

Shoshana left them at the entrance to the brightly-lit, Shul, and went upstairs where the women sat separately, partly concealed behind a semi-transparent curtain.

Meir and the two boys put on their prayer shawls and took their seats in row fifteen facing the Holy Ark, the sanctuary in which the sacred scrolls were kept. All around them friends nodded their heads in greeting and wished them 'Hatima Tovah' – 'a good inscription', meaning that when God came to weigh up their sins over the past year and their repentance on this solemn day, He would in His infinite mercy ensure their survival and well-being for the coming year.

Shoshana found a seat near the back next to Shula Singer, her neighbour and best friend, whose husband Chaim worked in the same office as Meir. She craned her neck to see the place where Meir and the boys were sitting, but she was too far back, and the curtain cut off her view. In any event she had the clearest picture of them in her mind, all in their best suits, and the quiet little smile of satisfaction which Meir would have as he 'showed off' his boys.

Shoshana knew that the boys were not really keen to come to Shul, but they accepted it for Meir's sake. Although after all these years Meir had not advanced to an important position at the factory where he worked, and had not achieved material success, somehow the boys did not seem to mind. They often teased their father, and occasionally there had been serious family arguments, but there was no doubt about their affection and respect for him.

Perhaps this was a result of his infinite love and patience with them, or perhaps it was in response to the strength of his character, which belied his mild outward appearance, and which had been like a rock for the family to lean on; and for her personally, a haven from all her darkest fears.

Her biggest difference with Meir over the years had been on the question of reparations from Germany, and the boys had instantly sided with him. Shoshana never mentioned this any more, but when times had been really bad she had argued with him about making an application.

'We're not asking them to do us favours,' she would say, 'just to give us back a little of what they stole from us.'

But his answer was always the same.

'I will not take money from those swines.'

'But Chaim made an application. He says they may get a pension of ten thousand lirot a year, and almost everybody who is entitled has made one. Why should we be different?'

'What Chaim does is his business, nor do I care how many others do it. It would be like letting them pay for what they did to Hilda and the twins. How much money would you take to square the debt for Janos and your two boys?'

Shoshana knew it wasn't the same thing, but she had no answer.

The excited murmur of the worshippers gradually died away to be replaced by a solemn, reverent silence, out of which emerged the age-old lament, the Kol Nidre. The Cantor sang the words, his voice beseeching the Almighty for forgiveness, with a sincerity that pierced to the very depth of feeling of those present. Meir felt a shudder running down his spine. When the last eerie note died away, the congregation again chanted the sacred verses, each person offering God Almighty his humble life to be weighed, judged and discarded, if He so decided.

It was dark when the crowd emerged from the Shul, and began to break up into family units, walking towards their homes or visiting friends and neighbours for a chat before retiring. Gadi and Rina had already left. Uri was walking with Aliza, and as they passed Meir and Shoshana she smiled and greeted them and Meir thought how pretty she was.

'Meir!' He turned and saw Chaim Singer and Shula and their fourteen-year-old son Eitan. They walked together, Shula and Shoshana a few steps behind the two men and the boy.

'Did you hear?' asked Chaim.

'About Danny?' Meir enquired.

He knew that Chaim's older son, Danny, a pilot in the airforce, had been called back to his base early that morning, but he had not attached any significance to this. The airforce was often 'on the alert'.

'No, about the five Syrian Migs we shot down this afternoon.'

'Who told you? Danny?'

'No he hasn't phoned, but everybody's talking about it. And they say Egged put all its bus-drivers "on alert" today.'

'Well I certainly haven't heard anything about Migs. And I can't see what Egged's drivers have got to do with a few planes that get shot down.'

'Neither can I, but so many people have told me, that they can't just be rumours.'

'Forget it Chaim. Let's go home and have a good night's sleep.'

Just before they entered their apartment block, a car dashed by at speed, its lights full on. And just behind it, a heavy truck.

'Bastards!' cursed Meir. 'Haven't they got any consideration for people's feelings, even on a night like this?'

Meir and Shoshana went to bed early, and were soon fast asleep. The neighbourhood was quiet, although peculiarly the silence was broken by more and more cars speeding by.

Saturday, 6th October

Meir and Shoshana were suddenly woken out of their sleep by a deep, angry rumble on the road outside. The sounds penetrated the room with startling harshness, and fumbling for the light, Meir switched it on, and scrambled out of bed. He glanced at the clock which showed just after four o'clock and threw open the window. Outside a number of trucks moved slowly along the road, their headlights cutting stark, white avenues through the darkness.

'Army trucks, Shosh. Full of soldiers. I'm going downstairs.'

'All right but put your gown on.'

On the sidewalk, he bumped into Chaim Singer, also in his gown and pyjamas.

'What do you think of that rumour now?' said Chaim.

'What do you mean?'

'About the five Migs.'

'What's happening with all those trucks?' asked Meir, ignoring the comment about the Syrian Migs.

'Nobody knows. I don't ever remember seeing army vehicles travelling on Yom Kippur. An ambulance maybe, but not troop carriers. For God's sake! It must be something serious.'

'What do you mean, "something serious"?'

'I don't know. Maybe the terrorists thought they would be clever starting something on Yom Kippur and we're going into Lebanon to clean them out. I wish Danny would phone, then we'd know for sure.'

'Well, whatever is going on there's not much we can do about it. Let's go back to bed and try to snatch another hour or two of sleep.'

All over the country Israelis were waking up to a highly unusual morning. It wasn't so much the odd car or truck that sped by as the shock it gave people to see such a thing happening on Yom Kippur. Many devout Jews on their way to prayers, were enraged and shouted angrily at the drivers for their apparent blasphemy. Meir arrived at Shul about seven o'clock. It was already three-quarters full, and the worshippers seemed to be chanting their prayers with a singular anguished fervour, which was more justified than most of them realised.

At that moment the general mobilisation of Israel's defence capacity was already under way. Soldiers on leave, like Gadi, were being contacted and told to rejoin their units as quickly as possible. In addition there was an emergency call-up of Israel's vast civilian army – tens of thousands of reservists, and a variety of vehicles – buses, trucks, bull-dozers, delivery vans of all descriptions and even private cars with their drivers. From early dawn, offices, relay-stations, communication centres not used since 1967, were being activated. Call-up orders and lists of names were issued to couriers who rushed out to deliver them to officers in charge of different units or cells. The officers started phoning their men, setting into motion arrangements includ-ing private cars to round them up, and deliver them directly to their assembly points. It should have been a well-rehearsed, smooth operation. In fact there was a great deal of confusion, errors and misunderstandings.

Israel Radio, with special code signals for each unit, was an important factor in the efficiency of the mobilisation process. On Yom Kippur it was closed down during the vital morning hours.

The orders for Gadi to rejoin his unit, and for Uri to make his way to a pre-arranged assembly point reached them at around nine-thirty, while they were still in Shul. One of the youngsters who lived in their block brought the news, and after a brief whispered discussion they indicated to Meir that they were leaving.

Meir, already knowing the answer, asked, 'What is it boys?'

'We've been called up, Dad, we must go.'

'Today, on Yom Kippur?'

'Come out with us for a moment. People are watching us.'

In the courtyard a few other men were also leaving and Meir felt his heart thumping in his chest.

'What is it Uri?'

'Nothing to worry about that we know of, Dad.'

'If it's nothing to worry about, then why are so many being called? And why on Yom Kippur?'

'Dad, I honestly don't know,' said Uri patiently. 'The boy who came to call us said there was trouble up north. Gadi heard a rumour this morning that something's happening down at the Canal. There's no point our worrying at this stage, but we must go immediately.'

'I'm sorry. I'm a bit shocked. Can't you even stay for "Yiskor"? Mom will be upset. You've got to go home anyway to change. I'll go with you.'

'No Dad, please! Mom will get a fright if you're not here when Shul comes out. You'll have to say goodbye to her for us.'

'What about money?'

'No. We've got enough, thanks. We'll try to phone you. Shalom.'

Uri and Gadi tore themselves away. Meir stood watching as they walked quickly down the road and disappeared from view. Then he went back into Shul, just in time to join the 'Yiskor', the sacred prayer for the memory of the dead. There were so many that he had to remember. It was like a compartment locked in his mind that he had to force himself to open – for his parents, for his brothers and sisters, for Hilda and the twins. Also for Shosh's Janos and their two boys.

Some hours passed. Thoughts about the boys kept intruding and Meir found himself unable to concentrate on the prayers. He went outside and started pacing up and down the courtyard, and was joined within a few minutes by a visibly disturbed Chaim Singer.

'I saw your boys leave,' Chaim said, 'do they know anything?'

Meir stopped pacing, and turned abruptly to face him.

'No! Nobody seems to know anything, just rumours. What do you think, Chaim? What do you really think?'

'I wish I knew. Yossi Shimon came to Shul only a few minutes ago. He heard the BBC news at one o'clock. They said that there have been tremendous troop movements, thousands of tanks, in Syria and on the Canal – and the Cabinet's meeting in Tel Aviv!'

'The Cabinet! Good God . . . !'

22

Suddenly he stopped talking. Shoshana was approaching them.

'Where are the boys?'

'They were called up, Shosh. They left in a tremendous hurry. You were upstairs. They didn't want to . . .'

'Are you all crazy? Why didn't you call me, for heaven's sake! How could you let them leave like that – without saying goodbye. All these rumours! What's going on?'

She was shaken and did not try to hide it. The men looked at each other. Before either of them could answer, something almost unthinkable occurred. Somebody had brought a transistor radio to the Shul, and the sharp intermittent beeps signalling the beginning of an Israel Radio news broadcast, sounded shrilly across the courtyard.

It was 2.00 pm. Without a word they hurried to join the cluster of people, many wearing their prayer-shawls, anxiously trying to catch every word the announcer was saying.

'The Egyptians and Syrians have launched simultaneous attacks at the Suez Canal, and the Golan Heights respectively. They opened fire around 1.50 pm on both fronts. Israeli troops are fighting to hold back the massive onslaught of the enemy . . .'

Suddenly in the middle of the announcement, the radio was drowned out by a much more sinister sound: the up and down wail of the air-raid siren.

Israel's radar system had picked up an unidentified object on its screens and within seconds the red button was pressed activating every siren in the country. Two fighter planes circling fifteen thousand feet above Tel Aviv received urgent instructions, banked sharply westwards and headed out at maximum speed over the sea.

The public shelter underneath the synagogue was locked, and there was a moment of confusion and panic until the Cantor came running up with a key, and the crowd hurriedly forced its way in. Everyone was strangely quiet, their faces pale and strained. Many, especially the older ones, simply continued their prayers.

The planes soon had the unidentified object on their radarscreens and when they actually sighted it, it looked like a relatively small, slow-moving plane. It was in fact a Kelt missile, which had been released by a lone Egyptian

Tupilov 16 bomber, flying low over the Mediterranean eighty kilometres out to sea – and, packed with three hundred kilograms of high-explosive, was heading directly for the heart of Tel Aviv.

Tense with excitement and over-eagerness, the pilots' first bursts of fire missed the target, but rapidly adjusting their controls the subsequent bursts hit home deflecting the missile downwards and causing it to plunge harmlessly into the sea less than two minutes away from its destination.

The all-clear signal came half an hour later. Unaware of the danger that had been avoided, the congregation of the Herzliya Shul, trooped noisily and somewhat relieved, back to continue the service. Quite a few had left but more started to arrive. The people of Israel had a new, urgent reason to appeal to their God through prayer. The dreaded event which lingered always at the back of their minds, had burst upon them once again. A new war had begun, and the name of it came naturally to the lips of everybody – The Yom Kippur War.

* * *

As soon as they entered the apartment Uri phoned Zeev, but Vered said he had left two hours earlier, after trying unsuccessfully to contact him. Gadi and Uri spent only a few minutes changing into their uniforms. Outside they were picked up by a private car, which took them to the Tel Aviv–Haifa expressway where they alighted and said goodbye to each other. On a sudden impulse they embraced and then parted without a word, Uri remaining on the right of the highway, heading north towards the Golan Heights. Gadi crossed to the opposite side to get a lift in the direction of Tel Aviv.

There were already many vehicles travelling in both directions. Uri was the first to hitch a ride when an army command car halted. Gadi could see that there wasn't too much room but the soldiers in the back moved over and Uri climbed in as it sped away.

Several cars passed Gadi before a white Volvo pulled up and the driver opened the door for him to climb in. At the Ramat-Aviv junction, he got out and began walking towards the Sde Dov Airport. Instead of hitching to his unit, he had decided to take a chance on getting a flight south to one of the army airfields in the Sinai desert.

He wasn't the only one to have thought of this. A large number of reservists dressed in civilian clothes, crowded the small departure lounge. Some had not had time to go home and change, others didn't even have uniforms and would only be issued with them when they got to their bases. A few still had on their prayer-shawls and while they were waiting, continued praying, oblivious to the surrounding turmoil.

Gadi was reminded of the feverish atmosphere preceding the Six Day War, when he was only a high school student, enviously watching the reservists heading towards their units. Now he was a member of Zahal, the Israel Defence Force, and he felt a distinct pride at being grown up and belonging.

He elbowed his way through the hall hoping to meet somebody from his own unit, but had no luck until he headed back towards the entrance, and suddenly felt a strong slap on the back. He turned and excitedly greeted Shmuel, the first lieutenant and commander in charge of his tank.

'It's good to see you Shmuel,' said Gadi.

'You too! Are you on a flight already?'

'No, are you?'

'I've got my motor-bike outside. I hoped I would find someone from the unit here. I think we should go to Rafiach before we go to Tasa. Some of our tanks are there and we may need them.'

'What good will they be unless we get some tank carriers?'

'If we're on the spot we've got a better chance of organising carriers – and in any event, we'll know more of what is happening by the time we get there.'

'You talk as though you really believe there's going to be a war.'

'I do!'

For a brief moment Gadi was silent. There had been other call-ups before, not quite as dramatic – but still – in his heart-of-hearts Gadi didn't really believe that this might be it. It was unreal, like a bad dream, but not really frightening . . . just a feeling of excitement, mixed with a vague chill of apprehension. Gadi tried not to show his confusion.

'I'm with you,' he said to Shmuel. 'Let's get going. In any

event it doesn't look like we've got a hope of getting a plane out of here.'

On the way out they passed the flight desk, where there was complete bedlam. An unruly crowd was pressing around a sergeant-major wearing an air-force jacket. 'Patience,' he kept repeating, 'there will be flights down, but it may still be an hour or so.'

Two telephones were ringing beside him, but he paid no attention to them. From outside the overpowering roar of a plane landing, momentarily drowned out the commotion in the lounge. It was a Nord, a fairly old French transport plane, used for paratroop training. The lounge doors almost flew off their hinges as the uncontrollable crowd surged out on to the tarmac and surrounded it, trying to ensure that they would get a seat.

Shmuel and Gadi climbed on to the motor-bike, a 600 BMW, and set off towards the Geha Road, which would take them straight down towards Ashdod, Ashkelon, Gaza and the Sinai desert. The highway was already packed with vehicles. There were giant-sized tank carriers without tanks, and other trucks trailing artillery pieces. Drivers fumed and cursed as they got stuck behind these monsters, some of them occupying the entire width of the road.

Shmuel laughed with pleasure as they zig-zagged easily through the narrow gaps between the vehicles. For a while it looked like they had overtaken the main traffic, but soon there was another long column, and then another, a seemingly never ending line.

'This is one hell of a way to spend Yom Kippur, isn't it?' called Shmuel, his voice trailing back in the strong wind, as the bike raced forward. They had already passed Ashdod and Ashkelon, and were entering Gaza.

It was deserted, a sure sign that something serious was happening. The shops were closed and the market-place was devoid of people. The Arab population was sitting inside their houses and wondering with mixed feelings how this new crisis was going to hit them.

Near the end of the town they came upon a real traffic jam. Two private cars had become entangled in a head-on collision, and the highway was totally blocked. The crew of a police tow-truck was working to sort out the mess and even Shmuel's motorbike wasn't allowed through. A military transport plane flew by at near tree-top level. The boys looked at each other. 'Lucky bastards,' murmured Shmuel.

'I don't know,' said Gadi, 'I think this is much more exciting.'

About ten minutes later the police started to wave the traffic through. Shmuel was the first to be able to shoot out of the long bottleneck down the now empty highway ahead of them. Suddenly he slowed down, pulling over to the side of the road and braked to a halt.

'Listen to that!' he said.

Softly, but unmistakably, they could hear the sound of air-raid sirens in the distance. A small army coupe approached and Shmuel, wanting to know what was happening, signalled for it to stop. As it pulled up they heard the radio turned up full giving a news commentary. Afterwards the driver filled in the details of what had already been said, and the two soldiers felt strangely shaken at this final confirmation that they were heading straight into the middle of a full-scale war . . .

Half an hour later they arrived at the huge storage and assembly camp at Rafiach. Vehicles of all sorts, military and civilian, clogged the spaces between the army huts and the warehouses. The place was in a turmoil. Men hurried in all directions, most of them reservists dressed in civilian clothes, looking for the group to which they belonged, and the officers who could issue them with kitbags and tell them what to do. The kitbags contained a full battle uniform, water-flask, helmet, ammunition pouch and all the other essentials for a front-line soldier. At one warehouse an officer was yelling at his men to make up their own kitbags from the myriad supplies on the shelves around them.

Shmuel and Gadi, still on the bike, headed for the armoured section. The officer in charge was a giant of a man, a veteran of all Israel's wars since 1948, when he arrived from South Africa as a volunteer, and afterwards, had decided to settle. Every officer in the armoured corps, senior and junior called him 'Saffi', and he invariably remembered them all by their first names. He was one of the few people around that seemed to be working methodically without getting over-excited.

'Shalom Saffi,' said Shmuel, without wasting time on

27

formalities, 'what's the position with our tanks? Have you sent them down yet?'

'If I didn't think you were serious, I'd be laughing,' came the reply. 'Maybe you brought a couple of tank carriers with you?'

Shmuel had half expected this, and did not take offence at the sarcasm.

'But are our tanks ready to go . . . ? Ammunition, fuel . . . ?'

'Well, I'll have to make a confession to you Shmuel, I've sent three of them out already, but not to Tasa. They are needed desperately at "Pizza",' – he used the code-name of the northern-most stronghold on the Bar-Lev Line – 'and I had no choice but to send them off on their own tracks. I know you won't like it, but that's the way it is.'

Shmuel respected Saffi's judgement and didn't attempt to argue with him.

'What about the others?' he asked.

'How many do you need?'

'I can take two right now.'

'Okay. Give me thirty minutes.'

In between giving orders and organising a hundred and one details, Saffi told them that the units he specifically controlled had been caught in a bad situation from the supply point of view. His first division of reservists had been relieved from their position on the Canal only three days before. The second division had been due to arrive two weeks later so there should have been ample time for the uniforms to be laundered, all the equipment checked and fresh kitbags made up. Now everything was in a mess, and they were working frantically to get it in order.

Saffi complained that he had plenty of men sitting waiting to go down to the Canal, but not enough troop-carriers and other vehicles.

'We're sending tanks in without any back-up cover,' he said. 'It's just looking for trouble but we have no choice.'

Shmuel intervened to ask whose fault it was that there were not enough vehicles and received the unexpected reply that he should blame Sapir for all the budget cuts in the last two years.

Their tanks were ready in thirty minutes as Saffi had promised. Shmuel and Gadi had intended to drive down alone, but Saffi insisted that they take full crews even though the men belonged to different units. 'Better that they should be waiting at Tasa with nothing to do, than kicking their heels here,' he said.

It was five o'clock before they left the camp, and the two hundred kilometre journey to Tasa was one of the longest and most uncomfortable tank rides that Gadi had ever experienced. They arrived at three a.m., exhausted. Shmuel went straight to the major's tent to report. In a few minutes he returned, grim-faced.

'I want you all to try to get some sleep. You've got exactly two hours. We're moving again at dawn, and you're going to need all your strength, so don't fool around.'

Gadi needed no urging. He crawled into the nearest tent, put his head on his kitbag and fell fast asleep.

* * *

The driver of the command car that had stopped for Uri, sported a full British army-style moustache. He drove with the accelerator pressed down to the floorboard, and seemed to take a special delight in going through the red light at the Netanya junction. The back of the car was open with twelve men squeezed on to the uncomfortable benches. Including Uri only four were in full uniform.

A middle aged, pot-bellied man sitting opposite Uri kept shifting his gaze around, anxious and frightened, as though he was trapped and looking for a way out.

A Yemenite with a coal black beard and long, tubular curls, wearing a skull cap, was bobbing back and forth, mumbling his prayers.

Next to Uri two long-haired youngsters, their army shirts tucked incongruously into their blue jeans, cigarettes in hand, were talking to each other, and Uri couldn't help overhearing their conversation.

'My mom was absolutely shaken, you would have thought that I was going away for twenty years . . . '

'My family too. My dad crying – actually crying. I've never seen him like that before.'

'I don't understand them. First of all, it will probably turn out to be a false alarm. If the Arabs are crazy enough to start a war we'll walk right over them. Look what happened to those Syrian Migs a few weeks ago. Thirteen shot down in less than half an hour.'

'I agree with you. I doubt if we'll even be lucky enough to see any action.'

'I still can't get over it though! I mean how upset my parents were. It almost made me feel good – as if I were a big hero.'

'Yeah. That's it, all right! I felt the same way.'

Uri's thoughts drifted. He remembered that in all the fuss of saying goodbye to his father, he had forgotten to send a message to Aliza. Oh well, maybe he would be able to send her a card when he got back to base.

Uri intended to get off at the Afula turn-off, but as they approached it, he saw about a hundred soldiers waiting, and made a snap decision to carry on to Acre and go via Safad. The car sped swiftly past the golf course at Caesarea, and now the road ran very close to the sea. Uri's mind was in a turmoil. He wished he had the unthinking bravado of the two youngsters, but somehow he felt that things were happening over which he had no control. Was it possible that a war could really begin? So suddenly? So stupidly?

They passed Mount Carmel and entered downtown Haifa, where several large cargo ships were at anchor in the bay. At the old British checkpoint on the outskirts of the town, the pot-bellied passenger and two of the soldiers in uniform got out. Other soldiers standing on the side of the road took their places.

At the traffic island at Kiryat Bialik, they caught up with unbroken lines of trailers, army trucks, and half-tracks stretching north as far as they could see. There was nothing they could do except stay in line and crawl along. It took nearly an hour and a half for the journey from Haifa to Acre, and Uri cursed himself several times for not getting off earlier at the exit to Afula. On the outskirts of Acre the command car finally drew to the side and stopped. The driver shouted that he was going to Nahariya and they all got off.

Uri had a difficult time getting his next lift. The army cars were full and he began walking. It was a nice warm day, maybe too nice. A small NSU approached and stopped next to another soldier about a hundred metres away from him. Uri ran towards it waving frantically, and fortunately there was still room for one more. It was headed towards Safad. He felt ridiculously excited, at last he was getting somewhere. The driver, an attractive young woman, was talking to one of the passengers in a poor Hebrew with a marked foreign accent, which seemed to be Dutch.

Uri waited for the first break in the conversation, then asked tentatively, 'Is there any news?'

'Yes,' said the woman, 'according to the radio it doesn't sound too good. Both Syria and Egypt have attacked in force, and we are fighting to hold them back.'

Uri felt a sinking feeling in his stomach. Just at that moment two powerful sonic-booms shook the little car. 'Phantoms,' said Uri. At a tremendous height in the sky they could see two white smoke streaks racing northwards.

'They're going to pound the Syrians, aren't they?' inquired the young woman earnestly.

'I'll ask them just as soon as they land,' said the man sitting next to Uri. They all began to laugh, and for a while the tension seemed to slip away . . .

From Safad Uri made the next lap of his journey in the driver's cabin of a heavy truck, arriving at the gas station at Rosh Pina at about three-thirty in the afternoon.

The Syrian attack was already in full swing, having begun with an extremely heavy artillery barrage against the Israeli positions on the '67 cease fire line. Except in the north where the armour had been recently reinforced on Dayan's instructions, the Golan positions were manned by a pitifully inadequate number of troops, without a fraction of the equipment necessary to halt the massive assault of the enemy. Most of the eight hundred tanks which the Syrians threw into the first battles were modern Soviet-made tanks including the formidable T-62's, never before used in battle.

On that first day, for reasons of their own, the Syrian air-force picked on the undefended Druse villages of Majdal Shams, Musada and Bukata. They strafed and bombed them, killing several men and women and injuring fifteen. A mother picking fruit in the fields, and her small daughter were among the first casualties of the new war.

More serious from the military point of view, elite helicopter-borne commando units landed right on top of Mountain Hermon and stormed the supposedly impregnable Israeli-held strongpoint. With only about a dozen fighting men to defend it, the fight was short and savage, and the result inevitable. The Israeli public was not upset by this disaster. They were simply not informed of it.

When Uri got out of the truck, at Rosh Pina, the scene was a mixture of activity and great confusion. Army and civilian vehicles stood in a solid line stretching north in the direction of Kiryat Shmoneh. In the distance the rumble of artillery fire was unmistakable. There were no local civilians to be seen. The sirens had sounded, and they were sitting in air-raid shelters.

He hurried to the military checkpoint straddling the road, where a harassed, gesticulating military policeman was trying to get some semblance of order among all the converging vehicles. Uri tried in vain to get some information from him. He decided he'd better move on, and walked past the checkpoint enquiring from all the vehicles in the line-up until he found one that was heading for the Bnot Yaacov bridge. The driver was only too pleased to take him. There was a turn-off to the bridge about five kilometres out of Rosh Pina, which was the shortest route to Kuneitra, once the biggest town on the Golan. It had been partially destroyed in '67, and his unit was stationed in some of the deserted buildings.

The truck ahead of them lurched forward, and they followed. The driver was short and tubby with fat red cheeks, hair partly grey and with a bald patch in the front. He was munching a sandwich. The explosions sounded closer.

'It sounds like they're bombing Kiryat Shmoneh. Do you want a sandwich?'

'No thank you. I don't feel like eating.'

'Observant?'

'Not really. I don't feel like anything.'

'They told us in Afula that the Chief Rabbi waived the fasting for soldiers. Where is your unit?'

'Kuneitra.'

'There's been a lot of fighting around there. The Syrians have probably taken it by now.'

Uri felt miserable and irritated by the matter of fact attitude of the driver. Two sonic booms shook the windows of the truck. 'It looks like our flying boys have woken up. Doesn't it?' said the driver. Uri didn't answer. He was thinking about his unit, wondering where they would go to if they'd had to get out of Kuneitra.

At the Bnot Yaacov bridge they were waved through. The truck began climbing, its engine straining as it laboured up the steep hair-pin bends. Once over the Heights, the road levelled off and it picked up some speed. They passed the village of Nafach with its huge army camp, but a long line of vehicles indicated another road block. Uri jumped out and ran to the head of the column. There was a jeep across the road and a military policeman was explaining something to an officer. Uri tried to catch a few words of the conversation, but only heard 'Sukhois' and 'heavy artillery'.

The noise of the explosions was now very loud. They were close to the battlefield and he could distinguish the bursting of artillery shells and tank guns, as well as bombs.

Uri told the officer that he was trying to get to his unit at Kuneitra.

'Do you have any idea where they would be now?' he asked. The officer looked at him and Uri felt there was pity in his eyes.

'No, I'm sorry. We're diverting all the traffic to Waset.'

In desperation Uri requested permission to continue by foot.

'No,' replied the officer, 'It's absolutely forbidden: Under no circumstances!'

Uri turned back, and climbed into the same truck again.

'That's the way it goes,' said the driver cheerfully. 'Want a sandwich?'

'No.'

'It's my fourth war son. It's not worth getting yourself so tense at this stage. Take my advice, calm down a bit and try to eat something!'

Uri appreciated the common sense of what the driver had said. He took the sandwich which had been offered to him, a turkey shnitzel with a piece of green pepper between two slices of bread, and chewed it slowly. It was the first food he had eaten all day. Then he relaxed and settled back accepting the fact that he could do nothing more until they arrived at Waset.

3

Sunday, 7th October

It was after two o'clock in the morning when Meir and Shoshana finally switched off the radio and retired to bed. Meir had woken up again a few hours later, tired but unable to sleep.

Now, even more than in '67 he was frustrated by not understanding every word of the Hebrew news broadcast. There were services for new immigrants in other languages but not at frequent intervals, and important events might be happening at any moment. His thoughts wandered round in circles. Golda had spoken on TV. She looked exhausted. Yet she was as reassuring as ever. God bless her!

Shoshana was still fast asleep. He got out of bed, found his slippers, threw his gown over his shoulders and tip-toed out to the kitchen: A good hot coffee will wake me up. He filled the kettle, and lit the gas flame under it. How and where did the boys spend the night? He took out a packet of cigarettes. He knew he shouldn't smoke before breakfast, but this Sunday wasn't a day like other days. War! Again! He felt the awful burden.

Suddenly the air-raid sirens started their horrible up-and-down wailing. Coat over pyjamas, Shoshana appeared at the door, Meir saw that she was scared. She was holding her large leather shopping bag, in which she had put their savings-books and a few valuables the night before. Without a word they walked down the steps towards the shelter. The baby next door was screaming, and some of the other babies also started to cry. Civil defence workers tried to keep everybody calm, and helped a few older people who had difficulty with the steps leading down into the reinforced concrete shelter.

They hardly had time to seat themselves alongside the stark unpainted walls, when a long continuous wail of the siren signalled that it was all clear again. On their way out of the shelter Meir took Chaim Singer aside.

'When did you last listen to the news?'

'At six o'clock.'

'What's going on, Chaim, I'm scared I'm missing part of what they say.' Chaim's usually merry eyes were sober. 'It looks bad. They aren't giving details, but the Syrians have taken part of the Golan, and the Egyptians have crossed the Canal. Do you need to hear more than that?'

'No. I thought that's what it was, but I wasn't sure. Chaim I've had a bad feeling ever since all this started. I can't explain it. As though everything has gone wrong. Do you know what I mean?'

'Yes. I also feel that way. I've got no doubt that we'll win in the end, but I'm scared. Danny's up there somewhere. God knows what he's going through at this moment.'

'Are you going to work?'

'No. What about you?'

'I'm also not going; not today. I couldn't leave Shosh alone. And besides, I don't think anyone else will turn up either. I'm going to walk down and see if I can get a paper. Do you want to come?'

'No, I'd better go back to Shula. I think she's becoming a bit hysterical about Danny.'

Meir bought a copy of *Uj Kelet* and sat down on the bench near the news-stand. Opposite, a long line of people waited for a bus to Tel Aviv, but none came. Some of them tried to hitch, and most of the private cars were stopping.

Crowds of housewives were leaving the supermarket with overloaded shopping bags. Meir looked at them and was disgusted. He remembered wartime Europe, when food had become the only currency. A feeling of despair and gloom was beginning to take hold of him, and the more he tried to fight it off, the deeper it became.

He opened the paper and scanned the headlines. Moshe Dayan said we were fighting a total of nearly 350,000 enemy soldiers on the two fronts. The Israeli Navy had sunk four Syrian missile boats and a torpedo boat, using for the first time Israeli-made 'Gabriel' surface-to-surface missiles. The Egyptian strength was estimated at 700 planes, 2,000 tanks, and 1,500 artillery weapons. The Syrians: 500 planes, 800 tanks, and 800 long- and medium-range guns. Both armies were fitted out with the most modern Soviet equipment. He put the paper down.

Uri! Gadi! Where are you now? What are you fighting against? So many tanks! We didn't bring you up to fight Russian tanks. My God! Is this the new life that Shosh and I built up from Auschwitz and Maidahek? We were so happy your mother and I . . . Such fine boys. When I was your age I never wore a uniform. My father 'arranged' the matter . . . I suppose I did really wear a uniform, if you can think of a yellow star as a uniform . . .

Abruptly he stood up, and began walking home. Shoshana was in the kitchen cooking. He could smell fried onions. 'I'm making stuffed cabbages,' she said. 'You know how much they like them, even if one of them shows up during the night I can warm them up very quickly. Sarah Goldman said I'd better go and buy food. She's bought a full month's supply.'

'Let her buy. We won't be hoarders.'

'Don't be so touchy. I have two big boys to feed, haven't I?'

'You do, but not for the moment.'

There was a long pause. Both of them were thinking, trying to visualise just where the boys were and what they were doing.

'What's going on, Mickey?' she asked, switching affectionately to his old-country name. Suddenly she was crying. Her tears trickled slowly down her cheeks, as she stood in front of the hot pan.

'You're tired, Shosh.'

'No. I'm not. Just worried, like everybody else. Aren't you?'

'Yes of course I am, darling, but it doesn't really help.'

'Shula said that the Egyptians crossed the Canal. Is it true?'

'Yes.'

'What does it mean?'

'It means that things are serious. We thought our Bar-Lev line was so strong. We never believed they could cross.'

'Gadi is in Sinai, isn't he?'

'I don't know for sure, but I think so.'

'Why?'

'I'm just guessing. He told me once that they were stationed near a place . . . I don't remember the name, but I know it was somewhere in the desert.'

'Then you really don't know anything?'

'No Shosh!'

Silence. The onions were ready. She shut off the gas.

'We'll have to black out the kitchen, Shosh, I'm going out a little later to buy some tape and dark paper. Do you have enough candles?'

'Yes. We've got a whole box . . . Have you eaten yet?'

'No. I made myself a cup of coffee before the air raid siren went off.'

'It's nine o'clock, already. Why didn't you tell me?'

'I wasn't hungry.'

'I'll make you a nice cheese omelette. Okay?'

'That would be lovely . . . Shosh . . . ?'

'Yes?'

'It'll all work out, Shosh! Try not to worry.'

* * *

It was a cold misty day. A pale light began to brighten the edge of the darkness somewhere beyond the sand dunes. The distant rumbling of artillery had gone on right through the night. The maintenance men had refuelled the two tanks and gone over them trying to repair some of the ravages of the long run from Rafiach and they now stood ready with the other tanks of the unit. The men were already awake and sitting on the sand nearby.

Shmuel returned from the major's tent where he had received his final briefing. They were all feeling the tension. Until now, they'd hardly thought of death. Suddenly they were aware that they would be coming face to face with it, perhaps even within the next few hours.

'Well fellows, we've got a tough day ahead of us,' began Shmuel, 'but I'm not going to feed you any bullshit.'

Shmuel's unit was referred to as Group 1. It consisted of four tanks, each with a crew of four. The men listened attentively as Shmuel went on speaking in a voice that was reassuringly calm. 'I'm going to give you the facts exactly as they've been given to me. When the Egyptians started their attack at the Canal yesterday, the Syrians also started on the Golan Heights. There is no doubt that the attacks were deliberately co-ordinated and prepared with the utmost care. The Egyptians crossed the Canal at a number of points

37

and some of our positions on the Bar-Lev line were over-run almost before we knew what was happening. They've got at least three bridges across the Canal, and are moving infantry and tanks over them. Kantara is in their hands, and a big strip of the East bank – I don't know how big. Something that is of direct concern to us is that their infantry has some new type of portable anti-tank missile which they are firing in hundreds, and which have knocked out a lot of tanks and troop carriers. About the only good news is that the Egyptians suffered a disaster in a commando attack on Abu Rodeis. They used helicopters and we shot down eight of them, each carrying thirty commandos. That's all that I know up to now. Are there any questions?'

'Yes,' said Gadi, 'what's happened to the air force? How come their bridges are still standing?'

'Good question – and I'm not too sure of the answer. I believe we've lost a lot of planes because of their missiles, and in any event I believe that most of our planes are helping out on the Golan. Our job is to do everything possible to block the enemy until the reinforcements get down here, and I can only tell you it's going to be rough. I hope you're not all scared stiff already.' Some of them laughed nervously.

'It'll take more than a few words from you Shmuel,' said Itzik, a huge soldier with a sergeant's stripes on his sleeves.

'Well, let's go through our orders . . . ' Shmuel continued, pulling out a map from the pocket of his lined jacket, and spreading it on the ground. It was too small for them all to see, so he put the map back again, smoothed the ground in front of him and squatted down.

'That's better,' he said, drawing lines in the sand with a ball-point pen. He looked at his watch. 'In exactly twenty minutes we'll get the order to start moving. This is where we are now.' He jabbed his pen in the sand, a movement he repeated to explain each item of information as he gave it. 'This is the Mitla Pass behind us; this is where we think the Egyptians are at this moment. Our information is that they are moving forward in strength, maybe as many as a hundred tanks. We are dividing up into four groups. The major is going to move down along this side of the road and our four tanks will move with him in battle formation. Group 2's tanks will move south-west as fast as they can travel, and then swing round so that they can hit the enemy from the side. Groups 3 and 4 consisting of two tanks each will move north-west. Captain Rudel will act as second in command and his tank will lead group 3. When we sight the enemy, groups 2 and 3 will close in, and if possible, we'll all open fire together. Group 4 will continue to move north-west and circle round behind the enemy coming in to attack from the rear. Hopefully we will surprise them and knock a lot of them out quickly. In any event, they are unlikely to realise that we have so few tanks against them. Captain Rudel will keep an eye on what happens from his position, and will co-ordinate with the major. There is plenty of room for us to move – and I don't want to see any of you closer than a hundred metres to the next tank.' Shmuel stood up. 'Good luck fellows.'

The group dispersed, heading towards the tanks that made up their unit. Gadi was scared, but tried hard not to show it. His mouth was dry and his legs weak and shaky. He felt an irresistible impulse to urinate, and afterwards his hands were shaking so much that he had difficulty doing up his fly buttons. He clambered through the small special turret of the driving compartment under the barrel of the big 105 mm gun, and sat down trying to retain his self-control.

Itzik and Ami climbed into the main compartment of the Patton. Shmuel followed them but remained standing in the turret, listening for the major's signal. Through the head-phones of their special helmets they heard the major's voice using the code name for his tank. 'Namer here – Do you hear me? Let's go.'

Gadi released the brakes and they moved off relatively slowly, the major's tank behind and to the left of him. His turret was closed but through his periscopes he was able to see tanks 1-A and 1-B of their unit move into position behind and to the right of him. Tank 1-C was behind and to the left.

The other groups were moving much faster, their trails of sand rising in the air, as they fanned out to the south-west and north-west respectively.

They advanced for about half an hour. In practice manoeuvers they would normally enjoy speaking to each other using the intercommunications system built into their helmets. This time, however, they remained silent, tensely listening to the instructions from the major to the various commanders. Occasionally the major would exchange information with Rudel, whose code name on the radio was Barak. Suddenly the major said, 'There they are – north-west about two kilometres.' Gadi looked through the periscope but there were small ridges in front which blocked his view.

'Namer to No. 2, do you hear me? Start moving due north at full speed. Barak move due south. Let me know as soon as you sight them.'

On Shmuel's instructions Gadi moved to the shelter of a sand dune. From this angle they could see diagonally across the plain. A kilometre away there was a ridge which the enemy would have to cross, giving Itzik a clear target. He trained his gun on the crest of the ridge, and waited. Ami stood next to the shell racks ready to load new shells as Itzik fired. The other three tanks in their unit moved up into similar positions.

Gadi now saw columns of dust rising, and Egyptian tanks in relatively close formation began to cross the ridge. In a matter of minutes thirty to forty tanks came into view – advancing in a direct line to the left of where they stood waiting.

Groups 2 and 3 had closed in and the major gave the order for all of them to open fire simultaneously. The Egyptian tanks did not take long to return the fire. Shells screamed and exploded in all directions. Three times Itzik shouted excitedly through the earphones that he had scored hits, but Gadi was sitting too low down to see. Dust and smoke closed in on them. Shmuel remained standing upright in the turret, completely vulnerable, but still able to see and react to each new development. Itzik was now firing blind, relying completely on his instructions.

The major frequently checked with Rudel for information. From the conversations Gadi understood that two of their tanks had suffered hits, but not serious enough to put them out of action.

Meanwhile the two tanks in group 4 had completed their half-circle around the back of the enemy, and moved in swiftly, guns blazing, catching the Egyptians completely off-guard, and creating havoc in their ranks.

The major's jubilation came through clearly in the earphones as he issued a stream of instructions to capitalise on their advantage.

Group 1's tanks were ordered to move forward. They left the shelter of the sand dune. Gadi could see nothing. He moved the driving stick according to Shmuel's directions. Several times shells exploded near them and they heard the rattle of shrapnel against the armour plating. They reached the ridge where they had first sighted the enemy tanks. For a brief moment the dust cleared, and Gadi saw wrecked and burning tanks all around him. Through the earphones Gadi could hear the major ordering Shmuel to change direction. In the middle of the conversation there was a sudden crash through the earphones. Shmuel called out anxiously, 'Namer, Namer, do you hear me?' But there was no answer. Rudel's voice came through, 'Barak here. No. 1 keep moving forward. Namer has been hit.'

The battle seemed to go on endlessly, and Gadi lost all track of time. The noise was deafening, the inside of his cabin was hot and filled with fumes and smoke. In the dust ahead of them a huge Soviet T-62 loomed into view through Gadi's periscope, the first time he had ever seen one. Even as he recognised what it was there was a blinding light and a blast shook their tank and seemed to throw it up into the air. Gadi was half stunned. The tank had stopped dead. No sound came through the earphones. He pushed open the turret, jumped out on to the sand and half-rolled, half-crawled away from it. He felt a sharp pain in his arm and realised that he was bleeding profusely. Somebody was crawling towards him. He couldn't distinguish whether it was a friend or a foe.

'Gadi!'

'Shmuel!'

Shmuel's face was black with dirt and smoke, but he was obviously unhurt.

The battle seemed to be moving away from them. Suddenly, from quite close they heard a series of loud bursts from an Uzzi. They pressed their bodies even closer to the ground. After a few minutes they cautiously lifted their heads to take a look around. The dust had now cleared. They were surrounded by an inferno of wrecked tanks. Some were perched in incongruous positions as though they had been trying to turn a somersault, but got stuck halfway and couldn't come down again. The barrel of one cannon had exploded, its mouth splayed open into four wavy pieces of metal like a modern flower vase. And many bodies lying around, across tanks and under tanks and around tanks, some of them blackened beyond recognition.

In the midst of all this their eyes focused on a figure trudging towards them. It was Itzik, with his Uzzi gripped in his hands.

'Bastards,' he said. 'Are you fellows all right?'

'Yes. More or less. What happened?'

'I'm not too sure. I think I was knocked unconscious when we were hit. But somehow I got out of the tank still holding this. The next thing I knew was that there were four Gyppos walking towards the tank. I didn't ask any questions. I just pulled the trigger and killed the lot of them.'

'Where did they come from?' asked Shmuel.

'I think from that one over there.' Itzik motioned with his Uzzi towards a large T-62 about fifty metres away, on the other side of their wrecked Patton. It looked totally undamaged.

'Why would they do such a stupid thing?'

'I told you. I didn't ask questions. I suppose they wanted loot, or maybe they were a bit drunk with success and didn't believe that anybody could have lived through this hell-fire. Who knows?'

'What about Ami?' Itzik asked Shmuel.

'I don't know. First let's see if we can do anything with their tank. Then we'll try to find Ami.'

They approached the T-62 cautiously, but reasonably certain that the four that had been killed accounted for the whole crew. Shmuel leaned inside the turret with Itzik covering him.

'All clear,' Shmuel said.

The driver's turret also stood open and they went through the same procedure here. 'Do you think you could drive it?' Shmuel looked at Gadi, and his blood-soaked sleeve.

'I think so. I think my arm looks worse than it is.'

Gadi clumsily climbed in, his wound hurting him more than he cared to admit. The motor had been left running, and after moving the controls around, he saw that he would have no difficulty driving it. Shmuel appeared with the Russian first-aid kit, and cleaned and bandaged his arm. Gadi had lost a lot of blood but the wound itself did not appear to be serious.

They drove back to their Patton. It was smashed and still smoking, but Itzik climbed in. Grim-faced he re-appeared, struggling to pull Ami's body out. Shmuel jumped out to help, and together they pulled it into the T-62, and placed it gently on one side.

Nobody said anything. Shmuel went back again into the Patton to retrieve his special coded map and Gadi turned the tank around. It was late afternoon, and the sun was already low down on the horizon. He headed for the road and then turned east, back towards the Mitla Pass. Shmuel was inside the tank fiddling with the radio, trying to make contact with Rudel's tank. After about ten minutes he gave a grunt of satisfaction, and spoke rapidly into the mouthpiece explaining their position and referring to the coded map. They were ordered to keep moving slowly forward and to rendezvous at point X-33 on the road. It was almost dark.

Rudel's tank appeared suddenly about five metres off the road and fifty metres behind them. At the same time a command car came down the road and stopped a short distance in front of them with its heavy machine gun trained in their direction. Rudel instructed them on the radio to get out one by one, hands raised above their heads.

The long day was nearly over. About an hour later they were at the first-aid post. Gadi's wound was deep, but apart from needing a lot of stitches no serious damage seemed to have been done. Even as the bandages were being tied he fell asleep on the hospital bed, exhausted.

He awoke at six o'clock, having slept solidly for about ten hours. His body was bruised and stiff from the previous day's ordeal, and when he moved his arm he felt a swift stab of pain from the wound. He recovered quickly, however, when the medical orderly who cleaned and dressed it, gave him a message from the colonel. 'If you feel well enough,' he said, 'there's a special job for you to take something to Tel Aviv.'

It took Gadi just five minutes to be ready waiting outside the colonel's tent to receive his instructions.

*　　*　　*

Uri's command post was not at Waset. It had been moved to a temporary camp at Muweissa, one kilometre east of

Waset and about eight kilometres west of Kuneitra. He was found by a corporal from his unit who had been sent down to collect the arriving soldiers. In the next three hours they located seven other members of their unit. They climbed into the half-track and drove slowly without lights along the dirt road, arriving after midnight.

Uri was greeted with an enthusiastic hug by Zeev who was corporal on his half-track and had already started getting things organised. There was a great deal to do, no one slept. The ten men in his crew checked everything; guns, vehicles, ammunition, food and extra fuel. Uri and Zeev made a final inspection of the half-track. Satisfied, Uri went to report to Amos, the captain-in-charge of the company.

'Ready?' asked Amos.

'Yes. When are we moving?'

'Soon. The other two half-tracks aren't ready yet. Our orders are to move along this track south of Kibbutz Ein Zivan, to the point where it joins the main highway from Kuneitra to Nafach. A tank force is being sent to support our position at Tsarman, south of Kuneitra. They need extra troops badly, and our job is to link up with the tank force and move up behind them.' As if to emphasise the urgency of the situation, they heard the Syrian artillery open fire with a tremendous barrage of shells.

'Amos. How much do you know? Are we likely to have a lot of trouble?'

'It's all so confused – I don't think anybody knows what's going on. It won't be easy. Look after yourself Uri.'

'Thanks. You too!'

Uri went back to his half-track and waited. Less than an hour later they moved off, the three half-tracks keeping a distance of fifty metres between each vehicle. Amos was in front. Uri's half-track brought up the rear. They were travelling in the direction of the firing and saw shells exploding, but none fell close to them.

They reached a point a few hundred metres from where the dirt road met the Kuneitra–Nafach highway and Amos started looking for a place to shelter until they linked up with the tanks. Suddenly the artillery barrage shifted towards them. An ear-splitting whine caused them to duck down instinctively, as a shell crashed with a tremendous explosion in front of Uri's half-track. The engine was wrecked and the tyres slashed by the shrapnel but nobody was hurt.

Amos gave rapid instructions over the radio. 'Uri take a Bazooka, a light machine gun and three men, and get up to the top of the hill nearest you on your left. Also take your radio. Tell the rest of your crew to get over here as fast as possible. We're going to drive up the two hills on the other side of the track. Put yourself in a position where you can cover us and also fire at anything coming along the highway. Stay in touch, okay?'

'Okay.'

The vehicles halted just below the crests of the hills and their crews jumped out and deployed themselves in positions overlooking the highway.

The Syrian artillery barrage was firing at full strength, but the shells were passing above them. The Israeli return fire seemed to Uri to be weak and sporadic. Via the radio Amos informed Uri that the force they had to meet was coming up the road. Amos had established contact with the command post and been ordered to stay where he was and to await developments. The position they were going to relieve had been bypassed in the Syrian advance, and could not be reached at present.

Three Israeli tanks moved past them and a few moments later Uri heard intensive firing from tank guns. The Syrian artillery fire closed in on the highway, and shells fell opposite them. The Syrians were apparently aiming at the Israeli tanks but were overshooting them.

Uri took Zeev and two other soldiers. He carried a Kalatchnikov and his Uzzi. Zeev took the radio on his back, and a light machine gun, and the other two soldiers carried the Bazooka and six rockets. They were sweating when they reached the top. They placed the Bazooka in position, loaded it and lay down behind some black boulders, watching the two half-tracks slowly trace their way up the hills opposite them.

Formations of Skyhawks suddenly appeared to support the tanks. With ear-splitting roars they flew in one by one low over the road, firing their rockets a few seconds after they passed the hill where Uri and his men lay. Then they rose sharply and turned to come in again for another run. One plane was hit just as it started to make its turn. An umbrella of six missiles had converged on it and the pilot had been unable to dodge them all. He had ejected himself from the plane, but the parachute drifted down on to Syrian-held territory.

'Poor bastard,' Uri said to Zeev who was lying right next to him.

The battle raged on for more than an hour, and then suddenly the noise seemed to slacken. Uri saw two of the Israeli tanks returning. 'No ammunition,' he thought. He tried to call Amos to find out if they should also withdraw.

Before he could make contact, however, a line of Syrian tanks came into view, travelling at full speed down the highway. Without hesitation Uri fired his Bazooka and was thrilled to see the rocket crash into the rear section of the lead tank. It burst into flames blocking the road. His excitement was short-lived. A shell from one of the Syrian tanks burst next to them in an almost direct hit. Uri pressed his whole body flat on the ground. He heard the shrapnel whizzing all around him, and was covered in a rain of stones and dirt. One of the boys screamed with pain, but Uri could not see what had happened.

Amos's men on the hill also opened up with their Bazookas, and anti-tank missiles. In the first minute three more tanks were hit and caught fire. The crews of the damaged tanks jumped out and ran in all directions seeking shelter from the merciless fire of the machine guns. The burning lead tank blocked the road and the column was forced to a halt. The area around the road became dense with dust and smoke; shells and bullets flew in all directions and the attention of the enemy tanks was diverted away from Uri.

Still keeping his body close to the ground, Uri gingerly lifted his head and looked around. Zeev was apparently all right, but the other two boys were sprawled motionless a few metres away. One was obviously dead, his face and throat ripped into raw, red strips. The second lay face down, with blood pouring out on to the ground around him. Uri and Zeev crawled over to him, and struggled to stop the flow of blood, but it was hopeless. He died a few minutes later without having regained consciousness.

On the road the scene was one of utter confusion. The lead tank had been pushed out of the way, its ammunition exploded and thick black smoke poured from it. Altogether six wrecked tanks were lying on the side of the road, but the line started moving forward again. Three tanks had detached themselves from the main column. Two of them were pounding away at the positions occupied by Amos, and the other one was ominously facing in the direction of Uri's hill, looking for any trouble from that side. Uri and Zeev kept well down.

It was late afternoon, and rapidly growing dark. Uri could see only one half-track and it was badly damaged. There was no firing coming from the two hills. He didn't know if Amos was lying low, or whether he had managed to retreat in the other half-track. He told Zeev to try to make contact and when Zeev lifted the radio up, they both gasped with astonishment. A large gaping hole showed where a piece of shrapnel had lodged inside it. When the shell burst Zeev had been lying right next to the radio which acted as a shield, saving his life. The radio was beyond repair, and there was no way in which they could establish contact with the others. Their light machine gun was also wrecked, but the Bazooka and the Uzzi were still intact. The three remaining Syrian tanks moved down the road in the direction of Nafach. It was now dark.

Uri decided that it would be dangerous to try to make their way back to the Israeli lines. They broke off a half of the identifying 'dog-tags' on the bodies and Uri put them in his pocket. Together they pushed the bodies under one of the boulders. With Uri's consent, Zeev went back to their damaged half-track, returning half an hour later with a carton of battle rations and two flasks of water. They ate in silence, then Zeev went to sleep. Uri stayed on guard, his Uzzi on his lap.

The moon was almost full. The sky was so bright and beautiful that for a brief moment Uri was able to detach himself from what had happened. Then his thoughts returned to the two boys – their bodies lying just a short distance away. The world seemed suddenly cruel and ugly. A feeling totally foreign to Uri's nature welled irresistibly up and took possession of him – a bitter hatred against the Arab enemy, and a harsh unyielding craving for revenge.

Monday, 8th October

Gadi was given immediate permission to enter the colonel's tent.

'How are you feeling?'

'Fine Sir.'

'Do you think you feel well enough to deliver some important papers to Tel Aviv?'

'Yes Sir. If you think it's all right for me to leave.'

'Well, I've been told that you won't be much good to us for a while, and I need these papers delivered personally. This is strictly confidential, but because you helped to get hold of them, I'm going to tell you that they're Russian documents from the T-62 that you brought in. I promised they would be at Intelligence Headquarters before noon today. Room 232, Major General Sagorsky. To be given to him and only to him. Is that clear?'

'Yes Sir.'

'Just in case the idea occurred to you' – the Colonel smiled, 'you might as well get home so that your parents can see you're still in one piece.'

'Thank you Sir.'

'Twenty-four hours, Gadi. I want you back here tomorrow morning as early as you can make it.'

'Yes Sir.'

Gadi took the thick brown envelope from the Colonel and within a few moments he was standing at the gate of the camp waiting for a lift. It was six-thirty. He did not have to wait long. An ice-cream truck carrying ammunition picked him up and he got off again at Baluza, a small airstrip in the desert. Since Saturday it had handled traffic on a twenty-four-hour-a-day basis. Planes of all types landed, discharged troops and cargo, and took off again. The ground staff had three-day-old beards and eyes red from lack of sleep.

An air force sergeant eyed Gadi's arm in a sling and checked his papers. He was told to stand by, it would only be a few minutes. The 'departure lounge' was a hut with two pane-less windows and four empty walls, not even a bench. A makeshift notice over the door was inscribed 'Baluza Hilton'.

A Dakota finished off-loading and revved its engines. The air force sergeant told him to climb aboard, and once inside, Gadi was amused; it looked like this was going to be his own private plane. Just before takeoff, however, another passenger appeared and sat down opposite him.

The newcomer wore a battered khaki windjacket and his dense unruly hair was almost completely white. His face was lined, but a deep tan gave him a youthful appearance. It was difficult to estimate his age. On his right hip a service revolver was tucked into a canvas holster, and his shoulder tabs showed that he was a major.

'How bad is it?' said the major, looking at his arm.

'It's nothing Sir. Really just a scratch.'

'First battle?'

'Yes Sir.'

'I hope you were a little less scared than I remember being in my first battle. I nearly died of fright.'

Gadi laughed and dropped his reserve. The older man was genuinely interested and on his insistence Gadi described as much as he could from his confused recollection of the action which he had been in. The major was interested that the Egyptian tanks had not been preceded by infantry.

'When they crossed the Canal,' he told Gadi, 'thousands of foot-soldiers went ahead of their tanks, armed with portable anti-tank missiles controlled by some sort of wire apparatus. It seemed to make no difference to them that they were mowed down in their hundreds as long as some missiles hit home.'

Gadi asked about tank battles.

'There haven't been any real tank versus tank battles. Yours is the first that I've heard about.'

'How far have they advanced across the Canal?'

'About six kilometres – maximum ten. We're actually lucky they didn't get any further.'

The major paused for a moment and then continued with a peculiar expression on his face. 'Tell me,' he said, 'did any of your people down at Tasa consider the possibility that we might be defeated? That the Egyptians might overrun us completely and sweep right through the country?'

'Of course not. They couldn't possibly. They only got as far as they did because they surprised us.'

'You're right son. I shouldn't even have asked such a question.' The major suddenly seemed very tired. He leaned back against the seat and closed his eyes.

The flight took only forty-five minutes. As they were coming down to land the major asked Gadi where he was heading for.

'Herzliya,' he replied, having already decided that it was easier to go home first, and then to Tel Aviv to deliver the papers.

'I'll drive you there,' said the major. 'It's very little out of my way.'

Near the apartment block Gadi took off the sling and placed it in his pocket. He felt blissful, not even nine o'clock, and he had the whole day ahead of him. The major stopped the car, wished him luck, and drove away. Gadi bounded up the steps, opened the door with his key, and shouted, 'Anybody home?' to an astonished Shoshana, who stood there not knowing whether to laugh or to cry.

'Gadi. Are you all right?' Without waiting for an answer she burst into tears and flung her arms around him. Gadi had instinctively lifted his wounded arm to keep it away from her embrace. She released him and then the questions flowed. Gadi was very matter of fact indicating that he had not even seen any action, and that there had been no real danger where he was. He explained that he had stupidly cut his arm with a screwdriver which slipped while he was lying under the engine of his tank, trying to tighten a bolt. The doctor told him that he couldn't drive a tank for a couple of days, and that's how he came to have the luck to be given the job of bringing some papers to Tel Aviv, and getting home at the same time.

He would have to catch a plane early the next morning to get back to his base. Shoshana was so flustered and excited by his actually being there, that she didn't even query the explanation of his injury.

'Gadi. You haven't eaten yet. Sit down. I'll make you a Spanish omelette. And for lunch I've got stuffed cabbages . . . and . . . Oh! You'd better phone your father. I'm sure he'll come home right away . . . ' Shoshana was bubbling as she broke the eggs and turned the gas on.

In between Shoshana's questions Gadi established that there had been no news yet from Uri. He assured Shoshana that this was not cause to worry. 'We've got no telephones, and they haven't had time to organise the post yet.'

He phoned his father first, went to turn his bathwater on, and then went back to the phone for what was really uppermost in his thoughts. Rina answered the phone with the usual formula. 'Mr Leibowitz's office, may I help you?'

'Well, I don't know if I'm really looking for help.'

'Gadi! Is it you? Gadi! Where are you speaking from? How are you?'

'Take it easy. I'm all right. One question at a time. I'm at home and . . . '

'You're at home. Fantastic. How did you manage to get home?'

'Well. I explained to my commander that I'm very much in love, and that I haven't seen you for nearly forty-eight hours, and that I can't fight . . . '

'Oh. Shut up. Gadi, are you sure you're all right?'

'Yes. I'm sure.'

'How long do you have?'

'Until tomorrow 6 a.m.'

'Oh, Gadi. It's incredible. I didn't know I could get so excited just talking to you on the phone. When will I see you?'

'As soon as you like. Would you like to come here?'

'Yes. But don't your parents want to spend some time alone with you?'

'I'm sure they do, but I also want to be with you. Can you leave work soon?'

'I shouldn't, but I'm certainly not going to sit here when you're only home for one day.'

'Okay. Listen! I'm having a quick bath. Then I've got to take some papers to headquarters. Can you be ready by – say – eleven o'clock?'

'I'm ready now. I'll be waiting for you outside. Gadi! . . . '

'Yes?'

'Hurry!'

Lunch was a very happy affair. Gadi sensed the love and appreciation of all of them flowing out to him. It was a very special feeling. 'It's good to be home,' he thought. The table was laden with his favourite foods and everyone ate heartily. When the meal ended, to Shoshana's delight, Gadi thanked her with a loving hug and kiss. After coffee Rina and Shoshana got busy clearing up and washing dishes, and Meir and Gadi 'retired' to the living room.

At two o'clock, they switched on the radio to get the latest news. Meir concentrated hard just to get the meaning of the words. Gadi was more concerned with the implications of the different reports. The Syrians claimed that they had pushed beyond Kuneitra, penetrated deeply south-west in the Hushniyeh area, and were still advancing. Israel claimed that it had counter-attacked and the Syrians were retreating. Nixon had appealed to Brezhnev to join in an effort to restore peace to the Middle East, but had received no response to his appeal. Air raid sirens had sounded in Haifa. On the Suez front the Egyptians had three bridge-heads across the Canal. They claimed to have captured Kantara, to be in full control of the East Bank and to be advancing deeper into Sinai. Israel had bombed five Syrian airfields, and also Port Said on the Egyptian front. Syria and Egypt said they had inflicted heavy losses on Israel's air force, and even Jordan claimed to have shot down two Israeli planes which had violated its air space.

'Winning? Losing?' – Gadi found himself unable to make sense of the conflicting claims. He switched off the radio.

'Are our people telling us the truth?' Meir asked Gadi.

'Of course they are. Sometimes they may not tell us things like how many planes we lost or the number of casualties, but what they do tell us is true . . . Dad can we forget the war for a moment?'

'Yes, sure. What is it son?'

'Rina.'

'I've had a feeling you were getting keen on her. You're not thinking of getting married?'

'Yes, I am. You sound as though you're against the idea?'

Meir's expression was troubled. For a moment he thought of teasing Gadi about getting 'tied down' but Gadi was too serious, too tense. Meir was against the idea! But how to explain himself? Was he wrong in wanting Gadi to be somebody, to have something? He spoke slowly, searching for the right words.

'Gadi, I'm not necessarily against the idea – it's a question of timing. When are you thinking of?'

'Now. I mean after the war. What's the point of waiting?'

'You know why! I don't have to tell you. What are you going to live on? Where are you going to live?'

'It's not important Dad. What's happened in the last few days has made me realise that nothing else is as important to me as Rina. Other people manage to make do, why shouldn't we?'

Meir remembered how hard it had been for himself and Shoshana to manage. 'I'll tell you why. It's not enough just to "make do". Look at us! An immigrant flat. No car. No savings. Not even enough money to send you and Uri to university without taking loans from wherever we can get them. You used to speak about studying engineering when you were finished travelling and ready to settle down. How can you become an engineer if you get married and have to support a family?'

'We'll make a plan, Dad. Besides what's wrong with your position? We don't seem to lack for anything except a car maybe, and that's not so important.'

Meir knew he was fighting a losing battle. 'Mine is such a limited world Gadi, a day-to-day struggle just to get by. I'd like to see you do better. In any event this is not the time to talk about such a complicated matter.'

'But Dad . . .'

'Gadi, your Mom wants to know if we're staying for dinner!' called Rina, appearing at the living room entrance. A swift glance passed between father and son, and it was understood that for the moment the discussion was closed.

'Mom – would you mind? I wanted to take Rina out tonight. We'll come back after dinner.'

'No, you children go out and enjoy yourselves.' Gadi didn't notice the disappointment on Shoshana's face.

'Thanks Mom. I knew you'd understand.'

'Rina, how about going out for a walk?'

'Okay, Gadi. I'll just get my purse.'

A few moments later they were outside. With their arms around one another, walking aimlessly, Gadi felt her body next to his, and his heart-beat quickened.

'What would you like to do?' he asked.

'Let's go to my place. Mom may be there, but it'll still be nicer than wandering around the street.'

'Okay. If you want to.'

'Gadi I want to know what happened? Please!'

'What happened? What do you mean?'

'To your arm, to you, I don't believe your story about the screwdriver.'

Gadi was pleased that she had the perception to see that his story wasn't true. He needed to tell her, to get some of it out of his system, and share the burden of what he had been through.

'Rina, it's very hard for me to say, "Okay, I'll tell you the whole thing from the beginning!" I can't. It was bad, very bad. I was so scared, I can't even remember everything . . . '

For a brief moment parts of what had happened flashed through Gadi's mind, the explosions, the smoky air, the charred bodies. Forcing the words to come out, Gadi told her how their tank had been hit, and how he had suddenly found himself lying in the sand wounded, how they had found Ami's body in the tank, and how they finally made their way back to safety. Rina listened without interrupting, her mind boggling with the realisation that it was sheer luck that Gadi was still alive walking beside her. When he finished, she turned to him and, un-selfconsciously in the middle of the street, held him close to her and kissed him as though nobody could ever make them part again.

Eventually they reached Rina's apartment, and her mother opened the door and greeted Gadi effusively.

'Gadi. What a wonderful surprise! When did you get in? What happened to your arm? Come in, come in! Tell me all about it.'

'What a phony,' thought Gadi, 'Why must she always act this way?' Mrs Aronsohn went on. 'Please Gadi, sit down here. In the big chair. Only the best for our soldiers, eh?'

Gadi felt repulsed, nevertheless he humoured her, and sat down.

Mrs Aronsohn was on the point of leaving. Dressed in a pink slack suit which made her broad bottom look broader, she was also heavily made up. It suited her character, and fitted in with the perfumery she ran on the main street in Herzliya. Rina had excused herself for a minute and Mrs

Aronsohn launched into a farewell monologue to Gadi.

'You look changed, I think a little older, but then you're nearly twenty-two, aren't you? In fact you look a full grown man. Are you going back in the morning? Not very much time, is it? Just enough for a good hot meal, a kiss from your parents, and you're off again. I'd invite you for dinner, but I have to attend a benefit. I won't be back until very late. We all have to do something to help the war effort, haven't we? I suppose you know that Shlomo was also called up. He's an officer in the civil defence. Quite important, you know. Poor dear, he's on duty right now. Anyway, I must rush off. Take care Gadi. Hope to see you again before you leave.'

With that she was gone. Gadi sighed with relief. He looked around him marvelling, as always, at how an apartment could be furnished so expensively and with such bad taste. A few large modern oil paintings, in old fashioned gilt frames, hung on walls which were decorated with pink and gold wallpaper. The TV set was also framed in gold. Gadi wondered if there was a psychological basis for gold being Mrs Aronsohn's favourite colour.

'Gadi!' Rina called from another part of the apartment.

'What is it, Rina?'

'Please come here. I'm in my room.'

Gadi walked in the direction of her voice, and found her standing in front of her mirror, brushing her hair, stark naked. The lace drapes were closed, letting only the softest light into the room.

'Rina!'

She put the brush down and turned to face him. 'Gadi, there are so many reasons . . .'

'Rina you don't know what you're doing!'

'Yes, I do. I know I love you, and I know you love me. I know that there's a war, and that you could be dead tomorrow. I know that nothing makes any sense to me anymore, besides my belonging to you. It must be now Gadi. I want to be part of you now.'

As she talked she moved hesitantly closer, and Gadi could smell the fresh, perfumed scent of her hair and body. They faced each other for several moments. Gadi stood there unwilling to turn away, and yet afraid to touch her. He knew how he wanted it to be. He wanted to take her gently, to make her feel beautiful and natural. But he'd wanted to choose his own time. Now, he was uncertain.

'Gadi, listen to me. I want to go through with it. Look at me!' she smiled uncertainly, 'Please Gadi . . .'

'Rina, I love you,' his voice was quiet. 'I want to marry you.'

'Yes,' she nodded, 'I love you too.'

Rina took his hand and brought him into the room. She lifted her head and gently touched his face with her fingers. He closed his eyes, felt her lips brush his, and lowered his head to meet her kiss. Slowly she began to undo the buttons on his shirt. He kept his eyes shut tightly, aware of every sensation her touch created. She eased his shirt off carefully, to avoid hurting his wound. Gadi undid his belt and let his trousers drop to the floor. Together they lay down on the bed.

'You're so beautiful,' he said. With his right hand he traced an invisible line down the centre of her body. Then he bent his head until his eyes met hers.

'Rina?'

'Please Gadi!'

No more was spoken. Gadi's doubts were swept away as their passion became uncontrollable, reached its peak, then subsided; and they lay there, eyes closed, arms and legs entwined, trying to retain the sense of oneness for as long as possible.

Gadi was the first to open his eyes. He looked at the girl lying peacefully in his arms. 'Woman!' he whispered jokingly. The sides of her lips turned upwards into a smile, and she snuggled closer to him. She opened her eyes to search his face. 'Gadi – I'll never be sorry. I love you.'

'I wanted it to be special for you, Rina, not just bodies or desires, but love.'

'It was Gadi – it was full of love.'

They lay there for a few minutes longer. Then Rina got up to get dressed, and Gadi was sure her body looked different. It was somehow older, wiser. He wondered if anybody else could notice the difference . . .

*   *   *

Gadi and Rina returned to the Ishboneh apartment, and that evening watched TV with Meir and Shoshana. At a special news conference, at eight-thirty, the Chief of Staff, General David Elazar, summed up the situation, and answered questions put by some of the two hundred foreign and local military correspondents who were in attendance.

'The tides of war have turned,' he said. 'Israel Defence Forces are now on the offensive on all fronts and will attack and destroy the enemy wherever he can be found.' More specifically he stated that the Syrians had been pushed back along the '67 cease fire lines, 'although a few units may still be a few hundred metres inside our lines.' As to the Suez Canal, he stated that the Egyptians had three bridge-heads, but no bridges; and their forces on the East Bank were in fact surrounded. Queried about belated mobilisation orders, the Chief of Staff stressed that the attack had not come as a surprise, and that the front line forces had been ready and braced for the onslaught when it came.

With typically aggressive Israeli cockiness he summed up the aim as being to hit out at the enemy, to cause them as many casualties as possible, and to win a quick and decisive victory, in short 'to break all their bones'. Meir, and many other Israelis, felt a little uncomfortable at this extravagant phrase; but all of them went to sleep that night, feeling relieved and even excited. It looked like '67 all over again. In a couple of days the boys would return home and more wonderful victories would be celebrated!

*   *   *

Zeev had taken over the guard duty while Uri slept. The wind was bitingly cold, and a fine drizzle added to the discomfort. As exhausted as he was, Uri awoke at two-thirty, and they decided to make their way towards the army camp at Nafach, about four kilometres away. Uri did not have any particular feeling of fear. With Zeev next to him, he was confident that everything would turn out all right.

The moon shed more than enough light as they picked their way silently across the rock-strewn terrain. They walked parallel about a hundred metres to the right of the highway, Uri carrying the Uzzi and two rockets, and Zeev the Bazooka and the remaining three rockets. About half an hour had gone by when Uri touched Zeev's arm lightly, and they stopped to listen.

They heard the deep rumble of slow moving trucks, and the distinctive clatter of tank tracks coming towards them from the direction of Kuneitra. 'They must be ours,' whispered Zeev. 'Those bastards never travel at night, they're afraid of their own shadows.' Uri wasn't sure. At his insistence they moved further away from the road and up a slight rise, sheltering behind some large boulders.

The convoy of vehicles came into view. There was no doubt that it was Syrian. The huge shapes of Soviet T-54 and T-55 tanks were unmistakable. At this point the ground was relatively flat and the tanks had taken advantage of this, moving in groups of six on both sides of the highway. On the road itself, armoured troop carriers, trucks trailing huge artillery pieces, and behind them other trucks with infantry, were keeping pace with the tanks. In the light of the moon Uri could see about forty vehicles, half of them tanks, and there were more coming up behind them. Zeev wanted to take a shot with the Bazooka, but Uri restrained him. He saw no point in committing suicide.

As they watched, a bright red flare burst in the sky above the enemy convoy, and all hell broke loose. An Israeli tank force had opened fire from a hill about fifteen hundred metres away, which commanded the whole area. Brilliant yellow-white phosphorescent shells streaked through the air from both sides, lighting the scene brighter than a city square.

The Syrian troop carriers and trucks scrambled off the road, with soldiers jumping from them and running in all directions to seek shelter. Many tanks were hit, turning into torches in front of their eyes. The Israeli tanks also suffered casualties. Two were burning and the explosions from the Syrian tanks began bursting all over the hill. It apparently got too hot for the Israeli force because their firing died down and they were gone.

'What the hell's the matter with them?' whispered Zeev fiercely, 'They weren't all shot up. Why did they stop fighting?'

'Probably because the Syrians had zeroed in on the hill and they felt it was more sensible to go back and come up again somewhere else.'

The massive Syrian column was already regrouping. They could hear the soldiers laughing and shouting with relief as they climbed back into their vehicles.

Uri was afraid of being caught in the area when dawn broke. They moved away from the road to avoid being silhouetted in a position where the Syrians might see them.

The first sign of light was already creeping across the edge of the horizon when they came over the top of a hill, and stood aghast. The field in front of them was thick with wrecked and smouldering tanks, half-tracks and jeeps. Corpses were scattered all over. A sweetish odour hung in the air and Uri realised in horror that it was the smell of burning flesh.

They made their way slowly through the field. Just as they were passing a wrecked T-54, they heard a slight sound, and both dived for the ground as shots rang out. Uri whipped his Uzzi around and fired a burst at the tank, but he could see nothing. Zeev was lying motionless with blood flowing from the back of his head. Uri grabbed the Bazooka from the ground, and propped it against a rock. He fired another round from the Uzzi to make sure that whoever was in the tank would keep down. Then he loaded a rocket and fired the Bazooka at point blank range. The tank seemed to rise up and burst with the impact of the rocket, then all was still again.

Uri gave a quick look around to see if there was any other danger. Satisfied, he crouched down next to Zeev and turned him over. A trickle of blood spurted from his mouth and down his chin. Uri knew he was dead.

'Zeev! – Zeev!' he whispered. 'It can't be like this!'

Tears welled up in his eyes as he cradled his friend's head on his lap. He began to cry, silently at first, and then in harsh uncontrollable sobs filled with misery and complete, utter helplessness.

More than half an hour later an Israeli mopping-up patrol found him sitting in the same position oblivious to everything around him.

Tuesday, 9th October

Tuesday was an uneasy day. In the light of the press conference by the Chief of Staff, Elazar, the excitement should have been more obvious than it was. The reports in the morning papers were cause enough for patriotic gratitude and optimism. 'Israel Takes Offensive' was the big headline.

Supporting stories included one headed 'Golan Soldiers Hope to be Home by Shabbat', and described the hopes of some reservists that 'the football league would after all start as scheduled'. Another headline read 'Decisive Push to Canal Coming Today', and reported that the 'last of the bridges' across the Canal had been knocked out 'completing the isolation of the Egyptian units'. Immediately below it, under the headline 'Strain on Economy Expected to Ease' a report on the transport bottleneck stated that this would now improve as 'vehicles are released after moving troops and equipment to the fronts'.

And yet something was missing. An airforce pilot could have put his finger on it; or an infantryman on the Canal front who had taken part in the three-pronged Israeli attack against the Egyptian bridgeheads which was thrown back with heavy losses. But on the civilian front it was only a feeling that something didn't add up.

The United Nations Security Council was reported to have met during the night to discuss a call for a cease-fire, but the talks had been delayed while the countries searched for an appropriate resolution. Israelis are deeply cynical about the United Nations, believing that decisions are made promptly when this works against Israel, and only become difficult to agree upon when the Arabs have an advantage. It seemed strange that the Security Council was procrastinating when Elazar had indicated so clearly that the war was all over bar the shouting.

During the day the uneasy feeling deepened when a disconcerting story began to be spread by those who listened

to the BBC Radio Newsreel. A direct eyewitness account
by a special correspondent, reported that he had just been
driven across the Canal, and that a great deal of traffic was
moving smoothly and undisturbed over the Egyptian bridges.
He interviewed some Egyptian soldiers and it was clear that
their morale was very high. They eagerly pointed out signs
of a hasty Israeli retreat, boots left in the bunkers, washing
hanging out and food half eaten, and with special pride they
drew his attention to the Egyptian flag flying over an abandoned Israeli position. The correspondent travelled about
five kilometres east of the Canal, and was told that the
Egyptians had penetrated ten kilometres and more, but that
it was not safe enough to let civilians through.

Although Israelis generally regarded the BBC broadcasts
as 'slanted', it was hard to believe that the special reporter
had actually fabricated his story. And yet there was no way
of reconciling it with Elazar's speech or the morning headlines.

*　　*　　*

Shoshana was not troubled by thoughts that anything might
be wrong, and set about her day's business with a relatively
cheerful countenance. At the supermarket friends asked
about the boys and she had a momentary disquiet about
Uri when they told her they had received post-cards or
phone-calls from their children. But she was still basking in
the warm glow of Gadi's visit, and illogically her feeling of
security widened to include Uri as well.

She bumped into Sarah Goldman and received some
quiet satisfaction from her complaint that she had had to
throw away six loaves of stale bread and four plastic bags
of sour milk. 'When they announced that there was a plenti-
ful supply of everything, I was sure we were in trouble,'
confessed Sarah without embarrassment, knowing that she
had acted no differently from thousands of other women.

All the items on Shoshana's list were available, except for
batteries for Meir's transistor radio that he wanted to take
to the office, and dark paper to black out their bedroom.
Also, at the cash desk, they only allowed her four packets
of cigarettes for the parcels she was making up to send to Uri
and Gadi.

The weather was beautiful, sunny but not too hot. Walking home Shoshana saw few signs that the country was at war. The high schools had not re-opened and the youths were having a fabulous time volunteering for all sorts of jobs. One group passed her with a tractor-trailer piled high with garbage that they had collected, and were taking to the city dump. Two teenage girls were delivering mail.

Outside the Shul a small stall was selling the traditional 'four species' for the rites connected with the celebration of the Sukkot holiday in two days' time. Several flat owners were busy building makeshift huts or 'Sukkot' on their porches, so that they could eat their meals 'under the sky' and commemorate how the Jews lived when Moses led them out of Egypt and across the Sinai desert. 'A pity he didn't lead us a little further away,' she thought with grim amusement.

*   *   *

Sde Dov was as crowded as Gadi had seen it on the first day of the war, but it seemed better organised. The same sergeant stood at the flight desk, but a girl assistant was checking leave passes and determining priorities for the 'passenger lists'. Looking at the sling on Gadi's arm, she informed him that he had to get a medical clearance first.

'What on earth for?' protested Gadi, 'I'm perfectly all right.'

'I'm sorry. Too many wounded soldiers have been trying to return before they were fit to do so. These are my orders.'

Gadi saw that it would be useless to argue.

The entrance to the doctor's office faced the tarmac just outside the reception hall, and had a large red Star of David painted on the door. As Gadi walked towards it, a squat ugly-looking plane was coming in to land. It had a belly like a pregnant guppy and Gadi had no difficulty identifying it as an Arava, the new 'short take-off' plane built by the Israel Aircraft Industries and ideally suited to the small patches of desert used as makeshift airfields close to the front lines. The Arava floated gently down to land, taxied towards the building and cut its engines. A dozen ambulances which had been waiting at the gate drove up positioning themselves in line next to the exit door of the plane. The doctor hurried out of his office, nearly bumping into Gadi. He saw the sling and told Gadi to wait, he would be busy for at least fifteen minutes.

Gadi watched as the doors opened and the wounded soldiers came out. The first small group who had bandages mainly around the upper parts of their bodies, disembarked on their own steam. Then came the stretcher cases, some with nurses and medics walking alongside holding a bottle of plasma or saline solution, helping the life-preserving fluid drip into the bloodstream of the patient to counteract the effects of shock and loss of blood. In sick fascination he saw the flatness of the blankets where a limb should have been, the raw pink of burns . . . and he looked at their faces, pale and unshaven; their eyes expressionless, as though the fright of coming close to death had numbed their minds. The ambulances drove off at speed, most with their sirens shrieking. The doctor returned to his office and motioned Gadi to enter.

'It probably doesn't mean so much to you,' he remarked as they sat down, 'but some of those men are living medical miracles. I presume you were too young to be fighting in '67?'

'Yes,' Gadi answered, although he felt that the doctor wasn't so much expecting a reply, as speaking his thoughts aloud.

'Well I thought we were good then, but the medical organisation in this war is unique. I don't know if you noticed that last stretcher case that I examined before they took him away. He was caught in an air-raid yesterday morning near the Canal, and was wounded badly in the chest and his right leg broken. A helicopter was called, and by the time it arrived half an hour later, a field doctor had already cleaned the wound, splinted the leg and treated him against gangrene infection. On the flight back to the field hospital at Riffidim he suddenly stopped breathing, and the doctor attached to the helicopter squad operated on his windpipe and applied artificial respiration while they were still in mid-air. By all normal standards he should have died! It's quite fantastic!' Gadi nodded his head in agreement, still feeling a little shaken at what he had seen, and trying to rid his mind of morbid thoughts as to how he would react if he were to lose an arm or a leg.

The doctor turned his attention to Gadi who explained that his wound was really only a scratch, but the doctor made him take off his shirt, and then deftly unwound the bandage. 'Eight stitches – that's some scratch!' he said with a smile, 'but you're lucky. It's healing quite nicely, and you'll be fine if you look after it.' He cleaned the wound and started changing the bandage.

'What do you do in the armoured corps?'

'I drive a tank, doctor.'

'Well, we certainly need you at the moment, but if you put a sudden strain on your arm the wound could open and start bleeding again; and in a battle, alone in your driving cabin, you would be a danger to your tank-crew. What do you think?'

Gadi was worried that the doctor might keep him back. Trying to make the matter sound very important, he told the doctor in confidence that he had to get back to report to his Commanding Officer about some vital secret papers that he had just delivered for him to Intelligence.

The doctor made up his mind.

'All right,' he said, 'you can go back, but on the strict condition that you don't drive a tank for seven days. I'm not prepared to take a chance on this, so I want you to know that I'm sending a copy of my order to your commander.' He was writing as he talked, and when he finished he handed the order to Gadi, again admonishing him to look after the wound.

Gadi thanked him and left. He showed the order to the girl who had previously stopped him. She handed him a boarding card and wrote his name down on the passenger list. 'You're on the Arava,' she said, 'it's leaving in ten minutes.'

The plane was full, and the trip uneventful. Most of the way down Gadi was day-dreaming about Rina, the memory of their few hours together still achingly fresh in his mind. From Gaza onwards the plane flew almost at ground level to avoid any exposure to missiles. When Gadi got off the plane at Baluza it was nearly eight o'clock. It did not take him long to get a lift in the direction of Tasa. Throughout the hour long drive Gadi heard the heavy pounding of guns coming from the direction of the Canal.

At Tasa he noted that all the tanks were gone. His first

step was to report to the colonel. The orderly outside the tent checked what he wanted and told him to go right in. The colonel was deep in conversation with a good looking young captain with compelling brown eyes, deep-set under thick black eyebrows. Gadi knew him as Bennie, a former commander of one of the top scouting reconnaissance units, and had worked with him in practice manoeuvers.

Bennie had a tremendous reputation for toughness and intelligence. He was talking with great animation about a special task force that he wanted to form. The colonel saw Gadi enter and motioned him to come closer, but at that same instant the air-raid siren burst into a loud harsh wail and a tremendous blast seemed to hit the camp right outside the tent. For a brief second they froze, and then jumped into action. The major grabbed his steel helmet, putting it on as they ran to the bunker thirty metres away. By the time they reached it the whole area was trembling with a succession of explosions, the anti-aircraft guns were firing in loud rapid barks, and the screech of the enemy jets burst into their eardrums as they swooped mercilessly down on the camp.

In the shelter of the bunker they caught their breath again. Gadi was perspiring with fright, and his stomach was churning inside. There were about thirty men inside the bunker, and with a shock Gadi realised that Bennie wasn't among them. Instinctively he rushed to the entrance, brushing past a soldier who tried to stop him. Outside the air was dense with smoke and dust, tents and vehicles were burning. There was a body lying near the colonel's tent and a medic was bending over it. Gadi got there just as the medic straightened up. It wasn't Bennie, but whoever it was had died a quick horrible death, with a hole the size of a fist driven into his forehead. 'What the hell are you doing out here?' shouted the medic, 'and where's your helmet?'

Gadi started to say 'sorry' although he didn't quite know why he should be apologising personally to the medic, when he suddenly caught sight of Bennie. Instead of running for shelter Bennie had made straight for a half-track parked near the colonel's tent, and as the planes swooped down he fired at them with the heavy swivel machine gun. Illogically, instead of going back to the safety of the bunker, Gadi ran towards the half-track and jumped in with him. Two more Migs came screaming in at the camp, and Bennie fired away, methodically moving the gun, trying to keep them in its sights.

Then the noise and the explosions stopped as suddenly as they had started, and Gadi saw four silver dots streaking away towards the Canal. Behind them were two other dots which Gadi could only guess were Phantoms, and within split seconds there were two bursts of orange flame and clouds of black smoke trailed back from the enemy planes. It was too far away to distinguish whether they were shot down or not, but Gadi and Bennie felt like cheering anyway. Gadi's head was clearing now, and the realisation of his recklessness shook him.

'What got into you?' he asked Bennie, 'I came back to look for you, I thought you were hurt.'

Bennie showed no trace of fear, as though jumping into half-tracks and firing at planes were an everyday occurrence for him. 'Thanks,' he said. 'I've forgotten your name for the moment.'

'Gadi.'

'Oh, yes! Thanks Gadi. I've got a lot of scores to settle with those fellows. I didn't hit any of the planes, but one day I might, and I feel much better firing than just sitting in a bunker.'

The all-clear sounded and the colonel came out to join them. 'You both need your heads examined,' he said, but his tone of voice showed that he did not intend it as a reprimand. The colonel made a tour of the camp to check the casualties and what damage had been caused. He came back looking grim. 'Two dead and three wounded,' he said. 'I suppose it could have been worse considering that we had no warning. I've asked for a report, because they apparently came straight over Ismailiya, and our forward position should have been able to give us at least thirty seconds' notice. If we'd had this maybe there wouldn't have been any casualties.'

The colonel focused back on Gadi and Bennie again. Gadi reported that he had delivered the papers, and handed him the order from the doctor at Sde Dov forbidding him to drive a tank for a week. The colonel turned to Bennie suggesting that maybe he could use Gadi, and the two of them resumed their conversation.

Bennie had apparently been called back as a reserve

officer, but found that he had no clearly defined task. He had rounded up some other officers in the same boat, two captains, and two lieutenants, and wanted the colonel to allow them to form a special task force, to operate near the Egyptian lines, feeding back information and doing whatever damage they could. The colonel thought the idea a good one, and checked by field telephone with General Bardan, at the Divisional Headquarters, an hour's drive away at Riffidim.

General Bardan was in the 'war room' and could not be disturbed for any reason, but the officer assisting him felt that the idea was good in principle and ordered them to report to the General personally to finalise the details. Gadi was already completely under the spell of Bennie's charisma, and felt a surge of excitement when it was confirmed that he could join them. Together with the other officers they set off in a jeep for Riffidim.

Directly after they arrived Bennie went to the command bunker to report, but General Bardan was still in the war room. Israeli counter attacks had been launched early that morning, and the General was personally following and supervising their progress. Bennie spoke to the officer who had told them to come to Headquarters and he was given the names of four other officers available to join the unit, and told how to make contact with them. He was also given a requisition slip authorising them to take over a 'Zelda', a new type of armoured-personnel-carrier running on full tracks like a tank, and to load themselves up with all the food, fuel, arms, and equipment which they thought they could use. The whole group was to report to the General at six o'clock the next morning.

Gadi had used the few minutes waiting for Bennie to dash off two postcards. The one to his family was easy, the one to Rina more difficult. He wanted to tell her in a thousand ways how much he loved her, how glad he was that she had made the approach to him, how every fibre of his being longed for her; but he knew that Mrs Aronsohn wouldn't hesitate to read the postcard, and in the end he just wrote 'I can't get you out of my mind – Love, Gadi.' It seemed so inadequate, but he dropped it in the collection box anyway. The rest of the afternoon was spent scrounging equipment from the various supply stores – food, fuel, machine guns,

Kalatchnikov rifles, two Bazookas, ammunition, night binoculars, flares, radio equipment, detailed army maps, and emergency first-aid kits.

By supper time Bennie was satisfied that all was ready. They ate in the army kitchen. The atmosphere was a little subdued, the news filtering through from the war room indicated that the Israeli attacks had not gone well. One of the officers had a transistor radio and they decided to listen in to a news conference which was being broadcast that evening, and then to get some sleep. At five-fifty the next morning they would be meeting General Bardan, and they had every reason to think that there would be a long hard day ahead of them.

* * *

Bennie went off on his own, and arranged his sleeping bag outside, behind a tent where he would be sheltered from the wind. He crawled into it and snuggled down, gazing up at the clear desert sky, with its countless stars flashing pin-pricks of light in the inky blackness, and a halo of white light on the horizon where the moon was about to rise.

He wondered if Ruth was missing him. He was sure that he loved her a great deal more than she loved him. Probably this was very sensible on her part. A married man with two young children, what did he have to offer her? Even if he divorced Bracha like he had promised to do, what guarantee did she have that he wouldn't do the same to her a couple of years from now? Perhaps that's why she didn't let herself go completely, why she kept him at a distance. Sure, she had let him make love to her, but did it mean anything more to her than a physical attraction, and would she let him go when she found someone else attractive and perhaps a little more eligible?

And yet she had been sweet and loving to him, really loving. Why couldn't he just accept that? He had always been so sure of himself with women. What made him so doubtful about Ruth? And the more he doubted her the more he wanted to possess her and prove that she belonged to him, even if the feeling lasted only as long as they were locked together, and the doubts rushed back as their passion subsided?

In the month before the war he had felt as though he was going out of his mind. When he was with Ruth he would promise her anything, and believe that he meant what he said. Away from her, he saw how impossible the situation was. How could he divorce Bracha? Not that he loved her, but what about the children? How could he live with his conscience if he left them? And wouldn't it end up destroying his relationship with Ruth anyway?

The war had come almost as a relief to him. Not only could he postpone the problem, he could get far away from it. Maybe out here in the desert the answer would become simpler and he could decide what he ought to do. And yet at this moment he would have done almost anything to have Ruth in the sleeping bag with him.

Maybe he would get killed and the problem would solve itself. He had a brief satisfying vision of Bracha and Ruth attending his funeral together, weeping copiously. But he knew he wasn't the dying sort. He had never known real fear on the battlefield because he was absolutely sure that he would come through all right. In any event he wanted to live, and he wanted Ruth – badly.

It was late already. He knew that he needed sleep. To-morrow was liable to be rough, but at least the problems would be more clearly defined. He smiled in spite of himself – it was easier making war than making love!

* * *

Uri was lying on a stretcher in the field hospital at Nafach. He had been brought in the previous day by the patrol that had found him. The doctor examined him, saw that there was nothing physically wrong with him, and ordered the medic to put him to bed for a complete rest. Twenty-four hours had gone by, and the doctor decided that it was time for Uri to be brought back to reality.

Gently he placed his hand on his shoulder, and spoke softly. 'Come on soldier, it's time to get up.' Uri stirred slightly. The voice seemed to come from a thousand miles away, and he tried his best to shut it out. He didn't want to wake up. He needed time to sort things out, to understand what had happened.

It wasn't just Zeev, it was everything; the fighting, the

two boys who had died on the hill, and the acute fear that had crawled into his system and wouldn't let go. If only he could remain still and completely quiet he could cope with it. He could shut out the thought of blood trickling from Zeev's mouth. And Vered! Who would tell her? If he moved – if he showed that he could hear the voice that was pressing in on him – he would have to face it all. No, it was better not to hear the voice. He kept his eyes closed and felt himself slipping back again, farther away from the voice, to where it was still safe . . .

The doctor turned to the medic and asked for a big pitcher of water. When it arrived he lifted Uri into a half-sitting position, gave him a sudden firm smack on the back of his head which jolted Uri's eyes open, just in time for the medic to throw the full contents of the pitcher into his face. Spluttering and a little dazed from the shock, Uri was hauled to his feet by the doctor and the medic. 'Okay sergeant,' said the doctor in a clear authoritative voice, 'stay on your feet, and look around you. You're awake now and you've got work to do. You can't go back to sleep. What's your name?'

'Uri. Uri Ishboneh.'

'How old are you?'

'Twenty-three.'

'Where do you live?'

'Herzliya.'

'All right,' the doctor's voice softened, 'you've been through a rough time Uri, a little bit too rough for you. What was the name of your friend who died?'

'Zeev Ronen.'

'I'm sorry Uri. I've got to ask you these questions to show you that you're still alive and functioning. Nothing can bring your friend back – absolutely nothing! But meanwhile you've got a job to do. We need you. If you want to make your friend's life worth something, you've got to fight and play your part. Do you understand what I'm saying?'

'Yes. I understand.'

'All right,' the doctor turned to the medic. 'I want him to stay on his feet. Let him get dressed and see that he has some breakfast. Then give him something to do, I don't care what it is, but he's to keep moving – not even to sit down. Bring him to me in about two hours.'

The medic took Uri to the kitchen and personally organised two hardboiled eggs for him, with bread and hot coffee. The colour came back into Uri's cheeks and the medic sent him off on an errand to the other side of the camp. Threading his way through the hive of activity Uri found himself responding, and wanting to become a part of it again.

A tremendous barrage of artillery was taking place not far away, and there were frequent sonic booms, always in twos, linked with the beautiful and sinister shapes of Phantoms zooming at incredible speeds only a hundred feet above the ground in the direction of Damascus taking advantage of the terrain to avoid the missile screens, or cruising back high overhead, their missions safely completed.

Nafach was the Headquarters of the army command on the Golan, and on the Saturday and Sunday it had been in the direct line of the Syrian attack. Enemy tanks had been destroyed as close to five hundred metres from its barbed wire fences, but somehow the camp had held out, and had functioned all through those desperate first hours, organising, improvising and co-ordinating the limited defence forces available. Uri had been out of touch with reality for the last twenty-four hours, and had no idea of the progress of the war, and the changes that had taken place on the different sectors of the Golan front.

In the North on the 1967 cease-fire line stretching roughly from Kuneitra to Majdal Shams on the slopes of Mount Hermon, a tremendous tank battle had raged unabated since Saturday afternoon. For their initial attack the Syrians had massed six brigades consisting of a hundred tanks each, many of them T-62s. Powerfully supported by Sukhoi bombers and Migs and enormous concentrations of long-distance artillery, and aided by spotters on the newly-conquered Mount Hermon stronghold, the tanks advanced in wave after wave against the Israeli positions. Fortunately for Israel this was the one area where the armour had been reinforced on Dayan's instructions. A total of 110 Israeli tanks were available to meet the onslaught, six to one against the defenders, but these odds were twice as favourable as anywhere else on the Golan. In addition they were commanded in the field by some of the most experienced and brilliant tank officers in the Israeli Army.

On the Southern and Central sectors of the Golan between Kuneitra and Lake Kineret, the situation had been much more serious. The highly-fortified Israeli strongpoints on the 1967 cease-fire lines had put up a fierce resistance, and not one was actually captured, but their occupants were forced to retire below ground to the security of their bunkers. The Syrians pushed through in classic Soviet-taught style parting around the strongholds like water and continuing to flow on, their intention being to return later and mop up the pockets of resistance. The Israeli back-up armour and artillery was weak and spread far too thin. The terrain was difficult, with the field of vision limited and obstructed by hills, rocks, bushes and deserted villages. The roads were winding and one never knew what lay behind the next bend.

The Syrians fought with unexpected courage and determination. Two of their spearheads captured a huge bulge in the Hushniyeh region below Kuneitra. One spearhead linked up with forces which came down from the north-east around Kuneitra, overrunning the settlements of Merom Golan and Ein Zivan which had been hastily evacuated only a few hours before. They were beaten off in their attacks against Nafach, but swept onwards down the road arriving within a kilometre of the Bnot Yaacov bridge, from where they threatened the entire northern flank of the country. The other spearhead turned south, driving straight through the settlements of Ramat Magshimim and El Al, also evacuated just in time, and onwards until they were within artillery range of Kibbutz Ein Gev on the northern shore of Lake Kineret.

From the very beginning of the war the Israeli Command had given top priority to the Golan, not only because the threat was so immediate, but also to discourage King Hussein of Jordan from any illusions that the Syrians were in a winning position and that he should yield to the enormous pressure on him to open up a third front. On the Egyptian front Israel still had more than three hundred kilometres of desert to manoeuver with and play for time.

As a result of this determination of priorities the Israeli air force unleashed its full strength on the Golan, flying thousands of sorties; bombing, strafing, and supporting the defending tank forces and artillery; and at a heavy cost, destroying the many Sam missile bases.

The Egyptians tended to keep their air force behind the shelter of their missile bases, venturing out for quick sorties, and scurrying back home, but the Syrians were committed to an all-out initial effort and sent their planes out with all the power they could command. The Israeli air force drove them off and shot them down with such appalling certainty that the Syrian pilots who ventured out were almost committing suicide. Assad in desperation publicly offered a lifetime pension of three thousand dollars a year and free education for his children to any Syrian pilot shooting down five Israeli planes. There were no takers.

By Monday the reserve forces were gathering in full strength on all sectors of the Golan front. Israeli heavy artillery was brought up and co-ordinated attacks of artillery, air force and tanks started to put pressure on the Syrian forces. The momentum of the Syrian attack was ground to a halt. Their losses were enormous. In the north by Tuesday midday they had lost 250 tanks against the Israeli loss of 31 tanks. In the south the spearheads had been thrown back from El Al and the Bnot Yaacov bridge. Battlelines had formed along the 'tap-line route' (the anomalous American-owned oil pipeline that runs from Iraq to Lebanon right across the Golan Heights), and Israeli counter-attacks were forming about a kilometre below Nafach, working towards surrounding an entire Syrian brigade in the Hushniyeh pocket . . .

When Uri returned from his errand the medic sent him back to the doctor, who gave him the briefest of check-ups and wrote out a certificate that he was fit. By now Uri was determined to get into action again. The words of the doctor had stuck with him, that if he wanted to make Zeev's sacrifice worthwhile he should be out there fighting. He hurried off to the operations room at Nafach hoping to find out where his unit was, and how quickly he could join them.

In the entrance to a large prefabricated hut, a baby-faced sergeant was talking on a field telephone. With a wave of his hand he stopped Uri from going any farther, and when he'd finished the conversation, asked Uri what he wanted. Uri explained, and was told that he'd have to speak to Major Shaul who was busy in the operations room at the moment. The sergeant's name was Naftali. He told Uri to sit down, and in between phone calls asked Uri what had happened to him. Uri sensed that he was keen to talk, and it suited him as he also wanted to catch up with the news. After listening to Uri's story Naftali filled him in on what had happened generally, adding some local colour about the rocket attacks on the Hula valley settlements by terrorists operating out of Lebanon. The entire civilian population was sleeping in shelters. He also described the giant Frog missiles with their five-hundred-and-fifty-kilogram payloads, which the Syrians had launched indiscriminately at civilian settlements from a range of seventy kilometres. Only a series of minor miracles had helped to avoid great loss of life.

While they were talking the phone was going constantly, and Uri with a pang of longing heard Naftali having several conversations with Tel Aviv.

'I don't suppose there's a chance of your letting me speak to my girlfriend in Tel Aviv?' he asked hopefully.

'Absolutely not,' said Naftali.

Uri did not argue, but the hurt on his face was too much for Naftali, and he compromised.

'Look, I dare not take a chance now, but after the meeting, when the officers have gone off, I might be able to squeeze in just a moment. I'm not promising, but we'll see then.'

Uri's face lit up as he thanked him.

A few moments later a stream of officers started to come out of the meeting room, and Naftali pointed out Major Shaul. Uri went up to him and explained his position. Shaul told him that his unit was in the north, where they had just crossed the old 1967 lines and occupied a series of Syrian bunkers. He knew Amos personally, and thought he was all right, although the unit had suffered quite a few casualties. Shaul told him that some jeeps would be going there in about thirty minutes via the Kuneitra road, which was now free of the enemy, and he told Uri how to find a Captain Bar-Am and join them. 'Good luck,' he said to Uri, and then went off.

The officers had all gone and Uri turned to Naftali, who didn't need to be told what was on his mind. 'Okay, we'll try now, but please don't say anything about where you are or about the war, and keep it very short.'

Uri gave him the number and Naftali dialed a few times, then handed the receiver to Uri, who heard the phone ringing, and suddenly, his heart pounding, he heard Aliza's voice answering the phone. The line was beautifully clear.

'Thank goodness you're home, Aliza, it's me Uri.'

'Oh, my God. Uri, are you all right?'

'Yes sweetheart, I'm fine – please listen carefully, because I can only talk for a second.'

'Carry on . . .'

'I'm a hundred per cent okay, so you mustn't worry about me. I'm not allowed to tell you where I am, but it's where you'd expect me to be. Please call my family and tell them I'm fine. Okay?'

'Yes Uri, I'll tell them.'

'Do you know anything about Gadi?'

'He's okay. I heard he was home for a day. He's fine.'

'All right, I've got to put the phone down but I'll write to you as soon as possible. I love you – do you hear me?'

'Yes Uri' – he could hear the tears in her voice. 'I love you too Uri. Look after yourself.'

He put the receiver down. Uri had the strongest feeling that all would be well, and that it would only be a matter of days when he would be back with her again. He knew again, as he had always known, that Aliza was his life, that without her nothing was important, absolutely nothing . . .

Naftali was watching him sympathetically, not wanting to break into his thoughts. 'Thanks Naftali,' Uri said, 'you'll never know what this meant to me.'

Naftali brushed him away – 'I wish I could have done more. Keep well.'

Uri hurried off to say goodbye and thanks to the medic, and then found Captain Bar-Am who was almost ready to go. The captain made room for him in his own Jeep, and they were soon driving in the direction of Kuneitra, with two other Jeeps following them.

They passed Kibbutz Ein Zivan, and felt a thrill to see trucks already inside the kibbutz grounds, and people busy working and tidying up. 'That's a pleasant sight, isn't it?' the captain said to Uri, 'the men came back today, and apparently it's not too badly damaged.'

They drove through Kuneitra due north, along a narrow sand road. Uri was a little apprehensive about mines, but he figured that the captain knew what he was doing, and he kept his thoughts to himself. A few kilometres past Kuneitra they crossed the 1967 cease-fire lines and passed through the Syrian village of Jubtata el-Kleshab. The village was not quite deserted, a few stray goats wandered around, and on the threshold of one dilapidated dwelling Uri saw an old man

75

peering anxiously out at them. It was now almost dark, and they were not sorry when they arrived at their destination about five minutes later. Captain Bar-Am called a lieutenant over to him, and in a few words explained Uri's situation.

Lieutenant Israel Cohen, or Izzy, as the Captain called him, led Uri to a deserted bunker. 'You'll sleep here tonight,' he said. 'I'll show you where you can get something to eat, and then make sure you get some of the Russian blankets that the Syrians very kindly left behind for us. They're not good quality, so don't be shy to take five or six.'

While he was still talking, Uri suddenly felt a hefty smack on his back. 'Uri, you bastard! Gosh it's good to see you.' It was Amos. The two of them hugged each other with genuine love and relief at being together again, whole and well. Uri felt as though he was back on the team again.

*   *   *

Meir came home as usual in Chaim Singer's car. He hadn't felt well all day, but said nothing of this to Shoshana, who was busy in the kitchen. She was baking three chocolate cakes, one for each of the boy's parcels, and one for the Singers who were coming to watch TV with them after dinner.

Just as Shoshana was putting the icing on the cake, the phone rang and she picked it up.

'Aliza? . . . Yes! . . . Oh wonderful, where is he? . . . Is he all right? . . . Is that all he said? . . . But how did he sound, did he seem all right? . . . He didn't even say when he might get back? . . . Oh . . . Thank you Aliza, thank you for calling!'

She put the phone down. There were tears of joy in her eyes. Meir had been hovering around trying to get his ear as close to the mouthpiece as possible to pick up any scrap of information.

'Nu! Tell me! Is he all right? What did she say?'

'She says that Uri called her ten minutes ago. He's all right. He asked her to call us. He wasn't allowed to say where he is, but he said it was where she would expect him to be, so Aliza thinks he must be on the Golan Heights. And that's all.'

'Nothing else?'

'No. He wasn't supposed to be using the phone. He had to make the conversation very quick.'

'I wonder why he called her. You would have thought he would call us!'

'Oh Mickie, how can you be so silly? Of course he would phone Aliza. You know how crazy he is about her – don't you?'

'Yes, you're right! I don't think I'd mind if Uri came to me and said they wanted to get married. I think she'd be very good for him.'

Shoshana finished icing the cakes and put them in the fridge. Then they had a quiet dinner, contented that both their boys were safe, and Meir lay down for a short sleep . . .

The Singers arrived just before the eight-thirty news. They had left their younger son, Eitan, watching the television in their apartment because they had not heard from Danny since five o'clock the day before, and like all other pilots he called home every evening from the base to save them worrying about him.

As on the previous evening the news began with a conference attended by a large number of overseas and local correspondents, and televised live from Tel Aviv. The central figure, however, was different – tonight it was General Aharon Yariv.

'I've never heard of him, who is he?' asked Meir.

The announcer saved Chaim the trouble by stating that General Yariv was a former Chief of Military Intelligence who had been recalled to the army to serve as special aide to the Chief of Staff, Elazar. The significance of his appointment and the purpose of the conference soon became clear.

In crisp, blunt terms, speaking first in Hebrew and then in a good English, Yariv tactfully but decisively shattered the illusions created by Elazar the night before. Instead of Elazar's statement that the Israel Defence Forces 'were now on the offensive on all fronts', Yariv suggested that 'a certain stability on each front' had been achieved. Yariv did not directly criticise Elazar's exciting 'the quicker we advance and the stronger we attack, the fewer casualties we will suffer and the more the enemy will suffer'; but he went out of his way to warn the country against 'visions of elegant and rapid conquest of the Arabs'. Asked whether the war was likely to be a long one, Yariv replied, 'it will not be short.' For the first time it was publicly admitted that the Bar Lev line had been 'evacuated'.

At one point in the conference Yariv was asked a question about a statement issued by the Army Information Services. His first reaction was that such a statement couldn't have been made, but when it was shown to him, he shook his head and said, 'It's just not true. It should never have been made.' The shock effect of this admission shattered any further illusions which the Israeli public might have been trying to hold on to. The uneasy feeling which had been hanging ominously over them was finally and irrevocably spelled out. They had not been told the truth! Facts had not only been held back, they had been distorted and twisted, and apparently in at least one instance there had been a blatant lie!

Yariv did his job well. He made it clear that the existence of the State was not in danger, and explained carefully why the situation was so different from the 1967 war. He didn't use eloquent phrases like 'blood, sweat and tears', but by the time the conference was concluded Israel understood that a big price had already been paid, and that the struggle would not end easily or soon.

Chaim and Meir tried to find some sense in what they had heard.

'How do you see it?' asked Meir.

'I don't know. I can't believe that what Elazar said last night isn't true.'

'Well, did he actually say it was so good, or did it just sound like that to us?'

'What's the difference? It's obvious we've been living in a fool's paradise. That's why they appointed Yariv, to tell us the truth and not treat us like children . . . unless maybe they've got some other motive . . . '

'Such as?'

'I don't know. Maybe to fool the Arabs that things are tough with us, or maybe to fool the United Nations. If they think things are going well with us, they might force us to make peace before it suits us.' Chaim's attempted explanations didn't sound convincing to either of them. They continued to talk in circles, confused and frustrated. Chaim was more depressed than Meir, because there was still no word from Danny.

Shoshana served coffee and cake, and the late movie started, so there was no more conversation until it ended at 11.30, when the Singers said their goodbyes and went back to their apartment.

Wednesday, 10th October

Meir woke up with a tremendous start. The sound of the air-raid siren was filling the room with it's bloodcurdling wail. Incredibly, Shoshana was still sleeping. He shook her awake and together they made their way down the stairs. Seconds later the Singers entered the shelter, with Eitan still sleepily rubbing his eyes. It was four thirty. Even before Chaim told them, they could see by the expression on his face that Danny had called. The phones at his base had been out of order, so he had only managed to contact them two hours previously, but he had assured them that all was well. With a bit of luck he might even be home on Saturday for twenty-four hours leave.

They sat around for twenty minutes, and Shoshana was trying to persuade Meir that she should go upstairs and make some coffee, but before he could make up his mind the all-clear sounded.

They trooped back to their respective apartments, and Meir got into bed but found himself unable to sleep. His forehead was covered with a cold sweat, and his stomach churned painfully, reminiscent of dreadful anxieties from the past. When his alarm clock went off at six o'clock, he lingered under the covers debating whether or not he should go to work, or to the Kupat Cholim, the clinic run by the National Health Scheme. Eventually he got up, put his robe on, and went across the Hallway to Chaim's apartment to tell him not to wait for him.

Shoshana was aware of the tension beneath Meir's apparent calm, and approved of his being examined by the doctor.

On the way to the Kupat Cholim Meir bought the *Uj Kelet* and scanned the headlines. Yariv's press conference dominated the front page, but nevertheless the news was reassuring. On the Syrian front Israeli Phantoms had bombed the army Headquarters and the radio station in Damascus. These targets were in the middle of residential areas and despite pin-point bombing, civilian casualties were inevitable. Further north other planes had inflicted devastating damage on the vital oil refinery at Homs and the important power station there. Also hit were the radar installations on Jebel Baurkh, in southern Lebanon, which Israel claimed was used to give advance warning to the Syrians of Israeli air attacks. The freedom enjoyed by the air force in making these attacks was attributed to the destruction of the extremely thick array of Sam missile batteries between the 1967 borders and Damascus.

On the Suez front the Egyptians were continuing to build up their strength, bringing troops and equipment across the Canal on rafts and new bridges. The Israelis were battering these forces causing considerable losses, but it was clear that crucial battles were yet to come.

The navy had been active again, sinking three Egyptian missile boats and a patrol craft; adding to its impressive score of five Syrian naval boats, three of them missile boats, on the first night of the war, all without a single hit on an Israeli vessel. The naval victories were doubly satisfying, because they resulted from the superiority of the Israeli-produced Gabriel missiles over the much vaunted Soviet-made Styx.

Soviet leader Brezhnev called upon all Arab states to join in the war saying that Syria and Egypt must not stand alone in their battle with the perfidious enemy. Meir wondered at the irony of fifty million people 'standing alone' against three million, not to mention their Russian advisers and at least double the planes and tanks and ships and guns possessed by the 'perfidious enemy'. Finance Minister Sapir announced a one thousand million pounds compulsory loan to help pay for the war, and Meir ruefully calculated that his take-home pay would go down by another ten per cent.

At the Kupat Cholim there was a long line of people, mostly elderly, looking especially pathetic and helpless in the harsh morning light as they waited to renew their prescriptions for medicine. Meir received a number and it soon became clear that he would have to wait more than an hour for his turn. He sat staring into space thinking of Uri and Gadi and feeling depressed and useless.

In the midst of his thoughts he became conscious that somebody had spoken to him. It was the man next to him, obese, white-haired, wearing a suit and tie. Meir knew him by reputation. He was a lawyer who lived in the neighbourhood, but they had never actually spoken to each other.

'What's wrong Mr Ishboneh?' asked the lawyer.

'I don't really know. I think I'm just run down, nothing serious I hope. And you Mr . . . er – ?' Meir was embarrassed, he didn't remember the man's name.

'Goodman. Call me Ernie. The doctor put me on a special diet, but I think he's out of his mind. He said if I don't stick to it I'll be heading for a heart attack. But if I do stick to it I'm going to die of starvation. I can't think of anything except food, I can't concentrate, I can't even sleep. There must be something better that he can suggest for me.'

Meir nodded his head in sympathy. 'What do you think of the situation Mr Goodman?' Meir was not just making conversation – he knew that the lawyer's opinion was highly thought of in local political circles.

'Ernie's the name. This is no time to stand on ceremony. What's your first name?'

'Meir.'

'Well Meir, you're asking a difficult question, but I suppose this is as good a time as any to discuss it. I think the situation stinks. I think we've been caught very badly off our guard, and that somebody should have the guts to get up and accept responsibility for it. We've been living in a world of make-believe. Dayan and all our other leaders kept telling us that we've never had it so good, that we could go on with this no-war-no-peace situation for fifty years, if necessary, and we believed them. The only pity was that Sadat didn't.' The lawyer paused, glancing at Meir intensely to see if his words were sinking in.

'Do you follow what I'm getting at, Meir?'

'I think so,' Meir answered, uncertainly.

'Well, let me put it differently,' Ernie continued, enjoying the opportunity to let off steam. 'What have my biggest problems been in the last year or two? I've been worried about inflation, I wanted to move into a larger apartment, I was thinking of buying my daughter a car, I was busy cursing all the groups who were striking and holding the economy to ransom, the dock workers, the bus companies, the electricity employees. But the real problem I forgot about. I buried my head in the sand and pretended that it didn't exist. Do you know what the real problem was Meir?' The question was rhetorical, Meir didn't even attempt to reply. 'The real problem was survival, to recognise that we couldn't live in a tiny postage stamp of a country, surrounded by millions of enemies who look upon us as usurpers, unwanted strangers who have stolen their land and threaten their very way of life. We kept increasing our strength, but unfortunately the more we did this the more impossible it became for the Arabs to live with it, and we ended up driving them into the wide-open arms of the Russians.'

'Well, I suppose we've got the Americans . . .'

'You're missing the point, Meir, look at the record. The Arab countries are fundamentally opposed to a communist regime because of its atheistic basis. And they distrust Russia, they've seen what happened to the countries that she "helped". Russia has always coveted a foothold in the Middle East, and we're the ones who made it possible. The Arab states distrusted and didn't want to get involved with her, but they couldn't go to war unless they did. And we gave them no alternative to war.'

'But Mr Goodman . . . Ernie . . . our government did try. Golda was always offering to meet them – anywhere, to discuss peace.'

'Well they didn't try hard enough. They convinced themselves that we were too strong for the Arabs to go to war, so they didn't feel that there was any real urgency to make peace.'

'And now?' asked Meir, 'how do you think the war is going?'

'I wish I knew. The trouble is I don't know what to believe any more. According to the papers things are quite good, but they haven't released the casualty figures yet, and I think we're going to have a shock when they do.'

Meir was silent. His thoughts went back to Uri and Gadi again. A few minutes later his number was called and he went into the doctor's office.

Dr Goldblatt knew him well. He asked a few general questions, listened to his heart, and took his blood pressure. '160/100, normal. You're suffering from the same disease as all of us Mr Ishboneh, you've got two boys at the front and you're worrying about them. And the trouble is that there's nothing more tiring than mental worries. If I could write you out a prescription that your sons should come home today, you'd feel fine right away.' Meir smiled, he had confidence in the doctor. 'You should be pleased,' Dr Goldblatt continued, 'you're in good physical shape. I'm going to give you a prescription for some sedatives, but I don't want you to take one unless you're really under pressure.'

Meir went out feeling better already. He went back to the apartment to tell Shoshana, and then walked down to catch a bus to work.

* * *

Saida Mizrachi arrived early at the Kfar Saba General Hospital, the largest in the Herzliya district. She smiled at the watchman at the gate, took the elevator to the third floor and sat down in the waiting room of ward 'E'. The large electric clock on the wall showed eight minutes to eight and she had arranged to meet Aliza when she came off duty at eight o'clock.

It was pleasant to sit on the comfortable leather couch and let her thoughts drift. It had taken a lot of convincing to get her to agree to have a gynaecological check-up. But the pains had been bad and Aliza had insisted. How different life was here. Who would have thought that her daughter would one day lay down the law to her on a subject so delicate as her womb. In her forty-four years Saida had not just moved from one country to another, but had crossed a generation gap of six thousand years. And Zachariah too, it hadn't been easy for either of them . . .

Saida remembered the first day she had met him – their wedding day. They sat confused and dumbfounded on their ceremonial chairs at the far side of the large stone building which served as the communal meeting house for the Jews of Hadeida, a small Yemenite town on the barren Arabian peninsula. Around them their clansmen were eating and drinking and enjoying the celebration. In one corner a group of men began a special wedding dance, graceful and light, slow at first, but gradually increasing the speed of their movements until it culminated in a wild exciting climax of exuberant leaps. The women, who did not often witness such a spectacle, joined in the jubilation and applause which followed.

Saida was fifteen years old. Her face was veiled, except for the slit through which her large black eyes shone with excitement. Her beautifully worked headpiece tapered upwards more than fifteen centimetres in row after row of delicate filigree silver threads, inlaid with blue and semi-precious stones. It was a family heirloom handed down from her great grandmother. Shyly she glanced sideways at Zachariah. He was a man already, eighteen years old, dressed in a long striped silk robe, a richly embroidered skull cap sitting on top of his thick wavy hair and carefully combed side curls.

It was the third day of the festivities. The evening before the women of both families had gathered at her house. Men were forbidden. Special songs of love and courtship and marriage had been sung, Saida's hands were painted with red henna to ward off the evil eye, and her mother had fed her seven times during the evening. Today in turn she had smeared henna on her father's finger. She knew that Zachariah's father had paid a more than generous price for her, and both her parents were pleased and happy.

That night when they were alone, Zachariah had been very gentle with her, and in the morning she gave her mother the bed-linen – with the spots of blood testifying that she had been a virgin.

She vividly remembered those first years in Hadeida, living in the little one-room stone hut. Who had even thought of a toilet in those days? She remembered how her initial shyness and fear had gradually faded away, and how she had come to respect Zachariah and to love him.

For her first two children she had only her mother to help her, and to their distress they were both girls. She marvelled at Zachariah's patience with her and vowed that she would bear him many sons.

Then the news started to trickle into Hadeida about a great war and how God had helped His people to win. The elders of the community took this as a sign that God was calling them back to the land of their forefathers, and the whole village had journeyed on foot to Aden, where they lived in the Hashid camp, until they were ushered into the

85

belly of the great bird that flew them to Israel – just as The Book had prophesied!

They were given a wooden hut on the outskirts of Herzliya, three small rooms and a kitchen, with an outside toilet which they shared with the family living next to them. The two girls slept in one room with Zachariah's mother (his father had passed away), her parents in the second room, and she and Zachariah in the living room. How hard he had worked, hammering away from early morning until late at night, at the fine silver jewellery which was so sought after. He had also used his skill with his hands to strengthen their hut and add on to it. And the small patch of ground around the house had become her special love; she had never grown tired of feasting her eyes on the green of the trees and the grass.

And then Aliza was born, and then to Zachariah's delight, five boys. And somehow Aliza had been mother to them all, even the two older sisters who were already married with children of their own. And now Aliza was in love with Uri, the young Ashkenazi boy. How different it all was. But she was grateful, for it truly was the 'promised land', and God had been very good to them.

Saida felt a light kiss on her cheek. 'Dreaming, at this time of the morning! Come on, we've got a lot to do.' Aliza took her by the arm, and they walked together to the Gynaecological department.

*　　*　　*

At exactly five-fifty Gadi and Bennie and the eight other officers stood at the entrance to General Bardan's Headquarters. In appearance the bunker looked much like any other ridge in the desert, except for the opening which was flanked by cement walls and stones and wire netting. An officer took their credentials, and they were left standing outside doing physical jerks with their arms and stamping their feet, trying to shake off the chill of the early morning.

Gadi felt his muscles tense with excitement as they were given permission to enter. They were in a large brightly lit hall with a wide flight of stairs leading further underground. They went down two levels and were then ushered into a large concrete chamber, with telephones and other communications equipment, and at the far end a huge map covered with a transparent plastic material, on which numerous coloured lines and symbols depicted the line-up and composition of the opposing forces. General Bardan sat on a plain straight-back chair, his back to the map. He looked tired, but well in control of himself. He wore a crumpled khaki fatigue uniform, with high boots, and no sign of rank on the shoulders of his shirt. He was a large man with rugged features softened by huge blue eyes, giving him an innocent expression that was dispelled as soon as he began to speak.

'Please be seated,' he said in a loud clear voice, indicating the rows of chairs in front of him. Then he got straight down to business.

'From this room we have an overall picture of what is happening on the Southern Front. Today is the fifth day of the war, and the map is not quite as pretty as I would like it to be, but it's a little healthier than it was a couple of days ago. We haven't been able to do much about pushing their positions back' – he pointed with a long stick to a red line on the east bank of the canal – 'but we've been building up our reserves, and we are pressing on the enemy and making life more difficult for him all round.' Here he pointed to a thick green line dotted with different symbols running parallel to the red line.

'We've been fighting a continuous battle for just on forty-eight hours, probing for weaknesses, and trying to ascertain if it would be worth while storming their positions at any particular spot. We've hurt them a little, but we've had virtually no air support because of their missile belt; and for the moment, we've decided to play a waiting game . . .

'The enemy is very excited, maybe justifiably so, at his success up to now. He's bringing more tanks and guns and equipment across the Canal, and in my view he is building himself a death-trap. Every tank on this side of the Canal will be destroyed, every man will be killed or taken prisoner. Sooner or later he's going to have to move forward, and when he does it will be the decisive moment. We're going to hit him with everything we've got . . .

'Meanwhile, I need information. I need to know his strength, what weapons he has brought over, where they are, and what they are doing. Your work will be mainly observation, and you will report back to me in as much detail as possible. Leave it to my people to judge what's important and what's not important. There are other special task forces operating like yours but we need you here in the north, between points P40 and 50.' He indicated an area on the map between Tasa and Baluza, roughly opposite Kantara.

'Most of you have had experience in the field, and you are all well trained. Bennie will be in command, and I am leaving it largely to his discretion how you operate. Your code name is "Meron". You will at all times stay in contact with Battalion 31 who are in control of that part of the front. That's all. Are there any questions?'

There were none. He picked up a half-full bottle of orange juice from the floor next to him, and toasted them with a large smile, 'Le Chaim! and good luck to you!'

Dror, a captain in the elite parachute commando corps, took charge of the Zelda with five men. Bennie climbed into the jeep with Gadi as the driver; Boaz, also a parachutist; and Shimon, an engineer. At seven-thirty they drove off, passing the airfield at Bir Gafgafa, and heading due west towards the Canal. At Tasa they turned north in the direction of Baluza.

Bennie was in his element. He believed that there was no greater mission in life than to fight for one's country. And he enjoyed being in command, with the special excitement of knowing that his men depended on and trusted him, even with their lives. He established radio contact with Battalion 31, and continuously consulted his map. The track they were on was at first clearly defined, but gradually melted into the surrounding desert scenery, its surface being covered by the shifting sands.

At the foot of a high sand-ridge they stopped. Bennie took Boaz with him, and they climbed slowly to the top. About twenty minutes later Gadi heard Bennie's voice come through on the jeep's radio.

'Meron 1 to Meron 2, do you hear me? Over.'

Dror answered affirmatively from the Zelda.

'Meron 2 to Meron 1, I hear you. Over.'

'Meron 1 to Meron 2, conceal yourselves carefully and leave the drivers on guard. The rest of you get up here with weapons and battle rations. End of message.'

Gadi was disappointed at being left out, but the noise of heavy artillery firing could be heard continuously, and he realised that at such a short distance from the front-lines action could come from anywhere, often from where one least expected it. He and Micha, the driver of the Zelda, manoeuvered their vehicles behind a smaller sand-dune, covered them with camouflage netting and watched the men climbing up the hill.

Micha was a short, stout man of about forty, with a receding hairline and an air of quiet toughness about him. He told Gadi that he thought they were opposite Kantara and that this was as good a place as any to lie low and see what was happening. The sun burned down on them and Micha decided it was time for a siesta. He lay down under the netting, while Gadi sat with the radio on one side of him, his Uzzi on the other.

* * *

Amos woke everybody up at six o'clock. Uri glanced sleepily around him, trying to adjust to his new surroundings. The entrance to the bunker was shielded by a massive slab of concrete about a metre away from the cliffside. The first grey lights of dawn penetrated from the narrow spaces on both sides of the slab, but the inside of the bunker was still dark and gloomy. He pushed his blanket aside and stood up, fully dressed in accordance with standard practice at the front, with even his boots properly laced. Putting on his windjacket, he stopped outside to look around.

The morning mist which clung to the contours of the ground, reluctantly rolled away from the bright rays of the sun, revealing an astonishing scene. Their bunker was next to a paved road which curved around about a hundred metres away in a large U-turn, and passed opposite them again about fifty metres across a steep wadi. Above the road all along its length, and below it, in the wadi enclosed by the angle of the curve, was a network of about thirty or more identical bunkers, each of them built like a small fortress into the side of the cliff. Scattered around them were the remains of about fifty wrecked tanks, burned-out trucks and armoured personnel carriers, the vast majority

Syrian with their distinctive light brown camouflage markings, and also a few Israeli vehicles.

The whole area was beginning to come alive with soldiers emerging from the bunkers, and Uri noted a force of at least a dozen Israeli tanks concealed under netting in the wadi, and also some half-tracks and jeeps. The site was so ideal for defence that Uri wondered what kind of fight had taken place before it was captured.

He went back inside the bunker and looked around. On the side furthest from the entrance a number of white pine ammunition boxes were stacked. Even in the dim light he could make out the Russian inscriptions. A separate pile was covered in what appeared to be Chinese lettering. In the centre of the floor the Syrians had left behind some half-eaten pittas and open cans.

It was still cold and the men lined up at the mobile mess for steaming hot coffee and stale bread. They had hardly eaten when Amos called them together and told them they would move out shortly on patrol. 'There's not likely to be much action today,' he said, 'our armour and artillery are moving up – it looks as though tomorrow will be the big day.'

They moved out in two jeeps and a half-track, driving back through the village that Uri had seen the night before. It was a bit more animated now. Smoke rose from one of the chimneys and a couple of old women, their faces covered with black veils, moved along the road with loads of firewood tied to their bent backs.

Uri was irritated by the poverty; no electricity, no water pipes, no telephone wires, and the farm equipment he could see was so primitive that it could have dated back a thousand years. It was impossible not to compare the standard of living of Israeli Arabs with their modern farming methods, their villages with schools and clinics and solid houses topped by TV antennae.

The patrol headed towards Khan Rinbeh on the Syrian side of the 1967 cease-fire lines, and almost adjoining the Kuneitra–Damascus road. Heavy guns rumbled occasionally, but on the whole there was an air of ominous quiet, as if a tropical storm was gathering strength, working itself up into a tremendous fury, ready to wreak destruction on everything in its path.

When they arrived at Khan Rinbeh, Uri saw that this wasn't so far from the truth. Huge columns of armour were taking shape, tanks, bull-dozers, Zeldas, mobile artillery, large mortars and Katusha rocket-launchers mounted on truck platforms. Some of the troop-carriers were inscribed in fresh white paint 'next stop – Damascus'. The concentrated power in front of them was awe-inspiring and Uri was sure that the end of the war, at least on the Golan, was very close.

Amos ordered the patrol to turn around, and they returned to their position without any incidents. They were told to relax, but to stay nearby in case they were needed suddenly.

Some of the soldiers decided to build a Succa for the next day's festival. They took one of the trucks and improvised by removing the tarpaulin at the back, and covering it with bright green branches. They had an ample supply of the 'four species' which had been distributed to the forward units by religious groups. The setting was completely incongruous, but they enjoyed themselves, laughing at each novel idea for decoration.

Uri had something else on his mind. He found a quiet spot, wrote a short letter to his parents, and then settled down to write to Aliza. It was not easy, and he tore up three attempts before he was satisfied. He placed the letters inside an envelope on which he had written 'Try to open this when you are alone', followed by her name in full, ALIZA MIZRACHI, her phone number and full address. Then he put it in his pocket. Later in the day his opportunity came when a group of war correspondents arrived at their base. Uri got into conversation with them, and a Mr Crawford, who represented a big London paper was more than willing to take his letter to Tel Aviv and to phone Aliza to come and pick it up.

* * *

Meir returned home from the office and was alarmed to find Shoshana red-eyed in the kitchen.

'What on earth is wrong,' he cried.

'I heard a terrible story today and I can't get it out of my mind.'

'What did you hear?'

'That when the Egyptians crossed the Canal we were so unprepared that there were about sixty girls with our soldiers when they captured the forward positions. Most of them were killed; the bodies were mutilated, and God only knows what happened to the girls who were taken alive.'

'It can't possibly be true, Shosh, who told you this story?'

'Sarah Goldman, she heard it from her husband, and he got it from a driver of one of the trucks that brought the bodies up here. She said that the details were so horrible that her husband wouldn't even tell them to her.'

'I don't believe it, Shosh.'

Meir was upset at the story and how upset Shosh was. He looked for reasons to convince her and himself that it couldn't be true.

'The newspapers would have carried it long ago Shosh. This is such a small country, they couldn't have repressed a story like that if it was true. There would have been a tremendous public outcry.'

'No, it is true. That's why they haven't released the names of the dead yet, because they'd have to include the girls' names as well, and there'd be such a scandal about them being in the front lines.'

'Shosh, it's only a rumour. I refuse to believe that such a thing could have happened and that we wouldn't have heard anything about it.'

'Well how can it not be true if the person who told the story actually brought the bodies back?'

'Wait a minute, Shosh, be logical. Our bunkers were overrun, right?'

'Yes.'

'So how did we manage to get the bodies? Do you think the Egyptians asked us to collect them so we could bring back evidence of their savagery?'

'I don't know, but why should Sarah Goldman's husband deliberately spread stories that aren't true.'

'I don't know, Shosh. There are all sorts of horror stories that go around in war time. You mustn't let yourself get upset by them, especially this one. It absolutely can't be true.'

Meir had convinced himself that he was right; but Shoshana was still shaken, and in spite of his logic, the pictures conveyed by the rumour were so horrible that they persisted in his mind and wouldn't go away. Shoshana served him supper and he dozed a while on an easy chair until it was time to go into Chaim's flat to watch television.

* * *

The Six Day War has often been referred to as the 'transistor war', because soldiers and civilians alike, spent those days with one ear glued to a transistor radio, following the news almost as it happened.

The Yom Kippur War acquired a new dimension through the TV screen. For the first time a war in Israel was brought right into their livingrooms, and the grim reality hit them hard. They saw young men with stubbly beards, sitting exhausted or sleeping at roadsides, while huge tanks rumbled past. The noises of war blended with the sight of guns firing, and showers of sand and smoke rising into the sky. They watched the wounded being picked up by helicopter; or interviewed lying in hospital beds, talking through bandages, describing actions and brushes with death, in simple everyday language, without bravado, but every word searing into the hearts and minds of their audience. Battles fought during the day were transmitted the same night, and people sat glued to their sets, hoping to see a loved one, father, son or friend, to make sure that at least for that day they were safe and unharmed.

The more discomfort and danger that was shown on the screen, the more uneasy and guilty the watchers felt in the safety of their homes. To counteract the impact of this, the network substantially increased the entertainment hours, and the quality of the programmes was much better than before the war. Good movies were screened almost every night, and viewers got their fill of favourite series like Ironside, Hawaii 5-0, Mannix and The Saint. Paradoxically, the violence and tension of fiction acted like a tranquiliser, taking peoples' minds off the violence and tension of the war.

The eight-thirty p.m. newsreel became a ritual, and new oracles arose. General Chaim Herzog commented on the military situation logically and intelligently, and the masses placed great faith on his pronouncements. As long as he appeared so calm, with all he knew, why should they worry?

His colleague, youthful looking Prof. Shamir, dealt with political matters, reviewing the Egyptian and Syrian press reports, and those of other Arab States, and expressing his opinion on their reactions, why they were doing what they were doing, what they hoped to gain out of it, and in particular what influence the Russians had on the entire conflict.

Tonight the Ishbonehs and the Singers, along with a million or two other viewers were watching another Golda Meir 'special'. Although she looked, and almost certainly felt frail and tired, she nevertheless projected an unshakable confidence in the outcome of the war, which gave a tremendous lift to sagging spirits.

'I am happy to tell you,' she said in her nasal, American-accented Hebrew, 'that the Golan Heights are back in our hands, the settlers are going back to their settlements, the enemy has been pushed back beyond the '67 cease-fire lines, and we will make them withdraw even further . . . In the South too, the situation is changing for the good. The war is not yet over, but I have no doubt that it will end with victory.'

Asked about the 'price', she suddenly appeared very close to despair, 'Every son who falls . . . That is a terrible price . . . For victory one must pay.'

She repeated the customary wish for a 'happy holiday' on Sukkot, pointing out that in the midst of battle the Jewish people had the capacity to celebrate a festival.

'Let us pray,' she concluded, 'that this may be the last war not only for ourselves, but for our neighbours and their children and their children's children.'

'From her lips to God's ears,' murmured Chaim fervently.

Thursday, 11th October

Because of the holiday Meir slept late, waking only when Shoshana brought him a cup of coffee. He switched on the eight o'clock news listening carefully for reports of tank or armoured infantry actions and was relieved that there were none. On both fronts there was a lull, although in Sinai the announcer referred to a war of attrition against the Egyptians – constant artillery bombardment, air force harassment and sniping at enemy concentrations. The navy had bombarded the Syrian coast, setting fire to fuel installations and tank farms at Latakia, Banias and Tartus, and sunk two more missile boats.

Meir was in a good frame of mind, for the moment it was reasonable to believe that the boys were safe.

'I'm feeling fine,' he told Shoshana, 'I think I'll take a walk down to the Kupat Cholim office to give blood. They said they'd be open today specially, and at least this is one thing I can do. Chaim might come with me.'

'What about me? Do you think they'll take my blood?'

'Why not? There's no law that says women can't give. I think it's a very good idea. Come along!'

When Shula heard that Shoshana was going she and Eitan also decided to go along. The town was quiet, although quite a few cars passed, the bright blue paint on their headlights being one of the few visible signs that this Sukkot holiday was different from others.

'They fined a driver two hundred lirot yesterday for not blacking out his lights,' commented Chaim.

Eitan was full of excitement about the fabulous concert he had attended the afternoon before at the Mann Auditorium, with Zubin Mehta conducting the Israel Philharmonic Orchestra and Daniel Barenboim playing the Beethoven Piano Concerto. Admission was free and Eitan had gone an hour early and been lucky just to get a seat. Hundreds were allowed to stand, but hundreds more were

95

unable to get in. He said the atmosphere was incredible, charged like electricity, the audience appreciating to the full such world famous artistes dropping all their commitments to rush to Israel and identify with it in its time of trouble.

Meir marvelled at people who could set aside their problems to go to a symphony concert at a time like this, but Chaim approved whole-heartedly.

'There's too much gloom around – we need to relax and go on living – if we don't bend a little, we're liable to break.'

At the Kupat Cholim they discovered that they were not the only ones who had thought of this way to observe the holiday. At least forty people were ahead of them, but they seemed to be moving reasonably, without the usual noise and pushing for position that made standing in an Israeli queue so unpleasant.

'It's a good job they're taking blood here, and not at the Egged bus station,' joked Meir.

A nurse came down the line and took their particulars. She asked whether they were all in good health, or whether they had had hepatitis or malaria. None of them had problems and they soon found themselves at the head of the line. Meir had a chronic fear of injections, but he controlled himself as he lay down on the narrow white cot, and fortunately the nurse found a good vein with the first jab.

The actual taking of the blood took less than ten minutes, and afterwards they sat down and relaxed, while some women served them with tea and home-made cakes. Shoshana asked if they needed extra volunteers to assist, but was told politely that they had turned down scores of willing helpers.

They left the office with the proud feeling of having given something of themselves.

* * *

For all his apparent impetuousness Bennie was a well-trained soldier. Capable of rushing into action in a split-second, he also had infinite patience. The whole of the previous day he and his men had sat on top of the ridge with their binoculars trained on the canal and the sand in front of them, and radioed back reports to Riffidim on everything that might be of importance.

At one stage they had acted as spotters to Battalion 31, in an artillery barrage when some Egyptian tanks attempted to move forward and dig themselves into new positions. Several of the tanks were hit, and the attempt was abandoned.

At midday they saw a strike by two Phantoms against what they presumed to be Sam 6 missile bases. The Phantoms came in very high, dived down almost vertically on their targets, and then swept away again in a sharp evasive 'S' pattern. They saw the tell-tale puffs of white smoke which were the special characteristic of the Sam 6 as it was fired, and counted at least eight missiles which exploded harmlessly in the air. The attack was over in a matter of seconds, and the Phantoms didn't even attempt to come back for a second run.

During the night Bennie organised shifts, and they continued with their observations, using special night binoculars which pierced the darkness with unbelievable clarity. Gadi and Micha shared a shift, and reported two helicopters flying across the marshes from Kantara in the direction of Baluza. They were identified as Israeli. It was bitterly cold up on the height and they were not sorry when the shift ended and they were able to climb down and snuggle next to the side of the Zelda, protected from the desert wind.

With the first light of dawn Bennie received special orders from Headquarters:

'Nachash to Meron, do you hear me? Over.'

'Meron to Nachash, we hear you, over.'

'Nachash to Meron. Proceed urgently to K42:20 – repeat, K42:20, two enemy pilots stranded inside our minefield. Stay concealed as long as possible – we have anti-aircraft guns covering the site to block any rescue attempts. Eventually your job will be to move in and take the pilots prisoners. The mines are type B2 only. Over.'

Bennie answered that they were leaving immediately. He detailed two of the men to remain on the ridge to continue their observations, and the rest climbed into the vehicles and set off. Battalion 31 had also picked up the message and cautioned them to be on the lookout for spotters. Accurate Egyptian artillery fire had been harassing them for the last twenty-four hours and it was clear that the Egyptian gunners were receiving correcting information from somewhere in the vicinity.

The jeep moved ahead, picking its way along the hard ground at the foot of the sand dunes. The Zelda trailed about fifty metres behind. Bennie was silent, concentrating on the terrain ahead of them. Gadi was a little awed and pleased that the awful fear he had felt going into his first tank battle was gone. In its place he felt a pleasant tension and excitement, and he was just beginning to congratulate himself that he was turning into a hero, when he was jolted out of his dreams by a sharp command from Bennie. 'Get the jeep to the right behind that dune as quickly as possible – hurry up, damn it!'

Instinctively Gadi jerked the wheel around and pressed down on the accelerator. Micha followed in their tracks sliding the Zelda in behind the dune about twenty-five metres past them. Bennie checked with Battalion 31 to make sure that no Israeli scouts were in the neighbourhood and explained that he had caught a momentary glint of reflected sunlight from a high dune about two hundred metres away. It could have been binoculars or just a bright stone, but he wasn't prepared to take a chance.

He arranged with Boaz and Dror, that they should make a detour on foot and come up around the back of the high dune, using the smaller dunes to remain concealed as long as possible. He and Rafi, a young Lieutenant, would advance openly, drawing the attention of any forces sitting there. The rest of the men would spread out, covering as wide an angle as possible with their machine guns trained on the top of the dune. If they saw any movement whatsoever they must open fire so that anybody on top would have to stay under cover and not be able to fire at the men climbing towards them. 'Just watch it when we get near the top though,' cautioned Bennie. 'I don't feel like dodging their bullets and yours.'

Boaz and Dror were already out of sight. Bennie gave them another five minutes and then he and Rafi set off. As they reached the foot of the dune a small spurt of sand rose on the ground near them, and the sharp bark of a rifle rang out. Immediately Gadi and the others opened up with continuous bursts of fire. Small fountains of sand shot up all over the top edge of the dune. It would need a brave man to stick his head up in the middle of that, thought Gadi.

Bennie and Rafi were moving very quickly not even bothering to crouch down. They had no shelter anyway. They reached a point about thirty metres from the top, and the men below were forced to stop firing. Gadi saw Bennie's arm jerk up in a wide circle and a few seconds later a burst of orange flame shot up from the top of the dune. Another followed a few seconds later as Rafi also threw a hand grenade. Like small dolls Gadi watched them making a wild dash for the top. They heard bursts of firing from Uzzies, but couldn't make out what was happening. A few minutes later four figures were standing there signalling them to come up.

When they reached the top they found one Egyptian lying dead in his foxhole, his body mangled and torn from a direct blast of one of the hand grenades. Another body lay about twenty metres down the slope on the other side. In trying to escape from Bennie and Rafi, he had run straight into the Uzzies of Boaz and Dror.

The equipment on top of the hill was quite extensive for only two men; a heavy radio set, now completely smashed, Kalatchnikov rifles, binoculars, water flasks and large packages of rations.

'They could have stayed here for a week,' Bennie said. 'Battalion 31 will be pleased, these must be the spotters who were giving them trouble. Let's get out of here.'

While he was talking he searched the body in the foxhole, and found what he was looking for – the code-map, stained red with blood. Dror and one of the other men dragged the body of the second Egyptian up the hill and dropped it unceremoniously in with the first body. They kicked a layer of sand into the foxhole and stuck a broken Kalatchnikov rifle into the sand as a makeshift tombstone. 'Come on,' said Bennie impatiently, 'that's more than they would do for us. We've still got a lot of work to do.'

They reached the vehicles and Bennie reported back to Battalion 31. He was informed that a helicopter had already tried to rescue the pilots but had been hit and managed to fly away again. Because they were so close to the enemy lines Bennie stopped frequently to send men climbing up on to high ground to check what might be waiting for them a little way ahead. Nearing the minefield they concealed the vehicles and left two men to guard them. Gadi was elated not to be left out of the action this time.

They moved forward across the uneven ground, tense and ready for anything. At a signal from Bennie they threw themselves flat on the ground. A loud chopping noise was heard, and two Egyptian helicopters came flying low over the minefield. Gadi saw the two pilots, one standing up, and the other lifting his arm, pathetically trying to raise himself up so that he could be seen. Immediately the whole area became alive; Israeli anti-aircraft guns fired rapid bursts like giant machine guns, and simultaneously a tremendous barrage of artillery fire came from the Egyptian lines aimed at the Israeli guns, trying to knock them out or to harass their aim and prevent them from hitting the helicopters. Within seconds, however, the one helicopter burst into flames, the pilot tried to lift it up but it crashed into the ground setting off some of the mines, and a huge explosion shattered their eardrums. The other helicopter pilot, understandably losing his nerve, flew back towards the Egyptian lines.

The guns stopped firing and the area became quiet, except for the two pilots calling to see if the other was all right; and the hissing and burning of parts of the helicopter, which had completely disintegrated, its remains scattered all over the ground.

Instructions were received from Headquarters to remain concealed, in the hope that the Egyptians might make another rescue attempt. The pilots were obviously terrified to move, and the one who had been unable to stand was groaning with pain. At three o'clock Bennie radioed for fresh instructions pointing out that there were not too many hours of light left if they were to try to cross the minefield. He was given the green light, and he and Ellie, a Lieutenant in the engineering corps, with a lot of experience in mines, prepared to move forward together. Bennie minimised the danger explaining that B2 mines meant anti-tank not anti-personnel, so that even if they walked right on top of one, their weight was unlikely to set it off. He told the others to stay concealed and cover their advance.

'But won't the Egyptians shoot at you?' asked Gadi, concerned.

'No. I doubt it. They know that we won't let them rescue

the pilots, so this is the only chance of saving their lives. If they make life too difficult for us, we'll come back and let the pilots sweat it out another day or so.'

The two men moved forward cautiously for about a hundred metres until they came to the fence, which marked the edge of the minefield. The wounded pilot was about thirty metres away and the other pilot another thirty metres further in.

'Keep your hands up,' shouted Bennie in a loud voice.

Both the Arabs turned towards them, and Bennie repeated his order, 'Irfa Eidat,' which was about all the Arabic that he knew. They did as they were told, but the wounded pilot was unable to support himself and fell back on the ground, his hands still in the air. 'Keep your hands up and don't move,' Bennie warned again.

Ellie had already crawled through the fence, and was expertly probing the ground in front of him, using a long sharp knife. There was a dull click as the blade struck the first mine. Ellie carefully scooped some of the sand away without touching it, leaving part of the mine exposed. In spite of the assertion that one could stand on an anti-tank mine without danger, he remembered being told about an instructor who had demonstrated this theory to his class one day ... and they were still looking for their instructor.

He moved forward probing the ground all the way until he located the next mine exactly a metre further on, and repeated the operation. After he had exposed another three, he already recognised the standard pattern in which the field was laid, and could probably have made his way safely through without much trouble, but knowing that mines sometimes shift slightly in the loose soil, he preferred to work slowly and methodically. As he moved he let out a roll of white tape behind him. Bennie followed a safe fifteen metres further back.

From time to time Bennie placed a small heap of sand on the white tape to keep it in place, but he never took his eyes off the two pilots, and several times repeated his warning to keep their hands up and not to move. The wounded pilot was in a state of terror, and in between groaning at his pain begged them for assurances that they wouldn't kill him.

It took a full forty minutes to reach him, and Ellie was soaked with sweat from the strain. Bennie searched the first pilot, but found nothing. His leg was doubled under him in a grotesque position, obviously broken. His eyes were wide with fear and he shivered uncontrollably. Bennie tried to speak reassuringly to him, but the words made no impression. Eventually he took out a packet of cigarettes, lit one and gave it to Ellie, and then lit another one and passed it to the Egyptian. The gesture calmed the man down, and he sat there trying to control himself.

Ellie started moving forward again. The second pilot appeared to be unhurt, and as they got closer Bennie called to him to turn his back to them and continue to keep his hands up.

'How do I know you won't shoot me?' asked the pilot in good English.

'If we'd wanted to shoot you it would have been much easier without going to all this trouble,' replied Bennie logically, 'you'll be in no danger as long as you don't try to cause us any trouble.'

When they reached him Bennie searched for weapons, again finding none, and ordered him to walk back slowly ahead of them following the white tape, and to help pick the wounded pilot up. Ellie assisted him, but a shriek of agony burst from the wounded pilot as his leg moved. His face was white with pain, and he hung like a sack while he was carried back.

Safely under cover again the wounded pilot was given a dose of pain-killing tablets, which he swallowed with some trepidation. They carried him in relays, two at a time, replacing each other every hundred metres, and in a short while reached the vehicles and placed him on the floor of the Zelda. The other pilot, who Bennie had established was a Major Ibrahim, climbed into the back of the jeep; a blindfold was placed around his eyes, and his wrists tied behind his back.

They travelled away from the Egyptian lines and Bennie decided to go at full speed without sending men ahead as scouts. He was anxious to reach their previous observation post, pick up the two men who had been left there, and get moving before it was too dark. Headquarters at Riffidim had instructed Bennie to come straight back, bringing the prisoners and the code map that he had taken from the spotters. By the time they reached Tasa it was pitch dark

102

and Bennie took the blindfold off the major's eyes and offered him a cigarette.

He had made no attempt at communication until then, but now he turned to him and said, 'Well, we didn't shoot you, did we? Are you still scared we might?'

'No. I am not afraid. In the air force we accept the fact that every man has his account with Allah. If it is decreed that he has to die, he will die, and nothing will help him. It seems that Allah is still keeping my account open.'

'You're right,' said Bennie. He had wanted to say something nice like, 'up to a hundred and twenty', but held himself back. How was it that he hated the enemy so intensely in the abstract, but the moment it turned into a living, human person, he found himself confused and unable to continue hating?

* * *

Amos and Uri, and the others who shared their bunker, were sitting wrapped up in their newly-acquired Russian great-coats, watching the shadows darken across the hills. It had been a frustrating day all round.

It began with the tension of Hussein's announcement that Jordan was calling up its reserves and mobilising the country's resources for 'the war effort'.

Speculation as to whether or not Jordan was being pulled into the war heightened with an announcement from Amman that its anti-aircraft guns had gone into action against Israeli planes at seven o'clock that morning, when they penetrated Jordan's airspace. The announcement claimed that the planes had been driven off westwards to Israel.

The men were on edge because they felt out of the action. They had been told that the big push would start early that morning, and had mentally prepared themselves for a rough day. The push did start, and the Heights reverberated with the rumble of artillery, but not on their sector of the front. The action centred largely below Kuneitra where the Hush-niya pocket was finally cleared out. The crack Assad armoured division, specially named after the Syrian President, was trapped by the co-ordinated Israeli tank, artillery and air assaults; and what was left of it retreated, leaving behind vast quantities of armour, guns, vehicles and other war machines, damaged and undamaged.

Many prisoners were brought in, some giving themselves up, asking for food and water. In spite of the tremendous defeat, however, the Syrian retreat was orderly, and showed no signs of turning into a complete rout like in 1967.

The Israeli force concentrated on a spearhead which pierced through the Syrian defences and during the day advanced ten kilometres north-east along the Kuneitra–Damascus highway. Hundreds of tanks locked together, the Syrians losing an estimated eight hundred, destroyed or captured intact.

Amos's men had sat the day out next to their vehicles, waiting to be told to move forward, but the order never came. The battle was essentially one of armour and artillery, aided by massive air support, and the mopping up by infantry was held over for the time being. The men sitting on the sidelines could not, however, complain about a lack of excitement. From early in the day Phantoms and Sky-hawks roared across the Heights, mostly at ground level, rising up just before they reached their targets, swooping in on them, and shooting out in sharp 'U' or 'S' turns to avoid exposure to whatever missile batteries were left. The Syrian air force came bravely out trying to blunt the force of their attack and eleven of their planes were shot down in brief murderous dogfights, two of them almost over the heads of Amos and his men.

As darkness descended the action died down, and only an occasional shell exploding, or short burst of machine gun fire, disturbed the silence.

At eight-thirty they gathered around a transistor set to hear a confident Moshe Dayan tell the nation what they already knew. 'The Syrians are practically broken,' he said. 'They are now learning a lesson – that the road from Damascus to Tel Aviv also leads from Tel Aviv to Damascus.'

'That's all very well,' complained one of the younger soldiers, 'but when are we going to get some action? I've spent three years being toughened-up for a fight, and now when it comes, I spend all my time riding up and down on a half-track, or sitting here on my backside.'

'That's right,' agreed Mokkie, who had been studying at Harvard University when the war broke out, and rushed back to join his unit; 'when I think of how I battled to get a seat on a plane to get here. Every second was important. I thought the war would be over before I arrived, and now we're not even being used – there's just no action!'

Avner, an unshaven, sloppy-looking reservist, with the rank of sergeant, told them not to be so impatient, they'd have lots of time to prove themselves heroes. As far as he was concerned, he had no objection to sitting the war out in the comfort of these bunkers.

'I've got a wife and two children at home waiting for me,' he said. 'They're relying on the law of averages that I'll come back like I did in the last two wars. I don't know how long a guy's luck can hold out, but every day I sit here gives me that much more chance. The way I see it, when I'm involved I do my best – when I'm not, that's my good luck.'

The others respected Avner; he was battle trained, solid and reliable in everything that he was called upon to do. They understood the logic of what he was saying, but emotionally they were keyed up and ready to go. Some deep basic urge was nagging at them and would give them no rest until they found themselves in the midst of battle. Uri felt the tug as strongly as any of them, events were moving so well and so quickly, it could only be a matter of days now before the war would be over and he would be home with Aliza again.

The sudden separation, and the heartache and futility of the war had left their mark, and he longed to have her arms clasped lovingly around him, shutting out all the tension and ugliness of what he had been through.

Friday, 12th October

It was twelve o'clock midnight. Aliza was a third of the way through her shift. She had already seen all her 'boys', and before starting on her next round, she snatched a moment in the nurses' room to freshen up and make herself tidy. She wore virtually no make-up, either on duty or off, except a light touch of green eye shadow.

Aliza knew she ought to feel tired, like in the agony of the first few days when the wounded had started to come in, and there had been no word from Uri. From the moment he had spoken to her, however, the nightmare that had built up inside her faded away, and she felt she could go on indefinitely. She wondered how Zeev was and again it irritated her that she had not asked Uri about him. The phone call had been so unexpected and so quick that it was only when she put the receiver down that she realised he had not said anything about him. She knew that if anything was wrong Uri would have told her, but now she was embarrassed to phone Vered and tell her about the phone call, because her first question would be about Zeev, and how could she explain that they had not even mentioned him? Putting the thought out of her mind she hurried back to the wards.

Aliza was born to be a nurse. Uri had once teased her that if there hadn't been such a profession it would have had to be invented specially for her. She started her second round with one of the 'burns rooms'. There were four patients, all serious cases still on the danger list. She had been shocked when the first casualties had been brought in, some with burns over more than two-thirds of their body-surface. In spite of their having received sedatives, they were unable to restrain their groans of pain, and her mind had conjured up horrible pictures of them burning like torches inside their tanks. She learned that the majority of these cases were caused by the RPG rocket, a new Soviet anti-tank missile constructed literally to burn its way through the armour plating of a tank and create havoc inside it, and she cursed the evil talent of men to find ever more horrible ways of inflicting injury on their fellow men.

Apart from the terrible pain they suffered, the visual shock of looking at them had been almost unbearable, raw pink flesh where skin had once been, pitted with huge blisters, hands swollen and deformed from the angry inflammation of the burn, eyebrows and hair burnt away. Their faces were ravaged like a parody of Frankenstein, a mass of red and pink amorphous tissue, with no distinguishing features except the red blistered lips, and the narrow crevices at the back of which the eyes peeped through.

It had taken all her training and special character not to cry out with horror, but she managed, and she was soon coping with the burden of looking after them, and the special treatments devised to help them heal.

The serious cases, and particularly those with facial burns, had to be fed intravenously. They couldn't open their mouths, and in any event they needed vast quantities of fluid and they were too weak to swallow enough themselves, or to retain it. At each bed an infusion set maintained a constant flow of special solution to keep the patient alive. They lay on special mattresses with inflatable and collapsible areas which were used to make frequent changes of the points of contact between the mattress and the patient's body, to avoid pressure sores.

As Aliza moved from bed to bed, all the men turned to her. At first many of them were unable to speak, and simply followed with their eyes, as she inspected their charts, checked temperatures, pulses, blood pressures, watched for haemorrhage, changed dressings, and where necessary, gave injections against pain. She had a word of encouragement and a smile for each one of them. Never seeming to hurry, she knew their names, she could flirt with them, tease them about their girlfriends, scold them if they didn't work at their exercises. Nothing was too difficult or too much trouble. There were several other rooms with less serious burns cases, and Aliza spent time in all of them.

Her next section was the amputations ward. This was where she originally expected to have the most heartaches, but from the time that the first casualties arrived, she had received help from an unexpected source. Veteran amputees from the Six Day War and other wars had organised themselves to be on hand to greet the new amputees as they were admitted, to show them immediately that their world had not come to an end, and that a reasonably full life was still possible. They provided irrefutable proof that the handicaps and difficulties that lay ahead of them could be overcome.

As a result of their constant presence morale in this ward was amazingly high. Games and activities were improvised in which the patients could participate, even while confined to bed. The volunteers were on call twenty-four hours a day. They laughed with the patients, and talked seriously to those who needed it, counselling them about the stages that lay ahead, the moods of undue depression or unreal optimism, and how to recognise and deal with them. It was all completely natural, and unbelievably brave and heartwarming.

In addition to her own wards, Aliza had also volunteered to help with a young boy who had been taken out of one of the helicopters when she was in charge of the admissions. He had been badly wounded and was operated on immediately. Aliza had been sure that he would die, and at one stage he was in fact clinically dead, but something deep down inside had refused to give up, and the small spark of life which survived the operating theatre still continued to flicker away, refusing to die down.

'Yankele', they called him, because he had no dog-tag when he was brought in, and this was the name used by the medic who had accompanied him.

Aliza never consciously had favourites, but sometimes, she had a feeling that she was specially needed, that the delicate balance between getting well or slipping back required just that much little extra faith or encouragement or love to tip the scales. Yankele was one of these cases. At the end of her second round she came to his room. He was the only patient, lying waxen-faced, eyes closed and his breathing uneven. He was talking, mumbling unrelated and mostly unintelligible words, trying in vain to express the agonies that had seared themselves into his brain. He twisted and turned uneasily, and a special nurse was on duty to make sure that he didn't tug loose from the infusion set that continued to feed a saline solution into his veins. Aliza told the nurse to take a break, and sat down next to him, holding his hand. It was badly bruised, the fingers were long and delicate like those of an artist, certainly not somebody used to doing physical work with his hands.

'Yankele,' she whispered softly to him, 'Yankele, fight a little, try to wake up,' and a little later, 'come on Yankele, the worst is over, as soon as you open your eyes things will start to get better.' Aliza wasn't sure if there was any response. For a moment she thought that she felt a slight pressure on her hand, but it may have been just an involuntary reaction. And yet he seemed quieter, and his breathing was more even. She sat with him for a full twenty minutes until the special nurse came back; then, reluctantly, she left to start her final rounds.

When Aliza came off duty at eight o'clock there was a message for her to call home. Her mother answered the phone and told her that a Mr Crawford had called, and said that he had a letter from Uri which she could pick up at the information desk at Beit Sokolov, the Journalists' Association Building in Kaplan Street, Tel Aviv. She decided to go straight to town rather than waste time going home first.

Aliza never had trouble hitching. She was still in her nurse's uniform, and the first car leaving the hospital grounds stopped for her. She recognised the Gynaecologist who had examined her mother.

'Shalom,' she said, 'are you going to Tel Aviv?'

'Yes. Hop in. Where exactly do you want to go?'

Aliza told him, and he said that he was passing close by and would drop her there.

'How'd your mother take her visit?'

'Better than I expected. I think she almost took a fancy to you.'

He laughed. 'Good. I haven't got the tests back yet, but I think the worst it can be is a cyst.'

'Thanks. I hope so.'

'And you Aliza?'

'I'll be all right,' she said, embarrassed.

A few weeks before the war started, she had been to see him, because she had missed her period. 'It's too soon to know anything yet,' he had told her . . . It seemed like ten years ago.

At the first crowded bus-stop they picked up more passengers who, seeing her uniform, bombarded her with anxious and concerned questions about the wounded. Aliza answered them in as much detail as possible, recognising the strange feeling that each wounded soldier was a part of them, a member of the wider group, that for all its diversity and contradictions constituted one large family.

At Beit Sokolov she entered the lobby, making her way past the striking paintings on the wall, to the information desk. The attendant was an albino, and she felt uneasy as he stared at her fixedly through his pale blue eyes, while she enquired whether a Mr Crawford had left an envelope for her. The attendant didn't know any Mr Crawford, and after a few more questions, it became clear that there was a different lobby for the foreign correspondents.

She walked through a courtyard and entered a large room containing three desks with typewriters, all of them in use. The switchboard operator had the envelope and handed it to her. She put the letter for Uri's parents into her purse, and sat down in an easy chair, a little puzzled by the admonition on the envelope to read her letter when she was alone.

'Aliza, my love,

First of all I want to assure you that I am completely well and there is absolutely no cause for you to worry about me, but this is not the reason why I have written to you.

Aliza, because I love you so much, and because you are such a very special kind of person, I am imposing a burden on you which I could not ask of anybody else.

There are no words to make the shock easier, so please forgive me for telling you bad news in plain simple language. Zeev is dead. He was hit by a bullet and died instantly, literally in my arms. The bullet that hit him could have hit me just as easily, we were less than a metre apart from each other. It was all over in a split second, so at least he suffered no pain in dying.

My heart is aching for you as I write this, because I know how you will feel. And my heart is aching for Vered as well. I don't know if there are any degrees of pain for a person who receives such news, and yet I believe that if you are the one who tells her, somehow you will find a way to make it more bearable.

Aliza, Aliza my only love, there is so much I need to say to you that will have to wait until we are together again, but

110

*please do not worry. I am well and healthy and my love for
you gives me a strength which can endure anything. I will
write to you again, in much more detail. There are other
good, positive sides to the experiences that I have been
through, but they just seem out of place in this letter. Forgive me again for the burden that I have placed on you.*

> *All my love,*
> *Uri.'*

Less than an hour later Aliza pressed the buzzer, and
Vered opened the door.

'Shalom, Aliza! What a lovely surprise,' she said, with a
warm smile which suddenly faded as she saw the set colour-
less face that looked at her.

'Aliza. My God what's wrong, come inside.'

She pulled her in and Aliza tried to get the words out.

'Vered I have bad news!'

'Did something happen to Uri?'

'No Vered. To Zeev!'

*   *   *

Bennie came back from General Bardan's bunker with news
that a commando group had just returned safely after an
extensive raid behind the Egyptian lines on the west bank of
the Canal. The commandos had crossed at night by helicopter, with a new type of light-weight but highly-effective
artillery, and had shelled supply bases near Fayid airport,
causing heavy damage and taking the enemy completely by
surprise. The raid proceeded like clockwork, although a
heavy mist came up unexpectedly, and there was a near
disaster when the pick-up helicopters couldn't find them.
Eventually they succeeded, however, and the raiding party
returned without casualties.

General Bardan was confirmed in his opinion that if Israel
could only get across the Canal, the Egyptian defence was
not organised or flexible enough to offer strong resistance.
The General was also pleased with their efforts, and task
force 'Meron' was given an unofficial holiday. Another group
had been sent out to cover their area, and they could relax
for the rest of the day and take things easy. Before they did

this, however, Bennie saw to it that they replenished their supplies for the Jeep and the Zelda, so that if necessary they could move out at a moment's notice.

Gadi went to the mobile phones to see if he could phone home, but there was a queue of at least fifty soldiers ahead of him, and he wasn't prepared to wait that long. He went to the camp post office and was overjoyed to find a parcel addressed to him in his mother's spidery handwriting.

Bennie was there, disappointed because he had received no post. Gadi opened the parcel, and they shared the chocolate cake inside, breaking it off in big pieces with their hands. Since the beginning of the war many soldiers had experienced a tremendous craving for sweet things. The army psychologists took official note of this phenomena attributing it to a desire to compensate for being away from home and the affection of their loved ones. Their stomachs loaded, the two soldiers sat down to write postcards home.

Bennie wrote to Ruth that he was having a good holiday and wished she was here. 'Seriously, I miss you more than you will ever know. I have only one thought in my mind, and that's to come back to you, and work out a future for us, together.' Even as he put the card in the box, he wondered how he would ever work his way out of the mess. He pulled out another postcard and began writing to Baracha and the children.

Gadi's task was simpler. He wrote an ecstatic thankyou to his mother for the chocolate cake and the rest of the parcel, and generally assured them that all was well. He also asked for Uri's address. He had never felt the urge to write to him before, even when they had been separated for months at a time. But now it was different, the family bond had become important, and very precious.

He also wrote to Rina telling her that he still loved her, although he hadn't received any letters. He explained that his unit had moved around, and he hoped the letters would eventually catch up with him, otherwise he'd just have to talk to his commanding officer and come in again to collect them personally.

At lunch time most of the group were sitting talking and drinking cold drinks at the soldiers' canteen, when a huge truck pulled up, loaded with loudspeakers and amplifiers, and word spread quickly that Yaffa Yarkoni and some other

Israeli artistes were going to do a show in the air-raid shelter at two o'clock. Over a hundred soldiers crammed themselves in, and soon the huge room shook to the beat of the electric guitars and drums, as the performance got under way with some rock music.

At the end of the first selection of numbers, the master of ceremonies, a well-known comedian, stepped out, introduced most of the performers, and told a few typical army jokes. He sang a song which started with the words 'Elazar, Superstar . . .' and proceeded to lampoon the Chief of Staff about what had happened to the bones of the enemy that he had promised to break? The audience shrieked its appreciation, and also applauded a funny story based on what had happened to Bar Lev's line. In all the tension, the Israeli enjoyment of mocking the dignity of the high-ups and being able to laugh at themselves was still very evident.

Suddenly the master of ceremonies announced that the next number would be a surprise. The lights went out, the group struck up the introduction to 'Bab el Wad', a favourite from the 1948 War of Independence, and a woman's voice rose warm and strong, filling the whole room with its vibrations. The young soldiers were familiar with the voice from records, the older ones remembered it with a deep nostalgia from previous wars, and a huge round of applause greeted Yaffa Yarkoni.

Song followed song, the audience joining in all the choruses, and clapping their hands in time to the music. For a wonderful hour, Yaffa and the other performers and the audience shut out the war, losing themselves completely in the joy of singing along with their friends. At the end of the show they gave her the characteristic Israeli slow hand-clap, which was even more deafening in the confines of the shelter; and, reluctantly, the audience and the performers parted from each other. Yaffa and her crew still had two more shows on their schedule for that evening.

*　　*　　*

Uri had not slept well. He had woken several times, trying to get his bearings in the dank moist atmosphere of the bunker. Finally, it seemed that he had just dozed off, when he felt somebody shaking him, and with an effort opened his eyes and saw that it was Amos. It was cold, and completely dark outside.

'Come on Uri, we've got lots to do.'

A few minutes later, with a cup of steaming coffee in one hand, and an open tin of sardines on the ground in front of him, he listened to Amos brief them on their orders for the day.

'We've got a tough day ahead of us,' he began. 'Yesterday our tanks advanced along the road to Mazrat Beit Jinn, but they encountered very fierce resistance from two zig-zag rows of pill-box type bunkers which straddle the road, and they were forced to detour around them. In effect they've cut off any retreat from the bunkers, but we've got the job of going in and cleaning them up.'

He paused for a moment, then continued: 'There are twelve bunkers that we know of, six on each side, connected by trenches and positioned in such a way that each one is defended by a cross-fire from about three others. The only effective way of destroying them is to get up close enough to drop a grenade through the aperture.'

'Anybody here got very long arms?' interjected one of the soldiers, and a few of the men laughed nervously.

'Let's save the jokes for afterwards,' Amos reprimanded him.

At the same moment artillery opened fire from the Israeli side. Amos checked his watch. 'We start our attack in forty-five minutes,' he said. 'I and five of my crew will take the right-hand side of the road, coming in from the rear against Bunker No. 1. Uri will take five of his men against No. 2 Bunker on the opposite side.'

Turning to Avner he gave instructions for four pairs of machine-gunners to cover bunkers 1 to 4, firing continuously to keep them pinned down while the attackers were moving in. A fifth pair of machine-gunners was to move around the back to cover any trouble which might develop from the further bunkers.

'The code name for this operation is Dov. My unit is Dov 1; Uri's, Dov 2; Avner, 3; and the extra machine-gunners Dov 4. That's all from my side. Are there any questions?'

None of the men had anything to say. It was clear that the action was going to be difficult and extremely dangerous.

114

Most of them had already seen some action but the symptoms were still there, the sweat under the arms, the dry mouth, the wobbly knees, the urge to urinate. They recognised them more naturally now, and were basically not ashamed, but nevertheless did their best to conceal them.

Amos got into the first half-track, Avner the second, and Uri took the rear position. He stood there with the heavy 0.5 machine gun next to him. There were fourteen men in each vehicle. A few minutes later Amos waved his hand, and the small convoy moved off down the road.

On their left the Hermon range of mountains towered a thousand metres above them. On their right the terrain sloped steadily downwards, but the terrain was uneven, with ridges on both sides of the road along which the Syrians were waiting for them.

About seven hundred metres from the first bunker, they left the half-tracks and started advancing on foot. Avner and his four pairs of machine-gunners, moved forward on both sides of the road, parallel to it. The fifth pair made a huge detour to the side to come around the first four bunkers. They were all using MAGs, an extremely accurate light Belgian-type machine gun. Avner carried his radio in a pack on his back. Behind him the rest of the men followed, carrying Bazookas and ammunition and their Uzzies.

Amos's unit crossed the road moving to the right, from where they were going to come in diagonally from behind bunker No. 1. Uri and his five men moved to the left to come in from behind No. 2.

The covering artillery barrage from the Israeli side had stopped, but the Syrian answering fire, probably directed by spotters on Mount Hermon, was beginning to land uncomfortably close to them.

After getting into position, Amos checked that Uri's men were ready, and instructed Avner to let the machine-gunners open fire.

Uri's group moved forward slowly, hugging the ground, trying to remain concealed. They managed to get within about a hundred metres of No. 2 bunker when a burst of fire from the direction of No. 3 hit one of the men in the shoulder, and pinned them down to the ground.

Uri called to Avner asking him to send the medic and a replacement forward, and also to keep No. 3 under heavier fire. Avner brought up two men with a Bazooka to fire a phosphorous rocket at the bunker which was causing the trouble. It exploded well short but a huge wall of flame and black smoke shot into the air and temporarily blocked the view of those in the bunker, enabling Uri and his men to move to a more sheltered position.

Amos was having trouble. He reported that he was about a hundred and twenty metres from No. 1, but the stretch of ground in front of them was almost completely devoid of cover. He was also exposed to fire from No. 6 bunker, which seemed to be placed higher than the others, so that their angle of fire also covered the area that he had to cross. He checked with the forward pair of machine-gunners, but they had been spotted and were having troubles of their own under a barrage of fire from three other bunkers.

Uri studied the ground around No. 2 and felt sure that he could get to a low cluster of rocks about thirty metres from the aperture of the bunker without exposing himself. It was still too far to lob a grenade through it, however, and if he tried to dash that last thirty metres, he would be cut down within split seconds after leaving the shelter of the rocks. He contacted Amos and Avner explaining what he wanted, and Amos gave him the go ahead, wishing him luck.

Uri pressed his body flat on the ground, crawling further to the left, looking for a better angle to move up behind the rocks. Amos moved back a short distance and fitted a phosphorous rocket to his Bazooka, training it on Bunker No. 3. Avner brought up Bazooka teams and did the same with bunkers 1, 2 and 4, his machine gun teams continuing to fire at all four bunkers without pause.

One of Uri's men had taken over the radio contact and reported his progress as he inched his way forward. 'Dov 2 here, fifteen metres to go,' and then a few minutes later, 'he's nearly there' and finally, 'he's in position . . . get ready . . . now, three, two, one, fire!' All four Bazookas fired at the exact same instant, the shells bursting with a tremendous roar immediately below the apertures of the four bunkers. Apart from the shock of the noise, the flames and the smoke temporarily blanketed all the bunkers, making it impossible for them to see what was happening.

Uri darted out from behind the rocks and dashed forward covering the ground in not more than three seconds, although

116

to those watching, it seemed as though he was moving in slow motion. They saw him reach the aperture and bend down slightly as his right arm moved towards it. Then he dived to the ground on the left, slightly behind the bunker. A ball of orange flame shot out from the aperture as the explosion reverberated in the enclosed space, and more black smoke billowed across it. To the relief of the watchers they saw Uri crawl rapidly away, back to the shelter of the rocks.

With Bunker No. 2 out of action, No. 1 became much more vulnerable, and using the same technique the attacking force took Nos. 1 and 3, but they found no bodies in No. 3. Its occupants had already fled down the connecting trenches. A few minutes later a white handkerchief was stuck out of Bunker No. 5 and Amos ordered the firing to stop. Obviously scared, but encouraged by the sudden quiet, a group of three Syrians came out with their hands up.

Amos called out to them in Arabic to walk forward slowly. He remained under shelter, allowing them to move up to his position. They were searched and one of Amos's men questioned them in fluent Arabic. Their spokesman, a lieutenant, said that he was the commanding officer, and that they wished to surrender.

Avner dealt with the prisoners. Eight of them had been killed and fifteen wounded. Another thirty-seven were unhurt. He radioed back for the three half-tracks to move up along the road, and for a special truck to be sent from the base camp for the prisoners.

One of the men in Amos's unit had been killed, and three Israeli soldiers wounded. When the first half-track arrived, the dead soldier was covered by a tarpaulin and placed inside it. The medic had finished treating the wounded Israeli soldiers, and turned his attention to the more seriously injured of the prisoners.

While they waited for the truck to arrive the men gathered into small groups talking excitedly, swopping their experiences and laughing uproariously at each little comment or joke, relaxing from the strain and the tension they had just been through. Uri was in one of the groups, and Amos went specially over to shake his hand and speak to him.

'Uri, I'm proud of you. What you did today was exceptional.'

Uri smiled happily as the rest of the men shook his hand and joined in the congratulations. He felt a warm glow inside. He had often wondered if he had the guts to deliberately risk his life without being forced into it, and today he had proved it to himself as well as to the others. For a brief moment the thought flashed through his mind that he had settled at least part of the outstanding account for the death of Zeev.

A short while later the truck arrived, and the prisoners climbed inside. The vehicles turned around to go back to the base.

Mokkie, the student from Harvard, who had complained the previous evening about the lack of action, took his seat next to Avner. He had been crawling forward with Amos's group, when the man in front of him had suddenly fallen backwards without a sound. His eyes were open, frozen in an expression of utter surprise, and there was a black hole between them. Mokkie had vomited with shock and almost passed out, but Amos had shouted at him in fury and he had managed to pull himself together, and carry on mechanically for the rest of the fight. Now that it was all over, he was thinking about it again, and Avner could see that he was still shaken. He put his hand gently on his shoulder, 'Nu! Do you think you've had enough action for today?'

Mokkie was about to give an angry reply, but he realised that there was no malice intended, only a kind of sadness from an older man, who'd had a little more experience of life.

'Yes, more than enough,' he replied, trying to keep his voice steady, and not show how close he was to tears.

Saturday, 13th October

In Leviticus, the Third Book of Moses, God called upon him to speak to the children of Israel, telling them that for six days they should work, but on the seventh they should rest. If they observed His laws their enemies would fall by the sword – 'five shall chase a hundred, and a hundred shall put ten thousand to flight'; but if, however, they broke His laws, they would be slain and 'those that hate them shall reign over them.' And He reminded them that they were His servants whom He brought forth out of the land of Egypt.

Many Israelis are truly observant, and do not work, handle money or drive on the Sabbath. The majority, however, regard these passages as curious echoes of history, a part of their common cultural heritage, not to be taken too seriously in the context of modern living. Thus, on a normal Saturday the roads are filled with cars, the beaches are crowded, soccer stadiums are packed with wildly enthusiastic crowds. Those who breach the Sabbath do it conspicuously, the observant ones go to Shul, sit quietly at home, or in the very religious quarters where no traffic is allowed to defile the atmosphere, they may venture out for a short walk down the road.

On the second Saturday of the war, it appeared as if the children of Israel were doing their best to observe the Sabbath. Only an occasional car flashed by, and some of the local factories producing ammunition and other war equipment continued to work around the clock. On the whole, however, there was an unusual quiet and serenity.

Meir was woken a few minutes before eight by Shoshana, with a cup of coffee. He held the cup with his one hand, and with the other automatically turned on his transistor to listen to the news. Amman Radio announced that it had despatched some of its elite forces to the Syrian front 'pledged to fight until death in defence of the beloved land'. The Israeli thrust on the Golan Heights had broadened into

119

a twenty-one-kilometre front east of the old cease-fire lines, about ten kilometres deep into Syrian territory. The commentator specifically stated that the momentum of the breakthrough was slowed down by the tenacious fighting of the Syrian troops and the thick lines of fortifications prepared by them over the last six years to protect the approaches to Damascus. Unexpected resistance was also reported south-east of Kuneitra, where the Iraqis had moved in three armoured brigades, a total of about twelve thousand men and two hundred and fifty tanks. Syria had apparently transferred its own troops to dig in around Damascus, replacing them with Iraqi, Moroccan and Algerian troops.

An Israeli commando force had gone in by helicopter far behind the Syrian lines, blowing up an important bridge, and causing severe damage and losses to an Iraqi convoy which happened to be passing there on its way up to the front. The raiding force suffered no casualties.

On the Sinai front the Egyptians were still bringing reinforcements across and strengthening their positions, digging anti-tank gun emplacements and laying minefields.

At a press conference in Washington Henry Kissinger had criticised the Soviet appeal to other Arab states to join in the war, as well as the massive daily air lift to Syria and Egypt of hundreds of tons of arms and ammunition. He did not, however, think that the Soviet's actions constituted a sufficiently serious 'irresponsibility' to threaten détente with the west.

At the opening of the Public Committee for the Voluntary War Loan set up the previous week under former Chief of Staff Yitzhak Rabin to raise a thousand million pounds, it was announced that all workers would be called upon to pledge two weeks pay.

Finally, the exploits of a cook on one of the new Israeli missile boats received a special mention. When the ship went into action he doubled as a machine-gunner, and in one engagement shot down two Styx missiles. They approached the boat like two immense fireballs and were only a short distance away when they were hit and exploded. After the action the cook went back to his galley to serve the crew with coffee and cakes ...

Meir had arranged with Chaim the night before to go for

a walk after breakfast and they set off in the direction of the sea, down a long stretch of paved promenade, hidden by tall rhododendrons. They passed the deserted vocational high school, the local fire-station, and now on each side of them stretched huge citrus groves and green fields. A short distance away white clouds of seagulls wheeled in the sky, dipping down every now and again to ferret out a snack from the municipal garbage dump.

Chaim spoke of his longing to see Danny, and Meir asked whether, being a pilot, he ever gave them any special news.

'No. He always says everything is fine, nothing to worry about. I don't know if he's unable to say more over the phone from the base, or whether he's just being patronising and thinks I can't take any unpleasant news.'

'Don't you think that it's for Shula's sake?'

'Maybe. He knows that she can get a bit hysterical. I'll see when he comes home today . . . I hope. What about your boys?'

'We've heard nothing from Gadi since he came home. Uri phoned Aliza last Tuesday, and since then we haven't heard from him either. Shoshana is worried sick about it. I try not to discuss the subject, because I can't hide the fact that I am also worried, and this only makes her more upset. Yesterday she wouldn't even go to the supermarket, because everybody asks her whether she's heard from the boys, and she comes home a bundle of nerves.'

'The news is much better though, Meir, don't you agree?'

'Yes, but I can't stop thinking about the boys, and I feel old and terribly useless.'

'I don't know which is worse, my position or yours. I know that Danny's life is in danger many times during the day, but at least I get a phone call from him and I sleep well at night. For all you know, your boys may be miles away from the fighting; but if you haven't heard from them for a few days you start thinking all sorts of terrible things, which are almost certainly totally untrue.'

'It's all so unnecessary, Chaim. For my part they could give back everything if we could have peace tomorrow, and my boys would come back safe and sound.'

'So would a lot of us, but I don't have to tell you that it doesn't work that way. It all depends what you mean by "peace"! What kind of peace? Where they can take a deep breath and then start the next round? Where we have to continue to guard our borders constantly, and seventy per cent of our budget goes to defence needs? Where our boys have to serve in the army three years after they leave school, and then another forty days a year until they're old like us? What would you give up for that kind of peace, the Sinai? The Golan Heights? Jerusalem?'

'You're right, Chaim, it's no good simplifying matters by just thinking of my boys. Somehow the government has to find a way of ensuring a real peace, maybe starting off with something like we've got with Jordan, where they can cross the bridges freely in and out of Israel – or, preferably where we can do the same with them. A peace where we exchange embassies, where our ships sail through the Suez Canal, where we can co-operate with Syria on water projects, or with Jordan exploiting the minerals in the Dead Sea. If we all worked together we could do so much for them as well as ourselves.'

'Has it ever occurred to you how much we've already done for their development simply by being enemies?'

They had been ambling along, enjoying the warmth of the morning sun. Reaching the one-track railway line connecting Tel Aviv and Haifa, they turned back again. Nearing the apartments they passed groups of people coming home from Shul.

'Maybe that's where we should have been,' smiled Chaim.

'It would have done us no harm,' agreed Meir. But both of them knew that they preferred each other's company, walking quietly, and letting some of the tension out of their systems.

The people coming from Shul said 'Shalom' as they passed. It was a different greeting from the one they might have received a few weeks earlier, more serious and more personal, something in the eyes, a feeling of togetherness. They were all in the same boat, and each worried for the other. They felt a bond even with people who had never greeted them before.

Nearing the apartment Meir saw Shoshana on the balcony watching for him. When she saw him she disappeared into the apartment and came into sight again running towards him with something white in her hand. She was laughing and crying at the same time.

'What is it, Shosh?' he asked, alarmed.

'Two letters – one from each of them. They're both fine.' And then she burst into tears again, and Meir, with his arms around her, was crying too.

When Shosh calmed down a little she explained that Uri's letter had arrived via one of Aliza's young brothers with a note saying that it had been delivered to her by a visiting journalist, who had been at Uri's base. She apologised for not bringing it personally but she had to go on duty and didn't want to delay their receiving it. Gadi's was a routine postcard, delivered by young high school volunteers who had received special permission to distribute army mail on a Saturday, because it was realised how important this was to the morale of families on the home front. Gadi wrote that he was not doing anything exciting because of his arm, but that this was now healing nicely. Uri's letter was a little longer, it told how being away gave a special significance to family feelings and how much he was missing them.

'I am not going to tell you that it has all been easy here,' he wrote, 'I have seen things which I do not want to describe in a letter, but which I will tell you about when I come home. Meanwhile, don't worry about me. I am fine and well, and there is every reason to hope that the war will be over soon, and I will be back again. Look after Aliza for me until then. Love, Uri.'

Shoshana was worried. 'Some terrible things must have happened to him, if he doesn't want to write about them.'

'What do you expect, Shosh, he's in a war, it would be strange if he only saw nice things. But there's no point our worrying. He says that he is fine and well. What more can we ask for?'

* * *

Gadi woke up half-paralysed with fright. The loudest noise he had ever heard forced itself through his whole body as though it was being pierced physically by a thousand needles. Struggling to recover his bearings he threw his blankets off, wriggled out of his pup tent, and stood up. It was dark outside and there was complete pandemonium, with men running about everywhere not knowing what had happened or what to do. To add to the confusion the air-raid siren started to wail. He grabbed his helmet and rushed for the air-raid shelter.

Within seconds the rest of the crew from task force Meron had all arrived and were gathered around Bennie trying to piece together what had happened. As he started talking they heard another tremendous explosion, but this time further away. Bennie guessed that it was a Frog, a ten-metre-long ground-to-ground missile which must have been fired at them from the other side of the canal, and which carried a warhead of five hundred and fifty kilograms. The Egyptians had launched more than a dozen in the past week, and the one that had woken them must have landed almost on top of them. It was five o'clock when the all-clear sounded and they trooped out to find that Bennie's diagnosis was correct.

The first missile had landed about eighty metres from Gadi's tent, tearing a deep crater in the ground and shattering the windows of all the huts in the vicinity. By a miracle nobody was killed, although several soldiers had been wounded by steel fragments and shrapnel, which had peppered the area for a hundred metres in all directions. Gadi found a hole on both sides of his tent which he was sure had not been there the night before. The second missile had exploded harmlessly in the sand a short distance away from the camp.

It was too late to go to sleep again, and they lined up in the chill of the desert morning to get some hot coffee and bread. For a special treat the cook dished out a square of cheese to each of them. Gadi was not terribly food conscious, but at that moment he felt a tremendous craving for one of Shosh's special omelettes.

While they were eating a message arrived for Bennie to report to General Bardan immediately. A full hour elapsed before he returned and they gathered around him next to their jeep to find out what had happened.

'Boy! is he in a foul mood today,' Bennie started. 'General Mendler was killed yesterday. His jeep was hit by artillery fire.' The men had not heard this news before and were shocked. He was a top officer, extremely popular and with a high reputation for bravery. He was also a close personal friend of General Bardan's.

'And secondly, he's just given instructions for the Port

Tewfik stronghold to surrender.' This was the last outpost of the Bar Lev line to fall. A group of forty-two soldiers had held out for more than a week totally surrounded and against impossible odds. Five of them had been killed, and most of the rest were wounded. They still had food and water but their ammunition was running very low, and the condition of many of the wounded was so bad that without prompt treatment there would be a number of additional deaths. General Bardan hadn't had much option but he was extremely bitter about being forced to make the decision.

Bennie's summons had not been connected with either of these events. At about the same time as the Frogs had exploded, a group of eight Egyptian helicopters had swept in across the Great Bitter Lake towards Riffidim. Six were shot down, each containing thirty commandos, all of whom were killed on impact. The problem was what had happened to the other two helicopters.

The evidence suggested that two helicopters had flown back across the Canal, but it seemed likely that they had landed first and discharged their commandos. General Bardan's opinion was that their target was Jebel Cholot, an advance radar post built into a high mountain from which all air traffic in the Sinai was controlled. It was a tremendous thorn in the flesh of the Egyptians, and General Bardan was concerned that the commandos had been sent to attack it. His instructions to Bennie were to verify if the helicopters had discharged the commandos and if necessary to liquidate them.

Bennie's expression was grim. 'Up to now we've had it comparatively easy,' he said. 'This operation may be a lot tougher. First of all we're dealing with highly-trained men, the best in their entire army. Secondly, they are desperate, because they have virtually no chance of retreat. They probably have enough food and water for a couple of days only, unless they capture more from us.

'Our priority No. 1 is to find them. The trouble is that we're no longer sure of their objective. Assuming the General is right about the original objective of the eight helicopters, would they still try to stick to it when they are reduced to only sixty men? My feeling is that they may settle for something less ambitious, such as an ambush, but unfortunately we can't afford to take a chance. A damaged convoy is one thing, a damaged Jebel Cholot is much more serious. On this basis we have to start our search from Jebel Cholot and work our way west.'

He took out his map and unfolded it across the bonnet of the Jeep. A large 'X' west of Riffidim showed where the six helicopters were shot down. Bennie drew a line from the radar post to the 'X' and explained that they were going to advance about two kilometres south of that line on the assumption that the commandos would move away from the road to dig themselves in.

'In case my guess is wrong General Bardan has agreed to send a unit of tracker scouts, between this line and the road, and a Piper Cub will try to spot the commandos from the air.'

Task force Meron moved off with Bennie's Jeep ahead of the Zelda, stopping every now and again to send teams of two men climbing high ridges from where they could get a view of the surroundings. They saw the Piper Cub flying low over the desert, searching, but with no apparent result.

Just past noon they halted at the foot of a high white sand-dune which resembled the beginners' slope at a Swiss ski resort. While the others pulled out their battle rations and started to eat lunch, Bennie asked Gadi to climb the dune with him. It was hard going in the soft sand. At the top they crouched low down and crawled forward on their stomachs. Bennie had the binoculars and he scanned the horizon slowly and methodically.

The Piper Cub was flying about three kilometres away. They paid no special attention to it until they heard a sudden loud explosion and a pall of smoke burst near where the plane had been. At first they thought it had been hit, but an instant later saw it flying away almost at ground level in the direction of Riffidim.

'Well that's one way of locating them,' said Bennie, fixing his binoculars on a low circular hill, directly below the tell-tale puff of white cloud. 'It can only be a Strela.' He was referring to the Sam 7, a ground-to-air missile not as deadly as the Sam 6, but highly portable. It could be fired from the shoulder by a team of two men, effectively fixing on to the exhaust pipe or heat-source of a plane, and following it until it made contact and exploded. A tremendous amount of publicity had been generated a few weeks earlier when a gang of terrorists in Rome had been caught in possession of one, with the intention of blowing up an El Al Boeing.

As expected a radio report came through immediately: The Piper Cub had observed signs of fox-holes on a hillock at H 38:40. Flying low down to investigate, they had been fired at by a missile which, by a miracle, had not destroyed them.

Bennie studied the hillock carefully. It was about twenty-five metres at its highest point. The east slope facing them was steep, but the south slope was moderate enough for a Zelda or half-track to ascend without difficulty. The hill was in the centre of relatively flat ground. Except for a long, low ridge a kilometre to the east, between the hillock and their present observation point, there was no cover for an attacking force.

He radioed back to Riffidim asking if they could send two tanks and as many infantry in Zeldas or half-tracks as they could spare. The answer came back that only one tank was available, a British Centurion, but that three half-tracks with a dozen infantry in each would be on its way within a few minutes.

Awkwardly they scrambled down the sand dune, arriving sweating from the heat and the effort. Dror had picked up the radio messages and the force was ready to go. Boaz, who was always keen to drive, suggested to Gadi that he should rest and let him take the wheel. Thinking that he would have more chance of being in the action if he wasn't driving, Gadi agreed and climbed into the back of the Jeep.

The sand was light and fine, and lifted high in the air behind them as they raced forward, taking up a position behind the long ridge at the edge closest to the south-east corner of the hillock. No time was wasted. Max, one of the lieutenants, set up a 2-inch mortar which they had brought with them, and within a few minutes the shells were coming down, raising huge geysers of white sand as they exploded, and forcing any soldiers dug in on the hillock to keep well down in their fox-holes.

Bennie was not in a hurry. Any hostile force approaching the hillock would have to expose itself before it could attack.

127

At the same time, however, the commandos were left without an effective line of retreat.

The tank and the three half-tracks moved quickly down the road, and Bennie guided them in, taking advantage of the ridge. The defenders could not have missed seeing the dust-trails of the reinforcing vehicles and Bennie expected to see a white flag raised at any moment, but nothing happened. The tank took up its position on the southern tip of the ridge and immediately started firing with its heavy machine-gun.

Max prepared himself with six smoke shells for the mortar while Bennie briefed the commanders of the half-tracks, who in turn, were given a few minutes to explain to their men the orders for the assault. At a signal from Bennie, who had taken over the Zelda from Dror in order to lead the assault, they scrambled into their vehicles.

Max fired a preliminary shell aimed at the southern slope of the hill, and they watched in fascination as its trajectory suddenly became visible in a trail of grey smoke coming vertically down exploding directly on target, and sending billowing clouds of smoke all around it. By the time the second shell was in the air, the vehicles had all moved out together, travelling at full speed in a line which left only the half-track nearest the hillock completely exposed to fire. The vehicles kept a distance of about fifteen metres apart, each one sheltering in the cover of the vehicle on its right. The Zelda was in the middle of the formation, with one of the half-tracks on its left, and the Jeep taking the last and most protected position in the line, with Boaz still at the wheel, and Gadi operating the machine gun.

Reaching a point opposite the southern slope Bennie signalled and the vehicles turned to the right still travelling at speed, but with each vehicle now moving forward along its own track towards the hillock, and all the machine guns blazing away in a hail of death through the thick fog ahead of them. A heavy return fire came from the hillock, but blocked out by the smoke, and affected by the terrible force of the onslaught, it was desperate, and mostly wild of the oncoming targets. A few hundred metres from the hillock Gadi sensed rather than heard a stifled scream from Boaz. The Jeep lurched to the side and almost turned over. He let the machine gun go, grabbed the wheel, pushing himself

128

past Boaz who had slumped across the seat, and continued to race forward with the other vehicles.

As they came to the edge of the smoke the vehicles stopped for an instant. Three soldiers jumped out of each of the back hatches taking up positions to the right of their respective vehicles, and methodically both men and vehicles commenced moving forward, firing steadily ahead of them.

Gadi took a quick look at Boaz, but there was nothing that could be done for him. He was dead, shot through the throat. He grabbed his Uzi and ran forward to join the men in between the vehicles.

The acrid smoke and dust got into their lungs, but they kept advancing, spraying all the foxholes as they stepped around or over them. The pandemonium was so intense that the attacking soldiers were unaware of any return fire unless they were actually hit. It seemed virtually impossible for any of the enemy to survive the merciless assault, but as they came towards the end of the hillock, a grenade burst behind them, thrown as a last gesture of defiance by a commando who had lain low in his foxhole and somehow escaped the first wave of death. Three of the men on foot were wounded by the shrapnel, and the first-aid men rushed to attend to them.

As the noise and dust subsided Bennie stepped down from the hatch of the Zelda to check what had happened. Hearing about Boaz he ran to the Jeep and found him lying on the seat in an enormous pool of blood. There were no other deaths. Eight soldiers were wounded, the most serious being one whose main artery behind the knee had been severed by shrapnel from the grenade. One of the medics attended to him, stopping the flow of blood at a pressure point on the groin, and then applying a tourniquet on his thigh, writing across it '15.35 hours' so that the doctor at the base would know how soon it should be released. A helicopter arrived from Bir Gafgafa, took the patient in and flew away again within a matter of moments.

Sixty dead commandos were counted, there were no survivors. They placed Boaz's body on the floor of the Zelda. Bennie called Gadi to drive the Jeep back with him. Reluctantly he sat down and took the wheel, his thoughts running round in circles about God and fate, and whether if he hadn't done Boaz a favour by letting him drive, it would

9   129

have been his blood spread out dark red and sticky across the front seat of the Jeep.

*　*　*

The room was dark, the lights blocked out by the closed shutters and drawn curtains. Aliza was resting quietly, realising with an insight that she had never previously understood, how painful intense happiness can be. Uri was lying next to her. He had dozed off for a moment, his hand resting on her shoulders, his right arm encircling her body.

As a nurse she was well aware that a person had to be sick to appreciate normal good health. But this was different because the sickness was due to return again. It was as though she had been tossed around in a wild frightening storm, and now suddenly there came a day of miraculous warmth and beauty, but with the certainty that tomorrow the storm would break out again in all its fury.

There are things we can't control, she thought. The sun will move across the sky, and Uri will have to leave and go back. I cannot stop this, but at least I can savour every second of his presence, the touch of his warm body which I held today in mine as though nothing could ever pull us apart again.

Tenderly she stroked back a lock of his hair that had fallen across his eyes . . .

Uri had spent a restless night, his mind going round and round in circles devising all sorts of fanciful schemes to get to see Aliza. He would steal a Jeep and go 'absent without leave' for twenty-four hours, claiming that it was the after-effects of his being shell-shocked; or he would jam the heavy machine-gun on his half-track and persuade Amos to let him take it away to be repaired and while they were doing this he would slip out and meet her somewhere. In the cold morning light he knew that his ideas were impractical but the terrible need to see Aliza was as strong as ever.

At breakfast at six o'clock that morning he drew Amos aside and asked if he knew what the day's programme was going to be.

'No fighting today,' smiled Amos, 'you did more than enough yesterday. All we're doing is moving to our new base at Mazrat Beit Jinn.' Suddenly he stopped speaking,

130

seeing the tense whiteness of Uri's face. 'Uri, what's the matter? Aren't you feeling well?'

'No. Not really. Amos, I've got to get away today. If you say "no", I'll understand. Please don't ask me questions. I will never again ask you a favour like I'm asking you now.'

Amos was taken aback. He didn't even have the authority to let Uri go, and he knew that Uri knew this. Something was making Uri desperate, something which was totally out of character for him. In the two years that Amos had known and worked with Uri, he had never known him to try to secure any special privilege. Abruptly he made up his mind.

'Until what time Uri?'

'This afternoon – the later the better.'

'All right, but I think I need my head examined. I'll give you a special warrant to go to Kuneitra for an aerial map of Mazrat Beit Jinn. If you do anything more than that, it's not my business and I don't want to know about it. There will be a Jeep leaving here at 5 p.m. See that you're on it.' He pulled out a book and started writing. 'Uri, I don't have to tell you – not a word to anybody other than that you were sent to get this map, or we'll both be in trouble.'

Uri's face was ecstatic. 'I'll never forget this.'

A few minutes later he was hitching a lift to Kuneitra. He finished the business with the map in thirty minutes, and after standing in line for about the same time at a soldiers' mobile phone booth, was able to speak to Aliza before she came off duty at eight o'clock. There were no problems from Aliza's side, a quick phone-call to her mother; another one to Vered's mother, where Vered had gone to stay, saying that she wouldn't be able to see her today because of an emergency at the hospital; and Aliza was on her way.

She arrived at the hotel before Uri and arranged for a room overlooking Lake Kineret. She wanted to take a bath, but she wanted to be outside when Uri arrived and she was too excited to think straight anyway. The problem was solved by a phone-call from the desk-clerk to tell her that her 'friend' had arrived and was on his way up. She flew to the door and they fell into each other's arms pressing tightly against each other, and repeating over and over again words of love which were only an echo of the tumultuous pounding of their hearts and bodies.

131

At one stage they drew apart for a brief second and his face clouded over as he started to say something about Vered, but she stopped him immediately. 'Not now, Uri. Please, we'll talk about it later.' They moved to the bed, and he was suddenly conscious of the fact that he was still in his army uniform, dusty and unwashed.

'Aliza. Shouldn't I take a shower?'

But Aliza was determined not to break the spell. 'No!' she said, almost fiercely. 'I want you now.' There was no more talk. They devoured each other with a hunger and passion that they had never before experienced, and afterwards Uri cried with relief, his fears and tensions flooding out leaving him exhausted and at peace, like the muscles of his body which had also been stretched beyond endurance and were now loose and relaxed.

Uri decided to take a bath. He went into the bathroom and excitedly called to Aliza to come and look. The hotel was old, dating from even before the British Mandate, and the bath was old-fashioned and outsize, quite unlike anything they had ever seen before. They opened the taps wide and got in together facing each other with child-like excitement.

They soaped each other's backs and fronts laughing and enjoying the warm water and the slippery feeling of the soap on their bodies. Uri got hold of the hand spray turning it full on to Aliza who shrieked with the first impact of the cold water and threw herself on to Uri trying to grasp his arm and turn it back on to him. They wrestled with each other laughing uncontrollably, the spray shooting water in all directions.

Eventually Uri turned it off and held Aliza down on top of him, and they lay there together loving and kissing each other feeling their bodies again begin to respond and tingle with desire. Their first deep hunger for each other had been satisfied, and now the novelty of the water lapping around them, and the different feel of their bodies as they soaped each other again added a dimension of fun and pleasure-seeking to their love-making. They took their time, allowing their senses to react to each new sensation, the excitement mounting higher and higher until they lost control and clung tightly to each other, yielding wildly and freely in an embrace which left them joyously and utterly drained of any strength.

Aliza got out of the bath and dried herself lightly, but Uri lay there protesting that she should phone Kfar Saba and ask the hospital to send an ambulance and stretcher crew to carry him to the bed. Aliza gave him a hand and they lay down quietly, and within minutes Uri had dozed off, a lock of his hair falling across his eyes...

Time passed. Feeling Aliza's hand stroking his forehead Uri stirred and sighed. He turned his head to look at her, the rich black cascade of hair that fell across them both, and her huge black eyes. Then he wanted to talk. He asked her about Vered and she told him she had broken the news, and stayed with her until her parents arrived and took her home with them. She had been very brave but too shocked to really understand that Zeev was gone. She wanted Aliza to tell her all the details, where? How? What had happened to his body? Why hadn't the army notified her right away? Aliza had shown her the letter, and could tell her nothing more.

'It was bad, Uri,' she said, 'there's no easy way. Only time will help.'

'I didn't believe he was dead either. One minute he was there, the next, he was gone. Just a body, a shell. No trace of him, no sign that he ever existed on this earth.'

Aliza hugged him close to her and let him talk. Several times he stopped to apologise. 'Aliza, I'm not being fair, by the time I leave I'll be fine and you'll be a nervous wreck.' But she laughed, pointing out that as a nurse she had seen more terrible things from the war than he could ever visualise, and she made him go on talking.

Occasionally she interrupted, asking once if any war could be worth the broken and disfigured bodies that came into the hospital – the limbs lost, the deaf, the blind, the crippled for life ... 'We make them feel like heroes while they are with us – but afterwards, six months from now, will they believe their sacrifices were worth while?'

'It's a question of luck, Aliza. For those who pay the price, it can never be worth while. But what's the alternative? Can you imagine what would have happened if the Syrians had swept across the Bnot Yaakov bridge to Rosh Pina and Safad?'

'Do you hate them, Uri?'

'Yes. They are a cruel, barbaric people. I don't hate the Egyptians, or the Jordanians, or the Lebanese, but the Syrians make shivers run down my spine.'

Aliza put a towel around her shoulders. The room seemed to have grown colder. She went to the window, drew the curtains apart and opened the shutters a little. Uri also got up and they looked out at the lake, shimmering, blue-green and calm, a tiny fishing boat bobbing gently up and down on its surface and a fisherman casting his net, apologetically stirring the water. A cool breeze drifted through the window gently caressing them.

Aliza turned to Uri, tears forming at the back of her eyes. She had gone over the pros and cons hundreds of times since her visit to the Gynaecologist, and knew that she had to tell him.

'Uri, listen to me a moment. There's something important you have to know.' He looked at her a little taken aback, not quite knowing what to expect.

'I'm pregnant, Uri. I'm going to have a baby. I didn't . . . '

'Are you sure, Aliza, really sure? Did you have any tests?'

'Yes. It's not a hundred per cent certain, but the Gynaecologist says he's reasonably sure.'

'Aliza it's incredible. You don't know how happy I am.'

'Truly Uri? You're not just saying this to make me feel good?'

He took her in his arms tenderly kissing away the wet tears as they rolled down her cheeks.

'Truly my darling. You know when I thought about Zeev afterwards, it disturbed me that he didn't have any children. I know it's easier for Vered in lots of ways, but it just meant that there was nothing left of him. Aliza I am truly happy. We'll get married straight after the war. Are you worried about your parents?'

'Yes and no. I'm not so worried now that you know about it.'

'How far are you?'

'About a month and a half.'

'I think it's terrific. The war can't last more than a few days now, and if I don't get leave straight away, we'll get married up here. Lots of fellows are doing that. It could even make everything simpler.'

134

A cloud passed across the sun temporarily throwing its shadow over the lake. Uri went to check the time on his watch.

'Two o'clock.'

Aliza felt her heart jump with fear, but she tried not to show it.

'How long more, Uri?'

'Maximum another hour. I can't take a chance on missing that Jeep.'

'An hour can be like a lifetime.'

They lay down on the bed again their arms around each other. She snuggled into him, playing her fingers across his body, teasing and fondling him. He grinned at her.

'I didn't know that I was getting married to such a wanton hussy. Are you serious?'

'Yes, I may not see you again for another week.'

They laughed together even though the joke had a slightly bitter taste.

And so she held him to her again, and they poured out their love for each other. There was a strange new exaltation coursing through Uri, a wordless chant repeating itself over and over, struggling to find a form which could express the tremendous emotions surging through his mind. This woman in his arms was carrying his child, she had taken his seed and it lived inside her binding her to him for all eternity.

They lay quietly afterwards, not talking, conscious that the seconds were ticking away and they would soon have to return to reality. Eventually Uri knew he could not procrastinate any longer. He reluctantly untwined her arms from around him and got off the bed. Aliza stayed where she was, she didn't want to see Uri leave. He started to get dressed, teasing her that when he staggered into base that evening he would have to tell the boys every detail of what had happened. 'They'll never believe me when I try to explain that the map was so heavy.'

A few more light words, a long kiss, and then he left. 'I love you, Aliza,' he said simply, and went out closing the door behind him.

'I love you too, Uri,' she whispered, with tears in her eyes. She had a terrible premonition that she might never see him again and she wanted to dash after him to plead with him not to go, or even just to cling to him for a few seconds more.

But she knew she was being hysterical. Everybody had these premonitions. Uri was fine and healthy, the worst was past. Just a little more luck, and they would be together again. And until then she would have the memory of this day of miraculous warmth and beauty that they had snatched from the storm.

Sunday, 14th October

In the Northern sector of the Sinai Peninsula lies a sandy coastal plain, narrow in the east opposite El Arish, and widening in the west until it reaches the Suez Canal. In the middle, starting at Jebel el-Giddi, a series of mountains rises about a thousand metres above a barren limestone plateau – and in the South, huge granite mountains, including Jebel Musa (the traditional Mount Sinai), tower more than two thousand metres above a moonscape which is awe-inspiring and absolutely desolate.

Altogether, it is about as unlikely an area of land for nations to fight over, as it is possible to imagine. From time immemorial, however, armies have marched in both directions across the Peninsula to establish or confirm their mastery over the land between the Two Great Rivers, the Nile and the Euphrates – the Egyptians, Canaanites, Philistines, Persians, Greeks, Romans, Arabs, Crusaders, Turks, French (under Napoleon) and British – a kaleidoscope of history, their names conjuring up romantic pictures of ancient and modern powers, of glory and destruction. And as silent witness to the battles fought here, the desert itself acts as a perfect mirror to the futility of it all. Its shifting sands relentlessly cover everything, restoring the land the way it was before, as if nothing had happened.

From the point of view of history, the Yom Kippur war was just another variation of an age old theme. Round One had gone to the Egyptians. Round Two had just started, and at Riffidim its progress was being marked with new coloured lines and symbols on the map in the General's war-room.

The Egyptians had been casting anxious eyes at the deteriorating situation in the north, and were beginning to re-assess the wisdom of their initial battle strategy. Instead of stopping within the shelter of their missile bases to consolidate their positions, it might have been better to punch through as fast and as far as they could, taking advantage of the enemy being weak and off-guard. Now they found themselves sitting on a narrow vulnerable strip of land with their backs to the Canal, facing an army which was methodically building up its strength, and which might soon be in a position to double it by bringing reinforcements down from the Syrian front.

By the second Saturday of the war, the Egyptians were at the peak of their strength – their air force was virtually uncommitted, and their army across the Canal had soared to a hundred-thousand men and over a thousand tanks. Deciding that it had to be now or never, their armoured divisions had launched a powerful two-pronged attack, along the road to Riffidim and lower down south towards the Mitla Pass.

The battle had raged all day Saturday, and well into the night. It was the first massive tank against tank battle on the Canal front. The Israelis had the advantage of defending, and punished the two spearheads mercilessly, out-manoeuvering and out-shooting the Egyptian tanks. By the end of the fighting sixty-five Egyptian tanks had been destroyed without making any indentations on the Israeli positions.

At daybreak on Sunday morning the Egyptians resumed the battle, this time over a wider section of the front and on an even larger scale.

When task force Meron returned from its encounter with the commandos the day before, Bennie had tried to report to the General, but the battle was in progress, and he couldn't get past the entrance of the bunker. During the night he made full use of his connections, and the next morning he was allowed to accompany a colonel friend of his into the war-room. He stood unobtrusively on the side watching, fascinated, as the radio reports came in.

The Egyptians made a number of sorties with fighter bombers. In one incident the Israeli radar picked up the patterns of four Mirages which were not supposed to be in the area. In the few precious seconds that elapsed trying to identify them, the planes attacked Israeli ground positions, inflicting severe losses, and confirming for the first time that Libyan Mirages were being used to assist the

Egyptians. The General exploded with anger when the report reached him.

'I don't know which I'd enjoy more,' he shouted across the room, 'kicking Pompidou's backside or Gadafi's!' But they all felt better a little later when two of the Mirages were shot down.

The Israeli planes were active in all directions. A total of fifteen Egyptian planes were shot down during the day. They bombed airfields deep in Egypt, and missile bases and military installations in Port Said at the Mediterranean end of the Canal.

Bennie was intrigued by the organisation of the air-to-ground support. Armoured units calling for assistance to the war-room specified the co-ordinates on the map where the planes were needed. The war-room decided which appeal should get priority and the air force control centre attended to the matter, calling in whatever planes were available and briefing them on the locations and action to be taken.

The Egyptians threw everything they had into the battle, wave upon wave of tanks trying unsuccessfully to break through the Israeli defences. Symbols were marked on the map, shifted and taken off, depending on what type of units were engaged where. At one stage the General pointed out to the officers around him that this was the greatest number of tanks that had ever been thrown into one battle, including the famous World War II Battle of El Alamein in which more than 1,450 tanks had been involved.

By the end of the day another two hundred Egyptian tanks had been destroyed, for a loss of only twelve Israeli tanks. The General was grimly satisfied. Leaving the room, he passed Bennie who saluted and said, 'Shalom Sir, when would you like to see me?'

'Shalom Bennie – you did a good job with those commandos. Be here at six o'clock in the morning. It's going to be a big day tomorrow!'

* * *

At Beit Sokolov Robert Crawford sat typing a telex incorporating the latest release from the Army Spokesman.

'Iraqis routed – Syrians hard pressed to defend road to Damascus: In a ninety minute battle at El Harra, less than ten kilometres south-east of Kuneitra, an entire Iraqi brigade consisting of over seventy tanks was wiped out. Israel claims that it suffered no losses. After a brief skirmish on Friday night a trap was prepared by the Israelis, and when the Iraqis attacked at dawn on Saturday morning they were allowed to advance northwards. Israeli armour made a strong thrust forward on one side, penetrating deep into a deployment of Syrian artillery, and then cut down behind the Iraqis boxing them in. Over seventy tanks were destroyed and many prisoners were taken. The Israeli armour continued to thrust forward mopping up the Syrian positions as well. A top-ranking Israeli officer commented on the low level of fighting ability displayed by the Iraqis, who had obviously been thrown into battle without adequate preparation. The officer claimed that the Syrians have been knocked off-balance by the strong Israeli attack in the north along the road to Damascus, and that their morale had sagged now that the intoxication of their imagined victory was beginning to wear off.'

Crawford asked for a connection and after being put through, pressed the button feeding the tape into the machine, which instantaneously transmitted the report a third of the way across the world to his paper in London. His duty done, he sat down in an easy chair to relax. His head was not as clear as he would have liked it to be. Drinking with the boys and then taking a broad to bed was not the ideal preparation for the next morning's work.

Over the years he had grown used to what he called the 'loneliness of the long-distance correspondent'. The glamour of the first few years, chasing to where the action was, the open sesame of his press card, had long since worn off. The illusions that he once held about truth and justice had faded, to be replaced by a weary cynicism which accepted men as self-seeking and dishonest, and their governments simply a reflection of this on a larger scale.

He felt that he was on a treadmill with not very much to show for all the effort he had put into his profession. Over the years his scale of values had changed, and given another chance he might well have chosen a different road. He recognised with painful clarity that the best thing he had ever had in his life was his wife Anne, and their two daughters. But he had divorced her five years ago when she gave him an ultimatum to choose between her and the profession which she maintained was ruining their lives. For a moment he had the wild idea of calling her and suggesting that they give it another try, but he knew it was useless. She hadn't remarried, but lived with another man, apparently quite happily, and the children seemed to have accepted the arrangement.

His general mood of frustration was intensified by the feeling that he was not being allowed to do a good job. The Israelis had clamped down heavily on the newsgathering and freedom of movement of foreign correspondents, confining them largely to official hand-outs from government spokesmen. His head ached. Thinking the liquor might still be affecting him, he went to the cafeteria, ordered a large black coffee and drank it without sugar, hoping that the heat and bitter taste would revive him.

On an impulse he went to his special pigeon-hole, and was pleased to see a large brown envelope. The censors had worked quickly. In addition to the news which he telexed as fast as it became available, his paper had cabled him for news behind the news, background anecdotes which would be of interest to their readers, and he had written a special report about his trip the previous Wednesday on the Golan Heights. The censor had blue-pencilled only two items, the name of an officer and the name of a place, neither of which were of great importance to his story.

Returning to the cafeteria he ordered another coffee, this time with sugar, and settled down to give the story a final reading before transmitting it.

Cameos from 'the war that nobody needed'

A report from the Syrian Front, by Robert Crawford. Ten of us squeezed into a small panel van which left Tel Aviv at six o'clock on Wednesday morning, the fifth day of the war, with our guide Chaim Topol, the Israeli movie star who took the part of Tevyah, the milkman in 'Fiddler on the Roof'. He had rushed back from London to join his unit, but had been assigned instead to escorting foreign correspondents.

All along the road we encountered bright home-made stalls, staffed by volunteers, old and young, with cold drinks, sweets, biscuits, and slices of home-made cake for soldiers passing by. With pampering like this, it's a wonder that Israelis have managed to acquire any kind of reputation for toughness.

By eight o'clock we were driving through Kiryat Shmoneh, a medium-sized town which has been a prime target for Katyusha rockets, fired by Palestine Guerillas operating from the Lebanese border a few kilometres away.

After Banias we turned up the winding road which had cost so many tanks and lives when the Israelis stormed the Golan Heights in the last days of the Six Day War. The valley below was dotted with large ponds for breeding fish, and sprinklers threw a silver canopy over green and white fields. The white was the cotton crop, and the men were busy harvesting it in the bright sunlight. Above us the roar of cannon fire rolled across the hills, and a pall of grey-black smoke drifted lazily upwards discolouring the clear blue sky.

Passing through the Druse village of Massada which had been bombed on the first day of the war, we saw no people, although washing on the lines and doors standing ajar, indicated that the residents were keeping indoors.

The road broadened out on to a plain, and the debris of war became obvious; burnt out vehicles and tanks (mostly Syrian, with their distinctive yellow-brown camouflage markings), cast-off shell casings and piles of empty ammunition boxes.

Within a few minutes we were in the middle of the action. On the side of the road, half-tracks were parked with men around them; sleeping, exhausted, or sitting eating apples from a plastic bag.

Wherever we stopped soldiers came over and gave us cards to post or a telephone number to call just to say that they were okay. One of them was on his way back to his Kibbutz which had been overrun by the Syrians on the second day of the war. He was worried about the turkey flock. 'We had five thousand birds,' he said. 'I've heard that the turkey shed is intact, but they haven't had food for four days, which is not far from the limit that they can stand.'

We asked some of the men if they were in favour of going on to Damascus. 'Who needs it?' said one of them. 'Who needed this war?' asked another and continued – 'The only reason we're fighting is because they attacked us. We're killing each other and doing as much damage to each other as we can. The mothers in Damascus and Cairo are going to cry just as hard as the mothers in Jerusalem. And when it is all finished, with a bit of luck we'll sit down and talk about the things we could have talked about without having a war.'

A Peugeot station wagon was parked next to a row of tanks, their crews crowded around it, and a fat man wearing civilian clothes dished out sandwiches and cold drinks. He had a team of mothers in Safad who organised the food, and every day he drove up to distribute it as close to the front as he was allowed to go. 'I haven't been under fire very often,' he apologised.

We reached a barbed wire fence with a black and yellow notice reading 'Danger – Border ahead'. The information was out of date, the border had moved forward.

Finally we arrived at our destination, a small rolling plain near the foot of the Hermon Mountains. Over a hundred tanks lay scorched and battered within easy walking distance. Around the tanks, and beneath them where they may have crawled desperately seeking shelter, were the charred bodies of dozens of soldiers stiffened into grotesque positions. One dead Syrian soldier near me lay on his back, his helmet still on his head, his mouth open, with his tongue swollen and protruding, and his right hand stretched out gripping his rifle. From the knees down, the ends of his trousers were flat and empty. There was no sign of the lower halves of his legs.

Chaim Topol pointed to a twisted piece of metal which was barely recognisable as a plane engine. 'That used to be a Skyhawk,' he said. 'A lot of the credit for what happened here belongs to them.'

Three soldiers from the Army Chaplain's unit were busy collecting and burying the bodies of the Syrian soldiers. The Israeli dead had been taken away immediately after the battle to a morgue, where they were carefully identified, and then buried temporarily on a special plot in one of the kibbutzim, to await proper reburial at a later stage.

Two salvage crews were at work on the more serviceable tanks. Questioned by Chaim one of the men proudly told us that his unit had averaged putting six tanks a day back into fighting condition. 'We work every hour of daylight and usually more than that. When you see a little of what we've seen in some of our tanks – we're not the ones who are making the sacrifices.'

Chaim had arranged for a tank-corps officer to brief us on the action. The battle had started in the late afternoon, lasting well into the night, which gave the Russian T-62 tanks a tremendous advantage because of their modern infra-red instrumentation. In spite of this the Syrians had lost fifty T-62 and a hundred other tanks, about three-quarters of its strength, to the loss of only twelve of the fifty Israeli Centurion tanks which had opposed them.

Scratching with a stick on the ground and using a few strategically placed pebbles the officer described how the Israelis had blocked the Syrian advance, called for planes to attack the column, and while they were distracted by the bombing, had sent two units to outflank and ambush them from the rear.

The fighting had been very fierce, especially at the beginning when the Syrians thought they had the upper hand. As reports came through about tanks being blown up and destroyed in the rear, many of the crew panicked, believing that their retreat had been cut off, and they simply abandoned their vehicles and vanished into the night.

The officer took us over to a completely undamaged T-62 which had been left as a showpiece for groups like ours. Even a layman could appreciate its low silhouette as compared with some of the lumbering giants we've seen. Four of us at a time were allowed to clamber in and examine its gleaming brightness. The smooth bore of its 115 mm. guns which enabled it to fire missiles as well as shells was apparently its most important innovation.

The T-62 had a speed of over fifty kilometres an hour and a cruising range of three hundred and fifty kilometres compared with the Centurions' thirty-five kilometres per hour and a range of a hundred kilometres. The point of the explanation we received was obvious – that the quality of the tanks was a factor, but when the chips were down it was still the quality of the men that counted.

It had been a long day and Chaim wanted to have us off the Heights before it was dark. We came back on a different road, where the Israelis were occupying a series of Syrian bunkers built into the hillside, with huge walls protecting the entrances. We stopped for a few moments intrigued by a group of soldiers in their makeshift Sukka on the back of an army truck. The Sukka is a small hut built of branches from a tree, used during the harvest festival of Sukkot, as a reminder of the forty years the Jews wandered in the desert when Moses led them out of Egypt. The soldiers had caps or hankies on the backs of their heads, and were praying and chanting, swaying back and forth with their bodies. The ceremony was serious, but seemed to include a large element of fun, as though they appreciated how incongruous it was to be observing their holiday in such a setting.

We wished them shalom, and our panel-van set off at full speed reaching the edge of the Heights just as the sun went down behind the mountains. The valley below looked even more beautiful and serene, with the fish ponds like smooth dull mirrors on the darkened landscape.

A long convoy of half-tracks filled with troops, and huge trucks carrying tanks and heavy artillery, passed us in the opposite direction – on their way to the war that nobody needed . . .

Crawford was satisfied with his article and got up to arrange for it to be telexed. At the same moment Chaim Topol entered the cafeteria, with a group of correspondents complaining angrily. 'We're fed up Chaim,' one of them was saying. 'Why can't you give us a pass and let us find our own way wherever we want to go?' 'Yeah!' said another one. 'We're not children, what's the point of taking us to places that are safe? Surely you can fix us up with something exciting for a change?'

'You're right,' said Chaim with a dead-pan expression. 'How would you like a date with Daliah Levi?'

* * *

Their new quarters were at Mazrat Beit Jinn, a large village, on the foothills of Mount Hermon north of the Kuneitra-Damascus road, and the principal water source for a large area. There were forests all around making it easy for enemy forces to infiltrate and set ambushes. The village had been evacuated before the Israeli army arrived. Amos's men were allotted a couple of mud huts, not as comfortable as the bunkers they had just left, but better than the tents that most other units were using. Uri slept a deep untroubled sleep, and had to be shaken awake by Amos. He climbed out of the blanket with a cheerful 'good-morning' and Amos with mock severity told him to get moving. 'You've done nothing since yesterday, except grin like a big Cheshire cat,' he said.

At breakfast time the men crowded around Amos to hear the schedule for the day. A slim blond, blue-eyed youngster, dressed smartly in the uniform of a scout, with characteristic red boots, and sergeant's stripes on his sleeve, was standing next to him. 'Meet Ibrahim,' said Amos, 'He'll be going out on patrol with us. Our instructions are to check the road through Charpah and Chalas, up to the Kuneitra-Damascus road. We're not expecting problems – the front line has moved about four kilometres north of our route – but I don't want anybody acting smart and taking chances. We're leaving in thirty minutes. Any questions?' There were none, and the men moved off to get ready.

Ibrahim stood waiting next to Amos's half-track. Nobody needed to explain that he was a Druze, a member of a minority sect with its origins going back nearly a thousand years to a Persian preacher who had broken away from the Moslem religion, and settled with his followers in a remote region of Lebanon. They had suffered a great deal of persecution from Moslems and Christians alike, and many had fled across the Golan Heights to Syria, or founded villages in Israel where they now numbered nearly fifty thousand.

Their religious precepts were largely kept secret even from the vast majority of their followers, but one of their beliefs was the transmigration of souls, that the number of true Druze in the world remained constant, and when one died, his soul entered a baby who had just been born, or if no baby was available, then it could also rest temporarily in a suitable animal such as a dog.

In Crusader times there had been a fair degree of contact between the Druze and the European invaders, which was the probable explanation of Ibrahim's blond hair and blue eyes.

Over the generations, the Druze had always sited their villages in high remote places, their activities had been largely agricultural, and they acquired an incredible knowl-

146

edge of nature. Their eyesight and powers of observation were exceptional. They could 'read' the ground around them, tell you what animals had passed, or sometimes in the case of human beings, details such as how many, what size they were, whether they were carrying heavy equipment and other facts which astounded those who saw them in action. The Israeli army had capitalised on these talents, and the Druze were invariably used as Border Police, or Scouts, enjoying an excellent reputation for reliability and bravery.

Ibrahim's home village was Daliat Ha Carmel, near Haifa, with a population of over five thousand Druze. He spoke Arabic at home, but his education had been virtually on the same syllabus as Israeli youngsters, and his Hebrew was fluent.

He had nearly finished his three years in the army, where he had been absorbed into and identified with the Israeli world, and in many ways his problems were just beginning. The girl who had been 'pledged' to him had been 'protected' in the community, her parents having removed her from school as soon as she passed the primary classes. Mentally she was now years behind him, with no knowledge of the kind of world that he had virtually become part of.

Ibrahim was extremely sensitive. He did not mix socially with Arabs or Moslems. He enjoyed the company of Israelis and his years in the army had been the happiest and most fulfilling that he had experienced. He did not, however, have false illusions as to the extent to which he was truly accepted in Israeli society.

Only just before the war, in the course of his work he had met an Israeli soldier-girl who had obviously liked him, and who, he was sure, knew that he was a Druze. The friendship had been relatively innocent, just a couple of meetings during the day, when they talked, laughed and drank cold drinks. Then suddenly through some remark which he had made about Daliat Ha Carmel, realisation had flooded into the girl's eyes, she burst into tears, jumped up and ran away. The humiliation still burned into him . . .

Amos and Uri were ready waiting to go, and spent a few minutes chatting to Ibrahim while the rest of the men climbed into the half-tracks. They moved off in their usual formation, with Ibrahim standing next to Amos in the lead half-track, Avner in the centre, and Uri bringing up the rear.

The road was gravel and in poor condition. As soon as they had passed the forest outside the village, Ibrahim climbed out and walked ahead of the column looking for signs that the surface had been interfered with and mines planted. A soldier walked on each side a metre or two behind him, their Uzzis at the ready.

After about forty minutes of travelling in this fashion they entered the village of Charpa, a village similar to the one where they were quartered. The local inhabitants had apparently fled, except the occupants of one reasonably solid cottage, which had a large white sheet on a broomstick projecting conspicuously from the roof above the door. The cottage had been built with spaces for windows, but these were now blocked with stones to keep out the cold. A little brown dog stopped eating from its bowl to bark at them and a chicken wandered about pecking at the scraps on the ground. An elderly couple sat on stools outside the door. The man wore a black and white check Kaffiya pulled down over his forehead and around his cheeks, showing only the deep-set eyes, a large thin nose and a peppery black and white beard. He looked straight at them, but without any expression on his face. The woman was dressed in black, her face wrinkled, and she kept her eyes averted. How they must hate us, thought Uri.

An Israeli army unit was stationed in the village, and they chatted for a while before moving on. The track to Chalas was in even worse condition. Tanks had gone over it, and its surface was chewed up and full of holes. Ibrahim's pace slowed down and he occasionally stopped to probe suspicious spots. Amos and Uri stood in their half-tracks, constantly sweeping the surrounding areas with their binoculars. The men were grumbling about the snail's pace at which they were travelling.

'It's a good job our tanks move faster than this, or we wouldn't get to Damascus until 1980,' said one of them.

'Amos, I've got a birthday in November. Do you think our patrol will finish in time for me to celebrate it?' called another. Amos smiled. He remembered one of his officers defining a mine as a bomb sitting in a hole waiting for a driver without the time or the patience to look for it. He had plenty of both.

Suddenly Ibrahim raised his hand to stop. He bent down

to examine the ground, walked ahead a few paces and then came back again. Amos jumped out to see what was bothering him.

'Mines?' he asked.

'No, I don't think so. But there have been some people using this road in the last few hours, probably before the sun came up.'

He showed Amos some shapeless indentations which meant nothing to him, but at one spot where a tank had pushed the gravel into a heap, there was a clear footprint.

'Do you have any idea how many?' asked Amos.

'At least two, but maybe three or four, not more than that.' Ibrahim inspected the sides of the track and pointed to a spot a few metres back. 'They came from this direction, so my guess is that it's some Syrian soldiers who got left behind in the retreat and are trying to make their way back to their own lines. When they came to the track they turned here, and started to walk down it. If we keep moving we'll eventually find out what happened to them.'

They moved forward again, cautiously, conscious that the enemy might be watching them from some vantage point, and setting an ambush for them. Further down the road they passed a low ridge, and in front of them lay the village of Chalas, a cluster of no more than twenty small stone cottages. There were some wrecked trucks, a burnt-out Syrian tank, and innumerable shell casings and empty ammunition boxes, testifying that Israeli artillery forces had paused here in their sweep forward. The cottages themselves were extensively damaged, some of the roofs had collapsed, and many walls had gaping holes blown through them.

Ibrahim raised his hand for them to stop again, and he walked back to Amos. 'Their tracks continue all the way down the road. I'm fairly certain that there are only three of them. They've probably taken shelter in one of the cottages, hoping that when it gets dark again, they can try to reach their own lines.'

Amos reported back to his base, receiving permission from his Company Commander to do a proper search of the village. At the entrance to Chalas, the track widened for a distance of fifty metres, forming the main and only street. They stopped about ten metres away from the first cottage. Ibrahim shouted out in Arabic that they knew there were soldiers hiding there, and ordering them to come out and surrender. There was no answer.

Amos signalled the men to leave the half-tracks. They knew the routine, having practised it many times in exercises. Some of Avner's men were posted on the flanks of the two rows of cottages where they could cover anybody trying to exit through an opening in the rear. Others covered the front entrances. The rest of the men formed up in threes behind Amos on the right-hand side, and Uri on the left-hand side.

On Amos's command, the first three men behind him positioned themselves along the side wall of the first cottage. At his signal they moved forward quickly round the corner, the number one man pulling the pin out of a grenade, throwing it around the side of the door, and keeping his body pressed against the wall. As soon as the grenade exploded, he jumped through the doorway and moved to his right placing his back to the wall and firing directly in front of him sweeping in a clockwise direction. At the same instant the second man moved in to the left side of the doorway firing in front of him sweeping anti-clockwise. The third man positioned himself at the entrance to make sure that in the excitement and confusion nobody else tried to enter the cottage. After about fifteen seconds the firing stopped and the men inside waited for the dust to clear. The cottage was empty.

Uri's first group of three repeated the action on his side, with the same result. They moved forward to the next two cottages, with fresh groups of three getting into position to take their turn.

They had reached the sixth cottage when suddenly a burst of bullets came from the doorway diagonally opposite it. Avner's men immediately opened up with their machine guns, firing non-stop at the cottage, and making it impossible for anyone inside to expose himself. Amos with hand signals moved his next group of three quickly up to where the shots had come from, and within seconds the grenade was thrown, the men had stepped in with their Uzzies and kept firing until they were certain that nothing could have lived through it. When the dust cleared, three men were lying dead on the earthen floor, their bodies riddled and disfigured with bullets.

Amos had held the other groups back under shelter, and gave them the order to continue moving forward from one cottage to the next, until they had covered the entire village. Only then he relaxed, and went back to where the men had been killed. Their uniforms and papers confirmed that they were Syrian soldiers, who must have been trying to get back to their lines.

Ibrahim was grinning all over as the men came up to congratulate him. Amos reported back to his commanding officer, and they moved out of the village, continuing at the same slow pace until they reached the road running from Kuneitra to Damascus.

The main Israeli spearhead was already ten kilometres past them, and a lot of traffic was moving up in the direction of the front, but the actual sounds of battle were muted, indicating little serious action.

The patrol returned the way it had come, this time travelling as fast as the track permitted. They arrived back at base in time for lunch, canned beef and a smaller tin of beans. One of the men looking at the beans commented in disgust, 'If they don't change our rations soon I'm going to be transferred to the artillery.'

*　　*　　*

Sunday was a difficult day on the homefront. There was no fresh news other than what had already been announced on TV the evening before, the tank battle in the Sinai, the defeat of the Iraqis on the Golan, and the speech of Golda Meir in which she declared Israel's willingness to consider a ceasefire any time the Arabs were ready, and then went on to castigate the callous disregard of the Russian and Arab leaders for the lives of thousands upon thousands of Egyptians and Syrians. 'The day that Sadat becomes concerned over the death of one man,' she said, 'the first step towards peace will have been achieved.'

A concern with death was the precise reason for the day being difficult. Israel is a tiny country, news – good or bad – spreads like wildfire, and from early morning stories had been circulating about families being notified of soldiers killed in action, in preparation for an official announcement that night.

Both the army and the government had problems in connection with the announcement. The army's difficulty was

151

technical. In the confusion of the first few days many soldiers had transferred freely from tank to tank, armoured car to armoured car, and unit to unit. Many soldiers had been lost trace of and were reported 'missing'. The army went to extraordinary lengths to establish the fate of such soldiers with certainty, to cut down to an absolute minimum the number of tragic mistakes of wrong notification.

The government's difficulty was political, the grim summary of losses usually being made at the end of the short wars which Israel had experienced since 1948. Reluctantly it had been decided to announce the losses while the fighting was still going on, partly to counteract the enormous imaginary numbers dreamed up by the Arab radio stations, and partly because the rumours circulating in Israel were beginning to have a devastating effect on morale.

The Israeli Army system of notification attempts to be as scientifically humane as possible. The idea of an official stereotyped telegram is totally unacceptable. Special units have the task of trying to study each case individually, in an effort to notify families in a way which will ease the shock as much as possible. The background of the dead soldier, the state of health of the parents, the choice of a time when both parents are likely to be home together, all these are factors which are investigated. Normally three persons form the official delegation, a special high ranking officer, a friend of the family or well-known public personality, and a doctor or at least a trained nurse. The medical people are ready to give an injection instantly, and are on their guard for attempts at suicide.

The army was given less than a day to notify the families of those who had died the first eight days of the fighting. From early in the morning their units had been busy doing their grim, unforgiving work.

In houses and apartments all over the country, people were aware of what was happening and dreaded every ring on the doorbell or unfamiliar visitors. At one house, two air-raid wardens pulled up in a Jeep to check a complaint from a neighbour that a light had been showing the previous night. A woman opened the door, took one look at their uniforms and fainted. The wardens almost fainted from shock themselves.

One team reported a woman opening the door before they

reached it. 'Come inside,' she said, 'I've been waiting for you.' When the doctor fumbled with his bag she told him not to worry, she'd be all right. Nonplussed they asked whether she'd been told already. 'No,' she replied, 'but I have been certain for at least two days now.' She asked them all the details, how it had happened, where and when, and then walked with them back to the door. 'I appreciate your coming,' she told them, 'I understand how difficult it must be for you.' One of the men in the team stayed behind a little while after the others left. 'Please listen to me,' he said. 'Don't place too great a burden on yourself. At a time like this one is allowed to cry.' 'I will,' she promised – 'as soon as you are gone!'

Meir and Shoshana had fortunately not been aware of the day's happenings. They finished dinner and were waiting for the news to begin. Eitan popped his head in to tell them that their family would not be joining them. Chaim was still upset because Danny's leave had been cancelled. He had a headache and wanted to go to bed early.

At eight-thirty the army spokesman made the official announcement. In the first eight days of the war six hundred and fifty-six men had been killed in action. Two thousand were in hospital wounded. All families had been notified, including those of soldiers who were missing and known to have been taken prisoner.

General Dayan appeared on the screen, his face somber, his message brief and to the point. 'We are in the midst of a war and cannot give public expression to our profound sorrow.' He expressed sympathy to the bereaved families, declaring that we are a nation 'whose destiny is shaped by its fighters and fallen sons' and that we would continue to move along the road they had helped build, to a secure state, and peace.

Paradoxically, because the rumours had depicted much higher totals, the first reaction to the announcement was one of relief. But the bitterness was there, the deep mourning and horror in every household, not just of those directly affected: a cold gloom settled across the land as people began to evaluate the figures. How many were dead and not yet accounted for? How long would the war continue? How much more could a small country pay in order to survive?

Meir turned to Shoshana. They were both white-faced,

and yet unable to contain the inner feeling of relief that at least their boys were safe.

'It will be all right Shosh. The war can't last much longer.'

There was light music on the TV. They spoke a while, tired from tension but unwilling to go to bed in case they couldn't fall asleep. Mechanically they continued to watch the screen, the adventures of Mannix seeming no more unreal than their own strange world.

Monday, 15th October

They came to call Aliza. Yankele had passed away. He had been identified two days earlier and his parents and younger sister had kept vigil at his bedside ever since. His name really was Yankele – in all the confusion the right name had somehow stuck with him. He was an architecture student at the Technion, and his parents assured Aliza that he was one of the most talented and artistic in his year.

At times it had seemed as though he was going to make it; the wild torments which racked his body died down, and he drifted into a quiet sleep. But the life force dwindled slowly away. He never regained consciousness, and a few minutes before they called Aliza he simply stopped breathing, like a candle blown out by a gentle breeze.

Aliza cried with the family, tears of compassion and love for a boy she had never known.

* * *

Shoshana felt uneasy after Meir left for work. The announcement of the casualties had upset her, and she needed to get out. She picked up her shopping bag and went next door. Shula felt the same way, and they decided to walk to the supermarket in the centre of town, avoiding all the familiar faces with the same questions and depressing rumours.

Only one bright spot had cheered Shoshana up – the army spokesman made a point of announcing that not a single girl soldier had been taken prisoner, and only one had been killed, dying of wounds received during an air-raid in the Sinai at the beginning of the war. At last she could forget about that stupid rumour that had given her so much heartache a few days earlier.

The supermarket was virtually empty. 'Probably they're all shopping at our grocery,' laughed Shoshana. They took their time, walking up and down the aisles, picking up items

155

they didn't really need and putting them back again. The only rationed items were cigarettes because of the huge supply the army was taking, and eggs. The blackout restrictions had obligated the farmers to turn off the lights in the poultry sheds, so the hens were sleeping more and laying fewer eggs.

It was good to be out for a while. They made idle conversation, women's talk about marriage ceremonies being performed near the battle centre, with the grooms getting twenty-four hours' leave, and about all the family announcements which were being broadcast over the army radio.

'I didn't realise how many babies are born every day,' said Shula.

'Have you noticed whether there are more boys than girls?' asked Shoshana, 'you know what they say about more being born in a war.'

Shula knew, but they both decided it was an old wives' tale.

Shoshana asked where one could apply to do volunteer work.

'I've got to get out,' she said. 'I can't even find the patience to bake a cake these days.'

'I know how you feel; there's a Mr Friedman organising volunteer work in Herzliya. I think Meir knows him.'

'Dov Friedman?'

'Yes.'

'I also know him. He's been very good to us. I'll talk to Meir tonight.'

At the checkout counter a high school student helped to wrap their parcels, and they walked slowly home again.

At the entrance to their apartment block Aliza was waiting for Shoshana with a happy smile on her face. 'Shalom,' she said, 'I came to tell you that I saw Uri on Saturday and he's fine and well.'

Shoshana was thrilled and started to ask questions, but restrained herself for a moment to invite Aliza to have tea with them. Aliza accepted gracefully, saying that she wouldn't stay more than a few minutes because she had just come off duty, and was very tired.

When they were seated Aliza explained that she'd received a phone message from an army exchange that Uri was being sent to Tiberias on a military matter and that if she went up to the Lake Hotel as quickly as possible, there was a chance she might see him. Aliza telescoped the meeting into a half-hour cup of coffee stating that Uri had wanted to call them, but just as he got up to do this his officer came back and they had to leave to go back to their base.

'But he's well Mrs Ishboneh, really well. You don't have to worry about him.'

Shoshana smiled. 'Please call me Shoshana. Mrs Ishboneh is too formal.'

'Thank you. I'll try.'

Shoshana asked whether Uri had been involved in any of the fighting, and accepted Aliza's answer that they hadn't had too much time to talk about it. He had seen some fighting at the beginning, but it was relatively quiet now and he thought the war would be over very soon.

'Why didn't you call me yesterday?' asked Shoshana out of curiosity, not intending any rebuke.

'I wanted to come myself because there's bad news about Zeev.' Shoshana turned pale.

'Zeev was killed in action Mrs Ishboneh.' Neither of them noticed that she was again addressing her formally.

'Good God,' said Shoshana, and Shula moved quickly over to her to hold her hand. 'And you're sure Uri is all right?' she couldn't help asking.

'Yes, I'm sure. '

'I suppose Vered knows?' Shoshana continued reacting mechanically, her mind spinning with grief for her son's best friend.

Aliza answered her questions as generally as she could, and then seeing that she was in good hands with Shula, decided that it was time to leave.

'Thank you for coming, Aliza. Please come again. We'd like to see more of you, especially when this horrible nightmare is over.'

'I'll try, Mrs Ishboneh.'

'Shoshana!'

'Shoshana!'

* * *

Meir had gone to work as usual in Chaim's car, and driving through the gates of the factory they were surprised to see for the first time since the war began, one of the two special trucks which brought the Arab workers from Kalkiliya.

Kalkiliya is a large Arab village situated about twelve kilometres from Herzliya. Previous to 1967, it had been a part of Jordan, and because of its proximity to the border, had formed an easy jumping-off place for hit-and-run terrorist raids inside Israel. It had also been the object of reprisal actions, the most spectacular of which had taken place exactly seventeen years earlier when eighteen Israelis were killed and more than fifty wounded in an expensive attempt to teach them a lesson. There was no love lost between the inhabitants on both sides of the border.

In 1967, in the aftermath of the Six Day War, Kalkiliya became part of the 'administered areas' and there was a great deal of apprehension about the possibility of friction and incidents. In practice, largely as a result of Dayan's imaginative policies, normalisation of these areas was achieved within a comparatively short time.

Under the guidance of Israeli experts, and with financial assistance from the Israel government, and a huge new outlet for their produce, Kalkiliya's agriculture blossomed fantastically. Clinics were set up, and medical services vastly improved, the Kfar Saba hospital receiving and treating hundreds of Arab patients a month. The inhabitants of Kalkiliya travelled throughout Israel; sat on the beaches, the men ogling the Israeli girls in their scant bikinis, while their wives noted the freedom of the Israeli women and began exerting pressure to improve their own social position. The workers found good jobs in the labour-hungry Israeli market, and were soon educated in their rights as workers, by the Histadrut, the Israeli trade union movement.

The Israelis did not fool themselves about the inner feelings of the Arabs, their humiliation at the defeat their armies had suffered, and the ignominy of being under Israeli authority. As a fact, however, there was harmony and cooperation, and the pre-1967 hostility of places like Kalkiliya seemed to fade further and further into the background.

At the factory where Meir and Chaim worked, two-thirds of the labour force was made up of Arabs from Kalkiliya, mostly men, but also some women. From the day the war started they had failed to turn up, and production was almost at a standstill. In desperation the factory owner had driven personally to Kalkiliya the day before, to speak to the representatives of the workers and persuade them to return.

'We would like to,' they told him. 'But we are afraid. The Jews will kill us because of what has happened.' The factory owner spent the best part of an hour, drinking innumerable cups of coffee, and arguing and pleading until they promised that they would do their best.

The representatives had managed to persuade about half of the workers to return. They were proved wrong about the Jews wanting to kill them, but the situation was distinctly unpleasant. It hadn't occurred to the factory owner to discuss the matter in advance with his Israeli staff, and their first reaction was one of angry hostility. 'If they work, we don't' was the ultimatum delivered by the works foreman to the astonished factory owner. And again he found himself arguing and pleading, but this time with the Israeli workers.

Reason eventually prevailed, and with apprehension on both sides, they agreed to try working together again. By the end of the day the atmosphere was almost back to normal, but it had not been an easy day for anybody . . .

Meir arrived home about four-thirty in the afternoon. He was tired, but in good spirits.

To his surprise Shoshana wasn't in the kitchen, and the apartment was ominously silent. He found her in the bedroom sitting in the large, old armchair in front of the window. She didn't even turn her head as he entered.

'Shosh, are you asleep?' he whispered.

'No.'

'Well what's the matter?' Meir's heart jumped with apprehension and even more so when she turned and he saw her eyes were red from crying.

'Don't get a fright Meir. Everything's all right. Aliza saw Uri on Saturday, and he's fine – but Zeev is dead.'

He sat down next to her holding her hand and comforting her while she repeated what Aliza had told her. He felt guilty that his own thoughts centred only around Uri, Gadi, and Shoshana. This was the world that he had retreated into. There were tears forming at the back of his eyes, but he knew they were tears of relief that Uri was still alive and well.

* * *

Sitting in the shade of the Zelda, Gadi was enjoying himself going through a batch of three letters which had all caught up with him at once, two from his family, and one from Rina which he read for the second time savouring its sweetness. It had been written the day after his visit – God, was it only a week ago? – the first letter he had ever received from her, warm and serious, expressing her love for him naturally and without reservations.

The three letters together brought back the memory of that day, not just what had happened between the two of them, but the feeling of being home, a hot bath, clean bed, food served on plates, and most of all the happiness of being with those he loved.

The camp was seething with activity. Since early dawn everything on wheels had been moving out in the direction of the Canal. At eight o'clock Bennie came out of the bunker with a group of paratroop officers, and walked over towards them. He carried a batch of papers and was smiling, a sure sign that they were heading for action and that it would not be routine or simple.

'Well fellows, it looks like we'd better get our passports and vaccinations fixed. We're going on a long journey.'

'To Egypt?' they burst out with one voice.

'No. To Africa. At least that's the way they kept referring to it while they were briefing us.'

'Bennie, that's fantastic. When?'

'Today. Hold it with the questions. There's a lot to talk about.'

The men gathered round him and squatted down on the sand. They had talked many times about crossing the Canal, and had no illusions about the dangers or difficulties, but their training over the years had conditioned them to wanting to be where the action was, and their over-riding emotions were those of excitement and pride at being amongst those favoured to participate in what would undoubtedly be the most dramatic operation of the war.

Bennie said a few words confirming their assessment of the importance of the crossing. The officers had been told to brief their men fully so that they would have an exact idea of where they fitted into the picture. They would retain their identity as a special task force, but would be crossing with units of paratroopers and co-ordinating with them, tak-

160

ing special targets and objectives, especially the missile batteries. The assembly point was just behind the hills where their present front line was situated, near the road from Tasa to the Great Bitter Lake. The projected time for moving forward was five o'clock that afternoon, but they would leave Riffidim as soon as possible to give themselves time to organise.

'Now let me go back to the beginning,' he said. 'First of all you know that General Bardan is commanding the crossing operation – it's his baby. He worked out the basic plans three years ago during the War of Attrition when we were contemplating going over and knocking out their missile batteries. The code name of the action is "Chutzpah" which is very appropriate.' The men grinned because the word was also a good description of their General.

Bennie took out a large aerial photograph from his papers. They shifted closer and some of them stood up to get a better view.

'I don't know if any of you recognise this point,' he continued. 'It's near where the Tasa road meets the Canal on the extreme northern tip of the Great Bitter Lake, opposite the Egyptian village and military airfield of Deversoir. By coincidence it happens to be the dividing line between the enemy Third Army which is spread out southwards along the shore of the lake down past Suez, and the Second Army which controls the north up to Ismailia, Kantara and Port Said.

'Now have a look here!' He pointed with his finger and they could plainly identify the long row of artificial earth banks bordering the Canal, about fifteen metres high, which had been constructed by the Israelis to give them cover from sniping and shelling during the War of Attrition.

'Three years ago General Bardan prepared special soft spots where our bulldozers could go in and push the sand away in a minimum of time. He even marked their borders with red bricks so there could be no mistake. This is where we're going to break through, cross over the Canal and establish a beach-head on the other side until we can put up a proper bridge. One of the biggest advantages of this crossing point is that the Great Bitter Lake covers us on the one flank, and we can concentrate on defending ourselves from the north.' Bennie paused for a moment and invited questions. The men were not slow to respond.

'How are we getting across?'

'The paratroopers will move over first on rubber boats with a squad of engineers to clear up any mines. The landing site on the other side is ready for use, because it's one of the places the Egyptians crossed over from when the war started. We'll go across after the paratroopers.'

'How big will the crossing force be?'

'About five hundred troops with half-tracks and Zeldas, a dozen tanks and some mobile guns.'

'That doesn't sound like much.'

'It isn't. We're counting largely on the element of surprise. The last thing they're expecting is a breakthrough in the middle. Our job is to hold the beach-head until the first bridge goes up which should be a matter of about ten hours, and from then onwards we're going to move our forces across as fast as we can.'

'What about the Second and Third Armies? We'll be in range of their guns and artillery.'

'You're right. Hopefully on the first night they'll be concentrating on our forces attacking them on the east side. Our rafts and bridging equipment are moving up after dark, and with luck they won't realise our real objective until we're across in reasonable strength.'

For the moment there were no further questions.

Their Zelda and Jeep were always fully equipped to leave at a moment's notice. They were loading the pup-tents, blankets and personal items when a large helicopter landed near the entrance to the bunker and a group of officers emerged and walked towards it. Catching sight of the General's large frame and white hair, a number of the soldiers gathered round spontaneously applauding and shouting 'good luck'. All the officers climbed into the helicopter and the General waved back at them, wondering wryly at the contrast between his popularity with his men, and his present extremely poor relationship with his own commanding officers.

Bardan had earned a name for himself as a brilliant soldier with a talent for unorthodox tactics and an uncanny ability to judge the fighting quality of his men, inspiring them by his own example, beyond their normal capabilities. He also had a reputation for being strong-willed and insufferably rude to his superior officers, ignoring their orders if he considered them less competent than himself, or less informed about the situation he was confronting. In the 1967 war he had been severely criticised for moving forward against orders to capture a particular position. His commanding officer felt that unnecessary casualties had been incurred, but refused to take disciplinary action against a man whose major fault was that he had too much courage and was too dedicated. The General retired from the army in 1972 and there had been talk of his going into politics in the ranks of the opposition.

Called back on the outbreak of the war to command a division on the Sinai front, he incurred the wrath of top government politicians and officers of the High Command by publicly criticising the unpreparedness of the country for war, and for his loud and characteristically tactless 'I told you so' when the Bar Lev line was over-run.

The General knew that he was putting his future on the line, and he was suspicious that certain 'high-ups' were anxious to ensure that he wasn't too successful. He was convinced that the only way to beat the Egyptians was to smash through to the other side of the Canal. Originally his mind focused only on destroying the missile bases because of the crippling effect they had on Israel's air force. Afterwards by a process of logic he realised the possibilities of cutting off the Second and Third Armies and even threatening Cairo itself. On the fourth day of the war, without authorisation, he tried to break through but his attacks were beaten back with relatively heavy casualties, and he was told in no uncertain terms to prepare defensive positions and to wait for the enemy to make the next move.

In retrospect he was not altogether sorry. The waiting game had enabled Zahal to knock out the Syrians, to a large extent freeing the air force to concentrate its activities on the southern front, and the Egyptians had meanwhile pushed almost all their tanks and men across the Canal, leaving their defence on the west side weak and thinly spread.

Landing at Tasa the General moved straight into the air-raid shelter bunker which would serve as temporary Divisional Headquarters. Checking the radio reports, all his forces seemed to be already in position or moving up on schedule.

Defying the missiles, Israeli planes had carried out heavy saturation bombing raids on both sides of the Canal. Sharp at three o'clock the artillery started its barrage in waves which spread along the entire front, giving the impression of an attack which was escalating rather than planned; and general, rather than concentrated on particular points. In two areas, however, it was powerful and constant, one in the north near Ismailia where a brigade was preparing to make a feint attack on the Egyptian Second Army, and one at the planned crossing point where the barrage grew more and more intense.

At five o'clock, with no more than an hour and a half left of daylight, the brigades in the north and the south, began to move forward; hundreds of M-60 Patton tanks, heavy self-propelled guns and mortars, trucks with batteries of Katyusha rockets, and behind them a miscellaneous group of other vehicles which gave no clue to the true objective of the assault, including armoured ambulances and tanks with 'cherry-picker' arms which raised artillery observers above the battlefield to direct the firing.

Still hiding in the shelter of the hills were the crossing forces, led by General Carmel, bulldozers, tanks with bulldozer blades, and huge trucks carrying the ferry barges. Some of the tanks carried inflated rubber boats for the paratroopers.

Units of engineers, responsible for all the technical details of preparing and fastening the vehicles to the barges were making last-minute checks to see that all was in order. Task force Meron was gathered near the Zelda. The paratroopers were divided into groups, some to cross the Canal, and the rest to support the armoured units pushing the Second and Third Armies apart.

Bennie sat with a friend of his, a lieutenant in the paratroopers listening to him briefing his unit. They had been detailed to capture some buildings in a small village known as the 'Chinese Farm'. Bennie was familiar with the area. It had originally been an experimental settlement, founded by a Japanese group doing research on irrigation methods, using sweet water from the Nile which flowed along irrigation channels through a pipeline running under the Canal to the other side. When it was captured in the 1967 war by the Israelis they found documents written in an Oriental language which was wrongly assumed to be Chinese, and the name had stuck ever since.

The lieutenant showed the men aerial photographs of the village and the particular buildings which they had been assigned to take. He told them that they could expect a few tanks dug in, but that the armoured corps would deal with them, and their job would be to search the buildings, cleaning out snipers or any other occupants. The lieutenant detailed a plan of attack starting with the third building which had two stories and from the roof of which they could control the other buildings. He pointed out that they would be moving on foot over flat sand with no natural cover whatsoever but they didn't expect too much resistance. When the area was in Israeli hands one small tank unit had been used to defend it. The attack would start in darkness, but an almost full moon would rise at eleven-thirty, and it was important to achieve their objective before there was too much light.

By six o'clock General Bardan was more than satisfied. The diversionary brigade in the north was holding the attention of the Second Army; and the main column in the south had swept aside all opposition, reaching the banks of the Canal. It split into two, one brigade moving south along the edge of the Great Bitter Lake, and the other turning north against the Second Army. With the gathering darkness the crossing units were already moving forward.

Within the next hour, however, the General became increasingly aware that things were not going according to plan with the brigade which had turned north. Commanded by Col. Reshon, a daring and efficient commander, it had been divided into three prongs, the left-hand one moving along the side of the Canal and the other two moving up parallel, in between an area of swamps and irrigation ditches towards the Chinese Farm. At first the column along the Canal had moved forward without interference and the enemy seemed to be taken by surprise. Then all hell broke loose and it became clear that they had fallen into a classical ambush from the area of the Chinese Farm. The Intelligence reports had been faulty and unbeknown to the Israelis, the Egyptians had dug themselves in with an enormous number of tanks, mortars and other heavy artillery, which was so well camouflaged that it had not shown up in the aerial photographs.

The enemy waited until the column had passed them, and then opened up a withering fire at its tail-end, cutting off its retreat and blocking the road to the planned crossing point. The two prongs sweeping directly towards the Chinese Farm were also bogged down under heavy fire.

Reshon called for a delay in the moving up of the crossing and bridging groups. He sent a battalion back to try to clear the road and evacuate the wounded. Anti-tank guns, mortars, field guns and missiles, in huge quantities created havoc with the armour. Tank battles took place at a range of thirty metres. In one case a tank commander reported to Reshon that he was so close to an enemy tank that he couldn't traverse his big gun to destroy it. He was ordered to open up with his heavy machine gun at point-blank range, and fortunately the enemy tank's fuel supply was hit and caught fire.

The engagement turned into the fiercest and bloodiest fighting of the war. The paratroop units assigned to support the armour and capture the village found themselves pinned down by murderous mortar fire with shrapnel spraying in all directions. Within a short time of starting their attack they had such severe casualties of killed and wounded, that there was no option but to try to withdraw. Armoured troop carriers sent in to assist were blown to pieces. Eventually the survivors crawled to safety on their stomachs.

While all this was taking place, but already over two hours behind schedule, the crossing party edged its way down towards the Canal, detouring across sand a few hundred metres south, to avoid the heavy shelling from the Chinese Farm which had zeroed in on the road. At the clearing next to the high artificial banks, the engineering corps put the bulldozers to work pushing the sand away. General Bardan had no thought of delaying the crossing. It had to be now while the element of surprise was still in their favour. The moon had risen, and together with the light and smoke from bursting shells and burning vehicles, the clearing was etched in a garish yellow colour as though lit by enormous fog lights.

Reshon called for reinforcements, without which he could not see any hope of subduing the Chinese Farm area that night. Bardan was reluctant to send in Carmel's forces which he was keeping for the crossing. 'Keep going anyway!' he ordered.

Within an hour the bulldozers had pushed the sandbanks away and prepared a track down to the water's edge. Some of the tanks were already in position on top of the high earth banks ready to fire with their heavy machine guns across the water. They were encouraged by the lack of any signs of activity on the other side, but had no way of knowing if it was genuine, or whether an enemy force was waiting in ambush.

Smoke flares were fired on to the west bank and released over the waterway. Huge grey-yellow clouds rose up blocking out visibility on all sides. The first rubber boats containing a group of two hundred paratroopers were pushed into the water and paddled silently across the hundred-metre stretch. The paratroopers fanned out from the bridge-head, digging themselves into defensive positions from where they could cover the landing site. The boats had gone back immediately and more paratroopers arrived, with a unit of engineers who checked for mines and radioed back that the tanks and half-tracks could come ashore directly off the barges.

The tank-dozers had been busy pushing the ferry barges across the soft sand down into the water. The engineers wore life-jackets and, working half in the water and half out, laboriously lashed armoured personnel carriers, one at a time, on to the barges. Task force Meron drove their Zelda across a platform on to one of them, and waited until it was securely fastened. The Jeep was lashed on to a separate barge. Salvos of Katyusha rockets and artillery shells landed with increasing frequency around the clearing damaging some of the bridging equipment which was being assembled, and forcing the engineers to seek shelter. On the edge of the Canal it was still completely quiet, the Egyptians apparently not yet realising that a serious crossing was under way.

Gadi was the first member of the task force to cross, going over with the Jeep, accompanied by eight paratroopers. The number of persons on each craft was strictly limited, to avoid too great a loss if it was hit. On the other side the Jeep was quickly released and Gadi experienced a tremendous thrill as he drove off the boat on to the soil of

Africa. The Zelda arrived shortly after, and the rest of the group shared in his excitement.

Suddenly they heard the sound of loud explosions from only a few hundred yards inland, followed by heavy machine gun fire. 'Looks like we're not going to have it so peaceful after all,' said Bennie.

A few moments later they heard that a force of four enemy tanks had approached the landing area and been ambushed and destroyed with missiles by the paratroopers.

After a short discussion between Bennie and one of the paratroop officers, ten additional paratroopers joined them, and the two vehicles edged their way out of the perimeter of the bridge-head, heading north-west towards a small bridge across an irrigation channel about one and a half kilometres away. Their instructions were to take it over and guard it from damage. The channel was not very wide, but without the bridge it could become a formidable obstacle in holding up the advance of the tanks.

At four o'clock Bardan made his report to Southern Command Headquarters. The fighting around the Chinese Farm continued with unabated fury. The losses already amounted to eighty killed and about two hundred and fifty wounded, many of them the paratroopers who had been sent in to clean up the village. He was ordered to abandon any idea of assembling the bridge that night, and to concentrate all of General Carmel's forces against the Chinese Farm. Those units which had already crossed were to dig in and not attempt to expand the bridge-head, until the farm had been taken and the Second and Third Armies pushed further apart.

Bardan agreed that there was no point trying to get the bridge up, but the bridge-head was a different story and had to be expanded as quickly as possible before the enemy realised what was happening and rushed in defending forces. The argument on the radio became increasingly acrimonious and was picked up by many different units. Bardan's use of four letter epithets didn't help, and eventually losing all patience he told his commanding officer that he should cut off his balls, if he had any, and that he was taking full responsibility for continuing to move troops across.

At five o'clock, when the sky was already a dull gold, General Carmel crossed over with the first tanks. As the craft hit the ground on the other side the fastenings were released and the Pattons lumbered on to the shore, arranging themselves in small units waiting for the signal to move forward.

General Bardan had a shrewd idea of the odds against them, and that depending on the outcome he would be regarded either as a total idiot or a military genius. When the twelfth tank completed the crossing safely, he sent a message to Carmel telling him to carry on and wishing him the best of luck.

Operation 'Chutzpah' was under way!

* * *

I wonder what the old man wants, thought Amos, when he received a message to report immediately to his commanding officer, Colonel Roth. It had been a quiet morning, a routine patrol with no unusual incidents. All the action was on the central and southern sector of the Golan front, east of Kuneitra. The Iraqi forces had been finally smashed, with another thirty tanks and several hundred other vehicles destroyed. The Jordanian troops were rumoured to be moving up to replace them, but there had been no contact as yet.

The colonel received him with a warm smile. 'Your unit's done some good work, Amos.'

Amos's heart leapt with pride; the colonel was not known for passing compliments.

'There's a big entertainment show planned for this afternoon at Ramat Moshe. I don't know how many of your men are fond of classical music, but the Israeli Philharmonic Orchestra will be there with Zubin Mehta, and in any event they might appreciate getting out of here for a couple of hours.'

'That's the understatement of the year,' said Amos, and went off to spread the good news.

By three o'clock they were at the Ramat Moshe Airfield, seated inside a huge aircraft hangar, packed to overflowing with untidy, tough-looking soldiers, most of them unshaven, talking with a relaxed excitement that they had not experienced for what seemed like ages. Floodlights and TV cameras were set up, and the men hoped that those back home would catch a glimpse of them. The chairs for the orchestra were all in place, and the seventy-five musicians received an enthusiastic ovation when they walked in and started tuning their instruments. They were dressed informally in dark trousers and white shirts.

Uri sat next to Amos, not talking, apparently completely at peace with the world. Amos was conscious of the deep bond which had grown up between them, and which had been sealed when he helped Uri to get away for those few hours that he needed so badly. It had to be something connected with his girlfriend, thought Amos, and a mental picture came into his mind of his own Yardena, freckle-faced, upturned nose, boyishly short brown hair.

A Youth Aliyah orphan smuggled into the country at the age of seven, Amos had been adopted by the kibbutz where her family had lived. They had grown up together, childhood sweethearts for as long as he could remember. It was taken for granted that they would get married, but when the time came to arrange the ceremony, Yardena made her position clear. No permanent army. She didn't have to explain why. Her father had been killed at Latrun in the War of Independence, and she wanted her husband beside her at night, not to have to worry whether he was out on an action, or sitting in ambush somewhere for a gang of terrorists.

He had agreed, even though the army was already in his blood, offering him opportunities for personal advancement which the kibbutz could never match – and he had stuck to his bargain. She was the one who went back on it, watching his joyous enthusiasm fade in the routine of farming duties. When Yardena couldn't stand it any more, she told him to go ahead and re-enlist, and in her sacrifice he became aware of her deep love for him.

But the war had had its effect. He knew he wasn't the same person any more. He wasn't afraid, he had proved this to himself many times. But he wanted to be near her, all the time, whenever he wished it, to be able to walk a few hundred metres and know she would be there. He didn't try to analyse why, whether it was some manifestation of his insecurity as a child, but he knew that he had had enough of the army, and that he could make the break now without regret...

A thunder of applause shook Amos out of his reverie.

The musicians were in their places, and Zubin Mehta strode confidently up to the dais. He wore a green Israeli Army shirt, and in a short introductory speech told the soldiers that he was prouder to wear it than any dress-suit he had ever possessed. He introduced another world-famous artiste, the violinist Isaac Stern, who also received a tremendous welcome, and the roof practically flew off when he invited the audience to join them on what he referred to as the 'first engagement of our Syrian Tour'.

Turning to face the orchestra, he allowed a few minutes for the excitement to subside, lifted his baton, and with the first bars of Hatikvah, the whole audience rose and listened to the wondrous music filling the hangar with its haunting melody. It was played with a majestic pride which surpassed any version they had ever heard before, and when the last note died away Isaac Stern wiped the tears from his eyes, and shook Mehta's hand, and the audience sat down moved by emotions and yearnings which no other medium could have evoked. 'That's really soul music for you,' whispered one of the awed soldiers.

The programme consisted mainly of light classical music, and the men responded to each number with deafening applause, which delighted and inspired the musicians. In spite of a generous number of encores the performance ended all too soon, and the soldiers spilled noisily out of the huge building.

Outside the first stars were twinkling in the darkening sky and a cold breeze played refreshingly on their faces, as they boarded their trucks and went back to the war.

Tuesday, 16th October

Shoshana woke up before the alarm clock went off. The news of Zeev's death pressed heavily on her and made her even more determined to get out of the apartment. She brought Meir his cup of coffee and he climbed reluctantly out of the warm blankets, and went to the bathroom to shave. He had slept badly, and his head felt thick and heavy. Reaching for the shaving cream his eyes alighted on a notice which Gadi had stuck on the mirror a few months previously. 'What can you expect from a day that begins with getting up?' In spite of himself he smiled, remembering the boys and the harmless everyday happenings that had been taken so much for granted.

At the breakfast table Shoshana spoke to him about Dov Friedman, and insisted that he come down with her to the emergency headquarters to persuade him to give her an interesting job.

'Do you have any idea as to what you want to do?'

'No, but I know what I don't want to do, and that's to stay at home alone.'

'And what if one of the boys phones?'

'I'm quite sure if nobody answers, they'll phone you at the factory.'

Less than half an hour later they were in the reception room of Dov Friedman's office. It was crowded with would-be volunteers, men and women from all walks of life, elderly people who had passed their prime, new immigrants who had not yet managed to get themselves attached to any army unit, and youngsters from overseas countries who had flown in to 'help wherever it was needed'.

Dov had been one of the first people to befriend Meir when he arrived in Israel and had helped him to find his first job. He was a character in his own right, sharp green eyes with a glint of a smile always at the back of them, contrasting with the deep creases in his face, formed by years of hard work toiling on the land under the unforgiving sun.

More than fifty years previously in the Ukranian village of Zuborska, his father and mother had been pulled out of their beds by raving Cossacks who found it hilariously funny to turn the tall, thin Jewish tailor and his wife into statues of ice. They tied them to a tree and poured tens of buckets of water over their nightclothes in a temperature of thirty degrees below freezing point, after which they set the house on fire and went looking for the next Jewish family. Dov had hidden behind a cupboard and watched, too terrified to utter a sound. Next morning, the twelve-year-old boy set out alone in the frosty dawn, and started his long journey on foot – all the way to the Holy Land.

Dov's wooden shack was one of the first buildings to go up in what later became the town of Herzliya. Now in his mid-sixties, knowing just about everything and everyone who counted in the town, he was ideally suited to organise the massive stream of volunteers.

Jobs available that day included helpers for kindergartens or large families; drivers for transporting military supplies; work in ammunition factories, bakeries, the fire department; loading and unloading shipments of fruit at the wholesale agricultural market, delivering goods such as sugar from government warehouses to retail stores and supermarkets; and filling sand bags for buildings without proper air-raid shelters.

When Shoshana's turn came, Dov greeted them warmly and came straight to the point. 'The best we can offer you Mrs Ishboneh is to help at the stall opposite the Sports Club, serving sandwiches and cold drinks to the soldiers. Do you think you could do that?'

'Yes, of course!'

'All right. You'll work a four-hour shift.' He motioned to one of his helpers, 'Yaffa will arrange all the details with you. Thank you and good luck.'

Ten minutes later they left the building. Shoshana's first tour of duty was set for one o'clock that afternoon. In a happy state of mind she walked with Meir to the bus-stop, and waited with him until he caught a bus to work.

*　　*　　*

Task force Meron picked its way at a walking pace towards the bridge, the paratroopers spreading out on both sides of the road, moving silently through a grove of high trees which towered above them, shutting out the bright moonlight.

Behind them, they were aware of the continual boom and thunder of rockets and shells exploding, and the noise echoing and re-echoing across the ground. Already, however, it seemed to come from a different world, and the relative quietness around them added to the eerie tension of not knowing whether the enemy was off-guard, or sitting silently in ambush, waiting for them to walk into his trap.

Gadi was driving the Jeep, Bennie stood in the turret of the Zelda scanning the darkness through his night-binoculars. A short distance from their objective they stopped and waited, while the paratroopers edged their way to the bridge.

Twenty minutes later a radio message came through to move forward. Two Egyptians had been found next to the bridge, one guarding it and one asleep. Both were killed before they knew what was happening.

The two vehicles were concealed under low trees in a position commanding the bridge. Two men were placed on guard, one on each side, and the rest were told to get some sleep while they could.

Less than an hour later they were woken by urgent whispers. Two faint lights were approaching from the north. Silently they took cover, leaving the bridge area clear. Four of the paratroopers crossed over with a Bazooka, taking up a position well off the road. Bennie climbed into the Zelda swivelling the heavy machine gun around until it pointed straight down the line of the bridge. Their hearts beat faster as they listened to the noise of the engines growing louder, and watched the dimmed headlights draw closer.

From a short distance away the bright moonlight silhouetted two trucks, and the red glow of cigarettes pin-pointed the black shapes of a number of men sitting in the rear, talking in loud voices.

The first vehicle approached and as it reached the bridge a Bazooka shell tore into the rear truck lifting it up in the air with a tremendous explosion. Bennie immediately opened fire on the lead truck and in an instant the driver's cabin was wrecked and the engine burst into flames. The rest of the

174

task force sprayed both trucks mercilessly, mowing down the Egyptians as they frantically tried to escape. Within moments the action was over. There were no enemy survivors.

Bullets and shells in the burning vehicles started to explode, and on Bennie's order they withdrew to a safe distance. There was no more thought of sleep, and taking out their battle rations, they ate a snap breakfast of sardines and cheese.

Dawn broke, and as the sky lightened, even the least poetic of the men were moved by the lush green of the countryside, in contrast to the desert they had just left. Near them rose huge date palms and a grove of old olive trees. An enormous mango plantation lay south of them; and over the bridge, fields of spinach and green corn stretched to the north.

Their enjoyment of the pastoral scene was shortlived. With a tremendous roar, Egyptian Migs came diving in at the crossing-point shooting their rockets at the bridgehead and the forces threatening the Chinese Farm. It was the first time since the opening day of the war that they had attacked in such numbers. Within seconds Israeli Mirages came to meet them, exploiting their knowledge that as long as enemy planes were in the sky the missiles would not be released. The Egyptians had not yet found a way of co-ordinating their firing to ensure that they didn't shoot down their own planes by mistake. At one stage more than forty planes could be seen. Six or seven spiralled down in flames, three of the pilots successfully bailing out and floating earthwards under their white parachutes.

Three Patton tanks came down the road to link up with the task force for its next objective, a large Sam missile battery two kilometres further north. Four of the paratroopers equipped with Bazookas and light machine guns were left to guard the bridge.

Bennie was in command of the operation. Moving forward cautiously over the bridge and along a road parallel to the Canal, he checked their position carefully on his map, and referred also to aerial photographs of the area. The site was fairly obvious, an enormous circular emplacement with the usual radar and scanner installations projecting from its centre. On the outside circle, half-submerged in protective trenches, the long missiles could be seen pointing skywards from their launchers.

The tanks moved ahead in single file about thirty metres apart, sticking to the road, which was narrow but had a good asphalt base. Gadi followed about fifty metres behind the tanks, and the Zelda brought up the rear.

Suddenly, without any warning they came under fire from two Egyptian tanks. The Israeli vehicles immediately deployed off the road, and a sharp battle ensued in which the enemy tanks were quickly destroyed.

The convoy resumed its journey, and at a point where they were still out of sight of their objective, Bennie sent two paratroopers forward to reconnoitre. They returned somewhat mystified. They had found the site easily enough, but from the outside had not been able to detect any signs of life.

Bennie decided to strike swiftly. He gave the order and the tanks charged down the road at full speed. The emplacement itself was not far from the road, on a flat plain, and the tanks swerved towards it in the shape of an arrow-head, with the Zelda not too far behind and the Jeep keeping close to the Zelda for protection. They raced towards the open entrance, going right through with their machine guns spewing fire in all directions, but there was no return fire. Bewildered, Bennie gave instructions to halt.

He then took a good look around him and burst out laughing. The others were not slow to join in. They were in the middle of six dummy missile launching pads, with long wooden missiles stretching ominously, but impotently, skywards, and in between them a large counterfeit radar installation. The Egyptians had fooled them.

Bennie reported back to headquarters and received orders to proceed to the next objective, another missile battery a kilometre away. Apparently the dummy was designed to mislead Israeli aircraft into attacking it, making themselves an easy target for the real missiles further north.

On their left the desert had reasserted itself and the dunes and ridges seemed to stretch endlessly away. Somewhere south of them a larger force was moving forward to capture the airfield at Deversoir. On their right on the other side of the Canal they could hear the battle raging in the Chinese Farm area. The road they were travelling was lined with bunkers facing towards the east, designed without any thought that a force might come from behind. They were deserted, their occupants probably having moved across the Canal, with the Second Army.

The road passed through a small village. It seemed to be totally deserted, but they proceeded cautiously, the vehicles going through one by one under the cover of those remaining. One ramshackle building looked like the local grocery, with wooden panelling on the outside of the door, and a faded mural showing Nasser framed by olive branches with a white dove of peace hovering near his head.

Approaching the missile site, two of the paratroopers again went forward. This time they returned with a report that there was a lot of activity outside the battery; half a dozen trucks and about thirty soldiers, who seemed to be moving normally, oblivious to the possibility of any danger.

Bennie's instructions were to try to capture missiles intact and he again decided to storm the position and rely on surprise. The result was a massacre. The few seconds notice that the enemy had, wasn't enough to allow them to do more than run for their guns. The tanks swept in, their heavy machine guns mowing down everything in sight. By the time Gadi pulled up in the Jeep, it was all over. Tens of Egyptian soldiers lay sprawled on the ground, a few as if they were peacefully asleep, but most in horrible unnatural positions, with blood all over them, dripping dark red in pools on the ground. Looking at the sight he felt nauseous, and began trembling.

Subconsciously he moved over to Bennie and stood there white-faced, feeling that being close to him would help him to retain his self-control. Bennie was reporting back to Headquarters and asking permission to move on again. He looked up from his map and saw Gadi was upset.

'You look like I feel,' he said, drawing a weak smile from Gadi and breaking the tension ...

* * *

At ten o'clock General Bardan ordered the engineers to commence building the bridge. He had received a report from General Carmel detailing the capture of some of the highly-advanced Russian bridging trucks. These carried special interlocking pontoons which could be lowered into place using hydraulic power. The truck then backed out allowing the next vehicle to drive across and lower an additional pontoon. A pity we don't have equipment like that, Bardan mused.

He was wearing a blood-stained dirty bandage around his forehead. A few hours earlier he had stood on a ridge between the clearing and the Chinese Farm, chilled by the scene of destruction that confronted him. Twenty-three wrecked Patton tanks lay muzzle to muzzle with Egyptian tanks, their guns intermingled in a kiss of death. Around them were scores of burnt-out vehicles, and corpses blackened from the fire that must have enveloped them as they tried to escape, screaming in agony.

Bardan did not often let his thoughts dwell on such matters, but in the unreal softness of the early desert morning, it held him like a modern painting bordered with beige squares and a blue sky, and in the centre patches of red and black leaping from the frame in an orgy of violence and cruelty.

He turned around and climbed back towards the clearing. At the same instant a mortar exploded about thirty metres away, and suddenly he couldn't see. A splinter had creased his forehead so lightly that he didn't even realise he was wounded, until the blood flowed into his eyes.

He hadn't slept for more than twenty-four hours, but he was buoyed up by the growing number of successes reported by Carmel. Six missile sites had been knocked out, creating an already reasonably wide corridor for the air force. Fifteen Egyptian planes had been shot down in the early morning and their air force had apparently retired for the day to lick its wounds. Now the Israeli planes could concentrate increasingly on supporting the ground forces.

He remembered one of his conversations with Carmel when the question was raised of the relatively small force that would be moved across the Canal before the bridge came into operation. 'If they really move in strength against us, we'll be wiped out in no time,' Carmel had said, referring to the possibility of the Second and Third Armies rushing some of their forces back across the Canal to mount a counter-attack.

'You idiot,' Bardan had replied, with Carmel not even noticing this relatively mild form of address, 'can't you see that our advantage lies in the relative insignificance of our forces? The Second and Third Armies are too inflexible to think in terms of pulling back, unless they are confronted by a gigantic threat. They'll assume that the First Army around Cairo can deal with our small "search-and-destroy" units. It should take at least thirty-six hours for their chain of command to wake up to what has happened and start organising their defences.'

The Chinese Farm which had come close to frustrating the entire operation had not yet been knocked out, but Reshon's main battalion had fought its way up the side of the Canal, and was now attempting to move east again, to cut off the Farm from the Second Army and effectively surround it. The resistance seemed to be lessening and Bardan hoped that the Chinese Farm would be subdued within a few hours. In the South the Third Army had been pushed back about eight kilometres towards Suez, and when the Farm was eliminated the wedge between the two Egyptian Armies would be fifteen kilometres wide.

The General had just decided that it was a good time to snatch a cat-nap, when disturbing reports started to come through. Both the Second and Third Armies were launching massive counter-attacks. Using the same tactics as they had at the beginning of the war – wave upon wave of infantry preceded the Egyptian tanks, advancing under the cover of a heavy artillery barrage, digging themselves in, firing their wire-guided Sagger missiles, and then advancing again. In the midst of trying to cope with their ferocious onslaught, the Israeli tank commanders were astounded and appalled by the reckless indifference to life of the Egyptian forces. Hundreds of men were cut down, especially round the Chinese Farm area, where they tried desperately to reinforce and prevent it from being encircled.

The Israeli forces were thrown back on both sides; the crossing area was subjected to a murderous bombardment, and for a while General Bardan had visions of a complete catastrophe with the two enemy armies linking up again, trapping all of Carmel's forces on the West Bank.

As if sensing victory the Egyptian air force swung back into action, and the Israeli Skyhawks which had been working with the armour were replaced by Phantoms and Mirages zooming in to engage the enemy Migs and shooting them down with merciless efficiency.

The battle continued with unabated fury, rockets and shells exploding ceaselessly. The Egyptians made truly heroic efforts but the Israeli tanks and infantry hung grimly on. Eventually the pressure began to slacken and in the late afternoon when the final reports were brought to Bardan, he commented with grim satisfaction, 'That brings the total to three hundred and sixty tanks – enough to keep a Russian factory working full-time for the next three years.'

Throughout the tremendous clash the engineers had continued to work on the bridge, and in spite of delays caused by damage and heavy casualties it was almost completed. An hour later General Bardan stood proudly erect in the turret of the first tank to rumble over the bridge into 'Africa'.

* * *

Aliza had been assigned an additional responsibility at the hospital. A half-dozen Syrian prisoners with severe burns had been transferred to Kfar Saba for specialised treatment. They were all in one ward, with a guard on duty, although they were hardly in a condition to cause any trouble.

Aliza had never had any difficulty with the hundreds of Arabs who came to Kfar Saba for treatment, but these were different. These were enemy Arabs, the ones who had caused the terrible injuries to 'her boys' in the other wards. Even with her training and background she needed to reason consciously that Syrian and Egyptian nurses were facing the same conflict of feelings with their prisoners of war, and that this was simply one of the accepted disciplines of their profession.

She faced a real problem, however, in winning over the voluntary helpers, young high-school girls, who were in a mild state of shock at having been assigned to the 'Arab ward'. Aliza spoke to them quietly, and took each one through the ward, doing their tasks together on their first round.

One of the girls told her afterwards – 'It was weird. At first I just did everything mechanically, trying not even to look at them . . . then I noticed the one next to the window . . . he couldn't speak, but he was signalling with his hand and I realised he wanted some water . . . something inside me made me want to ignore him . . . not to give him any . . .

I felt revolted and confused, but I took a glass to him, and helped him hold his hand steady while he sipped it . . . and then I could see his eyes looking at me, and they were filled with such gratitude, that I felt terrible because of what I had been thinking . . . And I realised that for the first time I was looking at him as a person, a human being suffering and in need of help . . . '

*   *   *

It was a strange feeling for Meir to return to an empty apartment, but he had the excitement and relief of finding a postcard from Gadi thanking them for the chocolate cake in the first parcel they had sent him. It was dated October twelfth and Meir's mind did a careful check-back on the events which had happened since then in Sinai. It didn't help very much, but at least Gadi was alive and well up to the previous Friday. It was like playing a children's game with dice and markers. The postcard enabled him to move Gadi's marker a few squares forward and it would be another day or two before the tension mounted again.

He made himself a cup of tea, and settled down in a chair on the balcony with his copy of *Maariv*. The *Uj Kelet* was easier for him but the afternoon paper was more up to date, and its news reports more detailed. For the last few days he had been buying it and labouring over the relatively difficult Hebrew.

The major headline reported heavy Syrian counter-attacks in the vicinity of Mount Hermon, but no details were yet available. In Sinai the position was static, except for a determined Egyptian attack on the only Israeli strong-hold still holding out on the Bar Lev line. Situated near the northern end of the Suez Canal, it was connected with the Israeli front-line by a road running along a narrow strip between the sea and perilous salt marshes. The Egyptians sent in a commando force to ambush a relieving Israeli convoy, and simultaneously attacked the outpost with artillery, tanks and infantry. The attack was beaten off with heavy enemy casualties, at least thirty Egyptians killed and more than sixty taken prisoner.

Most of the front page was taken up by a detailed description of the United States airlift which had started thirty hours before, but was now acknowledged officially. The State Department's chief spokesman on the Middle East crisis, Ambassador Robert McCloskey stated that this was a response to the massive Russian effort of two hundred and eighty flights in the last six days, delivering more than four thousand tons of equipment to Egypt and Syria. In addition Russian ships had been arriving at the Syrian port of Latakia carrying planes and tanks and missiles.

The Israeli spokesman confirmed that United States C5A Galaxies, the world's largest military transport plane, 'loaded with everything one needed for war' were landing one after the other at an Israeli air base, and that United States Ambassador Kenneth Keating had driven down there to take a look. An Israeli cargo ship, the Aben Dat, had sailed from a Virginia port laden with bombs and with three Skyhawks strapped to its deck. And reliable sources stated that Phantoms and other planes were being withdrawn from US units and flown direct to Israel.

We don't have many friends left in the world, thought Meir, but thank goodness the United States is one of them.

Also on the front page, was an item which Meir read without too much attention. It was a brief account of the death of an Israeli news-reporter who had been travelling on the Golan Heights with two German magazine photographers and a British Foreign Correspondent, Mr Robert Crawford. They had hired a private car, and been given a permit to tour anywhere within the old 1967 lines. Not suspecting any danger, they stopped at one point to get an interesting shot, the three visitors climbing out, leaving the Israeli at the wheel. Suddenly, like a bolt from the blue, a missile hit the car, killing the Israeli instantly. Mr Crawford was reported to have been seriously wounded and was flown by helicopter to Tel Hashomer Hospital. The two photographers were unhurt. The Army spokesman referred to the tremendous pressure from newsmen to get as close to the firing line as possible and expressed regret at the incident.

Feeling sleepy from the sustained effort of reading so much Hebrew, Meir dozed off, and it was nearly dark when he was awakened by Shoshana letting herself into the apartment.

She was bubbling over with good spirits, and the postcard from Gadi about how much he had enjoyed her chocolate cake, made her day complete. She fussed over Meir's dinner telling him about the work and the people who were helping and how much the soldiers appreciated what they were doing. After dinner she sat down to write to the boys, Meir switched on the TV and a few minutes later Chaim, Shula and Eitan came in to join them. During the afternoon Golda Meir had spoken at a special session of Parliament, and they were all anxious to hear the details.

The session started with all members standing and observing a two minutes silence in mourning for the fallen, after which the Prime Minister began her report. The TV camera moved close up to her, revealing clearly the lines on her care-worn face, but the watching audience was relieved at the strength and confidence that she projected.

'This is the best she's looked since the beginning of the war,' said Shoshana.

Mrs Meir's report ranged over a wide canvas. She stated that on the Syrian front the aggressors had been pushed back across the cease-fire lines, and on the southern front the indications were that the enemy's initiative had been curbed.

Without a change of expression she went on to announce that at that very moment an Israeli force was operating on the west side of the Canal and tantalisingly added that naturally she could not be expected to give details at this stage. It was done so casually that those listening had to mentally pinch themselves to make sure that they had heard right.

Mrs Meir was already well into her next topic, thanking the United States for the support it had given Israel to defend its existence and repel its attackers. In contrast she censured both Britain and France for their arms embargos, which she described as 'cynical and immoral acts by supposedly enlightened nations' for their own ends.

'If individuals did what they're doing, it would be called prostitution,' interjected Chaim bitterly.

Dealing with the question of a cease-fire the Premier was of the opinion that the Arabs were not yet ready for it. She was quite sure that when Israel brought them to the verge of collapse there would be no shortage of states 'volunteering' to save them by means of a cease-fire. She dealt with the role of world Jewry indicating the tremendous material

183

help, and the importance of the emotional and spiritual comfort which the people of Israel derived from the solidarity of their support.

She also singled out the identification with the State shown by Israel's Arab citizens. 'Offers of voluntary help have come from all communities and strata, from distant villages in the north to the Bedouin encampments in the south. They have provided manpower for vital work, given blood, and donations and subscriptions to the Voluntary War Loan. This was a tremendously encouraging omen for the future.'

Mrs Meir received a sincere ovation from the House when she finished.

General Dayan was conspicuous by his absence from the session and as they didn't feel like listening to any other speaker they turned off the set.

The two men went out for a short walk before turning in. They discussed the force on the west side of the Canal, speculated about its significance, and how large it was, and how it had been taken across. Whatever it was, they reasoned, it had to be good for Israel. Meir found himself worrying whether Gadi was with those who had gone across, but he said nothing to Chaim.

It was a perfect night; the complete blackout enhanced the brilliance of the moon and the stars, imparting a soft velvet beauty which was normally lost in the bright lights of the streets and surrounding buildings.

'Maybe when there's peace again we should have a blackout once a month or so,' said Chaim, 'just to remind us how lovely darkness can be.'

'Not for me,' replied Meir, 'I can't wait to go around putting on lights all over the place and not care whether they show outside or not. I never want to see another blackout.'

* * *

Two hundred kilometres north, the air was much cooler, but the same beautiful moon and stars shone over Mazrat Beit Jinn. The village echoed to the shouts and laughter of delighted Syrian soldiers celebrating its recapture. Next to one cottage five men stood shivering in their underclothes,

184

aching with the pain of their bruises and open wounds, and wondering numbly how soon their guards would carry out their loud jeering threats to shoot them . . .

Early that morning while it was still pitch dark, a thousand soldiers from Assad's guard, an elite infantry division had been brought up to within a few kilometres of the village, and made their way silently through the forest on foot. At four o'clock, a large force of tanks moved forward picking its way through the trees, and at dawn they launched their assault.

The battle for Mazrat Beit Jinn was only part of a tremendous counter-attack by the Syrians along the entire northern front down to Tel Shams, involving planes, tanks, heavy artillery, and thousands of well-armed infantry.

The Israeli Army had known an attack was pending, but had not anticipated the tremendous weight of armour and men that the enemy threw into battle at this point. The Israeli tanks were heavily outnumbered, and fighting in the forest made it difficult to keep track of what was happening. At one spot a Syrian tank emerged from the woods ten metres from an Israeli tank, surprising both commanders equally. The Syrian tank fired first – and missed. The Israeli tank made full use of its opportunity and hit its target full on, completely destroying it.

The enemy attack was so fierce, and its infantry thrown in with such reckless abandon, that the defenders were pushed back and the village abandoned. During the day the Israeli armour counter-attacked, advancing in some places, with their infantry backing them up; but with the mounting intensity of the battle, they were forced to fall back again to keep their line intact. In the confusion one of the supporting infantry units was cut off and surrounded by the Syrians . . .

Colonel Roth was sitting in his new temporary Headquarters at Charpa, writing his report on the day's fighting. Of the hundred-and-five Syrian tanks destroyed across the entire northern front, forty had been accounted for in his sector. Hundreds of enemy soldiers had been killed and twenty-four taken prisoner. Of the ten Syrian planes shot down, two had actually fallen victim to machine gun fire from his half-tracks. It was a good record by any standards, but the Colonel shuddered and found it hard to concentrate.

It wasn't the effect of his being forced to pull back from Mazrat Beit Jinn, or even the five men killed and eighteen wounded. He was a professional soldier and had learned to accept reverses and casualties as an inevitable part of war. What he had never been able to get used to, however, was the notoriously cruel and barbaric treatment by the Syrians, of prisoners unlucky enough to fall into their hands. It was the fate of the men he didn't know about, that was upsetting him.

Slowly he wrote: 'According to a report by Sergeant Avner Levy, the three vehicles in their unit were cut off during the fighting. They evacuated them and he was ordered to lead the men back through the forest to their lines. Five stayed behind to cover the retreat, the commander, Lieutenant Amos Perry; the second-in-command, Sergeant Uri Ishboneh; and Privates Yitzchak Mizrachi, Zelig Weiss, and Mokkie Porat. Their ammunition was limited and they could not have held out for long. There is a fair chance that they have been taken prisoner.'

Wednesday/Thursday, 17th/18th October

As soon as he awoke Meir turned the radio on, but was disappointed that only passing reference was made to the Israeli forces operating across the Canal. Golda Meir's speech was reported in detail. Also a speech by the Egyptian President, Anwar Sadat, in which he claimed that the Egyptian armed forces had performed a miracle by any standards; that they had missiles ready to launch into Israel's depths, and that they would continue fighting until they liberated all the land seized by the Israelis in 1967 and restored the legitimate rights of the Palestinian people.

The speech bothered Meir. It didn't sound like a man under pressure. He wondered if they were hearing all the news, or if the government was holding back unfavourable information like it had done in the first few days of the war.

Shoshana left the apartment before Meir. She had asked for a morning shift, and was picked up by a fellow-worker at six-thirty. Meir had the unusual experience of preparing his own breakfast, and leaving from an empty flat. It didn't bother him, as long as Shoshana's mind was occupied and she had no time to brood about the boys. They had an un-written understanding not to talk about them too much, not to wonder aloud what they were doing, or to comment on how many days it had been since they heard from them.

Meir had always regarded himself as a complacent person. The experiences he had been through had been so shattering that he had developed reflexes to insulate himself from the world and to avoid being involved or affected by anything.

The war swept all these defence mechanisms aside, leav-ing him helpless and vulnerable. Thoughts of the boys in-truded more and more into his mind, cold frightening thoughts which wrapped themselves around his heart with bands of steel. It needed a special concentration to push the terrifying images away. Sometimes he lacked the strength, and he would feel his limbs and then his body begin to shiver and a cold sweat break out on his brow. Always there was the connection of fear and cold, the physical symptoms of his day-time nightmares.

He knew that if he was feeling the pressure so strongly, Shoshana must be suffering unbearably, because she was a far more emotional person. He hadn't given her credit for having the strength to control herself, and he wanted desperately to reach out and tell her that he understood what she was going through, and to try to some extent to lessen her burden. But there was no way. He was afraid that if they discussed the subject he would not be able to stop himself from confessing all his own fears and premonitions, and that this would probably break her completely. No, it was better to wait, and say nothing.

Meir knocked on Chaim's door and arranged to be picked up at the news stand. He was just in time to buy the last copy of *Uj Kelet*. All the papers had been snapped up by people anxious to know what was happening on the west bank of the Canal and they were all equally frustrated by the lack of details.

Chaim arrived and they drove down to the factory. Meir got busy with a file of papers, thankful for a chance to concentrate on mechanical, impersonal things, and not leave his mind free to wander around in circles worrying about the boys ...

At lunch-time they were eating sandwiches in the canteen when Shula phoned to tell Chaim that Danny would be home later that afternoon. She had already told Shoshana that she expected the two of them for dinner that evening. Greatly excited, Chaim shouted out the good news to Meir, adding that maybe at last they might learn something about the war.

* * *

Meir came home early with Chaim, who wanted to be sure of being there when Danny arrived. He and Shoshana sat on the balcony talking, mostly about little incidents that had happened to her on her morning shift. Meir sensed that she was uneasy.

'Are you worried about tonight?' he asked.

'A little.'

'Would you rather not go?'

'It's difficult. I want to see Danny, and to join in their happiness, but I hope I won't get upset thinking about the boys. We can't not go.'

'I know how you feel. Just a few more days Shosh. It can't be long now.'

They were silent.

On the sidewalk outside, family groups were walking towards the Shul, mostly with small children, beautifully dressed. It was the evening of Simhat Tora, the festival to celebrate the reading of the last passage of the sacred scrolls, and of the first passage for the coming year.

There would be special prayers and 'hakafot' the traditional festive dances circling around the Shul, led by the Rabbi bearing the scrolls high above his head, with the members of the congregation and children waving flags moving in a procession behind him. Those who were nearest, would kiss their prayer shawls and brush them against the scrolls as the dancers passed by. Usually there were mass outdoor celebrations, especially in religious areas, but this year the blackout interfered, and as many Shuls had not had their windows papered over, even indoor services and celebrations were starting early.

At four-thirty a small army car pulled up outside, and Danny jumped out, looking very smart in his blue air force uniform. He had never been demonstrative, but he hugged them all, with a warmth which was completely natural. Looking at him carefully they could see no physical change. He was a tall thin youngster, who looked older than his twenty-five years, probably because his hair-line receded slightly.

'Well, Danny,' said Chaim proudly, 'we've been waiting for you to come home, so that we can get some reliable information on the war.'

'There's not much to tell, Dad. It's going pretty well now, and there's really nothing to worry about.'

Even Meir was irritated by the patronising way in which Danny had spoken. Chaim's face paled slightly and his eyes narrowed, but he said nothing. Only Meir knew how angry he was.

They went back upstairs, Meir and Shoshana promising

to be on time for dinner, and the Singer family entered their apartment. Shula hugged Danny again, and then at a signal from Chaim, went into the kitchen, and called out to Eitan that she had lots to do and needed his help.

When they were gone Chaim turned to his son, trying to keep his voice under control.

'I don't know how well you know me Danny, and I'm beginning to worry how well I know you. Maybe we've lost touch with each other these past five years, I don't know whose fault it is, and it's not worth trying to find out. I ask you seriously to tell me about the war, and you talk down at me as though it's a subject that I can't be entrusted with any kind of answer ... I remember when you were six years old, and frightened of something. You took my hand and asked what was happening, and I answered, "It'll be all right son, don't worry", because you could not have comprehended any explanation. But I'm not six years old, and I object to being treated this way ... Now you're not talking on the telephone from your base, nor is your mother around to panic. I'm feeling completely out of the picture. It's important to me to know what is happening, and I also want to know about you. You do happen to be my son and I want to know what you've been through. I don't care if it's bad. I just want to know.'

Danny was taken aback. His father had never before spoken to him like this, and he could feel the intensity of his hurt and anger. But for years security had been drummed into him at every level. He wanted to clam up, but instinctively he knew that it had become a test of whether his father was still a man, or a useless non-person who no longer fitted into the pattern of events which had overtaken them.

'You're not being fair, Dad,' he said defensively. 'You know we're not supposed to talk, not to anybody, including our fathers, but if you feel so strongly I'll tell you whatever I can. I prefer to talk to you, I'm quite sure you're not going to repeat it to anybody else.'

Chaim relaxed. He got up and and fetched a bottle of cognac, poured out a tot for each of them, and they drank 'to life'.

'You must have been through a rough time Danny, have you been very scared?'

'No. Not nearly as much as I expected to be.' Danny

spoke slowly, trying to recollect how it had been. It seemed as if it was ages ago.

'On the first Saturday morning it was a bit nerve racking when they briefed us, and we sat around waiting for a couple of hours, but as soon as I was strapped into the plane I felt better. We have to concentrate very hard when we take off, because the planes are loaded to their maximum capacity with bombs and fuel, and there's just no room for other thoughts. They opened fire at two o'clock that day, and at two twenty-six I was over the Golan, attacking one of the Syrian armoured columns . . . From then onwards it was sheer hard work – returning from a mission – de-briefing – being briefed again for the next mission – taking off again – incredible tension, but all the time a realisation that we were working exactly as we had been trained to work. I was afraid, but the fear was something right at the back of my mind, something that I could control, and if it affected me in any way, it was only to make me concentrate harder, to make sure that I didn't overlook anything, not to be off-guard even for a second . . . I think my first bad moment – my worst actually – came on the fourth day, Tuesday after-noon, when Morris was killed . . .'

'Morris Binder?' asked Chaim, shocked, the two boys had done all their training together and were best friends.

'Yes,' Danny continued. 'I felt terrible when his plane didn't come back and they said there was no hope for him. I didn't believe it possible. Luckily they didn't give me time to think. I was sent up straight away, and I remember the strange feeling as I taxied down the runway, as though I was physically pushing all thought of Morris out of my mind. It's bothered me since then, but only when I'm on the ground . . .'

Chaim watched him intently as he spoke, trying to grasp something of the pain Danny must have suffered. He felt a deep pride well up inside him, not only for his son, but for all the young men that he represented.

'Do all the pilots manage to control themselves so well?' he asked rhetorically, and then continued, 'do you think it's because of your training, or because you're all selected so carefully?'

'I don't know, Dad. I'm not sure how the others feel, whether or not they really are afraid. We don't discuss it.

Our training must help, but mostly I think it's a question of "no choice". We know we're Israel's front-line, that it depends on us, and we just can't afford to be afraid . . . I don't know quite how to explain it to you, but sometimes when I'm flying very high and I look down, I can see the entire country from one border to another. It's so beautiful and so small – I get a kind of protective feeling about it, as though it really needs me.' Danny stopped for a moment, a little embarrassed, he wasn't used to expressing himself so openly.

Changing the subject Chaim asked about the missiles, how bad they were and why they weren't better prepared for them.

'The missiles were a very ugly surprise. We were prepared, but not for the incredible quantities in which they were used. At first we accepted the fact we'd lose a lot of planes initially, but that pretty soon they'd run short of missiles. Only afterwards we realised that the Russian airlift was bringing them in faster than they could use them – especially the Sam 6's, they're the ones that did most of the damage.'

'Why is that?'

'Well, it's a new missile that's never been used before and we had no effective counter-measure for it.'

'Do we have one now?'

'No. It's a beautiful missile actually, very simple and very efficient. It works on about four different frequencies which we don't know, so we haven't been able to jam it yet. It also has a built-in heat-seeking guidance system, and the problem is they don't fire one at a time, but salvoes of three or four or more as if they were as cheap as rifle bullets. You dodge one, and another hits you. Or, if you manage to dive away they are almost always positioned near the new Russian 23 mm. anti-aircraft cannons which are just as dangerous. That's how Morris got killed. He was warned that a Sam 6 had been fired, and went into a steep dive straight into a barrage of anti-aircraft shells.'

'Isn't there any solution? You make it sound as though our pilots don't have a chance.'

'No. It's not as bad as that. On the Golan where the situation was desperate in the first few days we had no choice but to attack the batteries. We lost a lot of planes, more than we could afford, but we also learned quite a lot.

We knocked out fifty per cent of the Syrian batteries in the first three days, and the rest all pulled back to protect Damascus.'

'How many planes have we lost Danny? The Arabs say they've shot down six hundred and eighty.'

Danny laughed. 'We started the war with a lot less than that, so they've done pretty well. I can't give you an exact figure, but our losses are less than a hundred, and if it makes you feel any better, now that most of the missile sites have been eliminated, they've dropped to an absolute fraction of what they were in the first three days. I know it sounds unbelievable, but we've lost only three planes in dog-fights, as against about three hundred of theirs.'

'It's unbelievable. It sounds as good as in the Six Day War.'

'Are you kidding? Our record's much better. In 1967 for every hundred sorties four planes failed to return. Even allowing for the missiles our losses are down to one in a hundred sorties.'

'Incredible. I had no idea. I thought that 1967 could never be improved upon . . . I'm not sorry we've had this talk.'

'Me neither. As a matter of fact I'm very glad. I'm really sorry that I upset you, the way I spoke when I came in.'

Chaim wanted to take his son and hug him close to him. He felt a warmth and intimacy which he had not experienced, possibly since the day of Danny's Barmitzvah.

'Thanks Danny. I've only got a few more questions.'

'Go ahead. We're not in any rush.'

'What's the position now? Are we really close to finishing the war?'

'The Golan is practically finished already. Apart from the military losses, we've hurt them badly economically, their oil refinery, storage tanks, port facilities, bridges, radio station, power station – you name it, and we've hit it – this time the Syrians have really had a taste of what war can be like.'

'And Egypt?'

'We're working very hard. We put in a tremendous effort assisting the crossing, and now they've knocked out enough missile sites to make life much easier for us. We're punishing the Egyptians to such an extent that most of us don't believe they can last for more than another couple of days.'

Chaim sat silent, digesting the significance of what he'd heard. 'I hope you're right Danny. I don't know how much longer we can stand it either. I think there's only one more question I wanted to ask . . . '

'How many planes I've shot down?'

'You'd make a good mind reader.'

'None so far. The Skyhawk's not a very fast plane and we try to avoid getting into dogfights.'

'Thanks Danny. I'm sorry I lost my temper with you.'

'I understand Dad. I'm glad you did, otherwise for sure we wouldn't have had this talk.'

Chaim called the others in and Shula again put her arms around Danny and hugged him. A few moments later the front door buzzer sounded, and Meir and Shoshana arrived carrying a bottle of 777 brandy as their contribution to the evening. The meal was memorable. Shula had put on her best show, Chicken Goulash with home-made noodles, a special Crepe Suzette from an old East European recipe, fresh fruit salad with whipped cream and coffee brewed in a percolator. When he had finished, Danny sat back with a sigh.

'I can't complain about the way they look after us at base,' he said, 'but you don't know how good it feels to come home.'

The conversation at the dinner table hardly touched on the war except when Danny mentioned casually that he had refused an offer for a couple of million dollars.

'You what!' they chorussed.

'Yes. The Libyan radio announced that Col. Gadafi would pay more than the value of his plane to any Israeli pilot delivering it intact to an enemy airfield.'

'Can't we do a deal with him,' asked Eitan, 'and sell him back some of his slightly damaged Mirages?'

* * *

'I'm going crazy,' shouted Bennie angrily.

'How on earth do they manage to live with the things,' said Dror.

'Maybe the Russians have started bacteriological warfare,' suggested Gadi.

The three of them, and the rest of the members of task-force Meron stood rubbing away at big red weals on their stomachs and frantically scratching their skins just above their socks. The cause of their suffering was hundreds of tiny black fleas. On the first day they had hardly noticed the discomfort, but now suddenly they were covered with bites. They had been in Africa for just over forty-eight hours and had spent the night in one of the airport buildings at Deversoir. The field spread over several acres, containing a number of aircraft hangarettes, built with reinforced concrete walls three metres thick, designed to prevent planes being destroyed on the ground like in the Six Day War. There was also barracks for troops, storage buildings, ammunition dumps; and a two-storey brick structure which had probably served as officers' quarters, and was now General Bardan's temporary base. The floor of their barracks was cement, but they had taken some of the empty wooden racks of the storage buildings and spread their sleeping bags across them.

Gadi was boiling water for coffee. Washing was forbidden. Only a few water tankers had come across the bridge and they had been severely warned not to drink any of the local water, or even to touch it with any part of their bodies. Bilharzia, a debilitating disease rampant on the West Bank, was carried by fresh-water snails found in all the ponds and irrigation channels, and the spores of the disease could attach themselves to someone who even dipped his toes in the water.

Outside a light mist was lifting lazily off the ground, and the engines of the Zelda and the Jeep were already running. The three tanks were still attached to them, and in a few moments they would be moving north with some paratroop units, their objective being Serapeum, a large village and railway station on the edge of the Canal, about fifteen kilometres north of the bridgehead.

Phantoms and Skyhawks had been flying sorties since the first light of dawn. Using the narrow corridor which the task forces had opened, they were making a tremendous effort to widen it even further. The missiles had been arranged in an interlocking pattern. As soon as some of the pieces were knocked out, it became that much simpler to destroy the others.

In his new war-room General Bardan followed the quickening pace of the day's actions. The first major report made him grin broadly. During the night there had been extraordinarily heavy shelling of the bridge and surrounding areas, by Katyusha rockets coming from a direction which had at first completely baffled them. In desperation the artillery had stationed observers on both sides of the Canal to try to fix co-ordinates for the trajectory. In the first light of dawn they had matched these points to a deserted fifteen-thousand ton American freighter, the *African Glen*, sitting in the middle of the Great Bitter Lake where it had been stuck since the Six Day War. The air force was called in and bombed the ship, and as it began to settle in the water the planes flew off, and a small boat which must have been carrying the Katyusha crew scurried quickly away to the Third Army positions on the east bank.

The previous evening, an Egyptian major had been captured, and Intelligence Officers had been working with him, trying to get as much information as possible. The major had apparently talked freely, and the General was intrigued and pleased at the picture that emerged from the report on his desk. It confirmed his view about the rigidity of the Egyptian Command on the west bank, that the only person capable of making an important decision was General Ismail from his war-room in Cairo, and that there seemed to be no speedy procedure for giving him accurate and comprehensive information about what was happening. Bardan's small task forces had been roaming across the west bank, methodically attacking missile sites, fuel dumps and any other target that presented itself. The Egyptians did their utmost to fight these attacks off, and the engagements were becoming more difficult and fierce than in the first twenty-four hours, but there were no field command centres close to the fighting, and during or after such clashes there seemed to be no great urgency for the local junior officers to make detailed reports to Cairo.

Bardan, with his own experience and insight, visualised General Ismail sitting in front of his coloured maps. The only significant reports coming in would be those of the bloody battles raging on the east bank. On this basis he would not be in a position to evaluate the complete reversal of the strategic position, that the fate of the war would now be decided on the west bank, and that the east bank had become a minor side conflict.

General Bardan was well aware of his good fortune in correctly appraising the ineptitude of the Egyptian Command, but he also knew that the situation was crucial and could change at any moment. The unexpected resistance around the Chinese Farm had already placed the operation about twenty-four critical hours behind schedule, and the heavy Katyusha shelling had destroyed vehicles and blocked the bridge several times during the night. Each time tanks had moved down and pushed the wrecks into the water, but the progress had been slow and only thirty-five additional tanks had crossed over in the darkness, giving him a total of eighty tanks, a few pieces of heavy artillery, and three-thousand men, about a quarter of what he needed to give adequate protection to the bridge-head, and to proceed with their major objective.

The General had good cause to be concerned. Fresh intelligence reports showed troop movement and activity from the First Army on the outskirts of Cairo; and, a far more immediate danger, strong armoured columns were beginning to move from Ismailia down the west bank of the Canal, in the direction of the bridge-head. To meet this threat Bardan had ordered as large a force as he could spare to move north and attack Serapeum, which would be the most suitable place for blocking an enemy offensive ...

Task force Meron left their vehicles under guard, and proceeded in single file behind a line of approximately two hundred paratroopers. Silently they threaded their way through a dense mango plantation. They had never seen one as lush as this, and in spite of the tension had time to reflect on their bad luck, that it was the wrong time of the year for the fruit to be ripe.

A force of nine tanks had preceded them on the left, driving straight down the road, and opening fire on a military fortress-like building on the outskirts of Serapeum, which the colonel in charge had decided must be taken in order to control the village.

The lead tank had only just started firing when it was hit by an RPG Bazooka rocket, and caught fire. The other tanks deployed off the road in amongst the trees, but

although they were better protected it was difficult to manoeuver.

The building was well placed for defence, and a withering
machine-gun fire was directed at the mango plantation, as
well as mortar fire, the shells bursting around them and
scattering shrapnel in all directions. The colonel asked for
air support urgently, and within minutes Skyhawks came
zooming down on the building. One of the paratroopers near
Gadi suddenly staggered back and fell to the ground. Gadi
saw a huge hole in his helmet and thought he was dead, but
a second later he lifted his head a little dazed, took the
helmet off, and a bullet fell down on the ground next to him.
It had pierced the fibre-glass of the helmet and come to rest
against his head, causing only a slight flesh wound.

The planes did their work, and while they were busy the
tanks came out from the trees and added their shell-fire to
the walls of the building, methodically pounding away, leaving gaping holes. But the defence was stubborn. Casualties
mounted as the men tried to advance, two more tanks were
put out of action by missiles, their crews scrambling out
and escaping in between the trees. The colonel was wounded
but continued to direct the action. He reported back to
headquarters that their ammunition was running low and
without much heavier artillery support there was no chance
of achieving their objective. Reluctantly the order was given
to withdraw, and to regroup in defensive positions blocking
the route to the bridge-head.

Task force Meron was temporarily released. Rafi, one of
their members, had been hit in the shoulder. His wound had
been cleaned and bandaged by a medic, and Bennie and
Gadi drove him back in the Jeep and handed him over to a
first-aid station near the bridge-head. Before returning, they
stopped in the shelter of a grove of giant Eucalyptus trees.
Attached to some of the trees were wooden ladders used by
the Egyptians during the War of Attrition, to send 'monkeys'
with Kalatchnikovs or sharp-shooting rifles, to sit up high
above the Israeli lines and pick off anybody careless enough
to show himself. They decided to climb up one and found
themselves on a small makeshift platform with a grandstand
view of the tremendous activity going on around them.

On the bridge immediately opposite, three tanks were
lumbering over, about thirty metres apart from each other,

and military policemen with red arm-bands were doing their best to get some order into the line of vehicles waiting to cross. The assembly square on the east side was packed with bulldozers, trucks, fuel, tyres and ammunition, and for miles down the road a long procession of vehicles of all descriptions moved slowly towards the Canal. Dust rose up everywhere, and a number of shells dropped around the landing area, but nobody seemed to pay any attention. Hundreds of dead fish floated on top of the water near the bridge, killed by the concussion of exploding shells.

They climbed down the ladder and drove back to where the others were waiting for them. Gadi decided this was as good a time as any, and started to write a postcard to Rina. At first he found himself unable to concentrate; it was like trying to communicate with a different world, one which seemed more like a dream than reality. Gradually, however, he settled down and scribbled a few lines about how it would be after the war 'because the end can't be very far off now.'

He had just finished a similar postcard to his family when they were suddenly called back into action. The columns of Egyptian armour which had come down from Ismailia, had passed through Serapeum, and mounted a heavy attack on the defensive positions blocking the route to the bridge-head.

General Bardan ordered all the air-support available, and despatched all the forces crossing the bridge to reinforce them.

The sky became filled with Israeli planes, diving in to attack in greater numbers than Gadi or Bennie had seen since the beginning of the war. At first they encountered no opposition, but suddenly about twelve Egyptian Migs appeared flying in directly out of the sun which was already well down in the west. Some of the Israeli planes jettisoned their fuel tanks, which fell like long silver cigars towards the ground, and within seconds the air was full of dodging, twisting and diving planes mostly flying at an extremely high altitude, their vapour trails tracing intricate and beautiful patterns against the blue background of the sky. At first there was no way of identifying the four planes that came crashing earthwards, but within a few minutes, the air seemed suddenly to clear, and the inter-weaving vapour trails turned into eight straight lines streaking back to

199

the Egyptian side, most of them being chased by Israeli aircraft.

Almost without pause pairs of Skyhawks reappeared diving down to punish the Egyptian armour in front of them.

The Egyptian attack was aggressive and obstinate, continuing long after it was dark, but the co-ordination of the Israeli defences was too much for it, and eventually it petered out. Task force Meron had not been called upon to do any actual fighting, but the men were continuously under fire, and the heat and smoke fumes which penetrated everywhere left them exhausted. They were eventually released and allowed to return to Deversoir.

Tired and hungry, they opened some tins of 'loof', a kind of fatty mincemeat that they had learned to hate, but in their present state was more than welcome. Gadi boiled water for coffee, and they gathered round to drink it, and to listen to the news on the radio. The announcer commenced with a vague statement that the Israeli forces across the Canal continued to be active, enjoying freedom of movement despite enemy attempts to pin it down. In contrast, however, he quoted the Egyptian military spokesman, Major General Abdul-Asis Mukhtar, who claimed that the Israeli task force on the west bank had been 'completely destroyed'.

'It looks like we're dead but we won't lie down,' said Dror.

Bennie laughed, but his thoughts seemed far away. Dror looked at him carefully. For the last few days he had sensed that something was wrong.

'What's troubling you?' he asked quietly, drawing Bennie aside.

'Is it that obvious?' asked Bennie.

'Not all the time, but it was a minute ago. Do you want to talk about it?'

Dror was a few years his senior, a quiet person with a warm sincere personality, and Bennie felt an urge to talk, even if it was just a way of clarifying his thoughts.

'I don't really know!' he answered. 'Not here, anyway. Let's take a walk outside.'

It was a dark, chilly night. The moon had not yet risen. Bennie hesitated slightly, looking for the right way to begin.

'I think what's been bothering me the last few days is not my real problem, and I'm probably being very stupid, but I keep on thinking about it.'

He stopped for a moment, but Dror made no comment, and he plunged straight on.

'I've being going steady with a very beautiful girl – not my wife – I was really serious, I thought I was in love with her. I suppose I still am, but I think I'm beginning to look at the situation a little more clearly now. I phoned her a few days ago, the day before we came down to the Canal, at four o'clock in the morning. It was the only chance I had to get near the phone. A man's voice answered, and it was so unexpected that I couldn't open my mouth to say anything. Then she took the phone and I heard her voice clearly. She asked, "Bennie is it you?" I still couldn't answer. So her boyfriend took the phone again, extremely angry, swore at me, and called me a fucking coward, and then banged the phone down. I've got no claim on her. If she decided that she wanted to sleep around with somebody else, I suppose she's entitled. It's just the idea of some guy on the home-front in bed with my girl, and calling me a fucking coward, that's been bugging me.'

Dror agreed that it was rough. The home-front seemed so strange and remote, and yet they both knew that their present situation was the dream world, the one which would fade away in a matter of days and allow them to return to the only reality that mattered.

Having started, Bennie talked freely about his family and his feelings for Ruth, and whether at this stage he could go back and pick up the threads of his marriage again. Dror listened without interruption, understanding how bottled up Bennie's emotions had been, and how urgently he needed to let them out.

They had been out for about an hour when the sky on the east side of the Canal suddenly became alive with shooting. Red flares and anti-aircraft shells and a variety of night ammunition with tracers etched marvellous patterns of pink and gold in the sky, all concentrated on two bright orange trails of fire sailing slowly across the heavens like low-flying satellites.

'What are they?' gasped Dror in astonishment.

'I know,' said Bennie with a broad grin, 'they're Frog missiles, like the ones that nearly hit us at Riffidim. Have a look at the east bank, even the Egyptians go crazy firing at them. They know they're out of range but nobody can resist

201

having a try. Pity that we're so far away.'

The extraordinary display of fireworks lasted only another few seconds, when the orange trails suddenly broke up into a brilliant shower of fragments.

'Very few of them manage to get through,' said Bennie.

'What do you think hit them? Hawk missiles?'

'No. Probably Phantoms. Even if one wasn't circling around there would still be enough time to scramble and shoot them down.'

* * *

On Thursday morning with the first light of dawn, a giant Frelon helicopter flew low over the bridge-head, and landed at Deversoir. General Bardan was there to meet it, and warmly greeted his Very Important Visitor with the world-famous black eye-patch, who climbed out ahead of a group of twenty-four Israeli and foreign journalists.

'It's very good of you to come after that announcement yesterday that we were totally destroyed,' said Bardan.

Dayan laughed, and referring to the white bandage around Bardan's forehead, asked if he was getting careless in his old age. There was a genuine bond of affection and mutual respect between the two veteran soldiers, even if there had been some differences on policy. They disappeared together into the war-room, where General Bardan gave him an up-to-date briefing on the situation.

'Our strength is building up – we've got just over two hundred tanks and six thousand men as of this morning – but it's likely to be much harder going from now on.'

They discussed the various problems. Dayan informed him about Kosygin being in Cairo and having already had three long meetings with Sadat. He believed that Russia was urging Sadat to accept a cease-fire in place, which would be acceptable to Israel provided that it didn't happen too quickly. Dayan felt that any negotiations could be stalled for a while, but was nevertheless in favour of pushing ahead as swiftly as possible. It had been agreed that in the north Bardan would limit his operation to blocking the Ismailia–Cairo road. Irrigation works and channels created serious topographical difficulties, and it was unlikely that he would have sufficient strength available to go further and cut off the Second Army.

General Carmel would command the major objective, a drive southwards to Suez, with the object of encircling and cutting off the Third Army. The advantage of this move was that the Great Bitter Lake provided a natural protection against the Third Army, which could not come across in any strength. Also the terrain was firm and well suited to tank manoeuvers, and if the operation succeeded, it would leave a relatively small front of less than twenty-five kilometres to be defended against enemy attempts to break out.

It was also decided subject to General Elazar's approval, that Colonel Reshon's armoured units which had finally disposed of the Chinese Farm, should be reinforced, and strike out in a south-westerly direction towards Cairo. Politically this would be extremely effective, provided that the Second and Third Armies were properly contained.

'Not that we want to get there,' said Dayan, 'but to make some kind of impression on the Egyptians about what it's like to have a war on their doorsteps.'

They emerged in good spirits from the war-room. By this time word had spread, and a large crowd of Israeli soldiers had gathered to applaud Dayan's presence.

'With all those newsmen, it's going to be hard for Cairo to explain how they destroyed us,' said Bennie.

A few moments later he called to Gadi and the others to get ready. They had orders to move north again. While he was still talking, without any warning, a helicopter swept in low over the trees.

'It's Egyptian,' somebody shouted.

In horror they watched it moving straight down the field to where Dayan was standing near a palm-tree, casually stripping some dates from it. Ground fire was already battering the helicopter, which seemed to jerk as a crewman rolled a napalm bomb on to the edge of the open cabin, and pushed it out. It burst into a huge ball of yellow flame about twenty metres away from Dayan. Within seconds the helicopter itself crashed to the ground bursting into an even bigger ball of fire, and killing everybody inside it.

They all rushed to the spot, including General Bardan who had gone back to the war-room for a few moments.

'Wow! That was close!' he said somewhat breathlessly as he reached the Defence Minister.

General Dayan had already recovered his self-composure. 'In future I'll have to camouflage my eye-patch,' he laughed.

* * *

The Syrian soldiers were in their element. They had brought their prisoners in triumph into the village, their hands tied behind their backs with their own bootlaces. No attempt was made to question or identify them, but they were searched and everything taken from them, wrist-watches, photographs, money, boots, socks and all articles of clothing except their vests and underpants; even their dog-tags were torn from their necks.

Their captors stood around them in a circle enjoying their humiliation. One came up behind Mokkie and stubbed out his cigarette on his neck. Mokkie's choked cry of pain produced wild shouts of glee and encouraged a few more to step up and punch them, or spit in their faces. The first time this happened, Yitzchak Mizrachi spat back, and with cries of rage a half-dozen Syrians piled into them while they lay helpless on the ground. A heavy boot smashed into Uri's face, almost causing him to pass out from the pain. He felt the crunch of bone in his mouth and spat out some broken teeth. When their frenzy had worn itself out, the prisoners were hauled to their feet again and Amos cautioned them.

'Don't look for trouble, let's try to get out of this alive.'

A big hefty sergeant stepped up to Uri and ostentatiously pulled out his commando knife. To the great amusement of his friends, he launched into a diatribe in which the name of Mussa Dayan was mentioned frequently. In case the words were lost on Uri and the other Israelis, he held the knife only a few centimetres from Uri's eyeballs, pantomiming how he was going to gouge them out. Uri tried desperately not to show how afraid he was.

At that moment a Syrian officer walked by and issued a few sharp orders. The sergeant spat in Uri's face and put the knife away, and the prisoners were pushed and pulled into the nearest cottage, blindfolded, and their feet tied as well.

Uri's mind was in a turmoil. The cruelty of the Syrians

to prisoners was one of the facts of life he had grown up with. He remembered stories he had heard about Israeli airmen preferring to go down with their planes, rather than bail out and suffer the horrors of being taken into captivity by them.

Thoughts of his family came through to him, how they would react when they heard the news. His father in particular seemed to project strongly into his mind, the quiet man, who had suffered so much in his own time. Suddenly the occasional stories they had drawn out from him, of hatred, cruelty, and utter helplessness to fight against it, acquired a new significance. The unbreakable spirit with which his father had endured all the savage pains inflicted on his body and soul, and his mother too – how they had longed for death, but had willed themselves to hold on to life – he owed it to them to survive, no matter what. He thought of Aliza and his child that she was carrying. Tears came into his eyes, and he felt himself crying, but only strangled noises came through his bruised throat and bleeding mouth. His mind reeled with thoughts of vengeance. God! How he hated these barbarians.

He shivered from the cold. Amos spoke softly telling them to get close to him, so that they could try to create a little warmth for themselves, and plan what could be done. A door creaked open, a loud voice cursed them in Arabic and to add to their nausea, they felt the warm sting and unmistakable smell of somebody urinating on them. This was followed by a few extra kicks, and then the door banged shut again . . .

The first shell exploded with a tremendous crash, the air was filled with the sound of artillery fire and the cottage shook with the impact as shells burst all around them. From outside came the bedlam of shouts and cries. Uri felt Amos's breath on his face.

'Hold your head still,' he was told. Amos's teeth took a grip on the blindfold, Uri jerked his head, and the cloth slipped free. He tried to do the same for Amos, but couldn't get a grip with his broken teeth. The men shuffled around each helping the other, and in a few moments the blindfolds were off.

The noise of the shelling was deafening, and the air in the cottage was acrid with the smell of gunpowder. One wall suddenly trembled and a part of it crumbled inwards in a shower of stone and rubble, leaving a small hole through which they could see flashes of light in the blackness as shells burst around them.

Four of them sat back-to-back struggling with the laces around their wrists, but their arms were stiff with the pain of being tied so tightly, and their fingers struggled clumsily with the knots, working with their hands behind their backs and without being able to see what they were doing.

Amos moved around the sides of the cottage on his buttocks, feeling desperately for a sharp stone projecting from the wall, that he could use to cut through the laces. He suddenly found himself sitting on something hard, and his hands closed over an open tin which had been discarded on the floor. His heart pounding with excitement, he felt the sharpness of the raised lid, and gripping the tin with his fingers, worked it backwards and forwards against the laces. His fingers grew numb with pain, and he had to shift his grip several times, but eventually he felt the laces weakening and with a strong pull they came apart. Swiftly he set to work on the cords binding his feet, and a 'few moments later was able to get up and move over to the others, who were still struggling without success.

Uri was closest to him and he started to work on his wrists. The laces snapped apart, but at the same moment the door swung open and two Syrians came in carrying a flashlight.

'Amos, run!' Mizrachi shouted, and launched himself against the surprised Syrians. The flashlight dropped to the floor. Uri shoved Amos towards the hole in the wall yelling at him, 'Go quickly! Go Amos!' and almost before he realised what was happening, he was through the opening and stumbling in the direction of the forest.

In the shelter of the first tree he stopped to listen but could hear nothing. He thought of going back but realised that he would accomplish nothing except get caught again himself, and with a heavy heart he set out through the trees, his feet bleeding and his body numb with cold and pain. Shells were still landing around the village. Somewhere ahead of him he heard the rumble of tanks.

The forest ended a hundred metres from the village, and with the huge bulk of Mount Hermon looming upwards against a clear sky he had no difficulty choosing his direction.

His mind blanked out on everything except keeping moving. Several times he stumbled and fell, each time picking himself up and starting again, terrified that if he lingered even a few seconds, he would not have the strength to carry on.

Hours went by before he suddenly became aware of the sound of voices somewhere ahead of him. Cautiously he crept closer until he was sure that he was hearing Hebrew; and then shouting hoarsely not to shoot – he was Israeli, he staggered exhausted towards them ...

When he opened his eyes again, he was inside a bunker which served as a first-aid station. Colonel Roth stood at the side of his stretcher. 'Welcome back, Amos, you don't have to speak if you're not strong enough.'

'I'll be all right.' Amos looked around him trying to recover his bearings, and a horrible drawn-out groan came from deep inside as he remembered what had happened.

'They're still there. They'll kill them,' he said. 'Another ten minutes and all of us could have got away. God knows what they've done to them now.' A medic moved forward to see if he needed assistance, but Amos motioned him away.

He had been bathed in disinfectants, and iodine, given shots of anti-biotics and against tetanus, and several wounds had been stitched up. His body was covered with angry red and purple bruises, and part of his scalp was shaved, where they had cleaned and stitched a big gash caused by a Syrian boot. The soles of his feet were also cut to pieces and covered with bandages.

The doctor came in and told the colonel that in spite of Amos's frightening appearance he was really in pretty good shape. Within a week or two he would be up and around, and when the stitches came out he would feel a lot better.

Amos felt a deep anger rise within him. 'I'm up and around right now, doctor,' he growled. 'I've got an account to settle with those bastards, and no stitches are going to stop me. Do you understand?'

The doctor was taken aback by the violence of Amos's reaction. 'We'll see what we can do, but I'm not making any promises,' he answered. 'I'll come back later today and see how you are.'

When he was gone Colonel Roth made Amos relax and

gently questioned him until he had pieced the whole story together. Afterwards, the colonel suggested that the war was almost over, and that it would be sensible for Amos to go to a convalescent home; he'd been through enough for one person.

'Please don't let them send me away,' pleaded Amos, 'you've got to understand – I escaped and left them there. I must stay here, at least until I know they're all right.'

The colonel saw that there was no point upsetting him further. 'I'll talk to the doctor,' he promised. 'Meanwhile look after yourself.'

Amos was exhausted. The medic gave him an injection, and they left him to sleep. He felt dizzy, the room seemed to be turning slowly around and around. He heard their voices again. 'Amos run – go quickly – go Amos!' and he began to cry. Another ten minutes . . . It was so unfair . . . Why? . . . God – Why? . . . Why?

Friday/Sunday, 19th – 21st October

Somehow, without any special fanfares, or banner headlines in the newspapers, the atmosphere in the country had changed. The bewilderment of the first few days, the credibility gap and the bitter losses, had all left their mark, but imperceptibly the balance had swung around. The people knew that the war was going well, that it would end within a few days and that their loved ones would be coming home again. Those who had not yet been devastated by bad news, prayed quietly inside, even if they were completely unobservant, for just a few more days of good luck for their son or their husband.

Meir went into Tel Aviv early on Friday morning to the Head Office of Bank Leumi to arrange a credit on new machinery, which the factory had ordered before the war, and which was now awaiting shipment from West Germany. Coming out of the bank he purchased a copy of *Uj Kelet* and was on his way to catch the bus back to the factory when he passed an old friend sitting on a bench in Rothschild Boulevard, with a group of other grey-haired and semi-bald cronies.

Ferinand Lux was a 'landsman', born in the same small town as Meir, but who had emigrated to Israel as a young man. Meir was always happy to spend time with him, listening to his reminiscences of 'those days', when they built roads, drained swamps and laid the foundations for the State of Israel.

Today, however, the past was forgotten. The talk centred around the war, how it was going, and what the Israeli Army would do next, whether Dayan wanted to conquer Damascus or Cairo, or neither of them. These 'parliaments', composed of pioneers who had fought for the country as far back as the Arab riots in the 1920s, were remarkably well informed, basing their opinions on information from 'contacts' in every branch of the army and government, and also local phenomena such as the fall in value of the black market dollar from five Israeli pounds to four pounds seventy. Meir was happy to hear the general optimism, and the predictions of a tremendous victory if the United Nations would only continue not to interfere.

Reluctantly he tore himself away from them, and after boarding his bus, settled down to scan the headlines. Under the heading of 'Canal Partly Re-taken', mention was made of regaining control of part of the east bank, but only vague reference was made to the task force on the west bank.

Cairo Radio had announced that the Israeli task force was now surrounded and had been called upon 'to surrender or face destruction'. No attempt was made to reconcile this with previous claims that it had already been destroyed.

Syria had taken delivery of three hundred and forty new Russian tanks in the past four days. At least that didn't include three hundred and forty tank crews, thought Meir grimly.

A speech by Kissinger was reported, in which he stated that a 'decent and just' settlement of the Arab–Israeli conflict was possible, but that all hostilities would have to cease first.

And Kosygin was still in Cairo having talks with Sadat.

Meir felt himself divided into two. One part was exaltant that the war news seemed to be good, and the other, not having heard from the boys, gnawed constantly away at him. He had talked to Chaim and listened to his comforting and logical explanations, knowing that the law of averages was on his side. Nevertheless the calculations went ceaselessly through his head – no news from Uri for six days since Aliza last saw him, and from Gadi for seven days from the date that his last letter had been posted. He felt the pressure mounting up so sharply inside him that he had to make a physical effort to keep control and tell himself not to be a fool.

He remembered the Six Day War. How simple it had been then. His boys were at home, he had no mixed feelings and doubts – nineteen days of anxious waiting, then two days when they weren't sure if the news could possibly be that good, and the rest just a series of incredible victories culminating in the joyous restoration of Jerusalem. When the casualties were announced he was upset, but he hadn't been hurt directly; peace with the Arabs would be just a matter of days, and his boys would never have to fight in a war. What a foolish optimist he had been!

Meir decided to go back to the apartment. It was Friday, and there seemed to be no point going to work for the odd hour or two that was left. Shoshana was at home; she had been on an early shift at the refreshment stall, and had just come in from some shopping. She was brimming over with joy; there was a postcard from Uri, that all was well, and to let them into a small secret – as soon as the war was ended he and Aliza had decided to get married . . .

*   *   *

On Saturday, midday, Defence Minister Moshe Dayan spoke to the nation in a radio and television interview. Meir and Shoshana, and every Israeli who could get near to a TV set sat glued to it, anxiously hanging on to every word. They were not disappointed. Serious, but with his usual grin of cockiness always just beneath the surface, Dayan announced that the war was so bitter and intense that it could not last long. The military position was already that favourable, that if the Arabs seriously requested it Israel could accept a cease-fire in place, or even one where everybody went back to the pre-October lines. Israel, however, should not under any circumstances ask for one – 'Every additional day right now is to our advantage.'

Dayan discussed the position on the west bank, how over a period of years the Egyptians with Russian guidance, had built all their defences facing east, and now found that they were threatened from behind, and their missile system knocked out and ineffective. On the Golan, 'Israel had come as close as possible to smashing Syria's military power' which had had to be replaced by unprecedented quantities of Soviet equipment, and the forces of Saudia, Jordan, Algeria and Iraq.

He praised the Israeli soldiers, whose fighting was so 'intrepid and daring' and also 'sensible, not fanatic . . . performed fearlessly and without restraint . . . bringing us the advantage in every battle – for example the clash in the air today that ended in twenty-seven to zero.'

Answering questions, Dayan stated that the true intentions of the Arabs when they started the war had been to 'throw

211

us into the sea'. What they were now, he didn't know, but he hadn't discerned any wish to end the war.

Finally, asked to comment on a statement by an Egyptian leader that the Arabs had 'restored their honour' by launching the war, Dayan's quick sense of humour took over. 'Let them keep their honour, and lose the war. And if they salvage their honour, let them be ready to make peace!'

Shoshana went happily back to the kitchen. She was baking a strawberry cake for a 'party' she was giving that evening. The Soldiers Welfare Association had published an appeal for knitted snow-caps for the boys on the Golan Heights, and Shoshana had invited a group of women who worked at the refreshment stall, to come to her apartment and knit while they watched TV.

*　　*　　*

Aliza snatched a few moments off from work, and re-read Uri's letter even though she already knew it off by heart. It consisted of two pieces of rough paper, but somehow seeing the words, and knowing that he had written them, brought her closer to him. He had just come back from a symphony concert with Zubin Mehta conducting – 'a wonderful experience. The only thing missing was you. You're always telling me to look after myself,' he wrote, 'the same goes for you, too. It's hard for me to believe that I love you more than I did before, and yet I can't deny my sense of wonder and joy that you are carrying my child. There is so much I want to say to you, but it will just have to wait until we are together again.'

She went back into the wards. There had been a substantial drop in the number of new cases coming in, and her work-load was easier. In the orthopaedic ward she passed an automatic telephone wagon, which had been installed and was wheeled from bed to bed for the patients to phone home.

In the burns section, Shmuel, a young tank gunner, happily showed her the new set of prayer phylacteries that the Rabbi had brought him. Aliza deliberately looked straight at him while they talked, because she knew that he was desperately sensitive about his face which had been burned unrecognisably. He had a photograph of himself from before the war, which he insisted on showing to anybody who hadn't known him then, and it was heartbreaking to compare the beautiful laughing youth with the mummy-like mask in front of them.

Shmuel had turned intensely religious. The Rabbi had at first tended to discourage him, pointing out that if he was not observant before, it was unlikely that he would change basically because of what had happened to him in the war. Shmuel argued differently.

'I was the gunner in my tank,' he said, 'and the driver was hot and tired and asked me to change places with him. Soon after that we got into a battle, and a shell hit us in the rear, smashing the whole of the back compartment and killing everybody inside. The tank caught fire and the ammunition was liable to blow up at any moment. I wanted to climb out from the turret of the driver's cabin, but the gun had stuck just above it and I couldn't get it open. The flames reached me and I remember praying that the end would come quickly, when suddenly another shell hit the tank, slicing out the front of my cabin like a tin-opener, and I stepped out and was saved. How can I not believe that in some way God heard my prayer and wanted to help me?'

Aliza had spoken to the Rabbi. 'He needs your help and God's also. Look at his face! Give him something to cling to, that he can believe in, or he'll go out of his mind.' The Rabbi had obviously listened to her.

*   *   *

The movement of events on the west bank rapidly gathered speed. A second pontoon bridge had just been completed about two hundred metres below the first, and vehicles were pouring across it in an endless stream, which stretched miles back into the desert. On the Saturday morning General Bardan studied his logistics reports with satisfaction. In spite of the delayed start, there were now three hundred tanks and twelve thousand men across the Canal, not to mention the infinite variety of other vehicles, trucks, passenger buses, water-carriers, ambulances and troop carriers which a modern army needed.

The Israeli air force was operating virtually unchecked. In spite of the success of the air-lift there had been a shortage of tank shells, particularly those which Britain had embargoed and which were needed for the Centurion tanks. Special tactics had been evolved to call the planes in wherever possible, and conserve the firing power of the tanks.

Also of prime importance, were the huge mobile guns which had crossed the Canal, and were now deploying both north and south of the bridge-head, Bardan had several times turned them against the Second and Third Armies on the east bank, not only because they were needed, but because of his reasoning that nothing was more demoralising for an enemy than to be fired at from the rear. In the same spirit he had prominently hung out Israeli flags around the bridge-head and in other places where they would be conspicuous to enemy spotters or aircraft.

During Friday night his forces in the north had captured Serapeum, and the way was now clear for an advance towards the Ismailia–Cairo road. Meanwhile he was diverting almost all the new forces southwards. He had been tremendously concerned by the time factor, but the Assistant Prime Minister himself, Yigal Allon, on a surprise visit, had confidently assured him that nothing could happen inside of a week, and this should be more than enough time for him.

In the south General Carmel's forces had surrounded Fayid, twenty-five kilometres from the bridge-head, the biggest Egyptian military airport and supply centre in the entire region. As soon as it was taken, the dash for Suez could begin. Time was all-important. There were already some signs of a possible pull-back of the Third Army along the Suez–Cairo road, and it was necessary to close the trap quickly ...

Task Force Meron had taken part in the capture of Serapeum. Micha, who usually drove the Zelda, was hit by a shell splinter in his neck, and collapsed with his left side paralysed. The doctor in the field immobilised his neck so that it couldn't move and evacuated him by helicopter.

Instead of moving further north with the rest of Bardan's forces, Bennie was ordered to return to Deversoir, where the remnants of Colonel Rishon's armour were assembling and being reorganised, to launch a new spearhead in the direction of Cairo.

* * *

Shoshana's party was in full swing. Eight women had turned up, making ten altogether with Shula and herself, and Meir had hurriedly brought in some chairs from Chaim's apartment. The needles clicked busily away, and the women talked happily, enjoying the opportunity to socialise without feeling guilty about it. Most of them were younger than Shoshana, and the discussions centred on letters from their husbands, problems with their young children, unpaid bills, whether they would be getting pay-cheques from the army, and how much, the shortage of eggs and the irritation of the blackout.

Meir and Chaim, in self-defence, went out for a walk, but returned for the eight-thirty news. A surprise announcement informed them that Kissinger was on his way to Moscow, sent by President Nixon at the special request of the Soviet leaders. Washington officials stressed that there was no immediate plan for settling the Middle East War, but that the urgent Russian invitation could be regarded as a sign of progress.

'It's the best proof we've had yet that we're winning the war,' commented Chaim.

'The Russians must have heard Dayan's speech this morning,' added Meir, 'when he said that every additional day that the war goes on, will be to our advantage.'

'I don't care what their reasons are,' said one of the women. 'They can stop the war tomorrow as far as I'm concerned, just let them send my husband home safely.' The others all chorused their agreement.

The TV screen changed to show scenes of minor miracles which had occurred early that morning in the seaside resort town of Nahariya, north of Haifa. Two Syrian planes came in on a bombing raid and within seconds one was shot down, exploding and disintegrating in mid-air, right over the heart of the town, blowing out windows and damaging shutters and doors. The other plane turned tail and fled.

The camera showed the gaping wall in one apartment, where part of the fuel-tank had crashed into the bedroom of two sleeping children, wrenching off the headboard of the bed, which fell over them, protecting them from falling building blocks and plaster. The mother rushed in, and the children were pulled out completely unharmed.

In another apartment a man heard the roar of the planes,

got out of his bed which stood next to the wall, and dashed into the children's room where his eight-year-old daughter had woken up frightened. He told her to get into his bed, but instead she ran in and climbed into her mother's bed, which stood closer to the centre of the room. Seconds later the 30 mm cannon of the plane, with three shells still inside, crashed through the wall on to his bed. If either he or his daughter had been there they would have been killed instantly.

The Syrian pilot managed to bail out, and landed in an Israeli Arab village a short distance away. He was seriously injured and unconscious, and was rushed to hospital, but died fifteen minutes later in the emergency surgery.

During the day the Syrian radio announced that their air force had successfully bombed the Haifa oil refineries.

While the programme continued, Shoshana and Shula busied themselves bringing in the coffee and cake. There was a report about the oil embargo by Saudi Arabia, and then a relay via Telstar of an Egyptian film showing off Israeli prisoners of war. Two pilots were shown in hospital beds, and in answer to the commentator's pointed questions, praised the medical treatment they were getting. Another scene showed an Israeli private with his arm in a sling. In halting English he declared that the Egyptians had been right to want to recover their own territory, and that he just wanted to go back to his family and have nothing to do with wars any more. Finally there was a shot of about twenty soldiers marching with their hands held behind their heads, guarded by two armed Egyptian soldiers.

Only a small table-lamp was on in the room, and they had all been concentrating on the screen. It took a few moments to register that Ilana, one of the young women, had slid off her chair without a sound, and was lying on the floor. Quickly they switched the other lights on, lifted her on to the couch and dabbed her face with a cold wet cloth.

'Shall I call a doctor?' Chaim volunteered.

'No. Not for the moment,' Shoshana said.

Ilana opened her eyes, Chaim had poured out a small glass of cognac which they gave her to drink, and the shock of the strong liquor brought her back to her senses.

'Shmulik,' she said, 'my husband . . . ' and she began to cry.

216

'Ilana, for goodness sake stop crying and try to tell us what's happened. What's Shmulik got to do with this?' asked Sara, a close friend of Ilana's.

'You didn't see him? On the TV? He was there with the prisoners, with his hands behind his head.'

'Are you sure? I didn't see him.'

'Of course I'm sure. Don't you think I would recognise my own husband? . . . '

The next morning at eight o'clock Ilana and Sara and Shoshana, who had an illogical feeling of responsibility for what had taken place, presented themselves at the Manpower Branch of the General Staff Headquarters in Ibn Giverol Street, Tel Aviv. A young woman with the rank of captain received them sympathetically, and handed over a series of still photographs taken of the TV screen. 'We're trying to get a copy of the tape itself,' she told Ilana, 'in case these photos aren't good enough.'

The picture was remarkably clear. Shmulik's face was clearly visible in the second row of prisoners who had been marching with their hands held behind their heads.

The captain inked in a red 'X' above his head, and asked a number of questions, the answers to which she copied into a file marked 'Samuel Hirsh'. She explained to Ilana that her husband had been listed as missing, but there had been a report that he'd attached himself to a different unit, and they'd been trying to make absolutely certain what had happened, before notifying her.

'I know it's not easy,' she told her, 'but try to look on the positive side of things. The most important thing is that he's alive, and according to the photo he seems fit and healthy. Once the Egyptians have shown him like that on TV he's going to be taken good care of. At the present moment we're holding nearly two thousand Egyptian prisoners. You can be quite sure that one of the first things that will happen after the war is that they will be only too pleased to exchange the hundred and fifty they have of ours, to get all theirs back again. So please try not to worry too much. If you have any problems call me right away. In any event we'll be sending a counsellor to your home either today or tomorrow, to discuss what we can do to make things easier for you.'

Ilana asked a few more questions, and then they got up to leave. The captain walked through the lobby with them

217

to the exit. About a dozen other women were leafing anxiously through batches of photographs.

'In a way you're lucky your husband took such a good photograph,' said the captain. 'We've got a few situations here where two or three different women have identified the same photograph as being their sons or husbands. You can understand how terrible it is for them.'

Ilana tried to smile. She thanked the captain for being so helpful. 'The important thing is that he's alive!' – she clung hopefully to the words, and with Sara and Shoshana on each side of her, walked bravely out into the sunlight, wondering how everything could look so normal when her own world had just come crashing down.

* * *

It was Amos's third day at the first-aid station. He had made remarkable progress, and the doctor had given in gracefully about trying to persuade him to go to a rest-home. A Jeep turned up early in the morning with a message from the colonel to come back with the driver and report to him immediately.

When he arrived, Colonel Roth spoke firmly and to the point.

'Amos, I hope you can stand the shock. I think that the men who were with you have been shot by the Syrians, and I want you to come with me to identify the bodies. I would have preferred not to involve you, but you made it very clear that this is what you wanted.'

Amos turned white, but nodded his head and said, 'Yes, I do, Sir.'

They climbed into the Jeep and set out in the direction of Mazrat Beit Jinn which had been recaptured the day after Amos had escaped. The colonel explained that some wounded Syrians had been taken prisoner, and one of them told a story about Israeli prisoners being shot. He had received medical treatment, and been brought back to Mazrat Beit Jinn where he pointed to a spot, and a shallow grave had been dug up, exposing four bodies . . .

Amos found himself sinking into a peculiar form of detachment. He looked at the war debris on the side of the road, the burnt-out wrecks which had become as normal a part of the landscape as the rocks and trees, and he felt like a spectator, a bystander returning to a scene where he had been active somewhere in the long distant past. In his heart he knew what lay ahead of him.

Could he have saved them? Even if he couldn't, was it right to run away and leave them? Logically he knew that there had been no choice, but he also knew the question would haunt him for years to come.

Arriving at Mazrat Beit Jinn, they were taken straight to the field officer in charge, a Major Friedman. 'I'm glad you've arrived so soon,' he told the colonel. 'They've got a unit down there from Manpower, documenting the case and taking photographs. The men were quite obviously murdered in cold blood. They were dressed only in their underpants, their hands and feet tied and their eyes blindfolded. They were all shot three or four times in the back of the head. We found fifteen cartridge shells next to the bodies, and the powder burns around the wounds show that the weapon was fired from only a few centimetres away. The bodies are covered with bruises, cuts and stab wounds; and one of the corpses looks as though an eye has been gouged out with a knife.'

Amos felt sick, but took a firm grip on himself, knowing that he had to go through with it. Together they walked down to the edge of the village, to the cottage where the five of them had been kept prisoner. He identified it as in a dream, pointing out the hole in the wall through which he had made his escape.

About forty metres away, at the edge of the first row of trees in the forest, a group of men were gathered near a shallow ditch. Next to them were four new plain wooden coffins, used by the Israelis for army burials. As they approached, the men stood aside and Amos saw the four corpses lying face upward on the ground.

Bloated and swollen, there was no mistaking the faces; and on Uri's the horrible blood-caked hole where his left eye should have been. There was a shocking indignity to the smashed and disfigured bodies, their fists clenched as if in a rage at the injustice of it all.

The smell of dead flesh rotting hit Amos, and before he could control himself his stomach heaved and he was vomiting over and over again, until there was nothing left but green bile which burned and stuck in his throat. Too weak to stand, he sat on the ground with his head bent over, sobbing bitter tears. They left him undisturbed for about ten minutes and then Colonel Roth came back and helped him up.

'I'm sorry, Amos. They need you to answer some questions and sign the identification papers.'

Amos nodded, without speaking. He felt like a vegetable, absolutely drained of all emotion. A part of him had died and would soon be placed in the wooden coffins with his men. Especially Uri, thank goodness he had let him slip away from camp for the day . . . he had been so happy when he came back . . . what did it help now?

'Come on, Amos,' Colonel Roth took him by the arm. 'Let's sign the papers and get away from this place.'

Monday, 22nd October

Nobody in Israel doubted that the pendulum had swung in its favour, and that the war was drawing to a rapid and decisive close, but in spite of this the seven o'clock morning news hit them like a bolt from the blue.

Ten minutes earlier, after three hours of debate, with only the Chinese delegate criticising the failure to condemn Israel, the United Nations Security Council had passed a resolution calling on the parties to the present fighting to cease firing within twelve hours; immediately thereafter to commence the implementation of Resolution 242; and to start negotiations under appropriate auspices aimed at establishing a just and durable peace in the Middle East. Dr Kissinger and his party were leaving Moscow immediately, and flying to Israel for a special consultation with the Prime Minister, Mrs Golda Meir.

'It's incredible, Shoshana,' said Meir. 'Do you realise what this means? That the firing has to stop at seven o'clock tonight.'

'But who says we'll accept it, or that Egypt and Syria will agree, and what happens if they don't?'

'I don't know Shosh. It's all too quick for me. Nobody that I've spoken to even mentioned the possibility of a Security Council meeting. They said Kissinger would spend a few days in Moscow discussing matters, then he would fly back to get instructions from Nixon. I thought it would take at least a week. Anyway, I don't really mind, as long as the boys come home soon.'

They hadn't spoken about this subject almost since the war began and Shoshana hesitated a moment before continuing.

'Do you really think it will be all right, Mickie?'

'Yes, Shosh. I really think so.'

He kissed her goodbye, and went down to meet Chaim. At the news-stand where they stopped to buy a paper Meir

221

met Mr Goodman, the obese attorney whose opinion he valued so highly.

'Shalom Mr Goodman,' he greeted him.

'Didn't we agree that you should call me "Ernie"?' said the attorney good-naturedly.

'Yes – Ernie,' Meir hastily corrected himself. 'What do you think of the news this morning?'

'The cease-fire? I must admit I'm a bit shocked. That Kissinger's quite an amazing person. I just hope he's on our side, although it doesn't look very much like it to me.'

Meir introduced Chaim, and taking a chance on his friend's agreement, asked Ernie if he had a few moments to give them the benefit of his views. Flattered, and not averse to an early-morning snack, the attorney suggested that they have a cup of coffee together.

They settled themselves in a nearby restaurant, and without any further invitation, Ernie started speaking.

'I suppose the first question you want to ask is, "Is it good for us or bad?", and like most questions of this sort there's no easy answer. I think it's bad. I think we needed a few more days on the west bank to teach the Egyptians a lesson, maybe to get as close to Cairo as we are to Damascus. If we stop now the Syrians are defeated, even though they may not be too keen to admit it; but the Egyptians can claim a victory just as easily as we can. They're still sitting on our side of the Canal.'

'Surely if we need a few days more to defeat the Egyptians we don't have to agree to the Security Council resolution? We can make some excuse for delaying it, or ask them some questions which will take time to clarify?' asked Chaim.

'It's not as easy as that,' replied Ernie. 'If the boot was on the other foot – if the Arabs were winning – like at the beginning of the war, there would be no way of getting the Security Council to even meet. But we're in a position where our best friend – I could almost say our only friend – is a "good guy" and he won't allow us to play games.'

'But I thought that America also wanted to see the Arabs defeated. The papers were full of this yesterday when they spoke about Kissinger's mission.'

'I guess we all made a mistake. We believed what we wanted to believe. It seems to be getting a habit with us lately. Kissinger's an exceptionally clever man, and up until now I don't think we've really understood the way his mind works.'

'But is he our friend or isn't he?' asked Meir.

'He is and he isn't,' replied Ernie enigmatically, enjoying the playing around with ideas, and the obvious respect for his opinions. 'What I mean is that he believes he is doing what is best for us, but it's not easy for us to place complete trust in him. We've had too many disappointments in the past from people who manoeuvered us into accepting what they thought would be good for us.

'In 1956 the Americans forced us to give up the Sinai. They stationed United Nations observers between our forces and the Egyptians and the big powers guaranteed freedom of our shipping through the Red Sea of Eilat. And what happened in 1967 when Nasser blocked the Straits of Tiran? The United Nations Army obediently walked out, and then the big powers spent weeks arguing about how to implement their guarantees, while we were being choked to death.'

'But in what way does Kissinger think he's doing what is best for us?' asked Meir. 'Why did he act so quickly if he thought we needed a few more days to defeat the Egyptians? A man as clever as he is could surely have found a way of delaying a couple of days.'

'That's exactly the point, Meir, Kissinger didn't want us to defeat the Egyptians. You heard Dayan's speech last Saturday, when he said, "Let them salvage their honour and then they can sit down and make peace with us." That's what Kissinger is trying to do for the Egyptians. If they are defeated and humiliated like they were in 1967, Kissinger is afraid that we won't be able to get them to sit down with us and talk peace, and they'll go back to preparing for the next war.'

'Do you think he's right?'

'I don't know. I personally would prefer the satisfaction of giving the Egyptians a terrible hiding, but I'm emotionally involved. Kissinger is like a machine. He sits on the sidelines and manipulates everything to get the result he's trying to achieve. Maybe he's right. I'd like to believe he is. After all, the resolution does talk about "negotiation between the parties". That's better than we've ever managed to do before.'

'And will everybody accept?' asked Meir.

'I can't see why not! We've got no choice. Dayan himself said we could accept a cease-fire in place. Maybe he never thought it would happen so quickly, but it would be awkward for him to back out now. And Egypt is obviously desperate for one. Look how quickly Russia acted to get Kissinger there, and reach an agreement with him. Syria may have some difficulties because they've never accepted Resolution 242, but in practice I don't know if they've got much choice with our army sitting on their doorstep.'

Greatly impressed with their 'expert', Chaim looked at his watch, and reluctantly decided it was time for them to go to work. Ernie beamed as they thanked him, and told them with perfect truth that the pleasure was his.

*   *   *

At the first light of dawn, Colonel Roth slipped out of the prefabricated hut at the foot of the ski-slope on Mount Hermon, and peered anxiously through his binoculars at the peak of the mountain towering eight hundred metres above their temporary field headquarters.

Bleary-eyed and worn out, the colonel had been without sleep for more than twenty-four hours. His own units of tanks and armour had already played their part, and were now deployed in defensive positions around the mountain, to guard against a possible Syrian counter-attack.

Early the previous afternoon paratroopers had landed by helicopter in a surprise attack on the original Syrian positions on Mount Hermon, which were nearer to Damascus and a hundred and fifty metres higher than the captured Israeli stronghold. With shocked anger the Syrians sent in waves of planes to smash the attack, but nine were shot down, and with the help of artillery and tanks coming up the front of the mountain, the positions were soon taken.

As darkness fell the real attack began, with an elite Golani brigade climbing slowly up the forbidding mountain. The 'impregnable' Israeli position had been in their charge when it fell, and the Golanis had taken the disaster as a personal humiliation. Impatiently they had awaited the chance to avenge the stain on their honour.

The Syrians had had ample time to prepare their defences, and there was no possibility of them being 'surprised' like the Israeli defenders had been. Sensibly taking advantage of the terrain, they positioned their men outside the fortress, where they could snipe at the slow-moving climbers, using infra-red sights to pierce the darkness. The air force and artillery were powerless to help without hitting their own infantry. With incredible bravery the Golani soldiers crawled and dashed from rock to rock, paying for each small advance with their blood. As they approached closer the enemy lobbed hand grenades at them with devastating effect.

At six o'clock the sun rose above the mountain, adding to the difficulties of the attacking forces by shining straight into their eyes. The Syrians had no place to retreat, and fought bravely and with skill. Even after the attackers reached the crest of the mountain, the struggle continued fiercely for several hours, with the antagonists eventually clashing in hand-to-hand fighting, striking at each other with fists and the butts of their guns.

A few minutes before eleven o'clock it was all over, and the Israeli and Golani flags were raised above the recaptured fortress. There was a deep satisfaction but no joy in the hearts of the victors. Fifty Golani soldiers lay dead on the boulder-strewn slopes of the mountain, and more than two hundred were wounded.

* * *

'Goddam it!' Bardan cursed when the news reached him, 'how on earth could Kissinger have moved so quickly? With friends like that, who the hell needs enemies?'

Few people were in a better position to appreciate how spectacular a victory lay just within the grasp of the Israeli Army. The outside world was only just beginning to wake up to the fact that the daring Canal crossing was much more than an attempt to knock out a few missile bases, and that the so-called bridge-head had turned into a lightning pincer movement designed to cut off the Third Army from behind and completely surround it.

Everything had been moving so well. In the north Bardan's forces had reached a point within three kilometres of the Ismailia–Cairo road and the railway which ran alongside it, and nothing could move in either direction without facing instant destruction from the Israeli artillery. In the south,

Fayid had been captured, and General Bardan himself had been awed by the tens of thousands of tons of stores of all descriptions stacked in enormous warehouses, which had fallen virtually intact into their hands. General Carmel's advance unit had pushed further south along the shores of the Great Bitter Lake, to a point about fifty kilometres from Suez, and was only just beginning to pick up speed.

But time was running out, and Bardan knew there was no way of securing the total victory he had envisaged within the twelve hours' limit. He spoke to General Dayan on the field telephone urging him not to accept the cease-fire – it would be a national tragedy to let the Third Army get away. Dayan's answer was brief, 'There's no choice. We've already accepted it. The announcement will be broadcast in the next hour or two.'

'But I thought we'd have time,' Bardan persisted.

'We were both wrong!' came the grim reply.

Bardan was, however, given the go-ahead to exploit his forces to the maximum, rather than slow down in any way . . .

A crack group of ninety paratroopers was sitting opposite Kantara in the north, in readiness for a special mission that evening. Two giant Sikorsky helicopters picked them up six hours earlier than planned, flew back low over the Israeli lines and then changed direction again crossing over the bridge-head and heading almost due south.

There had been no time to brief the soldiers about the sudden change in their plans, and with the cease-fire only a few hours away, they had mixed feelings. They were excited to cross into 'Africa', but most of them didn't relish the idea of any special action. It was hard to avoid morbid thoughts of being among the last casualties of the war.

At two o'clock in the afternoon the helicopters flew low over the Suez–Cairo railway line, landing in the shelter of a line of sandy ridges parallel to the main highway joining the two cities. Immediately opposite them loomed the steep slopes of Jebel Ataka, a high mountain on the south side of the road, which dominated the town of Suez and the area around the Canal up to the Bitter Lakes.

As the helicopters came in to land, they were fired at from an Egyptian gun position on the same line of ridges, but about a kilometre further west, in the direction of Cairo.

They touched down and unloaded their equipment with tremendous speed, a special lightweight cannon, four heavy machine guns, some small mortars, Bazookas, boxes of hand grenades and other ammunition, and fifty anti-tank missiles.

The helicopters took off less than four minutes after they had landed, and the machine guns, Bazookas and missiles were deployed on the ridge facing all sides, as an attack was liable to come from any direction. They finished not a moment too soon. The men had already started digging their fox-holes, when they heard the characteristic loud bang of medium-sized mortar guns firing from the same position that had already given them trouble. Allowing for a ten-second time lag, the men dug furiously, flinging themselves to the ground as the first shell exploded, and then frantically shovelling more sand out of the holes, until their bodies were below the level of the ground.

Under cover of the firing, two tanks were seen approaching rapidly along the highway from the direction of the Egyptian gun position. As they came closer they veered off the road towards them, spraying the ridge with machine gun fire. When they were only about four hundred metres away, the officer in charge gave an order and a salvo of two Bazooka rockets and six missiles shot towards their targets. One tank exploded with a loud roar, completely disintegrating. The other continued to race towards them, but was stopped short by the next salvo. Its crew jumped out, and tried to crawl away, but were mown down by the fire of the heavy machine guns which opened up on them.

Throughout this time, the mortar barrage continued without pause, and the murderous fragments of steel shooting in all directions made casualties inevitable. One paratrooper was killed by the tank fire, another by a direct hit from a mortar shell next to his fox-hole. The wounds were mostly light, except for one soldier who was blinded in both eyes by shrapnel.

After about half an hour the shelling died down and for the first time the junior officers were able to brief the men about their situation. They had leap-frogged over a large segment of enemy territory, the object being to control and block the road from Suez to Cairo. Armoured reinforcements were already racing towards them, and could be

227

expected to make contact with them at any moment . . .

*   *   *

It sounded impossible to believe – a cease-fire at six-fifty that night – Gadi was thrilled. Thoughts of Rina and his family made him giddy with excitement and longing. In his mind he recalled what had happened after the Six Day War, when within a few short days after the firing stopped, the vast bulk of the army returned home.

The reaction of the remaining members of the task force were more controlled but also favourable. Only Bennie was upset, because he was more aware than the others of the tremendous victory that was being snatched from their grasp.

He briefed them on the special instructions he had received a few minutes earlier, to lead a unit of six tanks, which were being sent to relieve a group of paratroopers occupying an important position on the Suez–Cairo highway.

'I didn't know we'd reached there yet,' commented Dror.

'We haven't – the paratroopers are being sent there by helicopter in a few hours. They'll have no armour and could easily be wiped out if the enemy attacks in any strength.'

There was a brief delay while the Zelda was being loaded with a hundred blankets, jerry-cans of water, and cases of battle rations.

Initially they moved out with a convoy of armoured vehicles under the command of Colonel Rishon. Carmel's tanks were advancing along the shore of the Bitter Lakes towards Suez, and Colonel Rishon's orders to move in the direction of Cairo had now been changed to by-pass Suez and keep going until he reached the Port of Abidiya, effectively encircling Suez and the Third Army whether the town was captured or not.

The cease-fire agreement had scotched any chance of achieving these objectives in the time left, but their instructions were to redouble their efforts to cover as much ground as possible.

Progress was slow. The road was choked with every conceivable type of vehicle to back up the armour which had gone ahead, including milk-carrier tankers with their precious cargoes of water, ammunition and fuel trucks, Egged buses loaded with equipment and infantry, and even a private diaper-delivery van which had been crudely camouflaged by smearing it with brown mud.

It was the first time task force Meron had moved south. With Micha out of action, Gadi was driving the Zelda and he gazed in fascination at the countless bunkers lining both sides of the road, and the tramp steamers anchored in clusters on the Lake, where they had been trapped since 1967, some of them still with caretaker crew-members on board.

The road turned west taking them past Fayid, and the traffic became less congested. Gadi found that he could judge the progress of the war by the state of the Egyptian graves. Up to Fayid there had been several orderly lines neatly marked. Then the smell of death became progressively worse and they passed several open pits with the corpses stacked next to them awaiting burial by the special Israeli squad. Later the war debris increased tremendously and they passed masses of charred and broken vehicles, with dead bodies scattered in between where they had fallen.

They had become accustomed to the packs of wild desert dogs, white-grey mongrels, which must at one time have been domesticated, but now roamed around foraging for food in rubbish dumps and suspiciously shunning the attempts of Israeli soldiers to befriend them. Gadi thought he had become hardened to the sight of death, but passing a group of burned out vehicles he saw a pack of about ten dogs, snarling and snapping at each other as they tore chunks of meat from an Egyptian corpse. He turned his head away, sick at the sight.

As they advanced they became increasingly aware of the tremendous activity in front of them. Columns of white and black smoke rose high in the sky from the area around Suez and the sound of heavy guns rumbled constantly across the plain. An incessant stream of Israeli aircraft filled the skies, as though the pilots were flying against the clock, trying to cram in the maximum number of sorties before the cease-fire could take effect.

Occasional missiles rose into the sky, their tell-tale vapour trails tracing their path until they ended in harmless puffs of white smoke. They watched one rising towards the vapour trail of a plane flying at high altitude far to the south. It looked as though the two trails could not intersect, but suddenly the missile made a sharp turn, and a flash of orange

229

fire burst out against the blue sky. A few seconds later they heard the sound of the explosion, and watched the plane plummeting to the ground trailing black smoke behind it. No parachute was seen.

The power of the air force was simply demonstrated by the wreckage around them. The sand on both sides of the road was littered with smashed vehicles, whose drivers had tried in vain to elude the relentless attacks from the air. The area was also dotted with old T-34 tanks which the Egyptians had dug into ditches in the ground for protection, using their big guns to supplement the artillery. Unable to move, they had been systematically blasted out of existence by air-to-ground rockets.

Several times formations of two and four Egyptian Migs came streaking in to attack the Israeli ground forces, and with a ridiculous sense of certainty as to what would happen, they watched them being shot down, or fleeing desperately back again with Israeli planes in hot pursuit.

'Their pilots must have a lot of guts,' said Bennie. 'It must be like receiving a death sentence when they're ordered out to attack us.'

On the three o'clock news Egypt's acceptance of the cease-fire was announced.

'I guess that makes it official,' said Dror.

'Yes and no,' replied Bennie.

'What do you mean?'

'Well it can't just stop suddenly like that. Everything's all mixed up. Pockets of their troops are in areas which we control, and the same goes for us, like the paratroopers that we're going to reinforce. There'll have to be some sorting out and straightening of the lines.'

'You mean we're going to keep moving even after six-fifty?'

'If we don't run into any trouble we'll arrive before then, but we certainly won't stop until we've reached the paratroopers' position.'

At a point level with the southern-most tip of the Small Bitter Lake, they parted company with Rishon's forces, and moved south-west, travelling at full speed along the now deserted road, racing against the sun which was about to sink below the horizon somewhere behind Cairo.

Less than an hour later Bennie established radio contact

with the paratroopers, and was advised to turn off the road and proceed west as soon as they crossed the Suez-Cairo railway line. This would bring them in under cover of the ridges.

Shortly after six-thirty they pulled up in pitch darkness, at the foot of the ridge where the paratroopers were waiting to welcome them.

'What's the good of coming to help us when the war's over?' they were teased as they climbed out of the Zelda.

'Somebody had to bring you food,' answered Bennie.

'On the contrary, we can offer you Danish Cheese, Yugoslavian Beef, and there's even some Canadian tinned salmon which we haven't sampled yet.' There was an abandoned Egyptian supply base two hundred metres away, and the men had already explored it.

'And blankets?' Bennie asked.

'No. If you've got blankets, it was worth your coming. It's going to be cold tonight.'

Without wasting time Bennie gave orders for the men to dig their foxholes. While they were working somebody shouted out that it was six fifty-two, the official start of the cease-fire.

'Hey! Do you think it's really going to work?' one of the men asked.

They tuned into the seven o'clock news, only to hear the announcer state that the studio was still awaiting reports from the front lines as to whether or not the cease-fire was being observed.

As if to settle any doubts, a loud explosion sounded from the mortars which had been shelling their position spasmodically since the paratroopers arrived, and everybody dived for their foxholes. The barrage continued for a full hour and then stopped as suddenly as it had started.

Gadi's foxhole was about four metres away from Bennie's. The sky twinkled with thousands of bright stars and the moon had risen, lighting the desert sands with a pale silver glow, broken only by the dark mass of Jebel Ataka, looming above them. All around it was beautifully still, but from the direction of Suez the unmistakable rumble of heavy guns continued unabated.

'It doesn't sound much like a cease-fire, does it?' Gadi said.

231

'It's difficult to judge. Maybe there's a bit of line-straightening going on over there, and it will die down by tomorrow,' Bennie answered.

Gadi was silent for a few moments. He wanted to ask Bennie if he thought they would be involved in any more fighting, but he knew it was a foolish question. A new fear had begun to edge its way into his mind. Having gone so far, and stayed alive, the implication of the cease-fire was beginning to have an hypnotic effect on him. He had survived. He would be going home soon. He felt the joy of the nightmare being over, and suddenly he was ashamed because of those who would not be returning. And the fear came back, the feeling that from now on he must be specially careful. There was no sense to getting killed when it was really all over. To die now would be meaningless. He tried to push the thought away. Maybe if he spoke to Bennie it would help, but not about his fear, something else.

'Bennie, where about exactly are we?' he asked.

'Well, according to the map if you walked down to the highway, and then another kilometre towards Cairo, you'd have exactly a hundred kilometres more to go.'

'Is that all? A hundred and one kilometres to Cairo?'

'Yes. If we took the Zelda we'd probably get there in time for a late show of belly-dancing at one of their night-clubs. You feel like joining me?'

'Not now, I'm a little tired. Maybe tomorrow night.'

Tuesday/Wednesday, 23rd/24th October

It was three hours after midnight. Aliza was in the nurses' room taking a break. She had made herself a quick cup of coffee, and was dashing off a short letter to Uri.

Uri, my love,

I am so excited about the cease-fire – it came so quickly – I keep thinking of you coming back soon, maybe even in a few days. As I write this, the latest news is that there is still firing in Egypt but at least on the Golan it's quiet.

I was frightened yesterday when casualties started to come in from Mount Hermon, but then they told me that they were all from the Golani Brigade. I'm ashamed that I felt happy, because your units weren't involved. I can't help this, and I know you will understand.

I have re-read your last letter so often that I know it off by heart. You talk about our 'child' as though you are afraid to express a preference for its sex. I have no such inhibitions; I know that feelings can be wrong, and I will be happy whatever arrives, but I can only think in terms of 'him'. It will be a boy, Uri, just like you, warm, tender, handsome and strong.

I miss you so much, but I have had the same sense of 'wonder and joy' that you write about. I am not alone. I feel that you are with me all the time. I wanted to say 'inside me', but you would laugh and make a comment, and I would also laugh. But I am very serious and I love you – and him – so much.

Look after yourself, and be specially careful.

After all you've got responsibilities now.

All my love,
Aliza.

Meir and Shoshana were eating breakfast. They felt deflated. The morning news carried reports of massive Egyptian artillery barrages, and raids by Egyptian commando units during the night against Israeli tank encampments, most of the action taking place on the southern sector of the Canal zone. Israeli forces had returned the fire and the fighting was continuing.

'I knew it wouldn't work,' said Shoshana. 'We should have known that we can't trust the Arabs.'

'Well, if they were going to break it, maybe it's better now, than if they had waited a while and caught us unawares again. I told you what Ernie Goodman said, that every day the war continued would be to our advantage. Dayan also said that in his speech. Maybe we wanted the Egyptians to break the cease-fire, to give us an excuse for carrying on. It could be very good for us.'

'I can't think in terms like that, not while Gadi's down there.'

Meir stopped short: 'You're right Shosh, nothing else is important except that the boys should come back safe and sound.'

He finished his coffee and kissed her. 'When is your shift today?' he asked.

'Twelve till four. I'll come straight home.'

* * *

Robert Crawford moved restlessly on his bed in the orthopaedic ward of the Tel Hashomer Hospital. He had been there a week, and was not exactly their most co-operative patient. A huge bouquet of flowers from his newspaper, and a few smaller ones from friends, crowded the small table on either side of his pillow. He had hoped for letters from England but was informed that no foreign mail was coming in. The day before he had even written a short letter to Ann and the children, mentioning in a deliberately casual way that he was tired of running around and was going to resign from his post, and request a staff job in England.

He wriggled his toes as the Physiotherapist had instructed him. A compound fracture of the lower Tibia! When he first saw the bones sticking out of his leg after the missile struck the car, he couldn't believe that he had been hit, until he tried to move his leg and passed out from the pain.

He had been lucky, they said. When he was brought to the hospital they had suspected concussion and internal damage and bleeding, but in the end it had been just the leg. He gazed moodily at the crutches at the foot of his bed. It would be ten weeks before he could burn them, as he had vowed to do.

The doctor walked in, announcing cheerfully that he had a new medicine which might do him some good. Without any real show of interest he lifted his eyes, and there was Ann, smiling uncertainly at him, just as he had pictured her a hundred times in this last miserably drawn-out week. His jaw dropped. 'I know it's not true but please don't go away,' he whispered, as though if he spoke too loudly he might spoil the dream. She walked over and kissed him, and he held her to him.

Trying to keep his voice under control he said. 'They told me this was a land of miracles, and I didn't believe them.'

*　*　*

'We're moving again,' said Bennie.

It was twelve o'clock, and the seventeen hours since the official cease-fire had not been as peaceful as they had hoped for. They had been shelled with mortars several times during the night. The fox-holes were tremendously effective, but there had been one direct hit lifting the soldier inside into the air and depositing a mass of unrecognisable pulp into the sand ten metres away.

They had not returned the fire, but at the first light of dawn the tanks set off in the direction of the emplacement, and blasted it to smithereens. Most of the Egyptians fled on trucks when they saw them coming, and the remainder were killed next to their guns. The tanks returned without any losses.

A helicopter landed to evacuate the wounded, as well as the three corpses. During the night several vehicles had attempted to come down the highway from Suez in the direction of Cairo, and acting on express orders, they had fired on them with their heavy machine-guns, blocking the road with their wreckage. Several of the occupants had been killed or fled into the desert; others had come towards them with their hands raised, and been taken prisoner. Bennie briefed the men on their new orders.

'As you know the Egyptians have been violating the cease-fire, so it's fallen away. Carmel's forces are advancing, but the roads from the north are being shelled by the Third Army and reinforcements are coming through too slowly. The advance units have already entered Suez, but they're having trouble, and we've been instructed to get there as quickly as possible. We're leaving two tanks behind, and more armour is on its way from Fayid, so they should be able to manage here without us. We'll move out in exactly ten minutes.'

There were no questions. There was also no enthusiasm. It had been different before, but the war was supposed to be over now. Mechanically they checked their equipment, and the convoy of four tanks and the Zelda set off at top speed for Suez.

The battle was in full progress south of the city near the oil refineries, and also to the north where tanks and artillery were locked in a fierce clash with the Third Army. In the centre, opposite where they had entered, the operation had run into unexpected trouble. Advance patrols of paratroopers had moved into the town expecting it to be deserted. Halfway through they had suddenly found themselves surrounded on all sides by Egyptian soldiers. The leading tanks were hit by missiles and RPG Bazooka rockets, and burst into flames. The armoured personnel carriers tried to pick up their crews and withdraw, but they themselves were knocked out of action, and subjected to a murderous hail of machine-gun fire, Bazookas, and hand grenades from the windows and roof-tops of surrounding buildings.

In desperation they jumped out of the vehicles and about thirty of them had taken shelter in a police barracks; but they were surrounded and their situation was getting steadily worse. Bennie was requested to drive through with the tanks, to give the paratroopers a cover under which they could break out, and to evacuate as many of the wounded as possible in the Zelda.

Three of the tanks went up the street ahead of the Zelda, and turned into the courtyard of the police building. A Bazooka rocket smashed into the first one and it caught

236

fire. Almost immediately swarms of Egyptian infantrymen appeared from surrounding buildings, firing with light machine-guns as the crew scrambled desperately out and made a dash for the building where the paratroopers were besieged. Firing from his turret Bennie scattered the Egyptians, and saw three of the crew make it safely. The fourth one was hit and collapsed a few metres from the entrance.

The other two tanks blasted their way past the wrecked tank, then turned around and together with the fourth tank which had brought up the rear, fired at the surrounding buildings with their big guns, creating havoc as walls crumpled, masonry fell, and clouds of dust and acrid smoke filled the street. The Zelda had pulled up next to the door of the police barracks and opened the back flap, to give some of the men inside the building a chance to climb in. Three wounded paratroopers had succeeded in making it, when a Bazooka smashed into the engine of the Zelda. Bennie was thrown out of the turret, and landed unconscious on the street outside. The men inside scrambled out as it started to go up in flames and ran into the building.

Gadi and Dror were just about inside when they saw what had happened to Bennie. Without thinking they dashed back, each grabbed an arm and dragged him towards the open doorway. From across the street a hand-grenade was lobbed from an upstairs window, landing a few metres from them. The explosion caught them just at the entrance and catapulted the three of them into the building. The tanks found themselves sitting ducks for the vast quantity of Bazooka rockets and missiles which poured out at them from the surrounding buildings, and within a matter of moments the two leading tanks were destroyed and their crews cut down as they tried to escape. The fourth tank barely managed to reverse and extricate itself.

Gadi recovered consciousness a half-hour later. His mind was swimming in a red fog, and he had no idea of what had happened other than that he remembered going back for Bennie. 'How is Bennie?' he asked, and was shocked at the weak sound of his own voice. A medic went to call him. Bennie had not been badly hurt, he had been wounded in the back of the legs by small fragments from the grenade blast, but a doctor who was with the paratroopers had treated him, and he had insisted on joining the fighting,

237

standing at one of the windows on the third floor with an Uzzi which he sprayed in all directions opposite and the street below. Bennie came downstairs, took his hand and said 'Thanks Gadi, you saved my life. How are you feeling?'

Gadi obviously recognised him but was unable to talk, and fell back unconscious again. Bennie went to the doctor, who was working quietly and efficiently, with the number of wounded being brought to his 'room' steadily increasing.

'He's unconscious again, Doctor. Does he stand a chance? Is there anything I can do?'

'I don't know. I'll look at him again as soon as I'm finished this. You can hang on a few minutes if you like.'

Bennie wanted to but he was needed upstairs. The fighting had intensified. From one of the buildings opposite, Bazooka shells were being fired at the walls of the police building, but they were tremendously thick, and except for the demoralising crash as they exploded and shook the building, no real damage was done.

One of the men came around collecting water bottles for the wounded. They were also running short of ammunition and an order came through to control their fire. Their greatest comfort was that the radio continued to work, and they were able to keep contact with the command centre on the outskirts of the city. The messages they received were encouraging, telling them to hold on and that another attempt was being organised to rescue them.

Towards evening the enemy fire died down. Bennie seized the opportunity to get down to Gadi again. He was conscious and seemed better, but Bennie noticed the huge bandage around his middle. He spoke to the doctor who told him that shrapnel had gone through his back and damaged the kidneys, he didn't know how badly, but there was a fair amount of internal bleeding, and his condition was serious and couldn't be treated until they got him to a base hospital. Meanwhile he had dosed him up with morphine so that he would not feel too much pain.

Gadi was pleased to have Bennie there, but he felt disconnected, as though he was standing a little distance away, watching what was happening, but it wasn't really happening to him.

'You'll be okay, Gadi,' Bennie said. 'I spoke to the doctor, and he said you'll be fine as soon as we get out of here and get you to a base hospital, so all you've got to do is hold on. Okay?'

Gadi nodded his head.

'I'll stay with you all the time, Gadi. Just don't give in and you'll be all right – I promise you.'

Gadi smiled. For a moment his brain cleared.

'We've got a date tonight,' he said, 'to see those belly-dancers in Cairo.'

*　　*　　*

General Bardan was in his element. A brief report had just come in from Colonel Rishon that he was in full control of Adabiyah. No matter what happened now in the town of Suez, the trap was sprung. The Third Army was completely cut off.

In the north his forces had closed in to within one kilometre of the Ismailia-Cairo road and railway, and extended their line to a depth of thirty kilometres west of the Canal.

In the south, from early in the morning the Third Army had launched full scale tank battles and artillery exchanges in desperate but unsuccessful attacks to shake off the rapidly closing Israeli stranglehold. Hundreds of prisoners had walked across the lines, seemingly coming out of every second sand dune, with their hands in the air and asking for water. At two o'clock that afternoon and again at four o'clock, the Egyptian air force had come out in full strength, about thirty planes at a time, trying to help their hard-pressed ground forces to break through the Israeli ring of armour. The attempt had cost them ten planes in dog-fights, five in each encounter.

In the town of Suez itself the fighting had been exceptionally fierce, and he was concerned about the mounting reports of casualties. What had started out as a mild cleaning-up operation in a ghost town, had developed into a full scale urban battle, with the Egyptians fighting with great courage and skill.

Now with Rishon's report, General Bardan felt there was no point incurring further losses, and he issued instructions to Carmel's headquarters at Suez to extricate themselves from any forward position and to withdraw to a line in the city which they could hold, and where they could consolidate themselves with a minimum of additional casualties.

The Army Spokesman's office in Tel Aviv was put through to the general on the field telephone, with an urgent request from the foreign correspondents for his summing-up of the day's fighting. Without hesitation, and with a broad grin, Bardan answered. 'Tell them that the line may have changed somewhat, and not to our disadvantage.'

*　　*　　*

The Ishboneh and Singer families gathered around the TV set in the Ishboneh living room, in their standard routine, waiting for the eight-thirty news.

Addressing a packed special session of the Knesset, Mrs Meir warned Egypt that if it persisted in violating the truce, Israel's army would continue to act as military circumstances required.

Syria had not yet announced its acceptance of the ceasefire, but the Prime Minister did not link this to the position on the Suez front. Mrs Meir assured the house that there had been no special deal with Kissinger and Brezhnev, and that Washington's only plan was to bring the disputants together for direct negotiations.

'How can she be so sure?' said Chaim. 'Would Kissinger tell her if he'd made a special deal with the Russians?'

There was an ominous announcement from Egypt that all men aged 21 to 32 had been called up for active service. The Egyptians blamed Israel for the resumption of the full-scale fighting, claiming that she had exploited the cease-fire to improve her position.

The Security Council of the United Nations had met at the urgent request of Egypt; and the United States and Soviet delegates made a joint proposal urging that Egyptian and Israeli forces should observe the cease-fire and return to the positions they had occupied at Monday night's deadline. A part of the resolution urged that Secretary-General Kurt Waldheim should take measures for the immediate despatch of UN observers to supervise the observance of the 'cease-fire'. The session had been suspended without a vote being taken, after the Soviet and Chinese delegates began shouting at each other, but it was expected that it would reconvene shortly and the resolution would be passed.

240

Finally, it was noted that Ethiopia had broken off diplomatic relations with Israel, making it the seventh African State to take such action since the start of the war. 'They're all the same,' commented Meir bitterly. 'We were the best friends the African countries had, until they discovered that the Arabs had more money and oil than we have.'

'Why should we think badly of them?' asked Chaim. 'If Britain and France can switch sides according to the way the wind blows, why shouldn't they? At least we didn't rely on them for ammunition or aeroplanes.'

* * *

Inside the police barracks the strain was beginning to tell. It was completely dark outside and the Egyptians seemed to have given up for the night, but the men stood guard at the windows straining their eyes and ears for signs of a surprise attack. They were hot and thirsty, and most of them had not eaten all day. Bennie and Dror and several of the paratroopers sneaked quietly out of the building, crawled to the wrecked vehicles, and brought back water and food and ammunition.

At midnight word finally came through on the radio that there was no possibility of reinforcements being sent, and they were advised to try to move out under cover of darkness. They would have to walk a distance of nearly three kilometres to the town exit.

The commander of the paratroopers waited another two hours hoping the Egyptians would be less vigilant and then gave the order for the evacuation to begin. At first they tried to make no noise, but the streets were littered with broken glass and debris, and they soon realised that it was less suspicious to walk naturally. They went through back alleys, with four men marching in front and four behind. Those who were wounded walked on their own in the middle or were supported or carried by the remaining fit soldiers. Gadi was held in between Bennie and Dror, with an arm around each of their shoulders. He had received the doctor's last dose of morphine and was relatively immune to the pain, but he had a high fever and was semi-delirious, muttering away in Hebrew, but fortunately in a voice too weak to be distinguishable.

Several times they passed groups of enemy soldiers, sometimes only a few metres away from them, but in the dark the Egyptians assumed that it was one of their own units. In the distance they saw the flickering light of a lantern which had been hung up to guide them. Gadi had lost consciousness altogether and Bennie and Dror were staggering from fatigue and exhaustion. The sight of the lantern gave them additional strength, and a short while later they fell into the arms of willing helpers, laughing and crying with excitement and relief that their long ordeal was over.

Bennie's first concern was to get the doctor to arrange emergency treatment for Gadi, who was lying motionless on the ground, with Dror worn out, sitting next to him. The doctor bent down to examine him. It seemed ages before he lifted his head and looked grimly at Bennie.

'He's gone,' he said. 'Don't take it too hard. You did your best.'

*　　*　　*

General Bardan had lost all track of time. His job was done. The rest was just a question of detail. At the request of the Egyptians, General Dayan had fixed a second deadline for the cease-fire for seven o'clock that morning, but in spite of the fact that they were obviously in desperate straits, the Third Army had found itself unable to accept the situation. Throughout the day enemy forces had made desperate but futile efforts to break out of the ring which enclosed them. Hundreds of prisoners, totally demoralised, were still coming out of the desert to give themselves up.

At three o'clock in the afternoon the Egyptian infantry and tanks made a final tremendous assault across the twenty-five kilometre Canal front between Shallufa and Suez, and their air force came bravely in with more than thirty aircraft in support. Within minutes fifteen were shot down. Slowly the firing died down, and at five o'clock, nearly forty-eight hours after the first deadline, a strange and unnatural quiet descended on the battle-field.

*　　*　　*

Shoshana let herself into the apartment, and walked straight across to the window, opening the curtains wide and letting the light shine out on to the street.

'Shosh, what are you doing?' Meir cried out in alarm.

'Come and look,' she called out to him laughing.

He jumped up and ran to the window. Quite a few lights could already be seen, and more were coming on every moment, like a giant amusement park opening up for business, full of movement and excitement. People were coming out into the street to watch, fascinated, and deeply aware of the symbolism of light sweeping away the darkness.

'It's beautiful,' Meir said. 'Now I really believe that the war is over.'

Wednesday, 7th November

Dawn was creeping slowly into the room. On the bedside table the old-fashioned alarm clock ticked away with unceasing monotony. A dairy truck screeched as it drew to a halt at the grocery store down the street. Meir was asleep in the large double-bed, with the tall semi-antique headboard.

Shoshana, a thick warm robe over her cotton nightdress, sat in the chair next to the window, watching the first light penetrate the drawn shutters. In spite of the tranquilisers, she had woken early. She had thought vaguely of cleaning up the living room, which looked like a theatre after a show, empty chairs, empty soft-drink bottles and glasses. Only the ashtrays were full. When the last visitors were leaving, Shula had wanted to stay behind to clear the mess away, but she had refused. She only wanted to be alone, away from the helpless and overwhelming pity in their eyes. She knew they meant well. What else could they feel? What could they say? What could they do? Would any of it bring Uri or Gadi back?

Her mind was numb, as bleak and unfeeling as massive pain could make it. It was all an act, a play in which they had the central roles, in which they were supposed to mouth certain words, cry, break down, collapse, something, anything . . . and all the others had to do was look at them, not directly, but through the corners of their eyes, in swift glances, trying to determine how much suffering a human being could take, without falling completely apart.

Vaguely she recalled other dawns when she had known that the day would bring only tears, desperation and doom. Other early mornings where she had prayed to God (where are you?) – not to let the sun rise over a world soaked with blood, cruelty and hatred. But the sun had risen, and the misery and suffering had been endured. On the surface the wounds had healed, but deep in the body and the mind, they had simmered and festered like a witches' brew, waiting to bubble over and contaminate everything around them.

With inexorable certainty she knew that the day just brightening beyond the closed shutters would be the worst that she had faced in all her fifty-six years.

Only six days ago! It seemed like months, years. They had been worried and upset at not hearing from the boys, but there had been a postcard from Gadi, and others also hadn't heard, many of them. They had tried to shut out the ugly thoughts from their minds, concentrating only on the fact that the war was over, and soon the boys would be coming home.

And then the doorbell rang. A girl soldier, two officers, and the man carrying a black case, who turned out to be the doctor; and behind them Chaim and Shula, their faces contorted with shock and compassion, making the purpose of the visit hopelessly clear.

But both the boys! It couldn't be. Somebody was playing a horrible joke. There had been a mistake, some confusion. Shoshana had let out a wild scream of agony and despair, and the doctor had swiftly given her an injection; and also Meir, who had slumped silent and white-faced into a chair, with the room spinning round, unable to comprehend the enormity of what these people were telling them.

And they stayed with them and talked, and Meir and Shoshana heard the words, but they made no sense, only that their sons were dead. This they understood. And then they left. And Shula took over, making coffee, and opening the door for the people who started to come in, that night, the next day, a never-ending stream, close friends, some they knew only slightly; and some they didn't know at all, friends of the boys, teachers, soldiers who had served with them; Rina and Aliza, their eyes red with crying.

And the two officers came again, not once, but several times, Amos and Bennie. They spoke about the boys, directly, sincerely, you could see the love and the pain in their eyes. Each of them said that his own life had been saved by something the boys had done. They told her she should be proud of them. What good was it, if they were never coming back again?

And a Rabbi turned up, also in uniform. He asked Meir whether he was observing the customs relating to deaths, and whether he knew how to recite the prayers for the dead. He came to be of assistance, he said. They wanted to scream at him that they didn't need his assistance. Could he bring their sons back to them? That's what they needed.

The tears had dried up, and then inexplicably the wells would burst open again, and they would sob, their bodies racked with pain, conscious all the time of the people watching their naked grief. There were moments when Shoshana wanted to throw them all out, hoping that in this way she could end the horrible farce – like a nightmare, when she knew that she was dreaming, and if she could only force herself to wake up, it would go away, and everything would be all right again.

And Meir, sitting on the other side of the room, with the men around him. Smoking a lot, pale, with beads of perspiration gathering on his forehead. He would wipe them away, but later they would come back again. He seemed to have shrunk physically, as though he had tried to crawl back inside himself to avoid the torment.

Both of them were heavily doped with Libriums. They hardly ate or drank, only when Shula and Chaim forced them; or Aliza, who walked around emptying the ashtrays, collecting cups and saucers, and occasionally offering them a small snack from savouries which somebody had brought.

Aliza, who had been going to marry Uri! A deep uncontrollable moan escaped from the depths of her being.

'Shosh!'

'Yes, Mickey?'

'What are you doing there?'

'Go back to sleep . . . please!' She tried to keep her voice calm.

'I've slept enough,' his voice was thick, apologetic. She saw his dark shape moving around the room.

'Don't put on the light, Mickey.'

'I'm trying to find my lighter.'

'You shouldn't smoke at such an early . . . ' Her voice trailed off. 'I'm sorry.'

'Never mind.'

Meir sat down in the opposite chair. For a few minutes neither of them spoke. Outside the sun climbed higher, warming the ground, and drying the drops of dew on the trees and the flowers. It poured into the room, even through the narrow slits of the shutters.

'We're fooling ourselves, aren't we Mickey?'

'What do you mean?'

'By going on. By keeping on living. There really isn't any point to it, is there?'

'I don't know, Shosh. I just don't know.'

Silence . . .

'When did they fall?' she asked suddenly, and stood up. 'When did they die Mickey? Didn't they tell you?'

'Yes. Uri died on the nineteenth, and Gadi on the twenty-fourth. What's the difference?'

'I'm trying to remember what I was doing on those days. How is it that I didn't feel anything different? Surely something must have snapped inside me, given me a warning. I think when Gadi died I was baking a cake for him. I remember feeling that it was a peculiar thing to be doing when the war was already over, and he would be . . . '

'Stop it Shosh!'

'Why did they take so long to let us know?'

'I don't know. They said something about there being two of them, or trouble in identifying the bodies. I wasn't paying attention, it didn't seem to be important!'

'Maybe that's why they wouldn't let you see them.'

'They would have if I'd insisted. They just asked us not to.'

'You should have made them open the coffins.'

'For God's sake Shosh, our sons are dead. They're going to be buried today. What would have been the point of looking at them. Let me at least remember them as we knew them.'

Shoshana drew a deep breath as if she was about to scream, but no sound came. With a single violent move she tore off her robe and nightshirt. They fell on the carpet, and she stood there naked. 'Look at their scars, Mickey!' She pointed to her abdomen. 'Do you see them? This is Gadi, and this is Uri. That's all that's left of them, two scars on an old woman's stomach.'

'Shosh, please stop. You're only hurting yourself more.'

'Do you remember what Dr Goldstein said after Gadi was born? He said he can't open me up again. No more

247

children. Two boys were plenty at my age, he told me. Do you remember?'

'Of course I do. What do you want from me, Shosh?' His voice was desperate. 'What can I do? Blow my brains out?' Then, in a whisper, 'Shosh, I'm sorry. Please try to get dressed. We're going to need all our strength to get through the ceremony today.'

'I'm sorry, Mickey. I think I'd better take some more Libriums.'

'How many did you take last night?'

'Three.'

'You'd better take another three; I will too. We'll just have to hold on to each other. They'll think we're drunk. Come on Shosh, we've got to get dressed. It's seven o'clock already.'

An hour later, a shiny army limousine pulled up in front of their building, and an officer escorted them to the car. A silent corridor of neighbours watched them get in. At the cemetery they were led through a large crowd that opened up to let them pass, until they stood in front of two open graves with coffins beside them, and two white markers with the Israel Army symbol and Uri's and Gadi's name and rank inscribed on them, in plain black lettering.

There were three long rows of graves, each surrounded by mourning families, some weeping and lamenting openly, but most of them quiet and composed, as though bracing themselves for the ordeal to follow. A young wife stood near them, repeating softly over and over again, 'Why? Why?'

Shoshana leaned heavily on Meir, and he felt a cold perspiration cover his body. He pulled open his shirt collar, and tried to stand erect.

Loudspeakers had been set up at different points, and the service commenced with the reading of the psalm of David, on the death of Saul and Jonathan, the sound of the Rabbi's voice echoing mournfully, with unnatural force, above the subdued murmurs of the bereaved families.

'Thy beauty, O Israel, upon the high places is slain! How are the mighty fallen! . . .'

Shoshana began to shake, and Meir put his arm around her to support her. Throughout the crowd, anguished mourners burst into uncontrollable sobs and cries.

The Rabbi was followed by a General, who described the war as the worst ever launched against the State of Israel.

'Our enemies were encouraged by a great power, and their aim was to annihilate this nation and turn this land into a valley of death and slaughter. They started with every possible advantage, including those of surprise, and modern weaponry on a scale unknown in any previous war.

'With their very bodies, our soldiers stopped this on-slaught, turned back the attacking tide, and placed us in a position where we had the power to defeat and utterly crush the armies which opposed us.

'They were saved only by the intervention of the same great power that engineered this evil adventure. In the entire history of our people, there has never been a greater victory than in this war!'

Another officer stood up to speak. Apologising for the inadequacy of his words to comfort those who had lost a loved one, he pointed out that in the last two thousand years, when the Jews were scattered throughout the Diaspora, they had become accustomed to thinking of Israel as a place to which the faithful, at the end of their lives, might return to die, and be buried in its sacred soil.

'Since the founding of the State, Israel is no longer merely a place to die. Small as it is, it is the place where all Jews, everywhere, have the right to live.

'Jews from every community in the world have shown their understanding of this. They gave whatever aid their circumstances allowed, they prayed for our safety, and they mourn with us today for those who have fallen. Your loved ones have paid the price for them, and for us.

'There is something in the mystic history of our people which reveres life and clings tenaciously to it. Let us strive to make their sacrifice meaningful, that we shall build here a quality of life which will bring us closer to fulfilling the ancient prophecy of Isaiah:

'For out of Zion shall go forth the law,
And the word of the Lord from Jerusalem.
And He shall judge between the nations,
And shall decide for many peoples;
And they shall beat their swords into plough-shares,

And their spears into pruning hooks;
Nation shall not lift up sword against nation.
Neither shall there be war anymore . . . '

Prayers for the dead followed, the coffins were lowered, and the service closed with a guard of honour firing three salvoes into the cloudless sky, and a lone army bugler playing the haunting strains of 'The Last Post'.

It was over. Drained of all emotion, they were led back to the waiting limousine . . .

Afterwards, they took off their shoes and sat in the living-room, and it was the same as on the previous days. People came and sat down, the women next to Shoshana, the men around Meir. Embarrassed, the mourners talked quietly to each other, but were unable to find words for those they had come to console. More people arrived, and those who were there, were glad to give up their places and leave.

Shoshana and Meir were virtually insensible. They saw people come and people go, Rina and Aliza, Amos and Bennie, the same faces, the same pain, the same silences. There was nothing to say. Nothing.

At nine o'clock Chaim and Shula signalled to the last few visitors that it was time to leave. Shula kissed Shoshana lightly on the cheek, and said she'd come in early the next morning. The door closed behind them, and Meir locked it.

With a sigh he turned to Shoshana. 'I thought the day would never end . . . Did you eat anything?'

'No.'

'Would you like something?'

'No.'

'Let's go into the kitchen anyway. I'll make some coffee.'

Wearily, Shoshana raised herself and moved to the kitchen table. In silence they sipped the hot bitter liquid, feeling its warmth run through their bodies, gradually bringing them out of their stupor.

Meir looked at Shoshana, her face waxen and devoid of colour, the expression set and frozen like a death-mask. It was like gazing at a stranger, a caricature of the woman she had been. Aching with compassion, he leaned over and placed his hand on hers.

'You did well, Shosh. Nothing can be worse than what we went through today. We've just got to try to keep going.'

250

'What for, Mickey?' Shoshana spoke harshly. 'I told you this morning, we're fooling ourselves. We're two empty shells, moving around in a world which no longer makes sense. There's no reason – absolutely no reason – for us to go on living.'

'You're right Shosh, but we have no choice.'

'Why? Is it so difficult to die? The gas stove is just behind you. I can't think of anything better than going to sleep, knowing that I won't have to wake up again.'

'Shosh, stop torturing yourself! Time will pass. We'll find a way.' Meir's voice was strained. He knew she was serious, and in his heart he had no answer for her.

'Time won't heal this pain, Mickey. I can't take any more.'

'Shosh. If you're really sure . . . If that's what you want, I'll . . .'

Before he could finish, the doorbell rang. It wasn't a loud noise, but it was so unexpected that they both started. The intrusion was singularly unwelcome.

'Should I answer it?' Meir asked.

It rang again, and unwillingly he got up and opened the door. It was Aliza. For a moment they stared at each other.

'Please, may I come in?' she asked.

'Yes, of course Aliza.'

Meir took her into the kitchen and brought up a chair, but Aliza remained standing, her body tense and rigid. Her face was pale and thinner than they had noticed before, and her huge dark eyes seemed even larger.

'Is it all right to talk for a few minutes?' Aliza began uncertainly.

Bewildered they nodded their heads. Aliza had tried several times to rehearse what she was going to say, but now her mind went blank and the words came tumbling out.

'I'm pregnant . . . It's Uri's child . . . He knew about it, and we were going to be married . . . ' Tears started to run down her cheeks as she struggled to continue.

'I want to have the baby – that's why I came back tonight – I felt you should know. Uri was so happy when I told him I was pregnant . . . ' Unable to control herself any longer, Aliza burst into tears, and sank down into the chair, hiding her face with her hands.

There was a long, agonising silence, while her words burned into them. Crying, Shoshana gathered Aliza's head on to her shoulder and put her arms around her, gently stroking her long black hair.

Meir stood up, his mind in a turmoil. He wanted to say something comforting, but couldn't find the words. Awkwardly he said, 'I'll make some coffee.'

He filled the kettle, struck a match, and turned the knob on the stove. For a few brief seconds he stared as the gas hissed out of the ring, then he lit it, and watched it burst into a circle of tiny jets of flame ...

THE END

ABOUT THE AUTHORS:

LASZLO DEUTSCH – Professional Journalist and Clinical Psychologist. Born in Roumania, where he published a number of literary works including two prize-winning novels. Immigrated to Israel in 1960 and settled with his wife in Herzlia. At present, working and lecturing on a temporary project in Toronto, Canada.

HARRY BRODIE – Born in South Africa, where he practised as an Advocate in the Supreme Court, and played an active political part in the Liberal Party. In 1960, emigrated to Canada, established a successful import-export business, and worked as a writer and editor for a large legal publishing firm. In 1965, settled in Israel with his wife and four children (his two oldest sons served in fighting units in the Yom Kippur War). For five years, headed a special unit of the Ministry of Absorbtion, advising and assisting academic immigrants with their settling-in problems. Thereafter qualified as a Tourist Guide, and developed various business interests, including a unique pioneering fishing village on the Red Sea coast.

HORNED PIGEON by GEORGE MILLAR, D.S.O., M.C.

George Millar was an army lieutenant fighting in North Africa when he was captured by German soldiers. Handed over to the Italians, he was taken to Italy and imprisoned in a concentration camp at Padula. Despite dysentery and hardship, George's courage and determination kept him from despair. His first planned escape failed by a hair's breadth and he was transferred to a punishment camp. After the Italian armistice he and some fellow-prisoners attempted a second break-out, but were foiled by the Germans. Next Millar was moved to a German camp near Munich. He made his third daring bid for freedom at night, from a fast-moving and closely-guarded train. As he jumped, he was shuddering with cold and fear of failing once again . . .

0 552 09901 5 – 60p

HOW SLEEP THE BRAVE by JOHN BRILEY

Concerns the experience of five members of an American patrol, ambushed by the Vietcong and marched along the Ho Chi Minh Trail to a supply camp deep in the forests. There, intensive indoctrination – at the hands of an American defector – is used to persuade two of the GIs that America's cause is immoral and unjust.

This powerful novel tells the story of these traitors: their undercover trip to Saigon for supplies, a helicopter trip to free a Buddhist leader, the passionate affair between one of the Americans and a North Vietnamese girl. It captures all the terror of modern warfare in a land wracked by fighting for more than a quarter of a century.

0 552 09873 6 – 60p

THEY CAME FROM THE SKY by E. H. COOKRIDGE

The Special Operations Executive was created by Churchill in the summer of 1940 to 'set Europe ablaze'. Working secretly behind enemy lines to 'sabotage and subvert', they operated all over Europe, and some of the most active agents were in the French Section. It was dangerous work, and many agents did not return: a few, like Christine Granville, became famous names, but for the most part their exploits remain unsung. Here now are the stories of three members of the French Section – true stories that make more exciting reading than any novel . . . They had little training, and their unconventional methods were frowned on by the top brass of the Army, but what they lacked in style, they more than made up for in courage and initiative. . . .

0 552 10136 2 – 75p

THE SAVAGE CANARY by DAVID LAMPE

The Danish resistance movement was described by Montgomery as 'second to none'.
The Savage Canary is a fantastic but true account of the Danish efforts to help the Allies and cripple Germany in the Second World War. By May 1945, illegal newspapers had published a total of about 26 million issues; illegal broadcasts were transmitted regularly; boats were running a timetable service between Britain, Sweden and Denmark and 7,000 Jews had been shipped to safety. German ships were unable to move from Danish harbours; a vast number of German troops were kept from the main fighting points by Danish sabotage of the railways and aerodromes.
This book, the story of an impudent, almost foolhardy heroism, is a salute to the people of Denmark.

0 552 10101 X – 65p

A SELECTED LIST OF WAR BOOKS
PUBLISHED BY CORGI

☐ 10079 X	HITLER'S NAVAL WAR	*Cajus Bekker*	85p
☐ 09055 7	SIDESHOW	*Gerard Bell*	30p
☐ 09845 0	THE PASSWORD IS COURAGE	*John Castle*	40p
☐ 09674 1	THE BLITZ	*Constantine Fitzgibbon*	50p
☐ 09178 2	REIGN OF HELL	*Sven Hassel*	75p
☐ 08874 9	SS GENERAL	*Sven Hassel*	65p
☐ 08779 3	ASSIGNMENT GESTAPO	*Sven Hassel*	85p
☐ 08603 7	LIQUIDATE PARIS	*Sven Hassel*	85p
☐ 08528 6	MARCH BATTALION	*Sven Hassel*	65p
☐ 08168 X	MONTE CASSINO	*Sven Hassel*	75p
☐ 07871 9	COMRADES OF WAR	*Sven Hassel*	65p
☐ 07242 7	WHEELS OF TERROR	*Sven Hassel*	65p
☐ 07241 9	LEGION OF THE DAMNED	*Sven Hassel*	65p
☐ 10080 3	THE FIRST 100,000	*Ian Hay*	60p
☐ 08371 2	THE DIRTY DOZEN	*E. M. Nathanson*	85p
☐ 10035 8	THE BEARDLESS WARRIORS	*Richard Matheson*	50p
☐ 09778 0	NIGHT FIGHTER	*C. F. Rawnsley & Robert Wright*	60p
☐ 09932 5	PRIVATE NAVY	*David Satherley*	50p
☐ 09324 6	FIGHTER EXPLOITS	*Edward H. Sims*	40p
☐ 10057 9	THE DEATHMAKERS	*Glen Sire*	65p
☐ 08169 8	633 SQUADRON	*Frederick E. Smith*	65p
☐ 09308 4	THE JUNGLE IS NEUTRAL	*F. Spencer Chapman*	50p
☐ 08986 9	DUEL OF EAGLES	*Peter Townsend*	50p
☐ 09541 9	INVASION '44	*John Frayn Turner*	40p
☐ 09646 6	THE BATTLE FOR TWELVELAND	*Charles Whiting*	50p
☐ 09874 4	HUNTERS FROM THE SKY	*Charles Whiting*	50p
☐ 10016 1	GREEN ARMOUR	*Osmar White*	50p

All these books are available at your bookshop or newsagent; or can be ordered direct from the publisher. Just tick the titles you want and fill in the form below.

CORGI BOOKS, Cash Sales Department, P.O. Box 11, Falmouth, Cornwall.

Please send cheque or postal order, no currency.

U.K. send 19p for first book plus 9p per copy for each additional book ordered to a maximum charge of 73p to cover the cost of postage and packing.

B.F.P.O. and Eire allow 19p for first book plus 9p per copy for the next 6 books, thereafter 3p per book.

Overseas Customers. Please allow 20p for the first book and 10p per copy for each additional book.

NAME (block letters) ....

ADDRESS ....

(JAN 77) ....

While every effort is made to keep prices low, it is sometimes necessary to increase prices at short notice. Corgi Books reserve the right to show new retail prices on covers which may differ from those previously advertised in the text or elsewhere.